DARK PASSAGE

DANIELLE GIRARD

ITP

Dark Passage

Copyright © 2016, 2019 by Danielle Girard. All rights reserved under International and Pan-American Copyright Conventions

Fourth Edition: June 2019

Cover and Formatting: Damonza

ISBN-10: 0996308962

ISBN-13: 978-0996308960

Your Free Rookie Club Short Story is Waiting

San Francisco Crime Scene Analyst and aspiring Rookie Club member Naomi Muir is passionate about her work, especially the cases where she works alongside seasoned inspectors, like Jamie Vail. But this latest case has her unnerved. A serial sex offender is growing more aggressive. He attacks in the dirty underbelly of the San Francisco streets… and eerily close to Naomi's inexpensive apartment. Each crime is more violent than the last and also nearer to where Naomi herself lives.

To solve the case, Naomi will have to rely on her own wit and an unexpected new partner as the attacker gets too close to home…

Go to www.daniellegirard.com/newsletter to claim your copy now!

THE ROOKIE CLUB CAST, IN ORDER OF APPEARANCE:

Cameron Cruz, Special Ops Team/Sharpshooter (Also in *Grave Danger*)

Jamie Vail, Sex Crimes Inspector (Featured in *Dead Center* and Rookie Club Book 5, *Everything to Lose*; also in *One Clean Shot and Grave Danger*)

Hailey Wyatt, Homicide Inspector (Featured in *One Clean Shot*; also in *Dead Center, Grave Danger, and Everything to Lose*)

Ryaan Berry, Triggerlock Inspector (Also in *One Clean Shot and Grave Danger*)

Mackenzie Wallace, patrol officer (Also in *Dead Center*)

Linda James, Precinct Captain (also in *One Clean Shot and Everything to Lose*)

Jess Campbell, Immigration and Customs Enforcement (ICE) (also in *Dead Center and One Clean Shot*)

CHAPTER 1

HEAVY BOOTS DRUMMED on the floor, partially drowned out by the rasp of zippers and the sticky rip of Velcro. Inside the Ops van, the officers pulled on jumpsuits and tightened bulletproof vests. For Special Ops Officer Cameron Cruz, the red light had a calming effect. The raid was minutes away. In these moments, the energy of the officers built a charge in the air that was almost visible.

Despite it, expressions were guarded, cool. Tension was at a peak. As soon as they started moving in, the jokes would begin. The pranks and stunts would come after, the rowdy celebration that followed a successful raid.

Cameron was the only woman, always a little on the outside, and yet, she loved it. The adrenaline, the strategy, every minute a test. Then, reliving each second when it was done. No one talked about that beforehand. Superstition wasn't something any Special Ops member would admit to, but they all subscribed.

Tonight, they had a barricaded suspect. The red light protected their eyes, so they were ready for the darkness outside. Weapons loaded, Cameron smelled the acrid, grapefruit odor of sweat and the metallic scents of gun oil and ammunition. Already sweat ran along the line of her equipment belt and the weight cut into her hips. Two undershirts didn't prevent the familiar biting on her skin. The belt carried forty pounds of equipment, built for a man's hips, not hers. And even the extra-extra-small didn't hold the belt in place. Lately, though, it was getting easier. It had taken her until yesterday to figure out why.

"Four minutes," the sergeant called.

Silence buzzed inside the bus like the anticipation of tremors after an earthquake. Tonight, she would tell him. She surreptitiously crossed herself with a tiny motion of her index finger. It was a ritual for her. Everyone had one. She thought of Mama, Rosa, Diego, then of the unknown little person growing inside her.

The sergeant called the team's attention to a backlit board with a diagram that might have been for a complex football play. Cameron had intimate knowledge of the layout, as she had been on the reconnaissance team. On every job, the team was split into four duties: equipment; intelligence, who profiled the suspect; tactical, which coordinated the actual event; and reconnaissance. New officers began in equipment.

Reconnaissance was the fourth shop and the most dangerous. Not everyone was eligible for the recon team. Certainly they never risked the medics like Ambley. If something went wrong, medics were the last people the team could afford to lose.

"Lau, you're lead."

Ryan Lau's gaze swept across the team as he pulled his helmet over his black buzz cut. Lau was often lead. He was compact, maybe only five foot eight inches, but all wiry muscle, which made him easier to cover. The lead man was most at risk. He carried a fifty-pound ram to take out the door. If there was a shooter behind it, he depended on the team to cover him.

"Kessler does second, then Cruz." In many ways, Brian Kessler was Lau's opposite: taller and thick, built like a football player but also agile and quick. Sergeant Lavick went through the remaining list, eight in all. "Questions?"

Lavick ran his forearm across his face. He looked old. "Let's go, then. Gear on. We're moving in."

Cameron pulled the black helmet over her cropped blond hair. She patted her suit, fingered the reassuring bulge of her ammo. She signaled ready as the last of the weapons were checked, rechecked, and holstered. Hostile, agile, mobile was the recon credo. The door cracked open. The cool San Francisco night rolled into the van as the team moved out.

The perp was wanted for armed robbery. He had a weapons fetish and wasn't likely to go down without a fight. That's all she needed to know. Her job was to get him out. After that, he was someone else's problem.

The team stopped at the door, making their formation.

"Nuts to butts," Lau called back.

She tucked up against Kessler, felt Paules behind her. She was grateful it wasn't Diego. This was no place for distractions. Diego was behind Paules along with Daley, Ballestrini and Ambley.

The line was perfectly still. Sergeant Lavick stood to the side, his hand on his watch. After a beat, his hand went up. A breath shot through the group. He showed five fingers, then four, then three, two, one. Go.

The ram struck the door. The cheap composite buckled in the center, tearing the lock from the jam. Lau dropped the ram and drew his weapon. The wave of officers streamed in like high tide. The first two went right, the next two left, splitting to the two sides of the place. She and Daley cleared the first room, full of gym equipment, and then moved into the bathroom. She swung around the door, used the barrel of her rifle to pull back the shower curtain. Clear.

The next door was closed. She and Daley hesitated. Standing clear of the doorway, they waited for the team to gather. This must be the room. Lau arrived followed by Kessler. Lau raised one finger and pointed to himself. He would take the door. Cameron pointed right, ready to move around the doorjamb, keeping her back to the wall. Buttonhooking, it was called. Daley pointed left. He would cross the door to the left. It would leave Cameron in the best position to shoot. Gun raised, her finger resting flat along the trigger ring, she nodded to go.

Lau threw the door open and rolled into the room followed by Daley. Cameron came behind, then Kessler. She kept her back to the frame of the door as she hooked around the doorway and into the room. Her back was safe, her gun aimed and ready.

A string of shots fired from the closet. The angle was steep; the shots made a line of dust as they pierced high on the wall behind them. The shooter was sitting on the floor. Cameron aimed low and shot back. Three quick shots, then she paused. There was no response.

Cameron kept her aim still on the closet, while Kessler, Daley, and Paules moved past her. Daley took left and Paules right, as Kessler reached for the door. He nodded back to Cameron. She nodded in return. *Just try it, you son of a bitch. I'm ready.* Kessler slid the door open. A Heckler & Koch MP5 machine gun fell to the floor with a clank. Kessler and Daley pulled the shooter out. Dead.

"Suspect is down," Lau reported into his radio. "I repeat, suspect is down."

Without looking at the perp's face, Cameron lowered her weapon and left the room. Diego stood in the doorway smiling. "Nice work, Officer Cruz."

"Well, thank you, Ramirez," she said, trying not to grin like a schoolgirl. She followed him out of the house, itching to get him alone.

CHAPTER 2

DIEGO AND CAMERON were always careful to leave the station sepa-
rately. Usually she went first, but tonight, he begged off drinks with the
group. "Seeing my girl," he said without looking at her.

"When we going to meet this invisible chica?" Paules asked.

Diego shook his head.

"You afraid of a little competition?" Kessler joked.

"That's it," Diego responded. "You're so smooth, I'm afraid she'd fall for
one of you bozos."

Cameron took her time, packing up her bag and listening to the
male banter.

Sergeant Lavick came in and shed his coat. He stood in front of his locker
and stared at the lock.

Paules and Lau stifled their laughter.

Lavick spun the knob a few times. "Sixteen." Cameron folded her belt
into her locker. "Twenty-seven," she said.

Lavick frowned. "I know my own damn combination."

Lau burst out laughing. Lavick picked up a baseball hat off the bench and
flicked it at him like a Frisbee. "Watch it, Lau. Quarterlies are coming up."

Lavick turned to Cameron.

"Thirty-six," she whispered as her phone vibrated in her back pocket.
Diego.

"You sure you don't want to join tonight?" Kessler asked, leaning against
the locker beside hers.

"Not tonight."

She closed the locker and said good night. Only in the car did she read Diego's text.

PHNH in twenty.

Of course. She should have known they would go to the Potrero Hill Neighborhood House. It was one of Diego's favorite spots. During the day, it was a community center aimed at helping kids make good choices. It had been in use for more than fifty years. Diego had spent many afternoons there as a kid himself, before graduating and becoming a mentor. Now, he spent free afternoons at PHNH, talking with kids, helping with homework or playing basketball behind the house. At night, though, the center was closed, and the views of the city skyline were stunning. Tonight was the perfect night for it. No clouds and the temperature in the low seventies.

They might walk down the hill and have Cuban food at Fruitlandia. Maybe walk over to the park or climb the hill above the reservoir on the next block to get the extra twenty feet of view. The sun would set over the house, cutting down between the streets of the city and washing everything in pink and orange. And then, they would go home. Where in there did she tell him that he was going to be a father?

When she parked on De Haro, Diego was already on the porch, legs dangling over the banister exactly the way he told the kids they couldn't. He appeared lost in thought as she approached. He reached a hand back and helped her climb over the banister. She sat beside him, leaning into his warmth.

"Nice night," she said.

"Gorgeous." He smiled, but it faltered. Something in his brow was worried. He touched the hair along her face, slowly. Kissed her lips gently.

"What's wrong?"

He stroked her face, running his thumb along her jaw. "Nothing." He stared at the skyline and went quiet.

Normally, they would start in on the job, recount the moments from the day. He would talk about her kill shot. The banter before they got quieter, found the intimacy that they couldn't share at work.

Diego shook his head. "No, it's not nothing."

Cameron shifted away from him, waiting.

He didn't meet her eye as he spoke. "They're taking me undercover."

"What do you mean? Who?"

"ICE," he said. When she didn't respond, he added, "Immigration and Customs Enforcement."

She was in shock. "I know what ICE is."

"I offered to help with an ongoing investigation. Actually, I put my name in eight months ago. I got the call this morning."

"Where will you be?"

He looked at her without answering.

"You can't tell me?"

He held her gaze.

She thought about the baby, subconsciously crossed her arms. "How long?"

"Six weeks, maybe two months. It will seem like forever."

"It will." She thought about all the times her Papa had told her she shouldn't be training to be a police officer, when Mama pleaded with her to find a safe job. Telling him about the baby would be the same as asking him to stay. Two months from now she would be fifteen or sixteen weeks. It could wait. It would have to.

CHAPTER 3

Three months later

THIS WAS THE hardest part of the day at work, the time when she felt Diego's absence most profoundly. While it used to be a time of celebration, the job accomplished, now it reminded her that she was heading into another night when she couldn't see Diego, couldn't even talk to him. Cameron heaved her equipment bag back onto the top shelf of the storage room.

"Need some help getting it up there?" Daley joked.

"Mine's done, but you sure you can reach your spot? I can give you a boost," she joked back.

She'd originally been given a spot on the bottom shelf, but since she was one of the tallest members of the team, they eventually moved her to the top shelf.

Lau laughed out loud. "She's got a few inches on you, Daley."

"And on you," he sparred back.

She chuckled at them, more at ease in this environment than in any she'd ever known. As a kid, her brothers told her she could never be a cop. Not a girl, certainly not a gringa so unlike any of the police in her tiny hometown of Bleakwood, Texas. *Couldn't,* to her, meant *should,* and she'd been easily baited. What better way to make a stamp on the world than to make it safer?

Cameron rubbed her hand across her head. Tonight, she was ready to go home and get a shower. The changes in her body had pushed her to the outside of the group again. Sometimes, before Diego went undercover, she had gone along for the celebratory round of drinks. Careful to sit on the opposite side of the room from Diego, she'd listen as the men spun short tales into tall ones.

She was always the quiet one. Previous boyfriends had complained about her reticence. Women were supposed to ooze emotion, but that wasn't Cameron's style. No one had been worth talking to until Diego. He'd simply drawn her out, and it had felt as natural as exhaling.

Even after he went undercover, she still participated in some of the team nights out. She went to the bar and ordered a Coke. Mostly, she listened, laughed, and called out the really big lies. These men had no idea how far Cameron had come from the reticent girl she'd been. They called her the shyest tough girl on the force, but she was accustomed to feeling strange about her quiet nature. Being in the middle of the rambunctious group of men was no different from growing up the quiet, white girl in a raucous Mexican family.

"You coming out, Cruz?" Lau asked.

"Not tonight."

She caught Kessler eyeing her midsection and quickly pulled on her coat. She had to tell her sergeant. She'd been hoping to tell Diego first, to hold off until she'd heard from him. But, the bump was getting too obvious.

She grabbed her pack and said good night, heading to the sergeant's office before she chickened out again. As she passed the captain's office, she saw Sergeant Lavick sitting across from Captain Margaret Ahrens. Not wanting to interrupt, she kept walking, but Captain Ahrens caught her eye.

"You have a minute, Officer Cruz?" Captain Ahrens called out.

Cameron stopped in the doorway. The team had little interaction with Captain Ahrens. She was seldom in her office, as she coordinated the team's efforts with other departments. This meant she spent most of her time in the main station on Bryant. It felt especially strange since they were the only two women.

"That was nice work today," Sergeant Lavick said, taking off his glasses and rubbing the red marks on his nose with long, thin fingers. The skin on his knuckles suddenly seemed too loose, like an old man's. His face was thinner, too. Maybe he was sick.

"I heard you did very well," Captain Ahrens added. Even behind her desk, she was formidable. Taller than Cameron, she had the build of a basketball player.

"Thank you."

"Come on in," Ahrens said, motioning to the empty seat in front of her desk.

Ahren's office was largely sterile. Commendations and diplomas, as well as several pictures of Ahrens, including one with Michelle Obama, hung on the walls. But, the only personal picture was the one framed on her desk, an eight-by-ten of a large German shepherd. Cameron knew that dog was named Kleina, because the dog's tag hung from Ahrens' keychain.

"You okay?" Captain Ahrens asked.

Cameron didn't answer at first. It was now or never. She stepped into the office. "I'm going to need some time off."

Lavick put his glasses back on. "You mean vacation time?"

She considered telling them to forget it when she felt the strange gurgling of the baby moving. "More like leave."

"Medical leave?" Ahrens asked, folding her hands on her desk and leaning forward.

Cameron nodded.

"Are you all right?" Lavick asked.

"I'm fine. I have a—I'm—" Cameron hadn't said the words out loud, except to Rosa. Even Mama didn't know yet, although Cameron knew she had to tell her soon.

"Lavick," Ahrens interrupted. "Will you excuse us for a moment?"

Lavick frowned. "I should probably stay—"

"Please, Michael," Ahrens interjected. "I'll call you back in a few minutes. I would like to talk to Officer Cruz."

"Like woman to woman?" Lavick said, nodding.

Ahrens raised an eyebrow. "Sure."

Lavick got up and left.

"How far along are you?" Ahrens asked as soon as the door had clicked closed.

Cameron didn't blink. "Twenty-one weeks."

"Wow, you've kept it well concealed."

Cameron didn't answer. She felt huge.

"You're keeping it."

"There was never any question."

"And the father?" she asked.

"I think he'll be supportive."

Ahrens cocked her eyebrow again. "He doesn't know?"

"Not yet."

Ahrens was quiet before she said, "I have a son."

"I had no idea," Cameron responded as she scanned the room for some evidence of the child. There was none.

"We're not in touch," Ahrens added and Cameron didn't ask more. Ahrens opened her desk drawer and pulled out a notepad. "Twenty-one weeks," she said out loud. "You've got leave from the state—a portion of it paid and some unpaid. You'll be okay for money?" She asked this without looking up.

"Fine."

"You can take up to six months after the baby is born without jeopardizing your position. I'll get the paperwork started and get you in touch with the benefits group. They'll help arrange a desk position until you deliver."

Six months after the baby. A desk job until she delivered. That was twenty more weeks. She might be away for a year. In seven years, she'd never gone more than nine days without shooting. How could she last a year?

Outside Captain Ahrens' office, Lavick stood talking to Kessler. "Everything okay?" he asked.

"Fine."

He was heading toward Ahrens' office when he said, "Oh, you got a letter. It came in the department mail. It's on my desk. Go ahead and grab it."

Cameron went into his office and found the letter. On the front, in Diego's handwriting, it said her name and the words "Personal and Confidential." No postmark. No return address. It meant he was close. Maybe coming home. Thank God.

Kessler filled the doorway. His blonde hair was cropped short, his brown eyes wide. Women stared at him when they were out with the team and friends in the department had asked about him more than once. He was good looking, if in a Nebraska farm boy kind of way. "Hey." He glanced at the envelope, but she quickly folded it and put it in her jacket pocket.

"Hi, Brian."

"I thought you might want to see a movie this weekend," he said. "The new Bond is out."

"I'm going to have to pass. I've got company in town this weekend."

"Family?" he asked, hopefully.

She nodded.

"Maybe next weekend."

She thought about how the captain and sergeant would tell the others about her news. She was glad she wouldn't be here. "Good night, Brian."

"Good night, Cameron. Have a good one."

She hurried down the hallway and out the door. As soon as she was in the night air, she tore open the envelope. She flattened the note in her hand, wondering if he knew about the baby. She scanned the page and caught the words "love" and "miss."

She tried to calm herself and read the first line.

If you're reading this, it means I'm dead.

CHAPTER 4

Seven months later

NATE WAS EVERY bit the night owl his father had been. Cameron spent at least three nights a week driving around the city, trying to lull him back to sleep. Most of the time, he was out before she could drive to the Potrero Hill Neighborhood House and back to the house. Home again, she would lift his car seat out of the car and carry him carefully into his room and let him sleep in the chair on the floor. A few times, she had tried to get him back into his crib without waking him, but she'd never succeeded.

Sometimes, though, they were in the car for hours. Tonight was one of those nights. She tried the freeway down to the airport and back. Then, through the city all the way down Franklin to Crissy Field and back up Van Ness. Around the neighborhood and twice to the Potrero Hill Neighborhood House. She hadn't been into the PHNH since Diego's death, but driving by sometimes made her feel a little closer to him. As often, it made her feel worse.

It felt like a different world now. After his death, she had simply withdrawn. That their relationship spanned all areas of her life only made it harder. Plus, there was the growing person inside her. It was as though he was a shadow always behind her, at work, at home, in her dreams. Every new day had started with a fresh sense of devastation at his death. Worse, she couldn't talk about it at work because it had taken a month for the news to travel through the proper channels and come out publicly.

A week later, Diego was given an official department burial. With no wife or mother to claim his flag, she had watched it be carried away. Cameron sat in the third row with the team. None of them cried. Rosa and Mama Cruz were there too, weeping for the three of them only a few rows back.

Though Diego was gone, she wasn't without him. She had the baby. The week after Diego was officially reported dead, Cameron went to see Dr. Waterman to confirm the baby's gender. Originally, she had welcomed the idea of a surprise. But after Diego's death, she wanted to identify the baby as a boy or a girl, not a thing. When the doctor had pointed out the small penis, Cameron had thought she'd known all along that it was a boy. She imagined the joy Diego would have had at the news and she'd cried right there on the examination table.

Sometimes, when the ache for Diego became too much, she told herself that this was how it was supposed to be—just her and Nate. She didn't expect him to fill a void that Diego had left. People expected too much of their children—pressured them to reach unattainable feats, to capture their own missed opportunities. She wanted Nate to be happy—honest and happy.

Sometimes, when she would sink deeper into her shell, close herself off more completely, Nate was there to pull her out—to force her to be in contact with others—Señora Accosta and Rosa, Mama, even his doctor, who treaded so cautiously across the ground of how Cameron was coping with single parenthood. Maybe not in the way everyone expected, but she was coping.

Except at the moment, her eyelids were closing on their own. Nate continued to fuss in the backseat. She passed the Neighborhood House and followed De Haro through a neighborhood of small bungalows. Cars lined both sides of the street. She turned on 23rd as Nate cried in earnest. Down Carolina, she spotted the reservoir. Alongside it, the sidewalk was empty. "*Okay, cariño. Estoy aquí. Tienes hambre, pobrecito?*" She parked and got out of the driver's seat and climbed into the back beside Nate. She locked the doors, then lifted Nate, who had fat tears rolling down his cheeks, from his car seat. Never an SUV person, Cameron had to admit the tinted windows were handy. Hushing the tiny dark-haired bundle, she lifted her shirt, snapped open her bra, and let the baby find her breast.

She scanned the street. At one o'clock in the morning on a Monday, she doubted she'd see anyone, but keeping an eye out was instinct. She ran her finger across the dark brow on Nate's tiny face that reminded her so much of Diego's. When she and Rosa and Nate were together, people presumed Rosa was the mom and Cameron a nanny. It had become a joke between them. Everyone who saw Nate commented on how much he must take after his father. She agreed. Many stared openly, waiting for her to supply that last bit of information: who was the father?

It didn't matter now. She told them she was a widow. Most left it at that. The rude ones stared at her ring finger for a band. She wondered if they judged her more harshly because Nate's appearance was so different from her own. If it would be better if he, too, were blond-haired and blue-eyed.

To her, it was only natural that Nate would look more like her family than her. She'd long since stopped trying to fit in. At five foot ten, female, and blond, she was all too aware of how different she looked from the average Cruz, or even a typical cop. She had learned to deflect attention from her appearance with her ability, but standing out had started way before that.

For her first eighteen years, her blond hair and blue eyes had been a sharp contrast to the Mexican kids in Texas who were her adopted siblings. She had learned early to defend herself. She never wanted anyone to do it for her. Would Nate suffer the same way because he didn't look like his mother?

She'd proven herself with the Special Ops Task Force. She was as good as any of them. Sometimes better. And they'd be glad to have her back. At least that's what Ahrens had assured her on the phone. She'd heard very little from the guys in the past seven months. They were men, after all. Even those with children weren't going to call and swap diapering secrets. But, once she was back, she'd be in the thick of it again. Within a week, they would treat her as though she had never left. Or so she hoped.

She stared down at Nate's sweet face and listened to the little grunts and moans he made as he ate.

Outside, a car door slammed. Cameron flushed at the thought of someone seeing her breast-feed. The windows of the Blazer were dark, but if someone got close enough, they were transparent. She tucked her shirt down over Nate and searched for the source of the noise. Across the street, a man emerged from a dark green sedan. He started up the hill to the water reservoir. Peering between the seats, she saw another man waiting above.

Nate squirmed, and she brought him back to her breast without taking her eyes off the men. They met on the small path that circled the white, steel reservoir. The one who had come from the car was empty-handed while the other held a black gym bag. He dropped it on the ground between them, waving at it. She scanned the street for anyone else. Something was going down. Where was her phone? The man from the car grabbed for the bag. The first man pushed him back. They were yelling, but she couldn't make out their words.

It was too dark to make out their faces, but from the shadows, she saw the one from the car reach into his jacket. "Shit." It was a gun.

She thought her phone was in her purse. She tugged Nate off her breast to reach for it. Nate shrieked. Dropping to her knees, she brought him back to her breast.

Her heart was pounding. "Shh," she told him. "It's okay."

She peered out the window. The two men were looking around. Could they possibly have heard Nate?

She had to get to her phone. She counted to three and slipped Nate off her breast, cupping him against her as she sprang into the front seat and grabbed the strap of her purse.

Nate let out a piercing scream as she whipped the bag over the seat and dropped it beside her right knee. The man from the car came back down the hill, scanning the area. Cameron bent over, careful not to put her weight on Nate while trying to get him to feed. He wouldn't latch on. Come on, Nathaniel. His mouth widened for another scream. She tried to fill the open mouth with her breast. Her hands were shaking. "Please, baby. Come on."

One-handed, she rummaged through her purse for a pacifier. Why hadn't she bought one of those stupid things that attached to his outfit? Finally, she felt the soft latex of the nipple and pulled it out. Popped it into his mouth. She took a slow breath. The men were back on the hill. The one with the bag kicked it toward the other one. Where was her phone?

She scanned the front and spotted her phone on the passenger seat. She reached across and punched 9-1-1 without unlocking the screen. "This is Officer Cruz requesting a 406 at the water reservoir on Carolina. We have two 917s. One is armed. Repeat, requesting 406 at the reservoir on Carolina and 22nd." She lowered Nate toward his car seat.

If shots were fired, he'd be safer on the floor. She wrapped him like a burrito in a blanket and set him down on a burp cloth on the floor mat. She scanned the car for something else to cover him and remembered she'd thrown her equipment bag in the back so she could go train with the team. She reached over the seat for the bag, unzipped it blindly, and pulled out her Kevlar vest. She used it to create a semicircular shield of stiff Kevlar over Nate's little form.

She watched the man with the gun, waiting for him to make a move. She made mental notes of the differences between the two men. The one from the car had a slouch, a little rounder in the middle. He wore a light jacket, navy or black, and shoes that reminded her of the ones patrol officers wore. The other man was a little taller, more athletic. He wore sweatpants and a dark long-sleeved shirt. Nikes in gray. A baseball cap but no insignia that she saw. She checked on Nate, whose eyes were closed and moved back onto her knees. The police would be here any minute. Someone would drive by. There were easily a thousand people within ten blocks. Where the hell were they right then?

She took hold of her SIG with no plans of firing it. The car offered no cover. She'd never risk Nate. She couldn't leave either. They had to keep quiet until backup arrived.

Just then, Nate squirmed. She pressed the pacifier into his mouth and held it until he started sucking hard again. "Shh, baby. It's okay." She could sink onto the floor and feed him. The two men were still talking; the one with the gun held it barrel down. Maybe it was only a threat. Maybe he wouldn't use it.

The man in the cap shook his head and reached for the gym bag. The tension rose. The gunman raised his weapon. The man in the cap shouted. She scanned the streets, straining to hear sirens. Where were they?

Cameron was frozen. She had a decent shot, but she couldn't shoot from the car. No way. She gripped the gun, her mind racing. Come on.

A shot rang out. The man in the cap fell forward onto his knees. He dropped the bag and touched his chest. The shooter moved for the duffle, raising the gun. She was sure he was going to shoot again, but the man in the cap drew his own weapon and shot twice, quickly. The first shooter fell backward. The man in the cap dropped to the cement as though he were praying. After several beats, he lifted his head and rose slowly to his feet.

She pressed Nate's pacifier in again, then placed her hand on the door, switching the safety off on her weapon. The man shouldered the gym bag and started toward the far side of the reservoir. She paused again to listen for backup.

She couldn't let him get away. With a deep breath, she opened her car door and closed it silently. She rounded the back of the car and staying low, moved down the street until she was at a car two down from her own. A small Honda Civic wasn't perfect cover, but it would do. Using the car as a shield, she screamed, "This is the police! Get your hands up where I can see them."

The shooter turned around, the gun in his hand.

"Now!" she shouted.

The man dropped the gun and lifted his hands slowly.

"Put them on top of your head." He interlaced his fingers and rested his hands on top of his baseball cap.

Cameron left the cover of the car and started up the hill toward him. She watched his stance, the angle of his chin under the cap. She closed the distance and studied his face, the dark shadow of a week without shaving. Even under the baseball cap, she saw his eyes. "Get your hands up." Her voice cracked as she yelled. When he lifted his chin, she saw the scar beside his right brow. The air disappeared.

She was staring at Diego Ramirez.

CHAPTER 5

"YOU'RE ALIVE." SHE couldn't breathe. Diego was here. Alive. In the flesh. She felt frozen, yet her body leaned toward him of its own accord. How many nights had she dreamt of seeing him again? She scanned his body for injuries. There were none. He was alive. He was okay. He was here.

"Cameron."

She closed her eyes and let his voice echo through her. When she opened them again, he was a step closer. He reached out and touched her face. She heard a low moan that must have come from her. A brief flash of some past moment crossed her mind, some infinite fraction of emotion that compared to this. Behind it was the memory of his touch, of their closeness, of Nate.

Then, she remembered the shot. She turned to the man Diego had shot. Squatted and rolled him onto his back. "Ray Benjamin."

She tightened her grip on the pistol and Diego took a step backward. "You shot Ray Benjamin." She felt for a pulse. "You killed a cop!"

Diego touched his chest. "He shot me first."

A cop. Diego had killed another cop. On her feet, Cameron steadied her hand, and stiffened her thighs to ready herself. She hadn't shot outside the range in seven months. "Keep your hands up." She moved toward him. "Are you alone?"

Diego eyed the dead man. "Listen, Cameron. I—"

"No," she commanded. "Get your hands up." Not dead—alive. Her motions were habit, protocol. Call for backup. Disarm the perp. Check the wounded. Perform all possible lifesaving techniques until the arrival of paramedics.

He glanced down at his gun.

"Don't do it," she warned. "I swear I'll shoot."

"You don't want to do that," he said.

She tried to shrug, though it came out jerky and awkward. He watched her as though it was a normal day, as though he hadn't sent her a note to tell her he was dead, as though he hadn't abandoned her and shot another officer. She ached to throw her arms around him, touch his face, feel him solid and real. He'd been gone. He'd been dead. Now, he was alive.

He watched the gun again. "Really, you don't want to shoot me."

"Actually, shooting you seems like a good idea," she choked out, so desperate to feel nothing that she had the passing thought that if she shot him the old reality would be true again. "I thought you were dead. This way it would be true." She left the words hanging, giving him a chance to explain. As though it were possible.

He said nothing. He'd left her. She'd had his child, his son. Trembling with fury, she kicked the gun aside. Focused on his weapon instead of his face, hoping it would make the next step easier. *Get it done*. Get it done, and get out.

"I'm taking you in," she said. Saying it out loud made it real. It had to be real. She would do the right thing here.

He shook his head, his chin inching upwards the way it did when he was being stubborn. "I can't let you do that."

"You don't have a choice. Put your hands on your head and turn around." She needed to close the distance, to end this awkwardness, to be staring at his back and cuffing him rather than meet his eyes. But, the thought of physical touch gave her pause.

Forcing herself forward, she pushed him with her fist, wanting as little contact as possible. "Hands on head. Turn around."

He rotated. She felt under his arms and at his waist for a backup weapon. The rigid muscles in his back shifted against her chest. She struggled to move quickly and end the physical contact. She found his old .38 on his ankle and yanked it out. She remembered the piece. He'd been superstitious about it being his lucky backup. The sight of it, something he'd had before, something from when they were together, was excruciating. She wanted to say something flippant about the gun, some snappy comment, but nothing came. "Get down on the ground."

He hesitated. She pushed him. "Do it, now."

A moment later, Nate let out a shrieking cry from the car. Her stomach dropped. *Oh, God, Nathaniel.*

She pushed Diego toward the ground as Nate wailed. Finish with Diego, she told herself.

"What the hell is that?" he asked.

She didn't have cuffs. She'd have to sit on Diego until backup came. Where the hell were they? Nate was quiet briefly. Cameron took the .38 and backed away from Diego.

Nate cried out again. Without a word, she sprinted to the car. She didn't want Diego to know about Nate. She didn't want to explain—he had no right—not now, not ever.

As she looked back, Diego rose onto his knees.

"Get back down," she shouted.

He kept rising. She fired a shot. It cracked into the asphalt a foot from his head. "I won't miss again," she warned.

He dropped down again.

Cameron checked the safety and put Diego's gun in the rear of the car with her own. With the guns away, she leaned over Nate and wiped his fat, baby tears. "You're okay. *Todo está bien, cariño.*" She found his pacifier, and put it in his mouth.

Diego was climbing into Benjamin's truck. She grabbed her SIG and ran toward him as he threw the car into reverse and drove in a crooked line backward. Fifty feet down the road, he spun the car around and sped away.

Steadying the weapon, Cameron shot out his left taillight, then the driver's side mirror. Then, he was gone. The adrenaline faded. It was like losing her breath. She put her gun away and pulled Nate into her arms. Holding him tight, she rocked him. Diego was alive. Alive and gone. He'd left her. Jesus Christ, she'd let him go.

She kissed Nate's wet cheek. Nate had saved him. No, she'd made the choice to let him go. It was a relief that he was gone. She pictured his face, the way she'd imagined him when she missed him most. The way he was when he was determined and strong, when he was honest and passionate.

Then, she imagined him as she'd seen him—alive, after months of thinking he was dead, after having his child…

It was only instinct that brought air into her lungs.

CHAPTER 6

CAMERON SAT OUTSIDE Lavick's office and tried not to fall asleep. She hadn't slept. Not that she could have. It had been after two when she arrived home, rattled. Nearly an hour of answering calls. The Homicide Inspector who showed up was someone new. He'd been less understanding than suspicious about her story of driving Nate around to get him to fall asleep. How could she blame him? Who went for a drive in the middle of the night and happened upon her baby's dead father shooting someone? How could that be a coincidence?

Maybe some higher being wanted her to see that. But she wished she hadn't. She wished to that same God that she could put it out of her head. The thoughts of how much he'd missed, how different life with Nate would be if Diego were with her. If he'd been beside her when Nate was born. If he hadn't been dead.

Worse, she had made a mess of the investigation. She had the gun she'd taken off him. When the officers first arrived, she was so focused on explaining what happened, how surprised she was to know the shooter that she didn't mention it. Maybe she thought she was protecting Diego. By the time she convinced herself it was a bad idea to keep it from them, the Homicide Inspector, Patterson, was making her feel like she'd done something wrong. Bringing it up then felt like a sure way to dig herself in deeper. She didn't want to delay getting home anymore. Nate had to be put to bed. She was practically dead on her feet.

At five, she gave up the fight for sleep and went for a run in the neighborhood. Over to Mission Delores Park where she ran up and down the hill's steep slope until her legs wobbled beneath her. Every thought was about Diego. Why and how and when and where. That reservoir was in the middle of his old neighborhood. Why would he have chosen to kill a man there? Any one of three-dozen kids could have ID'd him. Would he have killed them, too? And how had he been in San Francisco all these months without seeing her? Or had he? Did the kids at the Potrero House know he was alive? Had he gone there? Did he go to mass at Mission Dolores on Sundays? Was he there, sitting a few rows away from her? No. Then, he would have known about Nate.

He didn't have the look of someone living on the streets. His hair was longer, but that was nothing unusual. It always grew out with some wave, and he'd often go months without cutting it, until it curled out over his ears and Lavick gave him a hard time. It had been cut since he'd died, though. The few days' beard growth was unusual. For someone who rarely cut his hair, he'd hated whiskers. She'd actually liked them—the scratchy feel against her face and neck and chest when they made love. The thought made her want to throw up, purge him out of her. She realized that he hadn't been wearing the ratty, navy tennis shoes. Buying shoes was such a mundane task, something they used to do together.

"Cruz."

Cameron started, straightening in her chair.

Lavick nodded to her as he pulled keys from his pocket and unlocked his office door. "Come on in."

Cameron sat in the chair that she'd sat in a lifetime ago when Lavick had offered her a job on the team. Lavick settled behind his desk. "Long night," he said.

She held her chin up. She so wanted to stare at her hands, to avoid a gaze that she feared might unearth some emotion that she'd held so carefully in check before last night.

The office door opened, and Captain Ahrens came in. Her navy suit was already heavily creased across her lap as she sat in the chair opposite Cameron. "You two started?"

Lavick shook his head.

The sergeant spoke to Cameron. "We heard about last night."

"Yes, sir." Cameron felt a little like a child with her parents. Captain Ahrens was intimidating. Sergeant Lavick, too, was tall and broad. In another life, they might have made a good couple. Attractive enough, though they each had a nose that was a little wrong for their face. Hers too broad with a rounded bulb on its point, and his more hooked and a little off to one side, maybe from an old fight.

"Now, we want to hear it from you. Why don't you start with why you were there at one in the morning?" Lavick asked.

Ahrens was silent.

Cameron sat up and told them about Nate's sleepless nights, about the Potrero House being somewhere that she used to go, that she often drove Nate around that area, as it was close to home and traffic was quiet. She also told them that she'd been all over town last night. She recounted how she'd been trying to find a quiet block where no one would see her feed Nate. She fought not to blush or drop her head when she said the words "breast-feeding" or to notice as Lavick shifted a little in his seat.

She recounted what she'd seen before she recognized the shooter. Could she say his name without a crack in her voice? She cleared her throat. "Diego Ramirez."

Ahrens frowned. "Diego Ramirez. The Special Ops Officer who was killed last year?"

"He's not dead, Captain," Cameron said. "I saw him. I spoke to him. He's alive." She didn't mention how she had him on the ground, had his weapons, then let him go.

The sergeant spun around to a cabinet and opened a drawer, thumbing through a number of files before drawing one out. He laid it on his desk and flipped it open. "Ramirez was killed on the border. I have the autopsy report dated August 22nd. They matched his dental records."

"I thought he was dead, too, Sergeant, but it was—"

Lavick looked up. "Diego Ramirez?"

She nodded. "And I have proof."

"What kind of proof?" Ahrens asked.

"I took his backup weapon off him."

Ahrens straightened in her chair until she was some six or eight inches taller. "You had contact with the shooter?"

"Not contact, exactly," she replied carefully.

"What exactly?" her sergeant asked.

"I had my weapon drawn. I told him to drop the gun. He did." She stopped talking. And then the baby cried and she ran for him.

"What then?"

"I was trying to call for backup and…"

"Where was the baby?" Ahrens asked.

"In the car."

Ahrens glanced at Lavick. The two seemed to agree on something.

Cameron sat on her palms to keep from fidgeting. "I should have given it to the inspector last night."

"And why didn't you?" Ahrens asked from her perch.

Cameron didn't answer at first. She'd been protecting him, but she didn't want to say that out loud. "I'm not sure," she offered. "He was one of ours."

"Where is the gun now?"

"In my car. I can go get it—"

Ahrens stood. "Get an evidence bag," she said, then turned to Lavick. "Have Ambley take it to the lab and babysit it. I want to confirm that Ramirez is alive for myself."

"If he is," Lavick said, "we have to assume he's not working for us."

"Right." Without looking at Cameron, she added, "Touch base with me as soon as you know something." She said nothing else as she stepped out of the office. Cameron had a strong desire to cry. Stupid. Of course they wanted to know why she wasn't able to capture him. Then, there was the question about Nate. Lavick opened a drawer and handed Cameron a large Ziploc bag.

Just as Cameron stood up, Ballestrini stopped in the doorway. Tim Ballestrini had a short, thick neck that someone had once likened to Italian sausage. He was also the team ham. The other guys called him Ballerina because of his fondness for show tunes and because he was anything but. Heavy-footed and clumsy, Ballestrini was permanently part of the intelligence team because he had a tendency to be too loud. The one time he'd gone on a reconnaissance mission, the perp had flown the coop.

"Cameron Cruz," Ballestrini said, bobbing his head from left to right like he did when he was being goofy. "What a sight. You coming back?"

Cameron nodded. "Hey, Ballestrini."

"Wow, you look tired, Cruz. You got the postpartum depression?"

"Ballestrini, give it a rest," the sergeant warned.

Tim raised his hand at the sergeant. "I'm being serious here, Sergeant.

Betty had it both times—crying all the time, couldn't keep it together." He put his hand on Cameron's shoulder. "It's real common. They got good meds for that stuff. You should talk to your doctor. Don't be ashamed or nothing."

"Can you excuse us, please," Lavick said, and Ballestrini headed out the door, whistling.

Lavick closed the door behind him. Cameron remained standing. "Ballestrini makes a point. Seeing a shooting is always tough. You want to talk to someone downtown?"

He was referring to a police psychologist. "I've been through it before. I'll be fine." It wasn't the death that struck her. It was the shooter. She wouldn't share the thoughts in her head with anyone, certainly not a stranger. Even she didn't want to be in her brain right now.

"If it's okay, Sergeant, I'd like to start back next week. Full duty. I'll start with equipment. I'm out of shape, but I'll work back up."

"Next week it is. You can take Ballestrini. He can yap your ear off about postpartum depression."

She walked through the station while her fellow officers hurried past her. A few greeted her quickly, but most were focused—head down. The job was priority. That's how it should be. Cameron jogged out to the car, feeling the burn in her quads and hamstrings from the morning's run. She was coming back to work. Suddenly, she couldn't wait.

She used her fob to unlock the car. With the rear hatch open, she turned the Ziploc bag inside out to use it like a glove. She scanned the back of the car, moving aside canvas grocery bags and a pair of running shoes. She had put the gun in the back corner and locked the car. Hadn't she locked it? She pulled things aside and searched again. No gun. Someone had taken it.

Diego. "Damn him."

CHAPTER 7

SHE STAYED IN the gym until the guys were gone and was slow to repack her gear. When she made her way to the locker room, it was empty. In the old days, one of the guys would surely have come by the gym to invite her out. But, these were new days. She had a baby now. She'd seen one of their own shoot a cop. Then, she'd lost the evidence. Lavick told her the lost evidence would be noted in her permanent file. It all made for a miserable first week back.

Worse, there was absolute silence on Diego. She had to believe he would show up somewhere but when? And where? Lavick and Ahrens spent large parts of the days up at Bryant, dealing with who knows what. She'd gotten no word on Diego. What did she expect? She'd failed to capture him, lost the gun. Without it, there was no proving to Ahrens and Lavick that she'd seen Diego. Her arms and back ached from lugging equipment around. With no active cases, Lau ran training drills. Kessler and Ballestrini led the team through strategy sessions. For all his goofiness, Ballestrini was a strong strategist. He was clever and had a head for planning. The team was uptight and antsy. Cameron had to remind herself that it happened when they didn't get any action.

The locker room lights were on, the fan running. A sink faucet dripped. The floor was littered with forgotten items—a stray sock, the cap to a deodorant, an SF Giants towel, two candy bar wrappers, a red poker chip, and an SFPD baseball cap from the squad's softball team. She picked up the garbage and threw it in the trash with the sock, folded the towel and laid the hat on top. With some finagling, the faucet stopped dripping. She shut off the fan. She wasn't ready to go home.

Nate was waiting for her. Rosa had the day off, so they were together. She should have wanted to go home. Nothing about this place felt right anymore. She scanned the row of lockers. Diego's had been the one on the end. The lock was gone. She lifted the lever and pulled it open. There was nothing inside. She leaned in and smelled, but his smell was gone. What did she expect after a year?

It was silent when she left. Special Ops was housed in San Francisco's Hunters Point, a few miles from the main police station. When the team was gone, the place could feel eerily quiet. She drove home slowly, knowing Rosa would be full of questions. She came in the back door and heard the TV on in the den. It was after eight, so Nate was probably sleeping. She felt guilty for missing him.

She needed to snap out of this, focus on what mattered. Her family, her job. Why was that so hard? In the kitchen, she poured a glass of milk. Where were the cookies? Her sister had a habit of loading up on sweets at the grocery store, then hiding them at home. Rosa tended to like the fancy sweets—Häagen Dazs and Godiva. Cameron preferred Oreos, Chips Ahoy!, and the vanilla wafers, which were surely full of high fructose and saturated fat. She opened the cabinet under the sink, pushing her way through the childproof lock Rosa had insisted on installing before Nate was born, and ducked under, in search of sweets.

"What are you doing?"

Cameron jumped and knocked her head into the underside of the counter. She sank onto the floor, holding her head.

Rosa was in the doorway. "You missed Ricky."

Cameron moaned. "Dinner."

"It's fine. I made us some enchiladas. But, be careful. Evelyn talks to Mama at least twice a week, so she's going to know you bailed on him."

"Shit." Ricky was Cameron's first mentor at the SFPD and his wife, Evelyn, was one of Mama Cruz's oldest friends from Bleakwood, Texas. Cameron knew that Evelyn had met Cameron's birth parents, but she hadn't known them well. Oddly, she and Evelyn had never talked about it.

When Cameron came out to San Francisco, Mama Cruz sent her to Evelyn and Ricky. Cameron stayed with them for five weeks while she interviewed for positions at the police department. Back then, Ricky was the captain of the Special Ops team, which had included both the Special Ops team and the Sharpshooters.

With Ricky's help, Cameron was hired on as a patrol officer. Recognizing her shooting ability, Ricky also helped her make Specials Ops in under three years, a record for the department. Cameron was no charity case. Her talent held up to the toughest critics, which was good, because Ricky had put himself on the line for her.

Now that he was retired, Cameron no longer saw him at the station, but they had dinner about twice a month, which gave Cameron the chance to talk freely about work. In addition, Cameron and Rosa usually spent Easter and Thanksgiving with Evelyn and Ricky. Cameron and Rosa got some motherly attention, and Mama Cruz got word back that her girls were eating well and not working too hard. A win, win. And now, she'd blown him off. "Was he pissed?"

"I am sure he understood, since you're just back and all." Rosa moved around the table, her perfectly coordinated outfit as pressed as if she'd just put it on. Rosa always dressed in colors—all blue, all red, orange, chartreuse, colors Cameron couldn't name. Each outfit had a patterned top or bottom mixed with a solid, perfectly paired. From living with her, Cameron knew that she kept them lined up in her closet, each ensemble together, shoes included. It was another skill Cameron lacked. Cameron wore jeans and sweatshirts, her boyish figure flat and straight. Rosa's was curvy, and she accentuated it with narrow skirts and fitted tops.

"I thought you'd be home at six."

Cameron shrugged.

"You guys get called out?"

"No."

Rosa stooped to pull out the slower cooker.

"I'm not really hungry," Cameron said, trying to cut off Rosa's mothering instincts to feed her. Ever since the pregnancy, Rosa's solution to everything was food.

Instead, Rosa removed the lid and retrieved a bag of unopened Oreos between her fingertips. "I thought you were looking for these."

"Oh, thank you." Cameron tore the bag open and rocked back on her chair to open the refrigerator and get more milk. She ate three without pausing for air. When she looked up, Rosa was staring, brow furrowed. "You seemed better until this last week. Maybe going back to work was a bad idea."

Cameron couldn't meet her gaze. Instead, she focused on twisting the top of an Oreo off without losing any of the filling.

"Does it make you think about him more?"

Cameron put the chocolate in her mouth. At first, she thought Rosa was referring to the shooting, but she hadn't told Rosa about seeing Diego. Why feed her theory that Latin men were all the same? But, that wasn't really why. If Rosa knew, it would mean hours of talking, trying to figure out why he would pretend to be dead. It was hard enough without that. She twisted the top off another Oreo and ate the chocolate, then pressed the two together to make a double stuff.

At the door, Rosa waited for an answer.

"Tell me about the day," Cameron said.

Rosa sighed and conceded. "For starters, Nate smiled at me in the park. He loves his Tía Rosa."

"That's wonderful," Cameron said, trying to sound upbeat. She didn't want Rosa to know how upset she was. She didn't want to get into everything that had happened. She was just so tired. "Of course he does."

"Well, he may be the only man who does." She sighed. "I went out with Jim from the bank again last night."

Cameron studied her sister, half smiling at the way she always described her men: Bill from the hospital, Dan from the pharmacy, and Jim from the bank. "Bad?"

"Horrible. Why are Anglo men so arrogant?"

Cameron waited for her to add to that. When she didn't, Cameron said, "If Anglo men are bad, why don't you date Latin men?"

Rosa looked horrified. "Oh, God, no. They expect women to be their slaves."

"I think you're taking the stereotypes a bit far."

"I'm not dating Latin men." The familiar refrain came out in a tone that didn't hide her disgust at the suggestion.

"They can't be that bad. What about Papa and Miguel?" She thought about their other brother, Juan. He could be a jerk. "So maybe Juan is a bit arrogant, but not Miguel, not Papa." Diego came to mind—the way he'd been before, and the way he was now. Maybe Rosa was right. Certainly Cameron could no longer trust her own judgment on the subject.

Rosa sank into a chair across from Cameron. "I want something different from what we had."

Cameron reached over and squeezed her sister's hand. They'd had their share of rough times—times when their jealousy of what the other had put them at odds. Cameron would have done anything to look like Rosa, to be the outgoing Latina instead of the silent misfit. Rosa somehow imagined Caucasian women to be more elegant, more sophisticated.

Rosa patted Cameron's hand, but Cameron could tell she wasn't ready to be comforted. Rosa picked up an Oreo and then put it down again, crossing her arms. "You can't understand, Cameron."

Cameron swallowed her cookie along with the lump that always came when Rosa reminded her she wasn't really one of the Cruz family. "Because I'm a gringa."

"Why do you always make it sound like an insult?"

"Why do you always make it sound like it's some sort of prize?" Cameron sighed. "I'm tired, Rosa."

Rosa got up. "Me, too," she said. "I'm going to go take a bath." She started from the room and paused in the door. "Oh, you're almost out of breast milk. I've been supplementing with formula."

Since the night with Diego, her milk production had practically stopped. "I have, too. I'm not producing enough." It felt like admitting to something shameful.

"It's got to be impossible to pump at the station."

She managed to do it a couple times a day, but her body seemed to have lost interest in it.

"Oh, and don't be too mad when you see Nate's toes," Rosa added.

"His toes?"

Rosa grinned.

"Rosa, you did not paint his toes."

"It's a very masculine color," Rosa said.

"Rosa Maria!"

"I had to try it out. I think you'll like it. Tangerine Dream."

Cameron took the last of her milk and headed down the hall.

Nate's room was dark except for a small moon-shaped nightlight in one corner. Cameron pulled the rocking chair over to the crib, sat, and stared down at him. She couldn't see his toes, but she had to smile at the image of his nails with polish on them. Rosa owned a little salon and loved giving makeovers. Cameron hadn't considered Nate as a potential client. Only Rosa could paint such tiny toenails.

Cameron kissed her son, and went to get ready for bed. Before she shut off the lights, she sent Ricky a text message with a bullshit excuse for missing dinner and hoped she wasn't as transparent to him as she was to Rosa.

CHAPTER 8

GRAVEL POPPED AND crunched beneath the tires of the truck. Ivana Pestova had no idea where they were. Three weeks since she left Šluknov. A truck from Varnsdorf to Germany then two—or maybe three—more trucks before the boat. It became difficult to keep count. On each journey, she and the other girls were stuck somewhere dark and cramped, unable to see outside. In the first truck, Ivana sat with a girl named Barunka from Rumburk, a town near hers. The two had whispered excitedly for the first hours of the journey. Though their towns were only a dozen kilometers from the German border, neither girl had ever been into Germany. They hoped to have a chance to spend a few hours or maybe a day in one of the cities there.

Instead, after a short break somewhere near Hamburg, where they were fed thick spicy stew at a long table in a dark back room, the trucks were reloaded. Barunka was not there. Ivana tried to imagine that they would meet up again on the journey to America, but they never had. After that, there were different faces at every stop. A boat to New York and then trucks—one after the other until she'd lost count. Fewer and fewer of the girls spoke Czech until it felt like she was the only one. The languages she heard now were foreign. Unable to communicate, the girls offered each other small, awkward smiles.

Two girls were trying to communicate with drawings. Ivana guessed they were talking about home. She was determined not to think about home. Still, she couldn't stop herself from imagining the narrow road that she and Michal ran down each day to catch the bus to work in Varnsdorf. The feel of cold, wet cobblestone under the thin soles of her black, lace-up boots. The tightness where her toes had long ago reached the end of the shoe and now curled against the soft leather, straining against the stitching. For more than half the year, the cold burned her lungs as she inhaled and breath slipped from her lips in waves of thick, white smoke. March in Šluknov and Varnsdorf—in the entire region—was bitter. Worse, the poor part of town was always colder, and things were worse lately. There were cutbacks at the factory where her mother worked on the line making machines for drilling.

Usually, her mother could afford new sneakers when her old ones got too ratty, but this year, Ivana had to make due. A hole in one of the soles meant her foot was soaking wet whenever it rained. The air stung her skin where the sleeves of her coat were too short to cover her wrists. Fighting the cold in her lungs, Ivana would sing the words to California Girls by Katy Perry, urging Michal to hurry so they didn't miss the bus. She couldn't be late. If Amira called her mother again, she'd be whipped worse than last time. The children at school had made fun of her for the way she'd sat after that day. No, she couldn't be late. But a whipping wasn't the only reason she longed to get to work on time. She secretly hoped the man who had asked her about going to America would be there again.

On the weekends when there wasn't extra sewing to do, Ivana would escape their drafty two-room apartment and go in search of American things in the shops in town. Michal was easily bribed with a treat to be quiet while she peered in the windows from the street and hunted for televisions playing American shows. She had been shut out of the shops and bars by storekeepers who knew she was too poor to afford anything inside. One day she would come back from America and turn her nose up at them.

In her memory, she saw the bus pulling to the curb up ahead. People swarmed on and off, wrapped in heavy coats and scarves against the harsh cold. Ivana turned back for Michal. He wasn't too far behind. She jumped on board and held her hand out for her brother.

He reached her as the bus started to move from the curb.

"Wait! My foot is caught," Ivana yelled so the driver would slow for Michal.

The driver grabbed her by the arm and yanked her up the bus steps. "Your foot gets caught again on my bus and I'm going to break it off," he warned.

Several of the old ladies on the bus laughed.

Ivana had pulled Michal to the back of the bus. Mostly older people took the seats and though there were a few empty seats, Ivana made no move to sit down. The last time she'd tried to sit in an empty seat, an old man with sour breath and nose hairs so long they ran into his mustache pulled her out of it by her ear.

She would watch the gray stone buildings pass, the dark sky casting shadows that always made it feel much later than it was. Michal would be stifling a yawn. Ivana would straighten his jacket, then fasten the top button.

"Stop, I'm choking," he always complained.

"Fine, but you'd better be good. I don't want you ruining my chances to go to America," she had told him.

"You can't go to America. You have to stay with Mama and me."

Now, sitting on the truck, she prayed he was okay without her. She pictured how angry her mother must have been about her leaving.

She'd left a short note under the teapot where her mother would see it before Michal. She'd packed up only enough to fit in a small duffle and left.

The truck rolled over a large bump and her eyes jolted open. A girl cried. Shivering, Ivana wrapped her scarf up over her head and tied it tightly around her face. She had expected America to be warmer.

To distract herself, she imagined herself in a fancy gown, serving drinks to the people she had seen on the television. The gown was the lightest of pinks, like the blush of the roses once delivered from the small floral store near Amira's bar. And silk. A perfect fit over her hips and into a full skirt that swayed heavily as she walked and danced. Huddled on the floor of the cold truck, Ivana prayed she would soon arrive at her new life.

CHAPTER 9

SATURDAY NIGHT AFTER Rosa came home from a night out with friends from the salon, Cameron told her she was going to help with a reconnaissance job. It was partially true. She was doing recon, just not for work. Diego was alive. She wanted to find him. Beyond that, she needed to. She needed to understand. She had believed in him—in them—and she couldn't let it go. Not until she knew why. Maybe then it would hurt a little less.

Perhaps it was so much harder to digest the deceit because Diego had been her first love. And maybe it was worse because it had taken her until she was nearly thirty to find it. Rosa had been in and out of love a hundred times by thirty, but Cameron was so bent on finding the perfect man that she'd focused on the things that would be the same on the surface—Caucasian, maybe adopted, some Latin connection.

Mama pushed her to be more open to differences, but it had never made sense to her until Diego. Diego's father had come to America with his twin brother, bringing only the boys—Diego, who was twelve at the time, and two male cousins. The women had stayed in Mexico—Diego's mother, his aunt and his sister, Claudia. Diego's father had died within two years of arriving, and Diego was left with two cousins he couldn't stand and an uncle he didn't respect. He had been desperate to get back to Mexico, but his uncle forbade it. He was eighteen before he returned. By then, his mother was dead and his sister married to a criminal.

It was a little past three a.m. on a Saturday, but one was never alone for long in San Francisco. Tucking her weapon into the pocket of her down jacket, she cracked the car door open and eased out. She pushed it closed until it clicked and made her way across the street and up the block toward the old appliance store. Duct tape crisscrossed the storefront of a Mexican take-out place, a last effort to hold the broken pane together. Next door, plywood filled in for broken windows. Bright red and blue graffiti decorated the wood, spilling over onto the chipped stucco storefront. It was all exactly how she remembered.

It appeared abandoned now, just as it had the last time she was there. They had come a few days before Diego went undercover. They were at a nightclub called Bruno's, also in the Mission. He had been called to do a drop-off, so he brought her by, swearing her to secrecy. That time, Diego said there were six undercover cops inside. She never went in. He never spoke of it again, but when she made a list of everywhere he had ever taken her, this was on it.

How many other places had she never seen? What seedy places had the undercover work taken him? What lies had he had to devise to keep himself safe? But the hardest question came again and again. Why hadn't he trusted her? At least while she was searching for him, there was temporary relief from the onslaught of unanswered questions rolling around in her head on repeat.

She was careful not to mention his name at the station, but she was doing everything to find him. Even if it meant coming to this shit hole in the middle of the night. She tucked her hand into her pocket and gripped her SIG Sauer, thumbing the magazine to be sure it was in place. Her badge was zipped into her breast pocket. She gripped a heavy-duty flashlight in her left hand. A single car key was tucked into her left shoe. Nothing with her home address or contact information—not on her person or in the car. Standard procedure for an undercover cop. But, she was breaking a lot of undercover rules, too. She had her badge and her police-issued SIG.

She wasn't an undercover cop. She was just trying to think like one. By putting herself in his mindset, maybe she could find him. The storefront was empty. That night, Diego had gone around back. After that, she had no idea what he'd done. She'd have to wing it. With one more look around, she moved swiftly down the alley, shoes popping softly on broken glass. Though she moved as quietly as possible, she was keenly aware of her footsteps echoing across the empty alley.

Halfway down the alley was a metal door, painted black. The alley was quiet, an old, green dumpster her only companion. Here, the walls were free of the graffiti that painted the street. Some places were too daunting even for street artists. Only the faint stench of vomit rising from the ground suggested someone else had been back there recently. Instinctively, she touched the door and tried the knob. It was common in reconnaissance. You could often get a feel for the door's weight. This one was locked and heavy, nothing she could take down, certainly not without a ram, unless she was prepared to pump it full of bullets. There didn't appear to be another side entrance. She stared into the dark. The light at the back of the building was out. She flipped on the flashlight and shone it into the blackness. Active. Aware. Adrenaline pumping. She was never on the ground alone. She wished she were sitting on a rooftop with her sniper rifle.

She moved slowly down the alley, watching with a soft focus to allow her peripheral vision to catch any movement. At the back of the building, she used the beam to scan the area. No sign of life. She took one last look at the street and walked along the back of the building. She buttonholed into the first doorway, giving herself a second to gather herself before moving on. She pressed against the side of another dumpster, this one halfway down the alley, a strange place for one since access back here was limited. She sensed a shadow behind her and tightened her grip on the gun in her pocket when a heavy hand grabbed her jacket, forcing her to let go of the SIG. She dropped the light, which rolled to a stop, pointing to the back of the building. Dragged backward, she fought for footing. Her attacker grabbed her under the arms. She threw her elbows one after the other. She missed and missed, then finally one elbow connected. The hit was followed by a drunken curse.

He let go momentarily. She ducked under his arms, scrambling for her weapon. She gripped the metal when a second set of hands grabbed her. One arm was tight across her neck, the other behind it. A rear, naked choke hold. She stopped moving and tucked her chin down to prevent him from getting access to her neck.

The first one stood. His head was shaved, but his beard stretched black fuzz from under his eyes to the place where his T-shirt collar began. His eyes were dark in color and hooded. "What the hell you doing out here?"

She didn't answer, going limp in her attacker's arms. Instead of pitching forward, he dropped her. She barely landed on her feet. When she raised her chin, he cracked her in the face. The blackness became blacker, then streaks of light swam across her vision. She touched her cheek. Blood. The eye was swelling. The second man was black, easily six-two and two-twenty.

She wiped the sleeve of her jacket gently across her eye as the beard groped into her pocket. She shoved her elbow toward him but missed. She stumbled back and reached for her pocket. Too slow. He pulled the gun out, letting it hang on one finger from the trigger guard. "What have we got here?"

"Ooh, wee. Um," the hitter said. He swayed slightly as though under the influence, but his eyes were sharp and clear. The pupils weren't dilated. Something felt wrong.

"I asked you what you doing way out here… pretty girl like you," the beard repeated, giving her a smirk that was highlighted by a brilliant gold tooth.

"I'm looking for someone."

He shrugged and waved his arms out to his sides. "We the only ones here, so maybe you looking for us."

The black guy nodded. "You looking for us?"

One or both might be undercover cops—maybe it was the swaying with the sharp stare or maybe it was the odd match they made for street thugs—a black man big enough to be a linebacker for the Raiders and a white guy with a shaved head and a gold tooth. One screamed street gang, the other White Supremacist. "I'm looking for Diego Ramirez," she said. The vision in her left eye was nearly gone.

"You the police?"

Just then, the beard moved his hand to her other pocket and pulled out her badge. He read it before announcing, "Yes, sir, she the police. Special Ops, it says."

The other man whistled. "That's pretty fancy for a lady."

"Do you know where I can find Diego Ramirez?"

The man watched her, unblinking, some kind of test she didn't pass. "No, ma'am."

Cameron waited for his next move. When no one made one, she reached for the gun.

The beard snapped it back. "I don't think so. We done with her, T.J.?"

T.J. shook his head and smiled gold again. "Oh, no. Girl this pretty? A shame to put those looks to waste." Not cops.

Feigning fear, Cameron folded in, drawing her right leg up into her stomach. With a deep hard breath, she launched the foot sideways, landing it fast and hard in the beard's stomach. He doubled over, then fell backward, landing on his back. Her gun clattered to the ground. She went for it, but the black man lunged forward. She took two long strides backward and grabbed her backup weapon, a little .22, from her waistband. She gripped it in two hands and tucked it up to the beard's head. "Drop it and back off," she yelled. She could take the black man if he didn't obey, but it would be neater if she didn't kill anyone while she was out there.

The black man hesitated, one hand on her gun.

"Do it, man," the beard said.

T.J. dropped her gun and raised both hands over his head. "Okay. Take it easy, lady."

"Down on your bellies. Both of you."

The beard groaned and rolled onto his belly.

T.J. got down on all fours.

"Down," she said, aiming the gun at his face. When both men were down, she kept the gun aimed and retrieved her SIG. She found her badge a few feet away. The flashlight had rolled down the hill. As she picked it up, T.J. lifted his head. "Don't tempt me to shoot you, asshole," she warned him.

His head dropped again.

She wanted to bring them in, but that would mean explaining why she was out here. "Count to fifty slowly before so much as blinking. If I see your face before I'm gone, I'll shoot it off."

"Sure," the beard said.

"We hear you," T.J. added.

With that, Cameron backed out of the alley, her heart pounding in her throat. Safe in the car, she locked the doors, revved the engine and pulled away from the curb. Only when she was stopped at a light a few blocks away did she pull down the mirror and examine her eye. Shit. How was she going to explain that?

As she drove on, the emotion leached out like poison. Where the hell was her reserve, her strength? He'd stolen it—that bastard had come back and ripped it from her. The windows down, wind whipped across her face. Maybe it was time to move on. A different job. Join the sharpshooter team permanently if Special Ops was too hard.

But, she would not allow herself to think about Diego Ramirez. She would push him from her mind. Maybe Diego Ramirez wasn't dead, but Nate's father and the man she had known was. Now, it was simply a matter of burying him.

CHAPTER 10

THE SORENESS IN Cameron's muscles stretched from her shoulders all the way to her ankles. As much as she hated to admit it, she hurt. She had forgotten how much training she had done on the job and how much she'd let herself go. Eleven months she'd been gone, longer since her body had been pushed to its limits.

During her leave, she'd practiced yoga and had run every day, sometimes more than once a day, but it wasn't the same. Having these men around her, having to compete with them, made her push herself. The men never said a word about how much Cameron could lift, for how long or how fast, but working out beside them was incentive to be better, stronger. She would never settle for being the weakest or slowest. Now, she was both.

In drills, her feet didn't cooperate; her breath was gone in ten or fifteen minutes. Worse, Ballestrini was competitive. He insisted they work out together, compare times and weights. Though no one expected her to lift more than he did, each comparison reminded her of how she used to be: faster, stronger, more in control, less alone. It brought on emotion she wasn't accustomed to. Maybe Ballestrini was right; maybe it was postpartum depression.

She knew that it was Diego. She wished she could trade it in for depression—anything but the feeling of being betrayed by him. They were partners, weren't they? Partners in work and in life. Could she have been so wrong? But, what kind of a relationship did they have if he would keep this kind of secret from her, knowing how devastating it would be? Worse, what if he had gone bad? It happened in undercover work. What if her Diego was now a dirty cop?

She was taking her share of razzing from the guys. A black eye wasn't something anyone was going to ignore. The barrage of questions felt endless. No one wanted to buy the story about walking into a door in the dark while trying to get to the crying baby. She didn't blame them. Even she had to admit it was pretty lame. Worse was Rosa, who watched Cameron out of the corner of her eye as though trying to solve the mystery with the force of her stare. It was starting to work. At least she had vision in both eyes again.

Beside her, Lau stretched like he was just getting going. "You going to shoot tomorrow?"

"Didn't hear about it," Cameron said.

Ballestrini strode by, singing, *"Now that I have you, I see it all so clear. The struggle inside me is nothing to fear. Now that I have you."*

He gestured at Cameron and Lau. "Come on, name the show."

"Don't know, don't care," Lau quipped.

"Now that I have you," Ballestrini continued, "Our love can't be denied. Now whatever may happen I'll be by your side. To love and see you through—"

"Ballerina," Daley shouted. "Cut it out."

Ballestrini stopped. "It's Diego and Carlotta from *Z. The Masked Musical.*" Cameron heard the name and faced her locker to avoid them.

"Who's up for drinks?" Kessler asked, coming into the locker room in his uniform pants and no top.

"Got to get home," Ambley said. "Wife's working tonight."

"I'm in," a couple others said.

"Cameron?"

"Rookie Club," she said, referring to an informal club of women in law enforcement who met once a month.

"I want to join the Rookie Club," Daley said. "I was a rookie once, too."

"No men allowed," Ballestrini said.

"Isn't that sexist or something?" Daley whined, half joking. He was the team's single guy, always watching out for the ladies, even on the job.

Cameron laughed.

"He's got a point," Paules said. "Maybe you could bring it up for vote, adding male membership. Think of how you could expand the group."

"You're engaged," Kessler said. "You can't be checking out other chicks."

"He's not married yet," Daley retorted, then winked at Cameron. "Maybe you can take a vote on it, Cruz."

"Sure," Cameron agreed. "I'll bring it up."

"Tell them we'll behave," Daley called after her.

"Daley, don't make promises you definitely can't keep," Kessler added.

Cameron headed to her car. She hadn't been to a Rookie Club dinner in almost a year. When she was a twenty-four-year-old rookie cop, the men outnumbered the women fifteen to one. Many of the women wanted nothing to do with their female counterparts. Cameron had been tempted to join that camp; she was never good with other girls anyway. Besides being blond and blue-eyed, Cameron was tall and lanky where the other girls growing up were dark-haired and eyed, petite and curvy. Little interest in clothes or music, Cameron preferred whichever sports she could convince the boys to let her join.

Her best friend growing up was the youngest of seven kids, the first six boys. Christina survived by being as low profile a female as possible, sort of how Cameron dealt with being a gringa. The two were creative at camouflage: short haircuts with baggy shirts and hand-me-down pants for Christina, a baseball cap pulled down over the blond hair and eyes for Cameron.

It was at a dinner with Christina's family that Cameron first heard Mama Cruz tell the story of how she and Papa came to adopt Cameron. Her birth parents had employed Mama and Papa Cruz. Papa had helped with farming. Mama Cruz had done housework and helped take care of Cameron after she was born. Cameron had been with Mama Cruz when her parents were killed coming home from a meeting with an accountant in the town of Beaumont, forty-five miles from Bleakwood. The two of them were hit head-on by a drunk driver, and all three were killed.

Mama Cruz didn't make a single phone call. She and Papa simply took Cameron home. No paperwork, nothing. Had the authorities known, Mama and Papa Cruz would never have been allowed to adopt an Anglo child, but Cameron had no other family and things were much different then than now, especially in Bleakwood, Texas. When she turned eighteen, she officially changed her last name to Cruz. Only then did Mama Cruz confess how many times she feared someone would show up at the door and take Cameron away.

The thought of losing Nate brought her blood to a halt. She considered going straight home, but she needed this companionship, too. Cameron had been part of the Rookie Club from the time she was a few months into the job. Two other rookies a few years senior invited her to join the group at Tommy's for Mexican. Cameron might have begged out, but she owed one of them,

Sydney Blanchard, a drink on a bet about time of death on a victim they'd found under a sewage drain. That first night, Cameron mostly listened as the others complained about the job, the crooks, the jerks, and men in general, surprised at how much she enjoyed it. Although she didn't always say much, Cameron found herself coming most months.

The women came and went. Jamie Vail had been absent a long time after catching her husband in bed with another member of their group. Cameron had assumed the group might simply disappear, but somehow the word about a woman-band of law enforcement officers had spread quickly. Over the eleven years Cameron had been on the force, the group had changed and grown, shrunk, and almost fallen apart more than a dozen times. The times Cameron showed up, she was often amazed at the crowd the group now drew.

Every time she entered Tommy's Mexican Restaurant, there was the same mixture of trepidation and anticipation. The conversations were always heavy. Their jobs were filled with death, disappointment in their fellow cops and in people, and a sense of disrespect from their male counterparts, including spouses. For a lot of them, it meant long periods of struggle. There were always a few in the bunch who discussed things openly, but mostly, like other cops, these women dealt with things on their own. The ones in crisis rarely came to find a shoulder to lean on. Instead, crisis was usually marked by absence. Cameron wondered if Jamie Vail would come tonight.

Cameron was prompt, as usual. Arriving at the table the restaurant held for them on the second Wednesday of every month, Cameron was surprised to see Jessica Campbell from the Immigration and Customs Enforcement (ICE). Jess was petite with dark hair and eyes. She looked Brazilian, but the name Campbell had always thrown Cameron off. Not that she was one to talk. Jess held a Bud between two palms, next to an untouched glass.

"Hey," Cameron said, sitting across from her.

Jess glanced at her, and it seemed to take a minute before Cameron's presence registered. "God, I thought you'd quit to have a baby or something." She shook her head before speaking again. "What a dumb thing to say. Sorry. Are you back on the force? Either way is great, I mean."

Cameron updated her on being back at work, then redirected the conversation where she was most comfortable, to work.

Jess pointed to her eye. "That looks like it hurts."

"Not too bad."

There was a beat of silence before Cameron asked, "Any progress on Ray Benjamin?"

Jess stiffened and blinked hard. "I haven't heard anything from Homicide, but they're keeping it wrapped up. You saw it, right?"

"Yeah. You know anything about the shooter?"

"No one's talking to me." Jess lifted her empty beer bottle and waved it at the waitress. "You want anything?"

"Soda water with lime, please," Cameron said, picturing Diego pulling the trigger. "Was he a good guy?"

"Benjamin?"

Cameron nodded.

Jess hesitated, picking at the label on her beer. Finally, she lifted her head and spoke. "He was the best. So intense, but completely dedicated to the job. Strong. A leader. He could be stubborn and an asshole with women, but he was good." Jess dropped her head. "Really good. And he cared." There was no question that there was more to Jess and Ray than a working relationship.

"He was directing an ICE move to crack down on human trafficking. You should have seen him. He was like a kid with it."

Cameron said nothing as Jess continued, clearly needing to talk.

"I'd like to see the bastards treated the same way they treat those women and children. Fine them every penny they've got saved, then stow 'em in the dirty hull of some boat with scraps of bread and barely enough water to survive. And when they get out, make 'em work for the rest of their lives like slaves. Makes me sick."

She took a drag on her beer. Cameron stayed quiet. She wanted to dig into whether Benjamin was really the good cop or the crooked one, but obviously Jess wasn't the person to ask.

"You hear how he got started?" Jess asked, setting the beer down.

Cameron shook her head.

"His first call as a rookie was to the port. Found a boat of women and children locked there. Twelve of them locked in some crate on a boat. The youngest was nine. He died. They'd been left there for days. Finally, someone walking down there heard them and called the cops. Ray responded." She blinked, and Cameron could see emotion glistening. "If you had seen him with my ten-year-old son, you'd know. The kid had so many problems when his father left, but Ray made it better. Ray took the pain away. You can't imagine how much it meant to see my son happy after his asshole father disappeared."

Cameron thought about her son. Maybe she did understand.

Jess drew a hard breath, then swigged the rest of her beer. "I hope they catch the son of a bitch who shot him." Jess lifted the empty bottle and tapped it against Cameron's glass.

She was relieved to see Mackenzie Wallace and Linda James come in together. Mackenzie had recently moved over to the Drug Enforcement Agency while Linda James had been the captain of the district near Cameron's house for two or three years now. Mackenzie was six-one and built like a violin—long with beautiful curves and strung tightly.

"Jack and Coke," Mackenzie ordered and pointed to Linda James, who said, "Just the Coke for me. I'm on call."

The two made comments about Cameron's eye, which she waved off. Sitting across from her, Mackenzie pushed a pair of narrow glasses back onto her nose and leaned forward. "You doing okay, Cameron? I heard about the shooting."

She nodded. "Hanging in there, thanks."

The bartender came back with the drinks. Stephani Wang from the bomb squad showed a few minutes later with two women Cameron didn't know. One seemed familiar. Stephani introduced her as Ryaan Berry of Triggerlock. It was likely Cameron had seen her at one of the specialist jobs. The second woman was brand new to the Bay Area. She'd moved to San Francisco from Chicago. Mei, Cameron thought she'd said, but it was loud. She did something related to computers.

The conversation shifted to city politics, case stories, and men. It always turned to men. Cameron mostly listened. It wasn't until they'd ordered that the person Cameron wanted to see came in.

Homicide Inspector Hailey Wyatt was short—not much taller than five feet—and full of curve. It was the curve that Cameron imagined had given her a hell of a time in school. As she walked in tonight, men ogled. Hailey might have acted oblivious, but she caught every stare. Perhaps they were the reason she spent most of her time around dead men.

Hailey's husband had been killed last year. In the last months before Cameron left on maternity leave, she hadn't seen Hailey at all. She looked better. Not straight-from-the-spa better, but this wasn't that kind of group.

Behind her was Shelby Tate, assistant medical examiner, in a pair of clean scrub pants and a UCSF sweatshirt. Though she had to be in her late thirties, her strawberry blond hair and freckles made her look like a college kid. Dinner arrived, and the conversation continued as Mackenzie talked about the undercover work. "During the bust, the guy turns to me as I'm cuffing him and throws up all down the front of me. Into my shirt, down my legs."

Linda James cringed while Shelby laughed out loud.

Jess was quiet, working on her fourth or fifth beer.

"Only an M.E. would find that funny," Linda said.

"Can't be as bad as what Hailey sees."

"Haven't had any really bad ones recently. Thankfully." She sipped her beer. "My favorite is the guy we found splattered all over a residential street in San Jose. Have I told you this one?"

A few shouted out "no," and Cameron leaned back.

"I've heard it," Shelby said. "It's great."

"What was it?" Mackenzie asked.

"Some guy literally in a dozen pieces all over. At first, we thought it had to be some sort of explosive. There was tissue on the side of a car, on the street," Hailey went on. "It was a mess, but we couldn't find any detonator. I was really new, but even the experienced guys couldn't figure it out. We ended up calling out Kjurkian." Kjurkian was Shelby's boss.

"We must have walked that street for an hour."

"What was it?"

"A plane."

"A plane hit him?" Ryaan said.

The tissue was spread out, no detonating device. "He fell off a plane," Cameron guessed.

Hailey nodded. "Hanging on to the wheels of a plane, and when the plane got too high, he fainted and fell off."

"Where the hell was he going?" Ryaan asked.

"No idea."

"That's one for the Darwin Awards," Shelby said.

Dinner plates were removed. They ordered another round—decaf coffee for some, drinks for others. Jess ordered regular coffee, black. The drinks had just arrived when a pager went off. Everyone reached for her belt.

Jess read the number. "Fuck." She excused herself and pulled a cell phone off her belt, taking a few steps from the table before flipping it open.

The others remained quiet, waiting to find out what disaster or death had called Jess from their meal. That feeling of anticipation and dread with the sting of adrenaline was something only another cop could appreciate.

Jess was off the phone in less than a minute. "Mrs. Hyde calls," she said, coming back to the table. She snapped her phone back on her belt and pulled cash from her front pocket.

"What've you got?" Linda James asked, standing from the table.

"Girl just off a boat, badly beaten. They think she's Czech."

"Mrs. Hyde?" Cameron asked.

"Jamie Vail, queen of sex death, mistress bitch."

Cameron didn't respond. She'd known Jamie Vail as a completely different person.

"Why Vail?" Shelby asked.

"Raped so badly she's half-dead. Doesn't look like she's going to make it, but for now it's Vail's. And because she's an illegal, they want ICE there."

"I'll take you," Linda offered.

"I've got a car," Jess said.

Linda gave a little shake of her head. Jess put both hands on the back of her chair, staring down at the table several seconds. "Okay. Thanks." She lifted the black coffee and took two drinks, twisting her mouth as the liquid burned.

Jess dropped twenty bucks on the table. Linda added forty more before the two left.

"What are you working on these days, Cruz?" Shelby asked.

She gave them her shoptalk, keeping her patience and hoping everyone would leave so she could catch Hailey Wyatt alone. The conversation returned to Ray Benjamin's shooting. Cameron told them an abbreviated version of what she'd seen. It was as though she'd told the story a thousand times and she was relieved when the conversation no longer focused on her.

"Jess is taking it hard," Mackenzie said.

"What was the deal with him?" Shelby asked before Cameron could. "She's picked some lemons."

"I hear he was an okay guy," Hailey said. "And clearly Jess fell for him. I don't know if it was a long thing, and I don't know if it had ended or not. He took care of his mother—supported her."

A few seconds of silence passed. Somewhere near the bar cheering erupted for some sports event playing on the TV.

The waitress came by and left the check. Shelby added cash to the pile and passed it to Mackenzie. "I've got to get home," Shelby said. "Tom's got the kids, and I'm sure he's ready to kill them by now." Mackenzie Wallace, Ryaan and Mei rose with her. Hailey started to move when Cameron leaned across the table. "You have a few minutes to talk?"

Hailey glanced at her watch and nodded.

The others made their way through the crowds and disappeared before Hailey spoke to Cameron. "It's good to see you," she said.

"You, too," Cameron told her. Then, feeling the awkwardness, she added, "I was sorry to hear about—"

"Thanks," Hailey said quickly. "What's going on?"

Thankful to return to shoptalk, Cameron pushed her coffee cup aside and laid her elbows on the table. "I wanted to talk to you about Benjamin's shooting. Who's working it?"

"It went to Nordenfeldt and Thomas. It was my call, but they pulled those guys in because of the situation." Hailey frowned. "They haven't talked to you?"

"I gave a statement to someone named Patterson."

"Alan," she said. "He's helping them out."

"They tell you I saw the guy."

Hailey watched her. "You gave them a description?"

"Didn't need to. I know him."

Hailey leaned forward. "And you told Patterson?"

"I did."

"Shit," Hailey snapped. Then, "Who was it?"

"Diego Ramirez."

"He was Special Ops for a while, right?" Hailey asked. "Then, he went undercover."

"Right," Cameron said.

"Jesus, a cop." Hailey's head popped up. "Wait, I thought he was dead."

"So did I," Cameron agreed.

"There was a service for him last year," Hailey said.

Cameron said nothing. Images from the service cascaded through her mind. The navy dress she'd worn so she wouldn't stand out, the way she'd stood in the middle of the crowd and fought back her tears. How she'd longed to tell people that they were together, that he was the father of her child.

"You're sure it was him?" Hailey asked.

"Positive." She hesitated, then said, "I know it was him, and he knows it was me."

"You're worried he'll come after you?" Hailey asked.

Cameron hadn't thought about that. "I want him caught for shooting Benjamin. I've tried to find him myself, but he's not in any of the old haunts."

"How long was he Special Ops?"

"Two and a half years after I started as a shooter. Maybe two to three before."

Hailey watched her. "So, he's been undercover for a year."

"About that."

"So, how would you know where to find him? He could be anywhere."

She nodded.

"And somewhere in there he's supposed to be dead?" Hailey continued.

"It was official—an autopsy and everything."

"How did he die?"

"Explosion in Mexico. They matched him with dentals," Cameron said, trying to sound like this was only a case.

"You knew him well," Hailey said.

It was not a question. Cameron didn't answer.

"And you want him arrested?" Hailey pushed.

"He shot Ray Benjamin."

"And what did he do to you?"

She met Hailey's gaze and shook her head.

"That's why you care, isn't it? Something personal?"

Cameron rattled the ice in her empty glass, trying to find a way to say it all in as few words as possible. "He made me think he was dead."

"Just that?" Hailey finally asked.

Cameron tipped the glass back against her lips and let the ice tumble into her mouth and crunched down on it, feeling it crack between her teeth.

"That, and he's the father of my son."

CHAPTER 11

LUIS ROSARIO WAS born in Chiconautla, Mexico. His father was a waiter. His mother cleaned rooms for gringos. He was going to America. A promotion, a raise and a one-bedroom apartment in San Francisco. Not just America. Luis Rosario was on his way to California. He took the last swig of Dewar's as the captain announced their descent. On the first page of his notebook, he wrote, "My life begins again today." Then, he closed the thin, blue book and tucked it in his inside pocket. They made fun of his notebook, called it a diary, but he felt important when he wrote in it. And now, he was important.

Enough listening to his wife's mother insult the way his boys "took after their father." His father-in-law always going on about how well he supported his family, listing all the things Luis couldn't afford to give Laura and the boys. Luis was never good enough for any of them. Well, he hadn't inherited a family business, so what did they expect? Mostly, he was sick of Laura's four brothers watching him like a hawk while they stayed out all night, gambled, and slept with other women. The one time Luis had talked to one of the hostesses, they'd taken turns bitch-slapping him in the parking lot.

He did his family duty. He provided for them. They had a nice house. She bought what she wanted most of the time, some of it with help from her dad. After Alejandro, she'd refused to have sex with him. Even on his damn birthday, she refused. Her brothers always had an extra girl on the side, and their wives were hot compared to Laura. Miguel's wife, Mariana, loved sex. He probably got it all the time and, still, he always had some young hottie. The rules didn't apply to Luis. He had needs, too. Now he was going to be free. Best part was it had all happened so fast that Oscar didn't have a chance to come over and stop him. His wife had barely had a chance to call her father. Fucking perfect.

Luis hoped to see Manny. He certainly owed him a drink. After all, Manny convinced Luis to take this job in the first place. He made his way out of the airport, searching for the man who was meeting him. They told him to pack for two nights. They needed to assess him, like a job interview. "Sure. No problem," he told them, although he'd never been through a job interview before. He'd worked for his wife's oldest brother at the family business after high school, then he'd lucked into this job when her brother decided he was no longer necessary—the asshole.

He'd been a gopher for her brothers, running out for lunches or supplies for the office, getting coffee. His wife's father and brothers imported small American appliances like toaster ovens and curling irons. He'd never gotten to handle his own account, not even a little one. Now, he was being promoted in a job he'd only had two months.

The business wasn't exactly legal, but he wasn't involved in any of the ugly stuff. He helped attract new clients, got the paperwork signed, then collected whatever portion they could pay up front and delivered the cash with their signed agreements to the room behind the bar. For that he got close to one hundred U.S. dollars a day. Now, they were going to pay him three times that, plus a place in California. If he got the job.

He pulled at his collar as he watched for his bag to come around the carousel. He hoped he'd packed the right things. He was wearing his best suit. He'd brought one other, a pair of khakis and three button-downs. All white, or they had been when he bought them. Considering the other travelers, his shirt was sort of yellow now. His best suit hadn't been worn since his wedding. The other one was a hand-me-down from his wife's second brother, Arturo, the shortest in the family, and so the closest to Luis's size.

The green U.S. Army duffle he'd swindled out of some American kid for twenty dollars came rolling down the carousel ramp. The sight of it made him proud. Slinging it over his shoulder, he made it through immigration without any problems, using the visa they'd sent him. He spotted a man with his name printed on a paper attached to a clipboard.

Luis raised his hand and cleared his throat. "I'm Luis Rosario."

"Mr. Rosario," the man said, reaching for his bag. "Please follow me."

Luis handed him the duffle. If Laura's asshole brothers could see him now. This job was going to be the best thing that ever happened to him.

The man opened the rear door of a black town car, and Luis got in. Luis stared at his surroundings, nothing like the shitty little town he'd come from: no dirt on the road, no smoking cars, and no farm animals in the streets.

The ride took almost an hour. By the time the car stopped, Luis was so pumped up about his new job he could hardly sit. The driver opened his door and nodded him toward a white door centered beneath a row of shattered second-story windows.

Luis frowned at the battered building.

"I'll take care of your bag, sir," the driver said, leaving Luis with nothing to do except get out.

He cleared his throat and crossed the gravel parking lot toward the warehouse. Maybe this was where they parked or something.

He knocked on the door, hoping someone would come out to meet him, but a loud voice echoed from inside. "*Venga.*"

Luis took a last look back at the driver, sitting behind the wheel with a newspaper, then pulled open the heavy metal door.

The smell inside was putrid—steamy and hot like a dead fish caught in the engine of a boat. How was it possible that no one else noticed it?

"Rosario."

Luis dropped his hands to his sides and turned toward the voice.

The man in front of Luis was easily six inches taller than he, easily taller than even Laura's tallest brother Juan. With sandy brown hair and light brown eyes, he wore a pair of jeans and a button-down shirt with the tan of an athlete. Despite the suit, Luis felt underdressed. "I'm so glad you could join us," the man said in Spanish, offering his hand. "You can call me Brad."

Luis shook it firmly, then rubbed his nose with the back of his hand, trying to get over the stink. His eyes watered. He blinked hard.

"Oh, I apologize for the smell. There was a little mess left from the last man in your position. It'll be cleaned up soon."

What would he be doing in his new job? If it was handling dead fish, he didn't want it.

"I run the operation here, along with three others. You'll never meet them," Brad said. "If you need anything, I'll be your contact. Mostly, you'll be on your own. Before we begin, I need to remind you of the nature of our business. Since you're here, you've agreed to take this position. You are to discuss the job with no one. Understand?"

Luis nodded. It had been like that with his last job, too. The money was good enough to keep his mouth shut then. It was three times better now.

"You've handled money for us before, but you'll be dealing with a much larger quantity and, more importantly, the cargo itself."

Luis wondered how much.

"The money was an issue for our last man. He felt the need to help himself to some of what wasn't his."

"I would never do that, sir."

"Good, Mr. Rosario. That's what I like to hear. Come. Let me show you the office before you go to your new home." The two walked across the warehouse to a boxlike office in the far corner.

Luis tried to be polite, but the smell was making him nauseous. He swallowed a mouthful of saliva and tried to quell the urge to gag outright. A few more minutes, then he'd be outside.

The man opened a solid door and stepped back as Luis passed him to enter the office.

A man was seated behind the desk. Luis halted and stepped back. Brad blocked his path. Luis stumbled, catching himself on the door jam. The man behind the desk wasn't moving. The room was filled with a low buzzing like the cheap halogen light in his living room at home. He glanced around the room, trying to place it.

When he turned back to the body, though, he found the source of the humming noise. The cloud of flies around the head was so thick, Luis had thought he was seeing the back of a man's head. Slowly the bloodied holes of the eyes and mouth came into focus. "Oh, God," he gasped. Luis recognized the half-eaten face. He vomited on the concrete floor.

Manny. It was Manny. Luis covered his nose and mouth, but the smell was overpowering. Brad stood off to one side, calmly, as Luis took a series of quick breaths. Unable to hold it, he retched again. He pressed his hands to his knees. "*Oh, Dios. Dios.*" He choked on a mouth full of sobs and let them out in a long, struggled chain. The tears ran down his cheeks. He couldn't contain himself. *Stop crying, idiota!*

"Oh, no. No, no, no," he blubbered.

He felt a hand on his arm. He tried to sop up the tears with the sleeve of his suit.

Brad handed him a handkerchief. Luis took it. The small gesture of kindness sent Luis into a stream of crying again.

"Shh," Brad said. "It's going to be fine. Really. Calm down."

Luis used the handkerchief to wipe his mouth. His heart pulsed a trumpet's beat across his chest and thumped like drums through his arms. It was pumping so hard, he felt it in his fingers and toes. "*¿Qué pasó?*" he asked without thinking.

"Mr. Hernandez didn't follow directions."

Luis was crying again. Oh, God. He never followed directions. He was going to die just like Manny. He didn't want this job. He wanted to go home, be nagged by his wife and annoyed by his children.

"I know what you're thinking, Mr. Rosario, but it was not something as simple as a little mistake. Mr. Hernandez broke the rules. He knew better than that. I left him here to help you understand how seriously we take the rules."

Luis tucked his head down like he used to when he got seasick on his wife's father's boat. It wasn't helping now.

"Here, breathe into this."

Luis took the paper bag and blew into it.

"Slowly," Brad directed.

Listen to what the man says. Do exactly what he says.

After several minutes, Brad gently pried the bag from Luis's hands and dropped it on the floor. Over his shoulder, the remains of Manny were buzzing at him. Brad closed the door to the office and with Manny out of sight, Luis was finally able to catch his breath. He felt like he needed to blow his nose, but looking down at the handkerchief that belonged to the killer, he didn't dare. He wiped his eyes and then his nose and sniffled quietly.

"The rules are simple, Mr. Rosario."

Luis shook his head.

"Yes, they are."

"No. It is not that, sir," Luis stuttered, the pressure of the man's hands like two concrete blocks on his shoulders.

"What, then?"

"I-I don't think I'm good for the job. Probably you need somebody different."

Brad lifted his hands off Luis's shoulders and for a moment, Luis thought everything would be fine. He closed his eyes and rested them for a nanosecond, hoping in another minute he would be on his way home. The thought of going home almost made him cry again, but he held himself together, barely. What he saw as he opened them made it clear he wouldn't be going home. Not outside a body bag, anyway.

Brad held a gun.

Luis didn't dare look around. There was nowhere to go. He caught his lower lip in his teeth. Oh, damn. Damn, he was going to cry again.

"You're the man for the job. And if you're not, I'm afraid that this will have been your last job interview."

Luis swallowed hard. The tears were streaming down his face, making it hard to see, but at least he wasn't sobbing. He didn't let himself think about how his father-in-law had warned him he would end up like this. Oh, Jesus. Laura's brothers would be laughing over his grave. He didn't want anyone to laugh at his funeral.

"Now, I'll explain the rules. Then, you can get settled."

Luis exhaled.

"Rule number one, don't ever steal money from us."

Luis wouldn't steal money. Stupid Manny. Stupid, stupid Manny.

"You understand?"

Luis nodded quickly. "Oh, yes sir. Yes, sir. I would never steal money, Señor Brad. I promise. Never."

"Rule number two is that if you get caught by the police, you know nothing, and you're on your own. You don't know me, you've never seen me, or anyone else who works here."

"On my own. I don't know you or them. I understand."

"Rule three is that you don't ever leave a voicemail about our work, and you write nothing down."

He felt his gut tighten at the thought of the little notebook. Already, he'd filled it with enough details to end up like Manny. Luis didn't move.

Brad smiled widely. "Good. Mr. Rosario, you're going to be great at this job."

Luis sucked in a few quick breaths, feeling them stick on something in his throat. "Thank you, sir."

"In fact, I've got so much confidence in you that I'm going to give you a raise."

Luis thought it was some sort of test. "No. It's okay. I make good money."

"I want you to take the raise."

Luis thumbed the edge of his pants, feeling the sweat tickle the small of his back. He didn't dare move.

"I'm giving you an extra hundred a day for the days you work. Okay? That's four hundred a day." The man grinned. The way it carved across his face reminded Luis of a jack-o'-lantern. "I want you to have it."

Luis hesitated.

"I mean it, Luis. You should take it."

Luis nodded. "Thank you, sir. Thank you very much."

The man reached into his pocket and pulled out a roll of bills that filled his fist. He carved off a stack with his thumb and handed it to Luis. "There. Here's a little to get you settled. Let's get you to your new place."

"Thank you." Luis took the bills and shoved them in his pocket without looking at them. He didn't want to act rude or greedy. He didn't want to do anything wrong.

"To welcome you to California, I've taken the liberty of having a friend of mine stop by your place tonight."

"A friend," the word came out as though it were hooked to a large chunk of food in his throat.

"Her name is Tami, but she's sort of like a younger Pamela Anderson. Do you know Pamela Anderson?" Brad asked as he opened the limo door.

Luis didn't answer.

"I thought you might enjoy getting to know some people. She'll show you whatever you'd like to see."

When they were both inside the car, Brad opened a cupboard and pulled out a bottle of Dewar's. "Your favorite. Shall we toast?"

Luis took the glass in shaky hands.

"To America," the man said.

"To America," Luis answered and let the liquid burn down his throat.

CHAPTER 12

SHE WAS HAVING the dream again. A long, black hallway. Only the smallest crack of hazy amber light at the far end kept it from being pitch black. Cars hummed past on the street. Doors slammed and people yelled in the distance, like couples fighting. Behind it was the faint sound of Diego's moans. Cameron sprinted down the hall, tripping over her own feet as she stopped to listen. She screamed his name but got no response.

Something streamed through her vision, but she wiped her face. It was dry. The farther she went, the cloudier her vision became until she no longer saw the walls and floor. Diego's moans grew more faint as though he were being moved farther away. The light dimmed until there was only darkness. Running grew more strenuous like the floor was sand. Then, her body was heavier, harder to move. She might have been in water, and she could make no noise. Finally, she quit. Dropped to her knees. A scream pierced the blackness. Light flooded the hallway. She woke with a start.

In her arms, Nate let out a small cry that kept her from jumping out of the chair. She surveyed the dark room, the back of her neck cool with sweat. Little more than an hour had passed. Pregnant, she had the dream most nights, but it was less frequent since Nate's birth. Perhaps the sleep deprivation of having a newborn had kept her sleep dreamless.

She laid Nate in his crib, wishing for the same deep sleep. Instead, it would take an hour or more for the adrenaline to fade enough to allow her to sleep again. She made her way through the empty house, the cool wood floor moaning beneath her feet. The sound welcomed her into nighttime wakefulness. In the den, she stared at the blackened TV and considered watching something. As she bent for the remote control, something snapped against a window.

She returned to the hallway and listened. In her bedroom, the clock on the bedside table read 12:12. Her blinds were down. She fingered one and lifted it slowly. The rain had started, a soft patter. She watched the tree beside the house for movement, but the wind was still. She saw nothing in the darkness that would explain the noise.

She went back toward the den. As she reached the doorway, she heard the same light clink. It had come from the direction of Nate's room. She checked the window again, this time stopping at the one farthest from Nate's room to check if the angle afforded her a better view. There, silhouetted against her son's bedroom window, was the figure of a man.

She dropped the blinds and sprinted for the front of the house. Her purse was on the entryway table. With breath pounding, she drew her SIG and threw the front door open. She jumped down the stairs in her socks, soaking them on the wet ground. She rounded the side of the house, gun out.

"Don't move," she yelled.

The figure wore a dark raincoat with the hood up. He turned toward Cameron, but it was too dark to make out his features.

"Put your hands up and move slowly."

He raised his hands.

"Now, turn to face me, nice and easy."

He shifted slightly, and she saw Diego's features. She drew in a sharp breath and held it, steadying her hand.

He moved toward her.

She kept the gun aimed. "You were dead," she called out. "You sent that letter to make me think you were dead."

His lips formed a tight line. "I had no choice."

"How about Ray? Was that a mistake, too?"

He shook his head without answering.

"Why did you come here?" Her chest deflated. "Just leave."

He motioned to the window. "I want to see him."

She didn't respond. There was nothing to say. Everything and nothing.

"That's my son, isn't it?"

She forced herself away. A month ago, this scene would have been part of some dream. And now, it was all such a horrible nightmare.

He took a step forward. "That's why you look different. You had a baby."

She had wanted to find him. She went searching for him. Even gotten attacked, and here he was. Now she had no words to confront him. There was no way to work out what he'd done. She wanted him out. Gone. "Leave, Diego, or I swear I'll get Homicide out here and have you brought in for Ray."

It was like he hadn't heard her. His eyes were fixed on Nate's window. "That's my kid in there, isn't it?"

Her breath caught in her throat. She forced it in, trying to build strength. "No. He's not yours. He's mine."

Diego pressed his hand to his stomach. "But, I'm his father."

"He doesn't have a father."

Diego's face fell, his eyes wide. "Please."

She walked back around the house toward the front door. "Leave."

Diego followed. "What's his name?"

"I said leave, Diego."

"I'll tell you his name," Diego said, his gaze landing on her with the force of a physical strike.

She didn't move.

"I called Records and pretended to be from the insurance company."

She shook her head, tears on her face or maybe rain.

The lines in his brow were carved deep with agony.

She had to turn away.

"That's my son," he said, barely a whisper. "His name is Nathaniel. My middle name, my father's name."

The gun quivered in her palm. She waved it at him. "Don't come back here. There's nothing here for you."

He raised his hands and moved toward her. "I just want to see him once." He slowed his movements. "I swear. One time, and I'll go."

"He's not your son. I don't even know who you are."

Diego didn't answer.

"Don't come back here." She started to shut the door. "I'll shoot next time. I swear I will."

She pushed inside and closed the door. Trembling, she sank to the floor and dropped the gun beside her. With her knees to her chest, she let go of all the emotion she'd been trying so hard to hold in.

CHAPTER 13

EVERYTHING ABOUT THIS thing had gone to absolute shit. All Diego wanted was to hold his son. A kid. He had a kid. A kid whose mother was going to shoot him. Not that he blamed her. He would have wanted him dead, too. Aside from being Special Ops, Cameron was also often loaned out as a specialist, which was a fancy name for the department's sharpshooters. Three years in a row, she scored in the top five of the department's sixty specialists. The shot she fired at the reservoir had missed him on purpose. There was no doubt that if he got near Nathaniel, she would shoot him for real. And all he kept thinking about was the feel of her full breasts against his back. What the hell had he done?

With Benjamin dead, the deal was as good as blown. Damn, he wished she hadn't seen him that night. It complicated everything. That noise coming from the car. It had taken him most of a day to realize that it was a baby. Then, the changes in her body. The math was easy. They'd been together for almost eighteen months before he'd gone undercover. Even nine months ago, it had been him. He'd felt a flash of terror that the baby was someone else's.

Not with Cameron, not a chance in hell. He had a kid. Jesus Christ. Nathaniel doesn't have a father, she'd said, and it was like some part of him had been severed. Like she'd taken another shot at him, only this one had hit. He had a kid he'd never know. He had sworn that his family would stay together. Now he had left his kid the same way his own father had left his sister and mother in Mexico.

He had to keep his resolve. He was doing what he had to do for Claudia.

Something was wrong. It was days since he'd heard from her. He replayed their last conversation, scrutinizing every word for some clue.

"Did you tape him?" he had asked.

"No."

He had pressed her. "What happened?"

"I think he saw me setting it up."

She'd cut the conversation short that day, promising to call him when it was safe. There had been no word. He waited, trying to plan how he would get her out of Mexico if her husband were on to them. He cursed himself for putting her in danger.

And they had been so close. A few more weeks, they assured him. Yes, it had gone so much longer than he'd thought, but it would pay back tenfold. Claudia would be safe.

He had forsaken Cameron when he'd made his choice. At the time, the assignment was for a few months at most. He knew it would be painful to believe he was dead, but at least she was safe.

Even that thought did little to settle his mind. He wasn't eating. He hadn't slept more than an hour or two since that night. The safe house was cold and dank. The only heat came from an old boiler. He had to shut the gas valve on and off by hand because it leaked. He paced the small space and called Claudia's number on the last disposable cell phone he had. No answer. The phone rang a double busy single like it had been disconnected. Two days of this.

He tried not to imagine the worst and dialed the other number. Someone named Tom Jones who was to be available 24/7. Diego didn't even know who the hell Tom Jones was. Certainly that wasn't his real name. The players weren't supposed to know each other. Which is why it was so weird when Benjamin called to meet him. Diego got Tom's voicemail, a computerized voice. No name. No way he was leaving any damn message. Not after what Benjamin had told him.

"They won't need you," Benjamin said. "With Vincente dead, they'll be in charge, just like they want. Unless we can stop them."

It made no damn sense. Vincente wasn't dead. It was Diego's job to bring him in when the evidence was solid and Claudia was safe. He didn't know enough about who the players were. Until he knew the tiers, he couldn't act. He'd told Benjamin he was wrong. Damn, Benjamin had been so insistent.

"You're getting screwed, Ramirez," Benjamin had said, drawing his gun. "How can you be so fucking blind? Vincente's dead by now, and so are you." Benjamin's shot hit him square in the chest. Diego rubbed at the bruised rib he had to prove it. Without the Kevlar, Diego would be dead. Benjamin had taken aim again. What choice did he have but to shoot back?

He dialed again. This time Tom answered. "Ramirez, that you?"

"Who the fuck do you think it is?" Diego snapped. "I've been calling you for days. Almost a year to set this thing up, and Benjamin almost blew it."

"Calm down, okay?" Tom said.

"He went nuts."

"You shouldn't have shot him."

"He put a bullet into my vest. I wasn't going to give him a second chance at a head shot."

"You should have controlled him."

"Fuck you," Diego said. He paced, his shoes silent on the floor. Undercover cops didn't pace and make noise. At least the ones who lived didn't. That's what they'd taught him, and he was good. Until now. Everything felt fucked up now. "I had no choice but to shoot."

There was no sound from the other end.

Diego drew a measured breath. "Vincente's going to want to know what happened to Benjamin. What the hell do I tell him?"

"You've got nothing to worry about."

"How can you say that? Vincente's not going to let it go."

"Vincente's not going to care about Benjamin anymore."

Diego halted. "Why?"

Tom sighed. "Vincente's dead."

Diego halted, a cold burning through him. He wanted to sit, but there was nowhere. He clenched the phone and made a noise that was barely a whisper. "What?"

"Vincente was killed in crossfire."

Benjamin had known Vincente was dead. How had he known that? Jesus, he'd been right. Why hadn't he said Vincente was dead already? "Killed in crossfire," Diego repeated. Benjamin had known someone was going to take out Vincente.

"He was in the wrong place at the wrong time. It was bad luck. You can come in now. It's safe."

It didn't make sense. "When?" he asked.

"The day before yesterday."

"The day before yesterday?" Diego repeated.

"I found out last night."

It didn't make sense. Benjamin had been dead six days. It wasn't just bad luck that Vincente had been killed. They'd taken him out before Diego could gather the evidence. Benjamin's voice echoed in his head. They won't need you.

"Do you have the money?"

Diego didn't answer.

"You need to come in," Tom said.

Diego lowered his voice and kept it even as he tested the waters. "What about Benjamin? People know I shot him."

"Come on in, and we'll see what we can do to clear it up."

"See what you can do? What the hell does that mean?"

"Calm down, Ramirez. Tell me where you are. Let's meet, and we'll figure it out, but you need to come in before someone misunderstands what you're doing, before something happens to Claudia."

Diego scanned the empty warehouse. "You bastard. We had a deal. I played your game. Where the hell is she?"

"Come on in, Diego. Let's talk. We don't want this to get out of hand."

Seething, Diego spoke through clenched teeth. "I'm not coming in. I'm keeping the money until I'm confident that I'm not getting screwed. And if you so much as touch a hair on her head, I'll hunt you myself."

"Diego, listen—"

Diego pressed end on the phone without answering.

Within seconds, the phone vibrated. Tom's number. Without answering, Diego removed the phone's battery. He tucked the battery in his left pocket and the phone in his right. Motionless, he felt his pulse beat the slow rhythm of dread in his chest.

CHAPTER 14

CAMERON AND HER partner, Tim Ballestrini, pulled up to the sixth marina of the day. Dressed in street clothes, they drove Cameron's Blazer. It was cold and damp, especially off the water. Being in and out of the car all day had left her with a permanent feeling of wet. Nothing had panned out. The suspects who were supposedly always at the piers were all on some kind of holiday, probably inside drinking cocoa. The few people who would talk to them knew squat. She believed them. Cameron hated to admit it, but she was discouraged. Ballestrini had been complaining about the wild goose chase since the second marina at nine that morning.

This was day four after the presentation from ICE and Sex Crimes. Jess Campbell and Scott Smith from ICE and Jamie Vail from Sex Crimes gave the team thick packets about trafficking statistics, the brutal details of the treatment of the victims and guidelines for what to look for.

What had surprised Cameron was that the girls were as likely to be American as foreign. She expected Eastern Europeans, Africans, and women from Middle Eastern countries. Jamie explained that the newest trafficking surge was kidnapping girls from local towns and selling them for sex. In other cases, girls were actually sold by family members or set up by friends. "They're as young as ten and eleven," Jamie said. "I left the images out of your packets." She had stopped by to say hello on her way out, congratulating Cameron on the baby. The mood was somber, and they agreed they'd catch up more soon.

The team had been surveilling marinas for the past three days without more than a permanent stink of fish for their efforts. This was going to get old fast.

It didn't help that she was tired. She was sleeping poorly, waking often, and creeping to her window to check for someone peering in. She couldn't keep Diego out of her mind. Each time he entered, she was both amazed and devastated that he was alive.

"One more?" she asked Tim.

He moaned and pulled up the list he had on his phone. "Looks like we might be able to miss this one. Let me find out what the deal is." Ballestrini was texting. Cameron turned up the heat and waited.

Every hour with Ballestrini made her long for another day with Diego as a partner, the way it had been back then. While they waited for a response, Cameron pulled out the map Captain Ahrens had given them and searched for the one marina they hadn't visited. Ahrens had set them up with a schedule on which marinas to visit when, but Bay Area traffic had been its unpredictable self and messed them all up. Ballestrini had managed to reorganize their visits to minimize the traffic delays, but it meant that the last marina they would see should have been their first. It was across the Bay in Berkeley. Cameron hoped they hadn't screwed anything up too badly by switching the order around. She certainly didn't want to bring it up with Ahrens, with the mood she'd been in since Ray Benjamin's murder.

"We've seen maybe six or seven Hispanics today, and I can't remember seeing a single Asian at any of these ports," Ballestrini commented.

He had a point. According to the intel they had, the main sex trafficking was happening by Mexican cartels and Asian gangs who were moving away from drug and gun trafficking into sex trafficking. As Jamie had said, "Guns and drugs can only be sold once. Girls can be sold as many as thirty times a day." The room was quiet after that.

Gangs imported girls with promises of legitimate waitressing and hostess jobs only to force them to work in sex clubs. With so many people around the world holding on to dreams of the rich life in America, it was easy to see how so many were sucked into the schemes. When she thought of it, Cameron couldn't help but imagine Mama and Papa Cruz and Juan when they'd first come to America. The Cruzes had come illegally from Mexico in the 1960s and had been illegals for almost a decade before receiving green cards two years before Cameron was born.

Working to enforce the laws that would today prevent her parents from entering the country sometimes felt hypocritical. Once, shortly after Diego had gone undercover, Special Ops had done a sweep, and an illegal immigrant had been caught up in it. Occasionally, Cameron still thought about her. She had never mentioned that part of her job to Mama Cruz or Rosa. Diego would have understood the strange push and pull. Diego wanted desperately to get his sister to America, but she was married to a Mexican man and had children. Cameron knew the job wasn't to judge the laws but to uphold them. Most days, she believed what she was doing was making a positive impact.

Ballestrini's phone buzzed. "All right," he said. "We're good to go to the last one. Traffic should be pretty quick."

After a few minutes of quiet, Cameron flipped on the radio. At least Ballestrini wasn't singing show tunes, although he did have a habit of rolling his neck until it let out a long series of pops.

Cameron hadn't been to the Berkeley Marina in ages, but it was mostly hippy vans and leisure fishermen along with a few parents and kids watching for diving birds and jumping fish. A lot of the places they'd been charged to stake out weren't large enough for a trafficking operation. As Jess had explained, part of the trick to getting away with any crime was choosing inconspicuous locations and changing the pattern often.

Cameron and Ballestrini walked the full length of the marina, then headed back to the car. At least, it was a little warmer in the East Bay, and this was their last stop. Cameron couldn't help but be encouraged by those two things.

Halfway back down the marina, Ballestrini stopped. "Look at this."

He gestured to a yellow Karmann Ghia. She stepped forward to peer inside. With the exception of the driver's seat, the entire car was piled roof high with trash. Burger King and McDonald's wrappers, newspapers, empty boxes.

"That's no way to treat a classic car," Ballestrini said.

"Can you imagine what it smells like?"

He wrinkled his nose. "Can't smell any worse than that second marina."

They moved past the trashed Ghia and back toward her Blazer. She assumed from the radio silence that no one had any luck today. Their group was used to high adrenaline, high action situations, and the pace of this one was too slow. It would take work to keep up morale.

Cameron and Ballestrini got into the car. Ballestrini took the binoculars he'd been wearing off his neck and put them in the backseat. Then, like an excited kid, he slapped his thighs. "I hope we're not doing this tomorrow."

"It's supposed to rain," Cameron said, starting the car.

Ballestrini hummed and within seconds he was singing, "*The rain can't hurt me now. This rain will wash away what's past. And you will keep me safe. And you will keep me close. I'll sleep in your embrace at last.*"

He paused. "Can you name the show?"

"No."

"*And I'm at rest. A breath away from where you are. I've come home from so far…*"

"Ballestrini," she interrupted.

He put a hand up, continuing the song, "*So don't you fret, M'sieur Marius. I don't feel any pain. A little fall of rain.*"

"*Les Miserables,*" she said.

He stopped. "You got it."

He was humming again. She ignored him, pulling along the frontage road.

Ballestrini stopped singing. "Freeway onramp is right there."

"I can get on down here, too. This way we can enjoy the water." Cameron always loved the bay, the boats like little pieces of paper scattered in the wind. It was early in the season, and the weather was cold for all but the hardiest of sailors.

One of the last times she and Diego had been together, they had spent the day at Crissy Field. They'd seen a yacht that he'd sworn had belonged to President Roosevelt. She had no idea how he'd known.

"You have an iPhone charger in here?" Ballestrini asked.

"I think my sister borrowed it."

She saw the black screen on his phone. "You can use mine."

"No. It's fine."

Cameron looked in her rearview mirror and watched as a white moving truck pulled into the parking lot of the pier they'd just left. Whatever words had been on the side of the truck had been painted over. Cameron put on her blinker and pulled over.

"Why are you—" Ballestrini started.

Cameron twisted around in her seat. "See that truck."

Ballestrini turned back. "What about it?"

"No logo. That was one of the things to look for."

Ballestrini stared at his phone. "But there's no boat. It's probably delivering produce to one of those farm booths."

"Pretty big for a local farmer. I say we check it out." She eyed Ballestrini. He nodded, a little frustrated.

Cameron made a U-turn in the road and sped back. The truck had backed up against the small port building. She couldn't see behind the truck.

"It doesn't look like anything is happening," Ballestrini said.

Cameron reached the parking lot as the truck driver was getting back into the cab. Another man rounded from the back and climbed into the passenger side. "Were there two men before?"

"Yeah," Ballestrini said. "They're Hispanic, but so is everyone else here."

She scanned the people selling fruit. It was true.

The truck pulled out past them. The men appeared normal. What did traffickers look like? Cameron pulled up to the place where the truck had been parked.

"What are you going to do?" Ballestrini asked.

"Look around."

Cameron walked to the door of the port building and knocked. When no one answered, she tried the knob, but it was locked.

"There aren't any windows low enough to get a look inside."

Cameron eyed the side of the building. The truck stopped at a stoplight. They were heading onto the freeway. It was probably nothing. The buzz of adrenaline she felt was the result of days of no action. On the way to the car, she caught sight of something on the ground. She stooped down and picked up a silver earring.

"What is it?"

The truck drove onto the onramp as Cameron ran to the car. "Come on."

"What are we doing?"

"Following the truck."

Ballestrini barely had his door closed before Cameron sped off. "Get the light," she said. "It's behind my seat."

"Are you sure? What did you find?"

She pointed to the earring in the center console.

"Shit. Seriously, Cameron. That could be from anyone."

"Get the damn light, Ballestrini."

Ballestrini put the light on the roof and switched it on. Cameron honked at the cars in front of her. As they slowly crept out of her way, she swerved around the line waiting to turn onto the freeway. "Do you see it?"

"It's up there. Get into the left lane."

Her view was blocked by an 18-wheeler as she moved into the left lane. "Where?"

"Get around this next truck and you'll see them."

Drivers were slow to acknowledge them as police officers, so Cameron kept one hand on the horn as she moved in and out of the lanes. Ballestrini had his window down and was waving cars to the side.

Cameron came around the second truck and scanned the lanes of traffic.

"Shit," Ballestrini said, peering out of the car. "Where the hell did it go?"

Cameron sped up and moved out of the fast lane in time to see the tail of the truck at the bottom of the off ramp. "Damn it, they're getting off. I've got to get over." The ramp was almost behind her, and a suburban was coming up fast. Cameron moved forward and changed lanes. Ballestrini was waving at the traffic in the lanes to her right, trying to help create space, but drivers kept passing.

Cameron had no choice but to keep moving forward as she tried to get right. By the time she was in the right lane, she'd missed the exit.

"What the hell?" Ballestrini yelled into the car. "Doesn't a police light mean anything to these assholes?"

Cameron drove onto the shoulder and put the car in reverse.

"What are you doing?"

She drove backward along the shoulder. "Going back for them. Honk the horn for me."

Ballestrini reached across and honked as Cameron backed along the freeway until she could exit the ramp. A minivan pulled ahead of her, the driver slowing down to take a good look. Maybe she was thinking she'd need to give a police description later. Instead, Cameron rode up on the van's ass and honked her horn until the woman pulled over and let her pass. They reached the bottom of the ramp. Cameron searched for the van.

"Where did it go?" Just then, she saw the truck heading east. She followed. She was maybe sixty yards back. The light changed to red as the truck approached, but instead of stopping, the truck blew through the light. A black sedan swerved to miss the truck and hit a pickup coming the opposite direction. Ballestrini grabbed the handset off her portable radio. Beyond the wreck, the truck barreled through a stop sign and kept going. The drivers of the other cars were getting out of their cars to assess the damage.

"They look okay," she said.

Ballestrini pointed toward the truck, then gave the dispatcher details on the wreck.

She tried to veer around the mess in the intersection, but one of the cars had ended sideways, completely blocking her lane. "Damn it," Cameron said, trying to maneuver around it. There was a narrow space between the accident and the curb, but a car that had stopped now occupied it. An older man got out and crossed to the accident. Cameron honked her horn, but the man kept walking.

The truck was gaining distance. "Can you read the plate?"

Ballestrini leaned out the window to yell at the old guy. "Get this car out of the road."

The truck made a left and vanished from view. Cameron cranked her wheel and drove up onto the curb. She went maybe half a block along the sidewalk, terrifying a pedestrian coming out of a shop. "Sorry," Ballestrini yelled. "Please step back."

She drove back into the street with a scrape and a thud. Rubber burned as she went after the truck. They swerved around the corner. Cameron eased off the gas to scan in both directions for the truck.

Her heart was pounding. "There," Cameron yelled, pointing to the frontage road which ran along the Berkeley side of the Bay toward Ashby. She yanked the car in a semicircle, then swerved to avoid a slow moving car. They exchanged honks. The other driver swore. Ballestrini waved his badge out the window as she punched the accelerator. She closed some of the distance, but there were two cars and a motor home between them and the truck. People on the streets stopped to stare. A homeless man yanked his shopping cart away from the curb and hurried in the opposite direction.

Cameron kept edging into the oncoming lane, but there was too much traffic. She gave the horn a long, hard hold. The motorhome's blinker went on.

"Finally," Ballestrini said.

The beast lumbered to the curb. Cameron sped past it, crossing into the other lane, and swerved quickly to avoid an SUV coming at her. As she came around, the truck shot right onto the freeway.

"They're going back to the freeway."

"Call for backup," Cameron said. "Tell him to get some black and whites on I-80."

Ballestrini got on the radio as they crossed two lanes of slow moving freeway traffic to pull in three cars behind the truck.

Almost there. "Come on."

The sedan in front of her made no move to pull aside despite Cameron's insistent honking. Damn, she wished they were in a black and white. She changed lanes and floored it past the sedan, cutting him off. From the corner of her eye, she saw the little old man mouthing what was probably a long a string of obscenities. Ballestrini continued to wave his badge, not that it was doing much good. On the dash, Cameron noticed the orange glow of the gaslight.

The truck was successfully swerving in and out of traffic. People slowed down to keep their distance. The result was that Cameron and Ballestrini got pushed farther behind.

She tried to move around a beater Neon, but the BMW she pulled behind threw on its brakes. They nearly collided. "Goddamn it."

"If you're going to hit one, go back to the Neon," Ballestrini said. He pointed. "There."

A hole opened in the traffic. Cameron moved through it and closed the distance to the truck.

Cameron checked her rearview mirror.

"Where the hell's backup?"

"We had to end up in Berkeley," Ballestrini muttered. He lifted the radio again and repeated his request with twice the venom and half the patience. "Stay with him."

Cameron was right behind the truck when the brake lights fired red. She pumped the brake and swerved right. But the truck stopped too fast. She hit the rear corner of the truck, sending it spinning counter clockwise. Cameron overcorrected left and skidded into the center divide. The impact knocked her toward the steering wheel, but the airbag exploded first. It was like being suffocated by a plastic bag. Her shoulder jammed against the door. The road outside spun by, then halted. When she opened her eyes, the airbag was deflated.

She tried to focus, but her vision was a blur. She examined her arms, touched her face. She was fine.

Behind her, the whir of sirens approached. She reached over and touched Ballestrini.

He looked as shaken as she felt. "Damn."

The truck had crossed three lanes of traffic and collided with a pickup truck. The moving truck was on its side.

A black and white pulled up beside her. She opened her door, using her shoulder when it stuck. Her back and shoulder ached, but she stepped from the car. A female officer met her. Cameron quickly explained how they'd come to follow the truck.

"An earring?" the officer asked.

Cameron flashed her badge and kept walking.

"Wait," the officer called after her, but Cameron didn't stop. The police were setting up cones to block off the freeway and routing cars to detour off the exit ramp. Cameron jogged stiffly toward the wreckage of the truck.

Another patrol car pulled up beside the truck. An officer emerged. "Excuse me," he said. "Please stand back."

Cameron pulled her badge off her belt and hobbled to the cab and pulled herself up to look inside. It was empty.

"San Francisco? What brings you guys way over here?" He handed the badge back.

"We're working with ICE on a series of boats that might be trafficking women." Cameron limped to the back of the truck and tried to open the latch.

"You should have called for backup. We could have helped."

She had no motion in her left shoulder, so she had to bend her knees and use her right side to lift it. It didn't budge. "We did call."

"We didn't—" He saw her face and stopped talking. He reached down and pushed the door up and open with a long screech. The noise was followed by human cries.

The patrolman stumbled back. "Holy shit."

Inside, the women had been thrown when the truck tipped over. Metal shelves were scattered among the bodies. There was blood. Two women rose shakily and moved toward her. Many didn't move at all. Some of the women were African while others appeared more Eastern European. One woman wore a burka.

"Oh, Jesus." Cameron kneeled in the truck and crawled through the bodies.

She acted as a one-woman triaging unit. Behind her, the EMTs arrived with gurneys.

Cameron looked around, trying to count. "We need more ambulances."

A paramedic was on his radio. He scanned the bodies as he did his own count. Their eyes met. Even for someone who dealt with disaster, this was extreme.

Cameron knelt and felt for pulses. As some of the women rose, she called to the officers to escort them off. In the distance was the cry of additional ambulances and police cars. She held her left arm to her stomach to immobilize the shoulder and moved on her knees through them. Beside her, the patrolman helped lift those who could move.

One woman sat huddled against the truck bed, which was now a wall with the truck on its side. Her head was lifted toward the ceiling. She was mumbling. Cameron moved toward her, lifted the edge of her skirt and saw bone pushing against the skin. "We've got a compound fracture."

The paramedics and officers worked to make a path for the gurney.

Cameron touched her shoulder. "You're going to be okay. Todo estará bien." She repeated the two sentences until the paramedics reached her. Other paramedics loaded up the injured. Several women held onto the others who moaned softly. Their friends held them and cried. Another onslaught of paramedics arrived, taking the injured one by one.

Cameron moved a metal shelf and saw one who had been hidden. Crumpled in the corner was a young woman who couldn't have been older than fifteen or sixteen. She had beautiful dark red curls and creamy white skin. Her eyes closed, she might have been sleeping except for the dark blood that ran behind her left ear and down her neck.

Her chest tight, Cameron moved toward her. She had to crawl over a bent metal piece and lost her balance. She threw her left arm out instinctively and winced when her weight shifted into her shoulder. She took a breath, shaky and nauseous. "Come on," she breathed. Cameron reached to touch the woman's neck. No pulse. She moved her fingers, praying to find it some-where. Nothing. A third and fourth try. Nothing.

Cameron sat back on her haunches. The woman's dirty hands were bunched in tight fists. Cameron touched one, feeling the woman's fear in her grip.

"Cruz!"

Ballestrini walked toward her, a gash on the side of his cheek.

"You okay?"

She nodded. Then, she shook her head, picturing the young woman in the truck. She crawled to the edge of the truck and stepped down, trembling.

"Cruz? Are you okay? Are you hurt?"

She fought the shaking, struggled against it. "No," she finally let out. She waved into the truck. "She's dead. There's a dead one."

The paramedics moved in. Ballestrini reached for her, but she pulled away. "I need air," she said, limping away from the truck.

Ballestrini followed. "We got a call back on the plate. Guess who the truck was registered to."

She couldn't think.

He waited to deliver the punch line until she met his gaze. "Diego Ramirez."

CHAPTER 15

IVANA'S ARRIVAL IN California was not how she had imagined it. The only bit she'd caught sight of was a wide slice of the bluest sky. After that, all fourteen girls had been rushed inside a tiny apartment where they had lined up for a shower that was ice cold before Ivana's turn. They were an awkward bunch. More than half were darker, some clearly African while others might have been from India, Pakistan, or Afghanistan. Ivana knew almost nothing about those countries. There was one girl from the Ukraine. She carried a small postcard of Kiev that Ivana recognized. Her mother had studied Russian for fourteen years, something required of all Czechs until the fall of Communism. Being there with no one to speak to made Ivana wish she'd learned a few Russian words from her mother.

Without a towel, she used her dirty clothes to wipe the water from her skin and wring her hair. When she emerged from the bathroom, two of the girls were gone. One was the blond Ukrainian. The remaining girls claimed small portions of the half dozen mattresses that lined the floor. Dinner was cold sandwiches and bottles of Coke and water that a man named Marty dropped in the center of the room.

As the women moved in for food, Marty studied each one. He took hold of one woman's arm as though to see how thin she was, placed his palm on another one's backside. The woman pulled away, but Marty yanked her arm and held her while he continued palming the full round of her bottom. Ivana looked away, feeling the woman's shame.

When it was dark, Ivana lay on the thin mattress and pulled her jacket over her. It was warm in the apartment, especially with all the girls, but she couldn't shake the chill she felt. The night was filled with sounds of the street, cars and horns, people screaming out, and despite the solid floor, Ivana still felt the rock of the waves beneath her. Someone was crying. Michal often had bad dreams and it was Ivana, not their mother, who got up to comfort him.

She slept fitfully and woke early. It was dark, but the orange hues in the sky indicated morning was coming. She lifted her head and scanned the room. The others were sleeping. She wondered how many of them dreamt of home as she had. She folded her coat to put it under her head when she saw the blonde Ukrainian sitting in the corner. Her head was down on her knees. Ivana couldn't see her face, but she was almost certain it was her. The girl who had gone with her wasn't there.

Ivana unzipped her bag loudly and the girl looked up.

Ivana offered a small smile, but the girl didn't return it. She didn't seem at all happy. When did she come back and why? Slowly, Ivana moved toward her.

"English?" she asked awkwardly.

The girl shook her head.

Ivana didn't speak Ukrainian or Russian. The only other language she knew was her own. "Czech?"

She shook her head again. Then, she dropped it back into her arms and cried.

Ivana went to touch her, but as she did, the door flew open and hit the back wall with a bang, barely missing her.

The room filled with the moans of the girls waking, but the man who entered wasn't concerned with them. In two giant steps, he crossed to Ivana and the Ukrainian. Ivana cowered at the aggression of his movements. He ignored her, grabbing the blonde by the arm.

She struggled, crying out, but he jerked her to her feet, holding her to his chest, then leading her to the door with one arm. Watching them leave, Ivana had the sense she had narrowly escaped something bad.

Sometime after noon, Ivana was called and paired with a smaller girl who she guessed was Romanian. Ushered by their escort, a man with a hooked nose and a face scarred by acne, Ivana and the other girl left the building. It was much warmer than Ivana expected.

They drove through the city in an old white pickup truck. Ivana took it all in without blinking. The streets were wide and filled with people. They wore bright yellows and oranges. Some barely wore anything at all. The women's shoes were high with straps and buckles like the ones in her favorite magazines. One day she would own a pair. They crossed a busy intersection, and she caught sight of a bridge a few blocks away. Not red like the famous one, but a huge, gorgeous bridge just the same. Down another street, she saw water with white crested waves and wondered if there was a beach there. Despite a lack of sleep and the incident with the other girl, Ivana felt a shiver of excitement. How lucky she was to be in California. If only the idiots at her school knew.

The man pulled over and double-parked. "Come," he said, motioning for them to follow. She and the other girl got out of the car. Ivana followed the man. The girl whispered behind her. "I'm so nervous," she said in Czech.

"You speak Czech?" Ivana asked.

The girl nodded. She was almost Michal's size. Her cheeks were white and pale, her lips almost blue.

Ivana touched the girl's arm. "You'll be okay. I'm here."

The girl bowed her head. She was probably younger than she looked. Ivana was fifteen, but she always considered herself older than her classmates. The other girl was probably only thirteen or fourteen.

"I didn't want to come," she whispered as though reading Ivana's thoughts. "My father made me."

Ivana felt both jealousy and pity. She had always dreamt that her father would return one day, but not a father like that. One who would send his daughter thousands of kilometers from home wasn't any better than no father at all.

"I'm Anna," she said.

"Ivana," Ivana answered.

"In here. Hurry," the man yelled and the two girls ran to catch up.

They walked down a narrow, dirty alley before he opened a heavy white door sprayed with graffiti. Ivana assumed they were entering the side of a restaurant, but she had been talking to Anna so she didn't notice the front.

She moved through the doorway with her chin high and nearly tripped over the threshold. Inside was pitch black and the transition from the bright sunlight made her feel blind.

"Here," someone yelled.

As her eyes adjusted, she saw an empty bar. To the left was a large stage surrounded by tables. Her stomach tightened with excitement. It had to be some sort of show club. She'd never seen a real one, let alone been inside. Would she recognize any of the actors?

The man pushed them forward. Ivana stumbled across the dark carpet. The room had the faint odor of the bar where she'd worked at home. She was instantly more confident. She could do this. Four men sat in a row of low, burgundy velvet armchairs lined up in front of the bar. The two on the ends were huge men, their frames spilling out of the chairs. She tried not to stare as she attempted to check if any of them was familiar. There were so many famous people in America; she would never recognize them all.

The biggest of them stood from the end closest to her and approached their escort. She tried not to stare at him. His skin was as black as she'd ever seen, and his eyes were light for such a dark man, almost green. The two exchanged a few words, but Ivana couldn't understand them. Then, their escort left. She didn't turn back. She didn't want her new employers to think she wasn't excited to be there.

One of the men in the center seemed to be the boss. Older than the others, he wore a suit and a bright tie in a color magazines called salmon like the fish. His shoes had sleek lines and long, pointed toes. The boss spoke, and the first man waved Anna forward. Ivana could feel Anna shivering. She willed her not to blow it for both of them.

The four men stared for a few minutes and then the boss twirled his finger in a circle.

Ivana frowned, unsure what he meant until he did it again. "Turn around," she whispered to Anna.

The two moved slowly together.

The men spoke some more, then another stood up. He approached them, and took Anna's hand. "Come with me."

Ivana gave her a look of encouragement, then faced the remaining men again. The black man pointed to her and pulled at his collar.

She shook her head, not understanding.

"Your top," he said. It surprised her that he spoke Czech.

Her chest tightened. She nodded, still unsure what he wanted. The man approached her, and she saw clearly the light color of his eyes. Like the glass that sold in the shops, like the pools at the fanciest resorts.

He touched her top button and pulled it open.

She swallowed a gasp and remained frozen. People dressed differently in

America. He wanted her to act more relaxed, more American. She forced her breath out, realizing she probably seemed like a ridiculous prude to them.

He reached up and pulled open the next one.

She stepped back and reached for her sweater, but he held her hand in a tight fist. The green eyes narrowed until she no longer saw the water or the glass. She pulled away without success, but he reached up and opened her sweater. One of the buttons popped and she hunted for it on the dark ground.

The boss said something. The black man pulled her from her sweater and pushed her closer to the other men. She stumbled without falling and stood in only a thin camisole, using her arms to cover herself.

"No," the boss said.

She felt herself cry. Stop. Be strong. She would leave. She went for the door, but the green-eyed man blocked her. Before she could reach for her sweater, he threw it into an empty chair.

She shivered in the thin camisole, terrified.

The boss said something and pointed to her camisole.

"No," she said strongly.

The man's breath was hot on her neck as he gripped the side of her camisole and tore it. Cool air hit her bare skin. Tears streamed down her cheeks as she wrapped herself with her bare arms.

The boss wasn't done.

She sobbed.

The black man gripped her shoulder and shook. Her head snapped back. She closed her eyes, crying and shaking.

Searing pain crossed her jaw as he hit her. She cried out and fell backward. He yanked her to her feet. She palmed the pain in her cheek. He moved her like she was a mannequin. He spread her arms and forced them to her sides, then he said something that made the others laugh.

They would be done soon. From a back room came a piercing scream. Anna. Ivana cried out loud, pushing her balled fist to her mouth to try to quiet herself.

The black man ignored her and shifted his attention to her skirt. He unfastened it in the back and let it drop. Shaking, she focused on the floor as the black man ran his hand over her skin and made comments to the others. She finally forced her eyes open and blinked through the tears. What did they want from her? She stifled a larger fear and forced it from her mind. They wouldn't kill her. They needed her to work, to pay for her passage. Surely, that much was true.

When she looked back at the boss man, he made a gesture to her chest. The black man cupped her breast in his hand and bounced it like spare change.

She turned away, humiliated.

Finally, the boss man nodded.

It was over. She reached down for her skirt, but the black man took her hand.

The boss stood from his chair. Not much taller than she was, he had a belly that grew out of nowhere when he got to his feet. He approached like a rat, with tiny footsteps. He touched her face. She bit down to silence her chattering teeth. With a smirk that showed off tiny, brown teeth, he took her hand and led her toward the back room.

She reached for her skirt, but he pulled her along. Oh, God. She yanked herself free and threw herself down for her clothes. The black man dragged her up and punched her in the stomach. She lost her breath and doubled over, struggling to fill her lungs. They didn't leave her alone. The boss had her hand, the black man pushed from behind while a third man followed.

They came to a small office with a desk in one corner and a couch and table along the far wall. A television rested on the desk. The boss waved her to the couch. She hesitated before sitting slowly.

The boss said something, and the other men left.

She watched him, frightened, as he did what she had feared most. He barely glanced her way as he slid his coat off his shoulders and unfastened his belt. She cried and tried to stand, but he pushed her down. She twisted and was able to escape under his arm. She reached the desk. He grabbed her. Snatching a pen off the desk, she spun back and gouged his face.

He screamed. The door opened. The two men lifted her, threw her down. She knocked her head on the floor. The one took a knife and cut away one side of her panties, then ripped them off the other side. The two men held her while the boss got on top. His face was bleeding as he reached down and choked her. The men held her hands and she strained, gasped for breath. He raised a hand and slapped her hard across the ear.

She stopped moving, then closed her eyes as he stabbed his way into her. He covered her face with his palm, pressing her chin to the side until she saw nothing but the leg of the desk. She focused on it, on the gouges around the base, on the dust that coated the wood detail. She studied the red and black nub carpet, the place where a loop had pulled out. A paperclip on the ground. She didn't know how long she stared, but finally it stopped. She didn't move. Finally, the man got off her. The pressure lightened. The worst was over.

Then, she heard another zip. From the corner of her eye, she saw the green-eyed man drop his pants. She was wrong—the worst wasn't over yet.

CHAPTER 16

AN HOUR BEFORE their shift ended, Lavick was called into an urgent meeting with Ahrens and a couple of suits Cameron didn't recognize.

"They're onto something with Benjamin's shooting," Kessler said without a hint as to how he knew.

"Guess it means quitting time's coming early tonight," Lau said.

Daley was at his locker, staring down the hallway. From that angle, he saw a slice of Ahrens' office. "What's that all about, anyway?"

"Word is that they've got a bunch of evidence about Benjamin's guilt," Kessler said.

Ballestrini glanced up at him. "Where did you hear that?"

Kessler went red and looked away.

"Your girlfriend up in Homicide?" Daley teased him.

"She's not a girlfriend." Kessler shrugged. "We went out a couple times is all."

Cameron wanted out of there so badly that she didn't even change her clothes before leaving. Her shoulder was throbbing from the car accident, so she winced as she hefted her equipment bag onto the top shelf. The effort made her eyes sting with tears. The job was always physical, but she felt so beat up now.

Cradling her arm, she grabbed her pack and keys, and left. As she passed the hall, she saw the meeting. Each of them was head down, nose dug in a packet. Must have been something interesting. Hopefully, it would put Lavick in a better mood.

Outside, she winced at the crunched front corner of her car. It drove fine, but it looked like hell. She got in, cranked the heat, and headed home. Something had shifted after the day with the truck. It was like Lavick was angrier than pleased that they'd had a break in the case. He wouldn't let go of the fact that the guys got away. How the hell it was possible was beyond her. They'd been on the freeway, surrounded by cops. The only way off that freeway was across eight lanes of traffic. Still, they'd vanished. The local squad had sent six cars after them and found nothing.

Ballestrini seemed deflated, too. Everyone did. She was off tomorrow. She didn't want to see this place or think about it until she had to be back.

Rosa would be at the salon until seven, so Cameron planned to drop off her car and walk down the block to Señora Accosta's and pick up Nate. Maybe they would go to Dolores Park, pick up breakfast for tomorrow at Tartin's. A morning bun for Rosa. Or the frangipane croissant with almond paste. A pain au jambon. Suddenly, she was hungry. Maybe they could eat at Tartin's for dinner. She put her key in the door and pushed it open slowly. The door had a low clearance. If too much mail had come through the slot, letters got caught underneath and ripped. But there was no resistance on the door today. She stepped inside. The mail was in a pile against the wall. Someone had opened the door but left the mail there. Rosa would have picked it up.

Instinctively, Cameron drew her gun and pushed the door shut with her foot until it clicked silently. "Rosa?" she called out. When no one answered, she stood still and listened. The house had been built shortly after the big earthquake in 1906. Though it was in great condition, the floor had distinct creaks. Perhaps worn down from the old forced air furnace, the top of the basement stairs made a high-pitched creak. Some old grout trapped beneath the bathroom floor made a gravely croaking noise while the hallway between her bedroom and Nate's moaned. The floor in the kitchen vibrated. By the back door was the sound of a small squeaky animal.

"Who's here?"

She heard the squeak.

She waited to hear it again. Unless he was standing on the threshold of the back door, a movement in any direction would create more noise. Those noises drove her crazy in Nate's early days as she tried to creep down the hall without stirring him. Meanwhile, he seemed to react to every change in the wind. Right now, she was thankful for the house's character.

The floor squeaked again. Cameron walked down the hallway, silently moving heel toe. Just then, the doorbell rang. Two, long insistent buzzes. The screen snapped closed on the back door. "Damn it." She ran to the kitchen and peered into the backyard. She went out the back door and peeked around the side of the house. Whoever had been there was gone. Her iPad sat on the kitchen table. She checked the den. Nothing was disturbed there either. The TV was on the wall, Rosa's Kindle on the table. Diego again? Why come when she wouldn't be here? The front lock hadn't been jimmied. She'd have to check.

The doorbell rang again, followed by a knock. She'd thought maybe it was a neighborhood kid selling something, but that would be one big kid. She tucked her SIG into the back of her pants, pulled her shirt down over it and opened the door.

Two men were on her porch. Each was the size of a small truck. Inexpensive suits, belts that pulled a little tight and shoes that hadn't been polished ever. Inspectors.

"Took you a while to get to the door," the bigger truck said, leaning back on his heels.

"Didn't know it was illegal to ignore the bell."

"Are you Cameron Cruz?" the other asked, a little Jersey nasal in his voice.

"I am." She shifted and felt the barrel warm on her back.

"We're from Homicide. When was the last time you saw Diego Ramirez?" Jersey asked.

"Maybe you should show me some I.D."

She got two badges flashed at her, barely enough time to catch their names. Unlike a civilian, she knew exactly where to look. Anthony Kelly and James Caltabiano.

They tucked their badges away and Caltabiano asked again. "The last time you saw Diego Ramirez."

"The night he shot Ray Benjamin," she said smoothly. "Now, if you'll excuse me." She stepped back to close the door.

Kelly slid his foot in the way of the door. Hands in his pockets, he studied her like this was all normal business.

Cameron stared down at the foot. "Unless you've got a warrant, you better get your foot off my property."

The truck slid his foot back onto the front porch.

Jersey put up his hands. "Let's not get excited. We are looking for Diego Ramirez, and we believe we saw him enter these premises."

She felt the familiar bump in her gut. "When?"

"Just before you arrived home," he said, "Uh, Ma'am."

"You've been watching my house."

The two exchanged a look like they'd said something they weren't supposed to. "You're saying he's not here now?" the truck asked.

"There's no one here but me."

"You're sure?" Jersey asked.

"Positive."

"Do you have any idea where he might have gone?" Caltabiano asked.

"I never saw him, and I have no idea where he would be." That was the honest truth.

"It's very serious, ma'am," Kelly said, his hands back in his pockets.

"Murder usually is, Detective Kelly."

She shut the door.

With the door bolted, she searched the house. What had he been doing here? Other than the mail, the house was exactly as it always was. No note under her pillow, nothing stuck into the book she was reading. Not in her drawers. At least not that she saw. Nate's room was the same. The circus mobile above his crib was still. Her blanket lay across the rocking chair from being up with him last night. She scanned the street through the front window. No obvious undercover cars.

In the kitchen, she pulled a Pacifico from the fridge. The desire to take Nate out to the park and down to Tartin's was gone. He was with Señora Accosta, which suddenly seemed like the safest place. The magnetized can opener she'd left on the fridge was not there, but in the drawer. It had been Diego's first gift to her. An opener in the shape of a pint of beer, filled with amber fluid. "Everyone needs an opener within reach," Diego had joked. Rosa hated the look of it.

Cameron went to put it up on the refrigerator and saw a handwritten note. Grocery, it said at the top of the list. Then, below it, "bananas, peanut butter, baby wipes." It wasn't her handwriting. It wasn't Rosa's. Four bananas lay in the fruit bowl on the counter. She hated peanut butter. Baby wipes. Leaving her beer, she jogged into Nate's room. The white plastic box of baby wipes was half full. She dumped them onto the tabletop and fanned through them. There was nothing inside.

"What the hell?"

There would be baby wipes in the diaper bag, but Señora Accosta had that. She started to leave the room when she remembered that she had a bag of refills in the changing table drawers. On her knees, she dug around for the extras. Where would they be? Nothing in the first drawer. The second was all sheets and burp cloths. She should know where they were; she organized this. She was too agitated to think. She sat back on her heels. "Calm down," she whispered. Top drawer was diapers and medicines. Second drawer. Bottom drawer. They had to be there. In the drawer she found a white plastic bag of extra wipes. Impatient, she tore it open. Halfway down the wet stack was a plastic sandwich bag.

She checked the window to be sure Nate's shades were drawn and shifted her attention to the bag. Inside were a small black jump drive and a bankbook from Bank of America. She dumped the two things on the floor and picked up the drive. She moved into her room and started up her laptop, pacing the room as it beeped and clicked. When she was logged in, she inserted the drive and watched as it lit up. The drive appeared on her desktop, and she double-clicked. A small black box popped up. Small white letters read, "Insert passcode." She stood back from the computer. "Damn it, Diego."

She went back to Nate's room and grabbed the bankbook. Maybe he'd written the password here. She flipped it open. The name typed on the front page was Nathaniel Cruz. Her breath stalled. He'd always said that if he had kids, he wanted them to have everything he hadn't. In the midst of all this, he had started an account for their son? She was flooded with dread that these men would find him.

She imagined Nate in his father's arms as she turned the page and scanned the numbers that lined the page. "God," she whispered. Six thousand, seven thousand, five thousand, nine thousand. The first one on the day after he'd come here. The total was $95,000. Her first thought was how much this would help Nate with college. Maybe graduate school, too. Then, she studied the numbers again. Stolen money. There was no way he had this much money. Diego had put his stolen money in her son's name.

She ran back to the computer and typed in "Nathaniel."

"Passcode incorrect. Please enter valid passcode."

She typed "my son."

"Passcode incorrect."

The door swung open with a creak and Rosa's voice called out, "Cameron, it's us. You here? I got off work early and picked up Nate."

She pulled the jump drive from the computer, which beeped at her and showed a big red stop sign. "The disk was not ejected properly." Like she had time to worry about that.

She turned to the door, gripping the book as though it were filled with gunpowder. A grenade about to explode. And it was. She had no idea what to do with it.

She heard Rosa's footsteps and glanced at the book in her hand. She shoved the book and drive back into the plastic bag and folded it into her back pocket, then headed for the front door to greet them.

CHAPTER 17

ROSA DRAGGED CAMERON out to meet Ricky for dinner at Puerto Alegre on Valencia. Cameron told herself that just because Diego had been at the house didn't mean he was coming back, but knowing that she had missed him by minutes made it hard to leave. Rosa swore she was going to die if she didn't get some coctel de camaron, something similar to ceviche that Mama Cruz made on Easter and at Christmas time.

Ricky had a table for four when they arrived. Cameron set Nate's car seat on one chair and pulled it beside her. He had already eaten and, miraculously, was sleeping. Rosa always had plenty to say. She and Ricky managed to hold dinner conversation almost exclusively without Cameron, which was good, because she couldn't focus on anything but the odd police visit. The more she thought about it, the more questions she had.

Rosa left before dessert to meet friends at Casanova across the street. She usually left dinners with Ricky early to give him and Cameron a chance to talk shop. Casanova was a raucous bar that she and Rosa used to frequent, but Cameron hadn't been there in more than a year. Going to a bar had stopped seeming appropriate when she found out she was pregnant. She was glad Rosa had plans. One less person to answer to. That left Ricky.

"You're the quiet sister, but this is extreme, even for you."

"Plainclothes detectives were at my house today. Two of them."

Ricky leaned forward. "About Ramirez?"

She nodded and explained about their visit, about the bankbook and the jump drive.

"What was on the drive?"

"I don't know. I can't unlock it."

"Why would he put stolen money in Nate's name? He knows you wouldn't accept that."

"Maybe that's why he did it," she said. "In case something happened to him, he knew I'd report it."

Ricky gave her his lopsided smile. The one that meant he saw right through her.

"I'm fooling myself?"

He shrugged. "You know how to follow evidence. Where does it lead you?"

"To feeling totally insane."

The waitress came back to the table. Ricky ordered another beer and asked Cameron if she wanted anything. "I'm good. Thanks." She'd already had one and there was no sense clouding her brain further.

"There was something about these plainclothes guys, too."

"What do you mean?" He thanked the waitress and took a swig of the beer.

She tried to identify what it was. "They didn't seem legit."

"Did you see their badges?"

"A flash of them, but I caught their names." Nate squirmed in his seat.

"Would be pretty bold to dress up like a cop and show up at the house of a real cop."

"I know. I'm losing it," she said, unbuckling her baby and lifting him from the chair. He arched his back and stuck his butt out, his little hands in fists, mouth wide in a yawn. Why was that so damn cute?

"Pass the little guy to Uncle Ricky," Ricky said, pushing his plate out of the way.

Waitresses stopped and cooed at Nate. "Wow, he looks just like you," one said to Ricky. He and Cameron shared a laugh.

There was a line at the door, so they relinquished their table and headed outside. Ricky carried Nate, and Cameron carried the car seat. This is what it would have been like to be a family. Little things like not having to carry everything yourself. Not that Rosa didn't help. No, she did more than that. Cameron would be lost without her sister.

"I'm parked a couple blocks down," she told Ricky once they were on the street.

He cocked his head toward the bar across the street. "You leaving Rosa?"

"She's young. She can stay out late."

"And you're so old."

They started walking. "Feels that way."

"It'll all work out, Cam," he said, giving her shoulder a little bump. "Important thing is to keep your head out of the clouds. Like what are you going to do with the bankbook and the drive?"

"Turn them in to Lavick?" As soon as she said it, she knew she had no intention of giving them to anyone. No matter what the outcome, they felt like some sort of insurance.

Ricky stopped walking. "Really?"

"Keep them?"

"I would," Ricky said. "It's probably breaking some rules, but until you know what side everyone is on, I'd put them somewhere safe."

"You think Lavick might be in on it?"

Ricky shrugged. "Ray Benjamin, Diego… How do I know? Lavick and Benjamin were close once."

She tried to remember if she'd ever seen them together. "Really?"

He nodded as they approached her car.

She opened the back door and snapped the car seat into its base. Ricky kissed Nate, who smiled broadly, showing off his mouthful of pink gums.

"You have somewhere safe to put that stuff?" Ricky asked as Cameron belted Nate in.

She thought about the house.

"We can store them in the big gun safe in the basement," said Ricky.

Cameron considered it.

"Might be a good idea to get them out of your house, anyway."

Sitting on the backseat, she faced him and he put a hand on her shoulder. "Hey, it's going to be okay."

"Swear?"

"You can call anytime," he said.

On the drive home, Cameron thought again about those cops. Beat up shoes and old, sloppy ties, it was all exactly what she would expect. But, there was something. She pictured them walking away. Had she seen their car? Then, she realized what it was. The suits. They'd been wearing the same suit. Almost identical. That sort of thing would be mortifying for a couple of detectives. She imagined the argument over who would have to go home and change.

She dialed Hailey Wyatt and left a voicemail with the names of the two detectives. Suddenly, she was stirred up. Something was off. She pictured the meeting Lavick was in today. Was he the one having her followed?

She eyed the clock. There was a way to find out. First, though, she had to hope Rosa had a miserable evening out and came home early.

CHAPTER 18

LUIS REEKED OF sweat. The new shipments were always the roughest days. Pay the guys on the boat, load the girls, and get them to the safe house. Sometimes as many as seventeen or eighteen girls. He had two helpers, who were anything but help. He'd fired five already, but the new ones weren't any better.

The first one, Dwayne, liked to pull his gun out and wave it around. The day Dwayne helped, they ended up with a mob scene. After that, Luis didn't let them have weapons at all unless he had problems with the guys on the boat. The word about Manny seemed to have gotten around, so there wasn't much trouble. Luis had only seen Brad two other times. Each time the sight of the man's face made him feel like he might be sick.

Still, the job was getting harder. For the first week, Luis met boats at the piers without any problems. Now, they had to go farther out or wait until nightfall. One night he'd ended up having to get on the boat and travel with them. He was so seasick. Then, there was the chase. Thank God he wasn't driving. He'd never been a good driver. He got too nervous. He panicked. But, Marty drove like one of the guys at NASCAR. Might have been the only thing Marty did well.

Someone screwed that one up. Not him. At least that's what Brad said when he called. Hearing that voice, Luis had to sit down on the floor right where he was. Middle of his apartment. He was sure he'd be sick. "That wasn't your fault, Luis. Our inside guy screwed that one up. It's on him." Luis wondered if that guy would get the same treatment as Manny.

At night, he drank Dewar's and wrote in the little book he wasn't supposed to be writing in. He had gotten a box at the bank. It required I.D. and a special key. Instead of keeping the book at home, he had unwound the wire that bound the pages and kept the blank ones at home. Each morning before work, he took the new pages to the box. He had put a little cash in the box, too. But, mostly it was just the pages. Laura's brothers would say he was like a little girl, writing in his diary. It didn't make sense to him, but he was afraid to throw them away. What if they found them? And he couldn't stop writing. He wrote and drank and wrote. One night, Brad sent over a new girl for him, Candi. Luis liked her better than the first girl, and so they saw each other a few nights a week. That wasn't so bad. He kept telling himself he would get used to it. Instead, he felt worse with each passing day.

Today had gone okay. He had just sorted the new batch, which was his least favorite part. They mostly got women and girls. The young ones were divided between attractive and unattractive. The attractive ones went to the clubs. The unattractive ones went to the shops and occupations like cleaning and working the fields, as did the sturdier, older ones. Some of them would stay in the area. Some would travel to other places in California and farther. They had clients as far as Nebraska, Michigan, and parts of Tennessee and Mississippi.

Each girl owed Brad and his partners almost twenty-five thousand dollars. Most had paid a little, but would need to work off the rest. Not in the jobs they thought they were getting—at restaurants or as nannies. Those jobs didn't pay enough to get Brad his money back.

The holding place for the ones who stayed local was in a nasty place down off 6th Street. In the next day or two, the new girls would get their first taste of what they were doing. They stayed in one city for a few weeks or months, then they were moved on. Luis had coordinated his first move last week. He hardly recognized the women he'd helped off boats.

They were ready to move as soon as the guys arrived. Freddy Jackson arrived first. No surprise. Marty was always late. Freddy was a huge, black man who almost always wore denim. Denim shirts, denim shorts and pants, overalls, even his T-shirts were denim-colored.

He came in, strutting. Luis was again impressed, as he was every time, with how big Freddy was. He had to be about six foot five. Luis couldn't begin to guess what he weighed. Luis had watched Freddy carry a woman under each arm without issue, so there was no question Freddy could bench-press a couple of Luises, too.

"How's it hanging?" Freddy said as he gave Luis the standard high five.

Luis laughed. "Yeah. How's it hanging with you?" He never really understood the question but didn't want to ask.

"Pretty good. Pretty damn good." Freddy checked out the shipment. He gave them all a big wave. His appearance had the tendency to make people nervous, and he didn't want them to be afraid to come with him. Sometimes, he did an imitation of Eddie Murphy in *Coming to America* that was hilarious.

Freddy made his way toward his group and introduced himself. "Freddy," he'd say, pointing to himself. Then, he raised his hands like a conductor and got them all to repeat it. "Fred-dy. Fred-dy. Fred-dy." After a minute, they'd be chanting. Freddy had gotten them going when Marty arrived. He and "his boys," as he called the two guys who always came with him. Technically, Marty was supposed to come alone, but Marty wasn't really big on rules. Freddy sent Marty a look, which Marty ignored, and launched into his own introduction. Marty waved and bowed to the women like a rock star starting a concert. Luis wished he didn't have to deal with Marty.

Today, Marty was wearing a bright orange-and-yellow-striped button-down that might have been made of plastic. Luis was curious about where Marty got his clothes. Worse than his clothes, Marty was greased head-to-toe. Occasionally, he ended up with little drips of hair oil that ran down his forehead. At first, Luis had thought it was sweat, but the drips stopped above his eyebrow and could be there for hours.

Marty walked right past Luis and over to where the women were eating. Until then, they had all been watching Freddy and giggling. Now, they stared up at Marty uneasily.

Marty walked slowly along the line of girls eating take-out Chinese food like he was shopping for corn at the supermarket. "Hello, ladies. I'm Marty." He gave them a little hip dance, which made them all laugh. "Marty," he repeated. "Rhymes with party, which is what we're going to do. Yeah!" He circled his belly around and ended with a big thrust of his hips.

The women continued to giggle, but Luis turned away, not interested in making conversation with Marty today.

Still, Marty came up, cackling at his own stupid humor. "A pretty good-looking group."

"I think they're okay to go," Luis said carefully.

"Yeah, sure." He paused and glanced back at the girls. "I like that one in the yellow the best," he said, pointing to a brunette with long hair that was pulled back from her face. She was pretty, but nothing Luis would ever touch. He wished Marty wouldn't talk about it.

He winked. "I'm starting tryouts with that one."

Luis didn't respond. "Things are outside. Freddy already checked." He tapped his watch. "You tell them when we are ready to go." Luis walked away.

Marty backed into his path. "Hey, what's the rush?"

Luis shrugged, trying to act cool. "Lots to do in the office. You need something?"

"I wanted to tell you about the beauty from last week."

"I don't remember," Luis lied.

"Sure you do. Gorgeous with dark hair." Marty shook his hands in front of his chest. "Huge melons."

One of Brad's people, Frank, had arrived to check through the shipment. Luis said hello.

Marty didn't bother to turn around. "She wore that flowered shirt that hugged so tight. Don't you remember?"

"Maybe. I'm not sure. I have to go help Frank."

Marty grabbed his arm. "Frank schmank, let him go spank."

Luis felt the sweat pooling at the base of his neck.

"He can wait. You got to hear this story."

Marty frowned like he meant business. Luis wondered if he was related to Brad. Maybe he should listen to the damn story. "Okay."

"So, I load them up last week to make my deliveries, and I invite her to sit up front."

The sweat trickled down his collar. He scratched at it like a fly.

"I tried her out," he said, like he was talking about a motorcycle.

Luis didn't answer.

"I mean kicking and screaming that really got me going. She was a feisty one, and so tight."

Luis looked around nervously.

"By the end, she was begging for it. You want me to hook you up?"

"I have a girl," Luis said.

"Fine, but that blonde one you're eyeing, with the blue shirt and the long hair—"

Luis tried to hide his surprise. He had to admit he'd been admiring that one. She was so small and pretty.

"I'm going to have her all to myself." Marty grabbed his groin and walked away.

Luis watched Marty wave over his boys and gather the girls. Marty seemed aware that Luis was watching, so he paid special attention to the blonde.

Luis walked to the office without looking at Marty again.

"You want to go for a ride?" Marty asked.

Luis didn't hear the response, but he knew exactly who Marty was talking to.

He couldn't wait to go home. He needed a drink.

CHAPTER 19

ROSA CAME IN a little past ten. She was stone-cold sober and pissed at men. This wasn't unusual, especially around Latin men. She was angry that they hit on her, that they wanted to buy her drinks and that they asked her out. Rosa with her five or six Latina friends in a Latin bar could not believe those men— she actually called them that—had the nerve to think she would date them.

"Are you in for the night?" Cameron asked, cutting off the rant.

Rosa frowned as though she wasn't close to done.

"I need to go back to the station quickly," Cameron said by way of an apology.

"I should go with you. I've seen the men you work with." She narrowed her eyes. "How come you never set me up?"

"You have to stay with Nate."

Rosa walked toward her room. "Fine, but you owe me a date with the blond one."

Both Kessler and Daley were blondish, but Cameron was sure Rosa meant Daley. He was her type—cocky, full of himself. Rosa didn't want a Latin man because she had decided they were all cocky and full of themselves. Then, she chose Daley. "Be back in an hour or so."

Rosa said something from the bedroom that Cameron couldn't make out. She was confident it had something to do with Daley. Since she had been in Special Ops, Daley had been through at least two dozen girlfriends. He was good, she had to give him that. He could turn it on when he wanted to, but it never lasted long.

Cameron made her way to the station in the dark and considered whether this was a good idea. No, she knew it wasn't a good idea. But, she also knew that there was a good chance that something in Lavick's office would offer a clue to what was going on. Lavick and Benjamin had been close. Why hadn't she heard that from Lavick? She tried to remember how Sergeant Lavick had looked the day after Benjamin was shot. Then, the meeting last night. That had to have been official, but why was no one talking about it? They were working this ICE deal, but other than being told where to go and when, there wasn't a peep about who the suspects were. They always got a big picture story. She needed to talk to the other guys, too. Maybe she would mention something to Ballestrini.

There was a single car parked in the gravel lot next to the bus and two squad cars. She recognized Kessler's truck, but she had seen him go out with Daley, so she was pretty sure he wasn't here. She let herself in with her badge card and walked toward the locker room. The hall was lit only by the dim glow of the emergency exit signs at each end. Ahrens' door was closed; the only light was a small blue spot where her computer was charging. Lavick's office was similarly dark. Cameron tried the knob. Locked. She went into the locker room and opened her locker, then down at Lavick's. What were the chances that Lavick had gotten a new lock? It had been a year. She held her breath as she went through the combination: sixteen, twenty-six, and thirty-six. She heard the click and exhaled. Same lock.

She put the lock in her jacket pocket and pulled the door open. She saw a picture of his wife and daughters, and deodorant. She didn't want the over-head light on, so she used the flashlight on her phone to search the locker. She remembered seeing him put his keys in the locker, but maybe he had stopped doing that. She stepped up on the bench and checked the upper shelf. Nothing but ten years of dust. Shit. No keys. She moved back from the locker and tried to figure out where the keys might be. He took them home. That would be the smart thing to do, but Lavick never had. His last stop was always his locker. He hung his team coat inside. She touched the coat hanging on the back of the locker door. A bulge in one pocket. She reached her hand in and pulled out his keys.

Moving quickly, she went to his office door and tried the first key. Bingo. The knob turned. She was inside. The desktop was arranged in piles. She started at the top right and thumbed through the papers. Budgeting. She stacked the pages neatly and moved on. Departmental memos in the next. Then, training materials. In the middle was a stack of printed e-mails covered in handwritten notes. So much for a paperless department, one of last year's top goals.

She went back to the hallway and checked both directions. She should have found something by now. Sliding into his chair, she dug through the stacks on the far side of the desk. Nothing. She opened the bottom drawer, but it was full of random equipment—a pair of gloves, a flashlight that didn't work when she tried it, an extra pair of clothes. Panicked, she opened the upper thin drawer. Through the clear plastic of his pencil tray, Cameron saw a manila folder. She slid it out, reading the tab: R. Benjamin.

Taking a deep breath, she switched on Lavick's desk lamp and scanned the police report on the shooting. Nothing surprising there. Behind it was Benjamin's personnel file. No awards, no merits, but no warnings or reprimands either. Clean, if maybe a little boring. Probably seventy-five percent of the force had records like this. Behind the personnel file was a 1099-INT dated from the year before. Benjamin had earned four thousand dollars in interest. Behind the 1099 was a bank statement for a Bank of America checking account 149-424 in the name of Ray J. Benjamin. She saw his Social Security number and an address she didn't recognize. She tried to commit both to memory as she scanned the page. Ending balance read $47,932.12.

Forty-eight thousand didn't seem like that much. Diego had put twice that in Nate's name, but four thousand dollars in interest was a lot at today's rates that usually approached zero. She flipped the page, which read like a grocery list of deposits and withdrawals. Nine thousand, eight thousand, four thousand, ninety-eight hundred, seven thousand, six, six, five, eight, four, nine and on and on. The next page was another account. Sixty-nine thousand and change, followed by a page with more additions and withdrawals. She glanced back at the other account's page. None of the numbers matched up. These were different deposits and different withdrawals. In total, there were five accounts, totaling over two hundred thousand and who knew where all the withdrawals had gone.

Did Jess know about any of this? Cameron would have liked to talk to her, but she had no idea who was involved, how deep it went. She turned back to the personnel file and searched for beneficiary information. She didn't see any. His emergency contact was someone with a 410 area code. She thought about the times she'd met Benjamin, with his Maryland drawl and his perfectly straight, little mustache.

The few times she had talked to him, Benjamin found a way to bring up Maryland. Some little place called Ocean Pride where they served the best crabs in all of Baltimore. He'd come to San Francisco in pursuit of a woman he then married and promptly divorced. Somehow, he ended up staying.

She flipped to the final pages of the file. The list of possible suspects only had one name on it: Diego Ramirez. His most recent address was listed up top, followed by his dates of birth and death. The last known addresses were all familiar. She flipped the page to the list of known associates.

"Shit."

The list included the entire list of Special Ops, herself included. The only difference between hers and the others was that her name was followed by another one: Nathaniel Cruz (Ramirez).

They knew Nate was Diego's baby. She felt a flash of panic. How would they know that?

The hinge on the front door creaked. She shut the file and flipped off the light and crossed quickly to the door, shoving the keys in her pocket. She considered staying in the office, but it would be worse to be caught inside. She slid out the door and closed it behind her.

"Cameron."

She jumped at the voice that seemed to come from on top of her shoulder.

Brian Kessler was directly beside her. What had he seen?

"What are you doing here, Cameron?" He drew the end of her name out like the country beside Nigeria. He'd clearly been drinking. For six hours if her math was right. Or, he was pretending.

Her heart was pounding. Lavick's door wasn't locked yet. Plus, from where they stood, Kessler had a clear view of the two open lockers—hers and Lavick's. "Forgot something."

He put his hands on her shoulders and motioned to Lavick's office. "You forgot Lavick?"

She stepped back. "No. I haven't seen Lavick."

He frowned at her, then looked at Lavick's door. "Huh."

She backed toward the locker room, but Kessler stepped forward and threw his arm around her shoulder. "You should have come out tonight. Was a party."

She tried to slide out from under his arm, but he held on.

"Me, Daley, Lau, even Ballerina was there for a while. You missed out."

She stared at the lockers. She didn't want him going into that room. He would notice Lavick's locker open. How could he not?

She stopped moving, frozen. Kessler stared straight ahead. She was sure he saw the lockers. He tilted his head sideways. "Would you go out with me sometime?"

He put his hand on her side and hit the pocket full of keys and the lock. He laughed. "What you got in there? A chain?"

She moved back and touched her lip, feeling the sweat there.

He touched his face, too.

"You have something on your face."

Kessler swiped at his face with both hands. "Chips probably. We had chips. And some pretzels. Is it a chip or a pretzel?"

"It's still there," she told him. "Go check the bathroom."

He jutted his chin out to her. "Just wipe it off."

She gave him a little shove toward the bathroom. "Okay, Cameron. So pushy."

As soon as the door was open, she moved quickly down the hall and into Lavick's office. She slid the file back under the plastic tray, straightened the pencil holder and carefully closed the desk. Fumbling with Lavick's keys, she hunted for the right one to lock it. It took three tries. All the time, she was waiting for Kessler to reappear. Or Daley or Lavick. She turned the key and checked the knob. Locked. She jogged to the locker room and shoved the keys in the jacket pocket. She halted. Left or right? She couldn't remember where they went. She dropped them in the right pocket and hoped it was where they'd been. She shut the locker, replaced the lock and took a long, deep breath. Then, she locked her own locker and put her hands in her pockets. Had she forgotten anything?

She heard the sink running and moved quickly down the hallway. Footsteps. She was almost at the front door.

"Cameron, where you going?"

"I've got to go, Brian. I'll call you an Uber. Probably be here in about ten minutes. Don't drive, okay?"

He reached his hand out toward her without moving. Cameron slid out the door and sprinted to her car. She locked the doors, started the car and pulled out in seconds and then, taking slow even breaths, she called Brian Kessler a cab.

CHAPTER 20

WITH NATE IN his Baby Bjorn, Cameron entered the San Francisco Sports and Swim Club. She stopped in the entry hall where a muscled twenty-something guarded the desk like it was a military post.

"Membership card?"

"I'm here to see the pool facilities for my son," she said, repeating Hailey's instructions.

"He seems a little young."

She glanced down at Nate. "My other son."

The guy laughed. "I was teasing." He pushed a clipboard toward her. "Fill this out and follow the signs to the pool. Pool only, though. If you want to go anywhere else, you have to come back to the desk first. And please wear this at all times," he added, handing her a sticker that read "Guest."

She pressed it over her heart and filled out the sheet, using a fake name, then made her way to the pool. The pool area was at least fifteen degrees warmer than the lobby. The bleach-like smell of chlorine and the splashing of kids in the water loosened the stiffness in her shoulders. She found Hailey Wyatt sitting up on the bleachers and peering down at a group of kids swimming in the deep end. Cameron watched the children, searching their small faces for one that looked like Hailey.

Cameron approached and sat awkwardly on the edge of the bleacher, leaving room for Nate's feet between her legs.

"The one on the far right," Hailey said.

Cameron followed her gaze to a little girl with white blond hair and a pale face.

"She looks like her father, only so much paler. When she came out, the first thing my husband did was to ask the doctor if she was albino." She shook her head. "She had this spiky blond hair and she was so pale. You never see a pale newborn, but there she was."

Cameron nodded.

Hailey leaned over and touched the thick hair on Nate's head. "Ali looks more like your child than mine, and he looks more like me than you."

She didn't speak. This was all leading back to Diego somehow. She couldn't make small talk about it. She needed to know what he was really guilty of, what they were setting him up for. Who they were.

Hailey sighed and sat back. "I talked to Jess last night after I heard your message."

"And?"

"Someone was in Benjamin's apartment," Hailey said. "They were careful though. If Jess didn't know the place so well, it would have been easy to miss."

"So, it's not the Homicide folks."

Hailey glanced back at Ali in the pool. "Nothing about this is official."

"What did they take?"

"Nothing that she can figure out, but Jess thinks they were on his computer."

"Why doesn't Homicide have the computer? Don't you guys usually collect that kind of thing for evidence?"

"Sometimes. Usually the evidence techs can get what they need at the scene."

Cameron thought about how Jess had been at the Rookie Club dinner. "Is she doing okay? I mean, is she sure that it wasn't the evidence techs who had been on the computer?"

"She's taking it hard, and the police can't find any evidence that someone has been there," Hailey said.

"So, maybe she's wrong."

"To be honest, I would be sure of it if it weren't for your call."

Cameron sat up. "What do you mean?"

Hailey seemed uncomfortable. "Kelly and Caltabiano."

"What about them?" she asked.

"They don't exist," Hailey said.

"What?"

"Not in Homicide, not in the department. How well did you see the names?"

"It was fast but I am pretty sure. I knew exactly where to look. James Caltabiano and Tony Kelly. My spelling could be wrong. Maybe Kelly was – ey."

"I tried everything," Hailey continued. "Even spelling Kelly with a C. Linda James helped me because captains have access to the different districts. We checked rosters going back a decade. We got zilch." She took a quick look at the pool. "They seem like cops?"

Cameron was thinking the same thing. "They did until I saw that their suits were identical. That was weird."

"It happens sometimes," Hailey said. "Usually means a lot of razzing at the station and one guy goes to change."

"That's what I figured, so it seemed weird."

"You see the car?"

"No. When they told me they thought Diego was at the house, I went looking for him."

"And?" Hailey put up her hand. "Never mind. Don't tell me."

Nate made little waking noises. Cameron thought it was time to go. "I appreciate the help, Hailey."

"I should tell you that there was another shooting. About six months ago."

"What? Who?"

"Another ICE guy named Axsater. He worked with Ray."

"Any lead on the shooter?"

"Not until last week," Hailey said. "They matched the bullet from Benjamin to Axsater."

"Shit."

"If you see Diego again, I'd ask him where he got that gun."

Cameron motioned around her. "Is that why we're here?"

Hailey sat up straight, pressing her palms against her thighs and stretching her neck. "I've been in Homicide eight years. This isn't my first dead cop, but it's the strangest. Hal and I don't have access to the files—not even for a quick glance. In fact, none of the guys do. When I mentioned Diego Ramirez to Captain Marshall, he said he was told there were dental records that matched Ramirez."

"It's amazing. How do they do that? Far as I could see, Ramirez still had his teeth in his mouth." Cameron thought about the file she'd seen in Lavick's office. "You didn't tell anyone that Diego was Nate's father."

"Not a soul."

"I figured," Cameron said.

"Why?"

"Somehow, the department knows."

"You never told anyone?"

"Just family." Cameron thought about Ricky. She'd always thought of him that way.

"Maybe Diego did."

"No," Cameron said, touching Nate's head. "Diego didn't know."

Hailey shook her head slowly. "I don't know where to go from here."

Cameron stood. "Don't. I appreciate it, but I'll handle it."

Hailey stared down at her daughter, then back at Cameron. "I believe you, I really do. Based on the other shooting and the ballistics, it's hard to see how Ramirez is going to walk away from this, but I hope he does. For your sake." She touched Nate's head. "And his."

Cameron blinked hard. "That means a lot. Thank you."

They both went quiet. Maybe Hailey felt that same heavy impotence Cameron did. As cops, they were accustomed to having some control over right and wrong. In some cases, though, what you knew didn't matter. What mattered was what you could prove.

Cameron got up and left without another word. She understood why Hailey would step back. As a mom, Cameron, too, understood that traveling down certain paths wasn't worth the risk.

CHAPTER 21

SHE LEFT RICKY a third message as she entered the department. If he didn't answer her soon, she was going over there to confront him in person. Around the corner, Ballestrini and Lavick were talking at the top of the station's cement stairs. Their backs were to her. Although the hall was empty, the men kept their voices low.

Lavick handed Ballestrini something. "Go check this one out, will you? They believe she's a recent immigrant, and she fits the profile of the ones from the truck. Give the area a run-through. Body's at the morgue. I don't expect to get much. It's a throwaway." Lavick mumbled something about the address as Cameron stopped and cleared her throat. "Sorry to interrupt."

Lavick winced when he saw her.

She frowned, hating the term they'd used. No life should be classified like garbage. "I was just finishing up that paperwork before the training drill. We got something else?"

"A European immigrant, no I.D., found dead in an alley down by 6th Street," Lau said. "There's a place nearby called the ORG Lounge. They've been known to use immigrant labor though we've never pinned them."

"A throwaway," Cameron said out loud.

"Shitty choice of words," Lavick admitted.

"Probably accurate," Cameron replied. Most of the people she dealt with were probably considered throwaways of one sort of another. "I'll go with you."

"Ballestrini can do this on his own," Lavick said. "We're running a drill today."

"If it's okay, Sergeant, I'd like to go."

"Make it quick, you two," Lavick snapped. "It's going from Sex Crimes to Homicide, not us. We're there to try to link it to our traffickers."

"That's going to be hard to do if we don't know who she is," Ballestrini said.

"Damn near impossible," Lavick agreed. He looked at Ballestrini and tilted his head.

Interpreting the message, Ballestrini nodded.

Cameron took the file from Ballestrini as they headed out to the black and white. "What was that all about?"

"Huh?"

"You and Lavick. He tilted his head, like he was telling you something."

"I didn't notice anything. Probably just telling us to be quick."

Cameron watched him. It sounded like bullshit.

Ballestrini was humming some show tune to himself. Cameron wished she could feel as cheery. She flipped through the pictures of the dead woman until she got to one where she could make out the features of her face. This was no woman. She was a child, fifteen at most. Her skin was deeply bruised, especially around the mouth. The bright color of the bruises meant she hadn't died immediately after her attack. The girl had long, thin brown hair and pale skin with dark eyes, a thin neck and an angular jaw. She was likely from Yugoslavia, Russia, or the Czech Republic. She was frail and trim. From the set of her nose and mouth, Cameron had guessed she was attractive. What false promises had lured her to America?

One hand rested by her face. Cameron could see the purplish-red ligature marks on her wrist. She flipped the images that showed how she had been thrown in the dumpster, her clothes tossed in beside her. Disposable. The perp would probably never be caught. Without families to report them missing, the immigrants had less hope for justice than the prostitutes, who sometimes met the same fate. Prostitutes could usually be ID'd. Families occasionally came forward to claim bodies.

Cameron closed the file and got into the passenger seat of the black and white.

"Okay, I got a quick one, cheer you up," Ballestrini said as he turned onto 6th. "*I got chills, they're multiplyin'…*"

"*Grease,*" she said quickly.

"I didn't even get to the fun part," Ballestrini said, sounding disappointed. *"And I'm losin' control. 'Cause the power you're supplying. It's electrifying."*

"Okay, Ballestrini, you better shape up."

"'Cause you need a man?" he sang out.

Cameron opened the file again. "No, because I need some damn peace."

Ballestrini went quiet.

The partnership with Diego had been so effortless. Instead of always working to fill the silence the way Ballestrini did, she and Diego had enjoyed it. They had communicated as much through silence as through words.

They debated their cases, what they thought was right and wrong. As a rookie cop, she had assumed the law was always right. Diego was constantly pushing her to see it from the other side. He was like Ricky that way. They had also agreed that their job was to uphold the law, whether or not they agreed with it.

When she started in Special Ops, Diego had been on vacation, visiting his sister in Mexico. The guys on the team had treated her harshly that first week, mostly in jest, but there was some real competition and a good deal of flirtation, too. This was nothing new for women in law enforcement. It was rare to find a man who didn't think of her as a potential sex partner before accepting her as a teammate.

When she met Diego, he shook her hand firmly and said, "I hear you're a hell of a shot. Welcome to Special Ops." Then, he walked away. No downward glance, no sly smile. Watching him stride out of the room, she thought he was incredibly sexy.

Ironically, it was during a debate about immigration policy that she and Diego hit on their first real disagreement. Cameron believed the U.S. had to limit the immigration for the country's economic viability. Diego thought there should be more opportunities for immigrants to come in legally. She had known nothing of his family, nothing of the women his father and uncle had left behind. That had come much later. It was through Diego's passion that Cameron had first recognized her real attraction for him. Their relationship had started shortly after.

Ballestrini pulled up to the curb in front of the ORG Lounge. The downstairs bar was a dive, but it was rumored that a more lucrative business ran upstairs. The club was suspected of having a second staff of girls who catered to that business. It was likely that their "throwaway" had been part of that.

According to Lavick, it had been a long time since the cops had successfully busted the place for anything illegal. She wondered if it was bad luck or if the current owners had some connections.

She let Ballestrini make his way around the car before following him in the front door. It was dark inside. Both she and Ballestrini waited a minute for their eyes to adjust before stepping farther inside. It took human eyes thirty minutes to become fully accustomed to the darkness. Had they been expecting anything other than a peaceful conversation, they would have been wearing special equipment.

Red, puckered velvet lined the walls. A man in a dark suit stepped forward as though waiting for them. He was thin and wiry with a nose that seemed almost as long and skinny as he was. His small dark eyes were narrow as he peered through a pair of triangular-shaped glasses. He had the look of a German accountant, not a strip club owner.

"I'm Officer Ballestrini, and this is my partner, Officer Cruz. We would like to talk to you and your staff."

"That's not a problem, but I'm the only one here right now," the man said, his voice free of the German accent she'd been expecting. He said problem like "pra-blem" with a slight nasal tone like someone from Chicago.

"And your name?" Ballestrini asked him.

Cameron asked him to spell out the name and wrote it down.

Just then, a back door opened, and a woman came out carrying a case of Budweiser bottles. She was stocky with short, blond hair and a figure not right for stripping. Cameron figured she must be the bar-back.

"Other than Roseanne." He shot the bar-back a glare, but Roseanne didn't appear to notice.

"We hope you might have some information about this woman," Cameron said, handing over the photograph. Ballestrini slid in and stuck the picture under the man's nose. It was a good tactic. The picture was striking and disconcerting. If the man was going to tell them anything, the shock factor might help him along.

The man stared at the picture, frowning in a thoughtful way that seemed practiced and shook his head. "She isn't familiar."

Ballestrini took the picture back. "Maybe I can check with Roseanne?"

"Of course." He led them toward the bar.

"You're the proprietor?" Cameron asked.

"One of them," he responded after giving her a flat expression. He was a good liar, if that's what he was doing.

The man grabbed the photograph from Ballestrini. "Roseanne," he said as though speaking over loud music. "These officers would like you to look at this picture."

Roseanne glanced up at him like he was an idiot as she wiped her hands on a dishtowel. When she was done, she pulled the picture from his hand and walked away from him with it. A few feet down the bar, she set it down and stared at it. "Who is she?"

"We don't know," Ballestrini said.

Cameron stepped toward the bar. "All we know is that she was brutally raped and beaten, then left in a dumpster less than a half mile away."

Like the man, Roseanne seemed resistant to the horror in the photo.

"No," Roseanne said. "I don't think I've seen her."

Cameron knew she was lying. As she met the woman's gaze, she could see her apology.

Ballestrini put his hand out for the photo. "We certainly appreciate your help."

Was he done?

"Some of the bouncers are out back," Roseanne said, handing the picture back. "You might ask them. Like Stuart says, I'm only in a few days a week."

"Of course," Stuart said. "Why don't I take you back there?"

"I'll wait for you out here," Cameron suggested.

Stuart's gaze shifted back to Roseanne. "Whatever makes you most comfortable, Officer." To Roseanne, he said, "Don't forget, we ordered the extra cases for tonight, so make sure we're topped off. It'll be the first thing Dominic checks when he gets in." He checked at his watch. "He should be here within the hour."

Cameron thanked him as he left with Ballestrini. He glanced back twice as her partner chatted amicably to him.

"I really can't talk," Roseanne said quickly. "Like he said, I've got a lot of work to do."

"I understand," Cameron told her, but she met the woman's eyes and stepped closer. "Dominic is an owner?"

"And my brother," Roseanne said. "He's why I'm here. If you can believe it, this is our inheritance." She gave a little nod as she spoke, as though to explain to Cameron why she couldn't say more.

"So, why are you backing the bar?"

"Because I do the buying and settle the alcohol bills. It's the only way the inventory doesn't go down my brother's throat. It's a shitty business to be in, but the money's not bad."

"And where does Stuart fit in?"

"Stuart is our partner because of the times when I wasn't doing the inventory." Roseanne slapped the towel on the bar. "Like I said, I really need to get back to work."

Cameron moved up to the bar. "And the woman? You're sure you never saw her."

Roseanne didn't meet her gaze. "I'm sure of it."

"They say she was raped by as many as six men," Cameron lied. Maybe it hadn't happened to this one, but it happened to some of them.

Roseanne lowered her head.

"They need to pay for what they did. This girl is maybe fifteen. She deserves some justice."

"Don't we all." Straightening her shoulders, Roseanne said, "I'm sorry. Like I said, I never saw her." With that, she threw the towel over her shoulder and walked out from behind the bar.

"One more question, Roseanne."

She turned back.

"Do you handle the alcohol for the business upstairs, too?"

Roseanne's eyes narrowed. "There is no business upstairs, Officer."

With that, she walked to the back of the club and disappeared through another door.

CHAPTER 22

CAMERON STEPPED OUTSIDE into the bright light and pulled her cell phone from an equipment pocket on her pants. She saw she'd missed a call from Ricky and played the voicemail.

"Cam, it's me. I promise I can explain," he started. His voice was like she'd never heard before. "I need a few days to talk to Evelyn first, but I'll call as soon as I can. I am really sorry, Cameron. It never occurred to me that it was a bad idea to share Nate's paternity."

What the hell did that mean? Share his paternity with who? What did she do now? Just wait? She deleted the message and called headquarters for Jamie's cell phone number.

"Inspector Vail," Jamie answered, sounding winded.

"Jamie, it's Cameron Cruz."

"Oh, shit. I thought you were going to be my snitch. Fucker was supposed to get me a name, and he hasn't called."

"Sorry. I wish I could help."

"Ugh. No. Sorry to snap. How are you? How's the baby?"

"He's great," Cameron said.

"Wait until he hits 12. I tell you, Zephenaya has math homework that I didn't do until college. We need an in-house tutor."

Cameron sighed. "I'm not ready for that."

"Thankfully, you've got some time."

The two women were quiet. It was tough to transition from their sons to dead women.

"What are you waiting to hear on?" Cameron asked her.

"Four dead prostitutes and one more in a coma who got the crap beat out of her so bad her mother swears it isn't her. We had to use dental records to prove it."

"Jesus."

"I hope to hell Jesus wasn't involved, but if he's around, I could certainly use some help."

"Well, I'm afraid I'm not going to be any use to you there. I've got a dead one, though, and I wondered if you had info on her."

"She have a name?"

"Another Doe, I'm afraid. She was found in a dumpster a few blocks from ORG Lounge, down at—"

"I know where it is. I swear I'm down there more than the working ladies. When'd she come in?"

"Last day or two, I think, but I'm not sure."

"I'm sure she's in a pile on my desk. I can call you when I get to her. I've got these four and then a bad ending to a first date in Noe Valley."

"I talked to a guy named Stuart at ORG Lounge and a woman named Roseanne. She knows something, but I can't get it out of her."

"Why are you guys in on this one?"

"Deceased is an immigrant, probably came off one of the boats we've been trying to track down."

"Sorry I don't have more for you."

Though she'd only met him briefly, Stuart had pissed off Cameron. She didn't like how controlled he was or how unhelpful. And it pissed her off that someone had treated the girl like a piece of trash. "She's under my skin for some reason."

"You're new to these. Give it time. Maybe it'll grow on you." Jamie paused. "Sorry, it's terrible. Listen, I've got to go. I've got your cell number now. I'll call if I find out anything."

Cameron was saying goodbye when Jamie added, "I heard you made it to the last dinner. I'll try to get to one, too. Would be good to catch up."

"I'd like that."

"Bring pictures of the little guy," Jamie said.

"You, too."

They hung up. Cameron remembered the days after Jamie found out about her husband's affair. The anger. So much anger. How would Diego's betrayal change her? Would she close up like a clam and dig into work like Jamie had? Was there something about women who went into law enforcement that made them such tough eggs to crack? Or was it what happened to them once they were there?

When he came out of the club, Ballestrini blinked wildly at the brightness. His arms out to his sides like he was blind, he looked a bit like a Weeble as he tried to get his eyes to adjust.

Cameron walked to the car. "Want me to drive?"

"Nope." Ballestrini pulled his sunglasses from his breast pocket. "Man, that place is like a dungeon."

"Think how much they save on electricity."

He grunted his amusement and opened up the car.

"You get anything else?"

"Nah. They say they don't know anything. We're not getting anything from those guys."

She glanced over as he started the car. "You believe them?"

"Nah. Everybody lies."

That was true.

"You get anything else from Roseanne?" he asked.

"No. She and her brother are partial owners. Sounds like her brother got them in some trouble, so they had to take Stuart on as an investor. I doubt she'd risk losing what she's got left. I guess they inherited it."

"Back on patrol, one of my buddies had this area as his beat. Said there was a rumor that it was partly owned by a cop at one time."

"Really, who?" she asked.

He shrugged. "No idea. I don't think he knew either."

Cameron pulled the file out from under the seat and flipped through the pictures again. "When's the autopsy on this one?"

"Should be done. Sergeant said he had called for a copy."

She probably wouldn't see it. If the case went to Sex Crimes or Homicide, there would be no reason. The sergeant likely ordered it as a follow-up measure, but she was interested. Surely there was enough evidence on the body and clothes to link it back to someone or somewhere. The question was: did anyone have time to pursue it? She shut the folder.

They got back to the bay in time to work the drill. Someone had come up with a scenario and set up a fake perimeter and a series of obstacles.

Cameron was on equipment detail now, her days of reconnaissance over. She would fight for it sometime, but not until she was ready. Maybe she never would be.

She and Zagrafis worked the equipment truck, checking for the necessary pieces. Zagrafis had started in Special Ops after Diego left. Quiet by nature, he had shared that he was married and his wife was pregnant and that he'd come out of the Army after serving two tours in Afghanistan. She liked him. They worked well together. The silence was a nice change from Ballestrini. She opened the pelican case, a hard, plastic briefcase where they kept their ammunition, and checked their supply of grenades, sting balls, and flash bangs. Zagrafis called out the shields, a sawed-off shotgun, rounds for the shotgun and less-than-lethal rounds, which were essentially a beanbag in a 37mm shotgun round.

They put on black, sub-fighting suits over their regular uniforms. She pulled on her aviator gloves, the thumbs and forefingers cut out so she had a good grip on her weapon. She pulled on a balaclava made with flame-retardant cloth. Then came the tactical goggles, which looked like ski goggles, only they were made by Kevlar with bulletproof material. Finally, she donned a heavy vest with a ceramic plate and her helmet. With her belt, it all weighed the equivalent of three bowling balls.

At least she didn't carry the ram. She passed Lau, carrying the solid iron tube. Cameron had only rammed one door with it, in training. That one experience had left her without the use of her right shoulder for nearly a week.

By the time it was over, everyone was exhausted. Lavick didn't seem in any mood to discuss the autopsy on their Jane Doe. She left before the talk of drinks. Her phone rang as she pulled into Señora Accosta's house to pick up Nate. "Cruz."

"It's Jamie."

"Hey, what's up?"

"Something weird about your Doe."

Cameron checked her rearview mirror, then wondered why she'd done it. "What do you mean?"

"No one's touching her. Autopsy got filed, but supposedly there's no evidence, no prints, nothing."

"No evidence?"

"Couldn't believe they told me with a straight face. Found in a dumpster, and they claim the body was clean."

Clean meant there was little trace evidence on the body. It was simply impossible unless the dumpster had been cleaned out and sanitized. "That's it? They won't do anything else?"

"Probably not, especially with our load. She gets put in the Doe file until we get missing ones who might fit her description. Then we try to match 'em."

"Who filed the autopsy?"

"Duane Grafton, know him?"

Cameron said she didn't.

"He's about the dumbest piece of shit on the planet," Jamie said. "If someone wants a body overlooked, Duane's their man. He couldn't see a bullet hole if it hit him between the eyes. And believe me, I keep hoping."

"So where did the body go?" Cameron asked.

"State burial. Oh, shit, Cameron. I've got to go."

Cameron leaned back against the seat. Triage happened in police stations and morgues, just like in hospitals. The less evidence and the less likely the victim was to be missed, the farther it fell on the list of cases to be pursued. It bothered her, but that was the reality of working with limited resources.

What disturbed her was the idea that someone was lying about evidence. How could a body come out of a dumpster completely clean? But if it wasn't a coincidence, what did the murder of two ICE agents have to do with a dead immigrant?

And how did it all tie back to Diego?

CHAPTER 23

"WE CAN'T AFFORD it." Michael Lavick pulled himself out of his comfortable chair and walked toward the garage. Maybe there he could find some peace. Ever since Ray's shooting, there was no peace to be had. His team was on marina watch with nothing to show for it. It was making him absolutely nuts.

His wife, Bela, followed, yapping in his ear. "I'm not having the girls grow up like we did. I want them to have the opportunities we didn't. We agreed on this." When she got angry, her accent was pronounced. It used to be charming. Now it was just irritating.

He turned around. Did she realize how she sounded? How could she not understand that it was too expensive? They had agreed she would stay home with the girls. Each of them had grown up in families where both parents worked just to make ends meet. His job had always supported both of them and the girls. They lived in a nice area of Berkeley; the girls went to good schools, got big Christmases. It was so much more than he'd ever had. But, Bela always wanted more. Sure, he did too, but he was the one trying to get the math to work. There had come a point where he couldn't.

They had to cut back. "Come on, you're not talking about opportunities. You're talking about extravagance, Bela. Dance lessons, music lessons, she has all those. And now you want her to have a private dance instructor? We can't afford it."

She crossed her arms and jutted her chin. She wasn't budging. "Mariela wants to be a dancer. Do you want to crush her dream?"

Michael took two steps toward his wife. "Do you hear what you're saying? You're talking about a private instructor. It's seventy dollars an hour. It's too much right now. Why doesn't she continue in the class she's in? I can't believe she really needs private lessons at this stage…"

His wife turned her back. "The instructor says she'll get much more out of private time."

So will he, Michael thought. Something like sixty dollars an hour more. He couldn't believe his wife was being so stubborn. His father had emigrated from Hungary with his mother before he was born. Michael was a surprise and not an especially welcome one. The story was that his parents let the nurse at the hospital name him. He remembered the struggles they'd had, especially before his father had been promoted to manager of the small shoe sole company in the town in New Jersey where he'd grown up. His mother worked as the secretary for a successful Hungarian banker until she was sixty and then only quit because the banker finally retired.

Lavick had always promised himself that he would do better for his own children. And he did. Much better. He'd made sacrifices to make some extra money, but for his wife, it was never enough.

"It's important to her, Michael."

He focused on his wife's face, knowing she was waiting for him to change his mind. He always did. He doted on Bela, bought her gifts for the birth of their children, for anniversaries, remembered flowers. She'd been good to him, too, but it seemed that with every present he gave her came a higher expectation for the next one.

Where had he gone wrong? Had the mistake been in not involving her in the finances? Not telling her how close they were to the edge? How hard it was to afford the things they already had. Along the way, he'd been smart and clever with the money. He'd been lucky on some business ventures. But, it all meant extra work. And it wasn't like he'd gotten anywhere. In fact, with each new success, he ended up deeper in debt.

"Michael?"

He was filled with resentment for the way she tried to trap him with those brown eyes. He studied the expensive makeup that added a rosy tint to the cheeks he had loved when they were pale. She touched his arm. All he felt were her long, fake nails. He saw the color she added to her hair, making it darker rather than the auburn tones he'd fallen in love with. Even the small, flat mole on her neck that he'd kissed so often when they'd first been together was now covered by makeup. She thought it was ugly. He'd thought of it as a mark of beauty.

"It's important to her," she said, breaking him from his thoughts.

"We can't do it."

She froze like ice beside him. It would be that way for some time. She was good at anger, but he'd long since passed the point where he would do anything about it. She didn't understand. They would need to address it soon. He'd been stupid to be so traditional and keep the situation from her. He'd wanted so much to provide for her, but he had failed. Now, he needed her to know where they stood.

She walked away as he knew she would. They would have something he hated for dinner. Chicken, probably. He hated chicken. Or tacos. Maybe chicken tacos. That was her way of saying he was in trouble. He was in trouble. He was in deep trouble, but right now, he didn't care.

He walked out the door to the garage. His wife never followed him. She could barely stand to park her car there because of his "heap," as she called it. It was actually a 1932 Ford V-8, three-window coupe. It was the only car his father had ever owned, and when he died, his mother had given it to Michael. His wife thought he should've had it scrapped, especially because his father hadn't gotten it running in the last ten years of his life.

But Michael refused. In hindsight, working on the car was the only thing he had ever done for himself. The car was about him—about his parents and him. He'd once hoped there might be a child who would want to help him with it, but Mariela and Alexis couldn't have been less interested.

He flipped on the bright, fluorescent garage lights and walked slowly around the car. It wasn't as though he hadn't made a hell of a lot of progress in fourteen years. When he got it, the frame was rusted and pitted. Almost nothing had worked. He'd joined a car club and learned how to do things. He'd sandblasted the frame. He'd primed it and painted it red. That's about when his wife's interest had peaked. She claimed not to have seen any progress since then. But, he'd been working steadily.

He subscribed to Hemmings Auto News. He'd found a replacement speedometer NOS, meaning new old stock. It was an original 1932 speedometer that had never been used. The thing cost him almost $500. He'd felt so guilty that he'd paid for it from his lunch allowance. Shit, he deserved something for himself.

Really, the car was coming along nicely. The big problem was the intake manifold. The one in the car had to be completely junked. But, he'd made a friend in a Heliarc welder who'd been able to patch an intake manifold he'd salvaged from a '37. Now, the problem was the fuel pump. He'd had to make his own gaskets, and they were leaking. Plus, the carburetor was messed up. He popped the side leaf and folded it back from the engine. Then he detached the fuel pump and pulled it out, his hands black with grease.

He set it on his worktable and pulled his stool up behind him. He loosened the nuts on the flange and worked the lock washers off. He tried to pull the fuel pump loose from the intake manifold, but it was stuck. He braced it between his knees and fought it.

"Damn thing."

He gritted his teeth. His mind drifted to his frustration with Bela as he gripped the two pieces and tried to detach them. He wanted the girls to be happy, to have opportunities. He never imagined that they would be spoiled.

Suddenly, the fuel pump loosened. One of the flange bolts raked across his palm. He dropped the pieces and grabbed his hand. "Shit."

He shook it and wiped the blood on a rag before leaning down to pick up the pieces off the ground. The light caught something disc-shaped and silver on the front seat of the car. A DVD.

"What the hell?"

He read the top. "January 11th, 10:30 PM."

He put the fuel pump down, and holding the rag, carried the disc into the house, trying to remember what he was doing on January 11th.

He walked past his wife in the kitchen.

"Are you ready to talk?"

He didn't answer her as he made his way to the family room. A swirling storm was rising in his head. The date was familiar. What the hell was it? Pressing the rag to his bleeding hand, he kicked the door shut with his foot and powered up the player.

He rested on his haunches and flipped the TV on, without bothering for the remote. He slid the disc in and pushed play. The screen filled with an image of a room. A card table was centered in the frame. A few chairs formed a circle around it. He watched as a gym bag was tossed through the door and knew exactly who had thrown it. The next bag came in. Then, a familiar face carried a third bag in and set it up on the table. He couldn't move as he watched himself unzip the duffel and take hold of a thick stack of bills in each hand, then wave them around.

"Oh, Lord."

CHAPTER 24

ROSA INSISTED ON going to a baby music class for kids age six months to a year. "He's not six months. He's not even four months," Cameron argued.

Rosa waved off the comment as silly. "He's extremely advanced for his age."

As it turned out, brains weren't required for the class, but more head control than Nate had would have been helpful as they bobbed and danced. Everyone thought he was Rosa's baby. Cameron mostly sat and watched. She was a good mother, she told herself, but somehow she never fit the mold of the good mother in her own mind.

These women did. Even the way they looked. They were rounded like the other women in Cameron's life had always been—had hips and breasts. They knew the words to "The Wheels on the Bus" and "Hush Little Baby, Don't Say a Word." All Cameron knew was that there was some reference to buying a kid a diamond ring and a horse and cart.

Rosa ate it up. She laughed and danced with Nate, drawing him to her like a woman in love. Cameron waved like a father trying to be involved but not knowing quite how. That was more her role. Thank God for Rosa.

They stopped for lunch on the way home at their favorite little Mexican dive where the chimichangas were almost as good as Mama's. Neither she nor Rosa ever ordered anything else. The shredded beef was so tender it was like chewing butter. Piled with cheese and beans and sour cream and guacamole with garlic and lemon and spicy salsa, it was enough to make the world right for a few minutes.

The owner called Cameron and Rosa "Las Chimamigas," some

combination of chimichanga and amigas. They rarely explained to people that they were sisters and Cameron knew they were an odd pair—this tall, skinny blond gringa and a curvy Latina. Then Cameron spoke Spanish and people figured she was somehow Latin, despite her looks.

Even with the distractions, Diego and the bankbook had not strayed far from her mind. She had texted Sydney Blanchard for ideas about how to disable the password on the jump drive, but she hadn't heard back. She hoped Diego knew what he was doing.

Full and tired, Cameron, Rosa and Nate arrived home as Nate was falling asleep. Cameron took the bags. Rosa held Nate as they made their way to the front door. Cameron inserted her key into the top bolt when she noticed deep gouges in the lock that shone like the copper of a new penny.

"Go to the car," she told Rosa.

"¿*Qué pasó*?" Rosa asked. Whenever Rosa was stressed or upset, she naturally spoke Spanish.

"Someone's been here," Cameron answered her sister in Spanish. "The lock's been tampered with."

Scowling, Rosa glared at her with familiar disapproval.

"Not now, Rosa. Just go."

Rosa cradled Nate close and ran back to the car.

Cameron knew people robbed houses in broad daylight. Her gun was inside in a lockbox in the front closet. Without her weapon, she pushed the door open and stepped inside.

Someone had been through the place. Pictures were off their hooks, pillows shredded, and books dumped on the floor.

Cameron scanned as she moved. It felt like she was on recon and yet, when she caught sight of Nate's favorite rattle—a black-and-white-striped stick with colorful rings on it, her throat seemed to close.

She opened the hall closet with one hand and spotted her lockbox. She stopped in a corner of the hallway, turned the combination and flipped open the latch.

Gripping the gun, she continued down the hall, the image of Nate's rattle burning like a brand. She said nothing, her breathing even, as she walked foot over foot. She cleared each room like she was on the job. But it wasn't. Someone had been in her home. Nate's clothes had been pulled from the drawers, his diapers strewn across the floor. She had an impulse to get down on her knees, to straighten and clean up. Her son's things, clothes that touched his body. She trembled with fury. Then, remembering, she ran into the kitchen and pulled open the dishwasher. Rosa's jewelry box lay at the bottom, but no bankbook. She hadn't taken it out of her pants.

In the laundry room, she pulled dirty clothes out of the washing machine by the armload before she found it. She tucked the plastic bag with the bankbook and jump drive into her jacket pocket and continued through the house.

When she was sure no one was there, she made her way outside. Rosa sat in the front seat of the car, holding Nate. Cameron saw the fear in her face. She couldn't take her sister inside. Not now, not looking the way it did.

She opened the passenger side and took Nate from Rosa's arms. Rosa started to get out, but Cameron stopped her. "We're not going in."

Rosa's eyes widened. "Someone's there?"

"Not anymore."

Though Cameron had expected it, Rosa didn't argue. Perhaps she sensed Cameron's own rage. Cameron buckled Nate into his car seat and got back in the car.

She pulled out of the driveway without knowing exactly where she was going. On the freeway south, she gripped the wheel and focused on driving. Ideas flashed by like the yellow lines on the road. They'd come for the bankbook and the jump drive. That much was obvious. But, who were they and why did they want them so badly? More importantly, which side was Diego on?

"What's going on, Cameron?" Rosa's voice was low as though she were trying to keep Nate from hearing.

Cameron glanced over.

"You have to tell me. You've been acting crazy ever since you went back to work."

Cameron searched for the right way to unload all of it.

"Don't treat me like a baby, Cameron. I'm your older sister."

"It's a lot," Cameron warned.

"I'm ready," Rosa assured her.

Cameron started with the night she'd seen Diego and the shooting.

"Oh, Dios!" Rosa had exclaimed after Cameron said his name. Then, Rosa was silent as Cameron explained the evidence that was mounting against him. The truck registered in his name, another killing with the same gun. She left out that he'd been at the house and had left her the bankbook and the drive. When she was done, Rosa asked, "You think he broke into our house?"

"No."

"The person who broke in is looking for him?" Rosa pressed.

"Right."

"What can we do?"

Cameron hesitated, unsure if Rosa meant what could they do to help put Diego behind bars or what could they do to help him. "I'm not sure," she finally said.

"I don't believe it for a second," Rosa said, her fire kindled. "There is no way he shot that man unless he had to."

Cameron reached over and grabbed her sister's hand and squeezed it.

Rosa squeezed back, but she was on a roll and it kept going. "I mean it. Someone is setting him up. Because he's Latino. You hear about that shit all the time. Oh, pardon Tía Rosa's bad language," she said to Nate in the backseat.

Cameron thought Rosa was right. Diego was being set up, but it had nothing to do with being Latin. If this wasn't a setup, why would he come to her for help? Surely he didn't take her for a total fool. Was she being a fool to believe him?

Cameron pulled off the South San Francisco exit and went down Sister Cities Boulevard. Cameron wasn't sure Ricky would be home. If he was, she had some questions for him.

She drove down Ash Avenue and into the wide driveway of the ranch house Evelyn and Ricky had owned since their move to California.

The garage was closed and like every house on the block, it was impossible to tell if anyone was home, as the streets were kept clean and car free, drapes neatly closed and a porch light set on a timer to illuminate each front door at precisely dusk.

Cameron came around the back of the car and opened the door where Nate was. Before she had him out, the front door opened. Evelyn stepped outside. She wore a pair of gray cords and a matching cable knit sweater. If not for the wool slippers on her feet, Cameron would have sworn she was on her way out.

"What a nice surprise." She turned back into the house. "Ricky, the girls are here with Nate."

Evelyn came out to meet them, peering down at Nate. "I swear, look at how big he is."

Cameron was grateful for Evelyn. She would be good at distracting Rosa and Nate, and she could do with some advice from Ricky.

"You just saw him last Thursday," Rosa said.

Evelyn didn't take her eyes off him. "But he's grown, I'm telling you. Come on in, I want to hold my little guy." Evelyn ushered them in. "I was about to put some coffee on," she said, though Cameron knew Evelyn didn't drink coffee. "Would you girls like some?"

"That would be great," Cameron said.

"Thank you, Evelyn. Let me help," Rosa said, taking her jacket off.

"What brings you down here in the middle of the day?"

"Someone broke into the house," Rosa said as Ricky entered the room. He glanced between Evelyn and Cameron. Whatever he had wanted to tell Evelyn, he hadn't done it yet.

Cameron set Nate's car seat on the kitchen floor and stooped down to unfasten him.

Evelyn didn't speak. Instead, she crossed the kitchen, arms out. "Let me take that little guy," she said, then looked at her husband. "Why don't you and Cameron go out back and talk? I'll bring some coffee out in a few minutes."

"Thank you," Cameron said, planting a kiss on Nate's head before handing him over.

Ricky and Cameron walked to the quiet bedroom that served as Ricky's office. It always felt a little like a child's room with its large white table and two chairs, a rocker in one corner.

Early in Cameron's own pregnancy, Ricky had told her that Evelyn belonged to a group for women who had lost pregnancies. Evelyn had joined in the eighties after her fourth miscarriage and was a member for nearly thirty years. It was the most Ricky had ever divulged about his marriage, and it gave Cameron the tiniest peek into what made them such a strong couple—years and years of difficulty. Most marriages would have collapsed under that kind of strain.

Cameron had worried that her own pregnancy might cause resentment for Evelyn, but Ricky's wife had never been anything but gracious and kind to her and Rosa, and seemed wholly smitten with Nate. More than once she'd called herself Grandma Evelyn.

Ricky didn't sit.

"You owe me an explanation," she said.

"I know," he agreed and sank into the chair opposite hers.

"And don't pull the 'trust me' shit," she snapped. "I'm sick of it. Diego, you. I want to know who you told and why."

Ricky exhaled. "It wasn't police business. It was social. Over drinks."

"Lavick?"

"I promise you, it was a mistake and it has nothing to do with what is happening now." He squeezed her hand. "Can you leave it at that a little longer?"

She didn't answer. She'd known Ricky for fifteen years. Her mother and Evelyn had been friends for forty. He was an uncle to her. Or closer. Just like Diego had been her partner. But where did she stop trusting and start demanding answers?

As though reading her mind, he said, "I know it's a lot to ask."

She blew out her breath. "Fine. But, I'm not letting it go."

"I'm not asking you to." He paused a beat and said, "Tell me about the break-in."

"Someone was looking for something."

Ricky walked the length of the room slowly. "Did they find it?"

"No. I got lucky." She pulled the bag out of her pocket and handed it to him.

Ricky opened the book and thumbed through it, then whistled. "Be nice to keep this, eh?"

"It crossed my mind."

"Don't suppose he made this from his undercover job."

"I think it was in the bag that he and Benjamin were fighting over."

"And he put it in Nate's name—clever."

"No, not clever. Stupid. He's a stupid son of a bitch if he thinks I'm going to sit back and let him use my kid," she whispered. And yet she had no idea what to do. She was so torn. Why did she still want to believe him?

"I doubt it's as simple as Diego using Nate. I suspect he has some sort of plan." He passed the book back. "You need to keep this part quiet." Ricky rubbed his face. "Call the police about the house. Let them print the place and see if they can identify who was there. I'm guessing it wasn't Diego who tore the place apart."

"But, keep the book and drive quiet."

"Sure. Do you want me to put them in the safe?"

There was a knock at the door. "Probably Evelyn with the coffee."

But when the door opened it was Rosa. At first, Cameron had wondered if Evelyn had sent her, but she didn't have coffee. She was holding Cameron's cell phone. "It's Jamie Vail," she said, holding the phone out. "She called three times. I finally answered. She said it's really important."

Cameron took the phone. Facing Ricky, she said, "Cruz here."

"Cameron, I'm glad I found you. We found something new at the scene at the ORG Lounge."

"Yeah, what's going on?" she asked Jamie.

"Hailey Wyatt said I needed to call you with this."

Anticipating something bad, Cameron sank into the chair. "Okay."

"We linked the girl in the dumpster to ORG's. A woman who cleans there brought forward a piece of floral fabric—matches the shirt that was in the dumpster with the girl. Crime scene tech found some prints inside."

Cameron knew what was coming.

"They belonged to a dead cop."

Cameron was silent. Inside, a million thoughts raced through her mind. A dead immigrant woman and two dead ICE agents.

"You know who I mean?" Jamie asked.

"Say it anyway," Cameron said as evenly as she could manage.

"Diego Ramirez."

Cameron wanted to vomit.

"I've got to go. They're putting out an APB. You going to be okay?"

No. Not ever. "Yeah, Jamie. I'll be fine. Thanks."

CHAPTER 25

CAMERON PACED THE kitchen floor, trying to ignore the police presence in every room. Already, she was questioning her own loyalty. From Ricky's, she'd rushed home to bury the book and the jump drive out by Rosa's tomato plants before the police arrived. Then, she proceeded to wipe her hands over every place she imagined Diego might have touched: the front door, Nate's door, the changing table and the wipes container.

Best case, Rosa was right, and they were saving his ass from some massive setup. Worst case, she was hindering a police investigation, assisting a fugitive, and putting herself, Rosa, and Nate in danger. The shooting she'd seen. She didn't know how to explain that away. Even if Ray Benjamin was guilty, she wished to heaven Diego had put a slug in his leg instead. Did he have to kill him? But Diego wasn't the shot she was. And surely he was panicked. It didn't seem like he had gone in expecting a fight. His gun wasn't drawn although he was wearing his vest.

Either way, she did not want the police to find Diego's prints. If he were smart, he'd have worn gloves. It was his smarts that were under question right now. Since she couldn't ask him, she made certain that her own prints were the only ones the police would find in those places.

The crime scene team had spent almost two hours fingerprinting and collecting evidence while Rosa worked to clean on their trail. Between the three officers and Rosa, the house felt like a city bus. And the noise. The clatter of broken dishes being swept away and the vroom of the vacuum running up and down the halls was enough to put her over the edge.

Thankfully, Nate was napping at Señora Accosta's house. Cameron had stayed in case there were questions. But, she had no answers. Nothing was missing. She was pretty sure they were looking for the bankbook and the drive, but she wasn't sharing that information with anyone until she knew what was on it. She texted Sydney at the crime scene lab again. Then, impatient, she left her a voicemail. She needed someone who could break into the files on the jump drive.

She had already told a pair of uniformed cops what she'd told the fake detectives, but there was no way of knowing if this was news to the department or not. Of course, the officers they sent knew nothing about the previous events. It was unlikely an inspector would show up to a B&E with no injuries and no missing property.

The only thing that made the scene unusual was the number of people. A case like this would normally warrant five or ten minutes with a couple of uniforms. No crime scene techs. Not without something missing. And even then, there seemed to be too many uniformed officers for the job. Two black and whites were parked on the curb outside the house and another one at each end of the block. Plus, the crime scene van. Did they know something she didn't?

Twice she went out to talk to the uniforms, but they weren't saying anything. Ricky was supposed to come by, but she was ready to leave. Giving up on the wait, Cameron went inside and found Rosa vacuuming under Nate's changing table. She shut off the vacuum cleaner and wiped a strand of hair out of her face.

"I need to get out of here. I can do that later."

Rosa waved her hand. "It clears my head. I need it. Why are there so many cops outside? There's one on the block behind us, too?" Rosa pointed to the window and Cameron joined her. Another black and white was parked on the next block down, just visible to one side of the neighbor's house and through the branches of a budding maple tree.

"I have no idea," Cameron said honestly.

"The time Elaina got robbed, it took four days to get someone to come down so she could file a police report for insurance."

Cameron thought about it. "Maybe they think he's coming back. Maybe you should leave, too."

"Hell, no. I want to be here if he comes back. Did you see what he did to my avocado tree? Killed it. Pulled it out by the trunk. Plus, there is dirt everywhere in there." Rosa pulled the vacuum cord from the wall and wound it on the back of the machine. "All those police—that's not normal. There's something going on that we don't know about." She studied Cameron. "Unless you are holding out on me."

Cameron raised her hands. "I swear."

"Fine, then. Go on and get out. We need eggs because that bastard broke all of ours."

"I'll stop at Yee's. Anything else?"

"Maybe a little bar of something dark chocolate." Rosa put her hands on her hips as though expecting a fight. "It's been a stressful day."

"I'll get wine, too."

"Good girl." Cameron pocketed her phone and grabbed the canvas grocery bag off the hook by the front door, then walked outside. No one stopped her. Her house was a crime scene and she was a cop, but it wasn't her scene and in this case, she wasn't a cop—not in the way that counted. It was no longer within her control. All those aspects combined to make her feel ready to crawl out of her skin.

She zipped her jacket against the cold wind of the clear day and waved at the two patrol cops as she passed.

For them, it was easy work. Today was the perfect day to be parked on the curb. The temperature was maybe sixty, cool enough to be comfortable in bulletproofing and heavy belts. The cool air acted like the oxygen pumped into casinos in Vegas—it made the cops more alert, more on guard. It made the crooks and the idiots feel cocky.

Two blocks from the house, Cameron stopped on the corner and peered out at the park where she and Diego had spent dozens of afternoons. She hesitated, unsure where to go next. She was in no rush to get to Yee's Market, the little convenience store they frequented for milk or eggs, or a late night ice cream treat. It was an errand she could do in ten minutes or less. One, in fact, she did at least three times a week in that much time. What she wanted now was something that would take an hour. Her life, especially over the past year, was always filled with plans. Between work and Nate, there was no time for frolicking.

Standing on the corner, she had absolutely no idea where to go. She stood for a good two minutes, scanning right and left, like a kid crossing the street for the first time alone. And then, as though she really wasn't up to the challenge, she continued down the block to Yee's Market.

She wandered in and waved hello to Mrs. Yee, who smiled but didn't speak. Mrs. Yee spoke English. Cameron had listened to her on the phone once and while it wasn't grammatically perfect, what bit of the conversation she'd heard had certainly made sense to Cameron. But she had never spoken to Cameron. Not so much as a word. She pointed to the register for the total, waved and smiled. That was it.

Cameron walked to the back of the store and scanned the row of red wines. She chose a pinot noir priced at ten dollars, which meant it wouldn't be great, but shouldn't be awful. The label was vaguely familiar, so she put it in her bag and slid open the Coke refrigerator. She selected a bottle of pink lemonade Snapple, before switching it for yellow. Maybe she'd go sit in the park for a while. The first thing that registered as she held the cold bottle was that Diego loved lemonade. Maybe he still did.

She cradled the lemonade and walked down the aisle where the Yees sold repackaged muffins from Costco. She chose a lemon poppy seed, then found a Dove chocolate bar for Rosa. She got to the counter and remembered the eggs. It wasn't as though she was in a hurry. In fact, nothing was less appealing than being ushered in and out of the rooms of her house like a stranger.

"One second," she told Mrs. Yee, who again nodded and waved.

She walked to the corner where the eggs were, searching for the brown ones Rosa always bought when she sensed someone move in beside her.

"Is Nate okay?"

Cameron jumped at the sight of Diego beside her.

She grabbed for something to hold onto and gripped a metal rack lined with little packets of Hostess donuts. Something jagged cut into her. She grimaced, glancing quickly at her finger, which was bleeding.

"Nate," Diego repeated.

"What are you talking about?"

"It's on the police scanners," he went on. "The B&E, a child kidnapped. An officer's child."

"We weren't there."

Diego stepped backward. "Nathaniel's okay?"

"He's fine. Asleep at the nanny's house. How did you find me?"

"I saw you walk in. I was in a cab. Shit. It's a setup." Diego took her shoulders. "Are you helping them?" Urgency bit into her skin along with his fingers.

"Of course not. I had no idea. Diego, what's the password to the jump drive? I can't open it."

He looked around. "I can't unlock it either. But it must be something good, because they want it back." He faced her. "Do you still have the DVD?"

"What DVD?"

"I wrote on the last page of the book—under the deck."

"Under my deck?"

"There's not much time, Cameron." He took her arm again. "Where's the setup? Who's involved?"

Her head was spinning. It was too much. She needed time. She glanced toward the back of the store, then the front. There was nowhere to go. "I don't know," she said quickly. "Supposedly they are processing the scene. Someone broke in this morning."

"What did they take?"

"Nothing. But, they tore the place apart."

She thought about all the cars. "There are four or five black and whites around the house. Two in front, one at either end of the block and one on the street behind. There may be more. All patrol guys. I haven't seen anyone in charge."

Mrs. Yee watched them intently, getting every word, Cameron was sure. She stepped away and lowered her voice. "They've tied you to a truck full of women, Diego, and now a dead girl in a dumpster. Everything points to your guilt. What the hell do you want me to think?"

Diego flinched. "You can't trust any of it."

"You died on me with no explanation. Then, I see you kill Ray Benjamin. A cop," she said. "How can I believe you?"

Diego pulled her close. The rapid beat of his heart pulsed against her ribs. The chest she'd slept against so many nights.

She exhaled against him.

"It's me," he said. "It's still me."

She was sucked in. She believed him. "Then, help me out, Diego. Tell me where I can get some proof."

"Watch the DVD. See if you can get the information off that drive." He gripped her harder. "But don't let them out of your possession."

"Okay. I'll do it." She tried to pull away. "You better go."

He didn't release her. "I've never stopped thinking about you. I did what I had to do after the explosion."

"They say they have your teeth. That they used dental records to prove you died in that explosion."

That made him smile. All the teeth still in his mouth. "I love you, Cameron." The pleasure vanished. "But, if I can't figure this thing out—what Benjamin and Axsater were doing, who else is involved, how high it goes…" He shook his head. "…I can't come back."

She felt empty—the same emptiness that sometimes came at the end of a work day when she longed for Nate—where the longing to see him or touch him or smell him was so strong that it was unbearable. Not like the passion of wanting someone you've never touched, but a need so deep it felt like desperation for something as basic as water or food. She stopped, wanting to sit down or sleep. The effort of thinking was like running through water.

Diego let go of her and walked away. A moan came out of her throat. It was meant to be a protest, some sort of loud rebuttal to his words. But, she couldn't manufacture it. Seeing him had melted her resolve. She wouldn't fight with him. Maybe he was a killer and a bastard. She was too levelheaded to love him after all that had happened.

But, she did love him.

So, she stood there without making a move, trying with all her strength not to watch him leave.

He pushed open the front door and, after pausing on the threshold to consider his options, disappeared onto the street. She kept an eye on Mrs. Yee as she returned to the counter. She pressed the cold Snapple bottle to her neck. The short pop, pop of gunfire came from the street. The bottle slipped from her hands.

Mrs. Yee dropped out of view behind the counter. Before Cameron could move, Diego burst through the door and pushed past her toward the back of the store.

She followed, but the liquid made the floor slick. She fell backward. There was a loud noise and pain in her head. The room spun, and it felt like things slowed down briefly. When she opened her eyes, faces swarmed like bees above her. Their voices hummed and droned. She couldn't make out one from the other. She could have sworn she saw Sergeant Lavick and Daley and Ballestrini, but one face was closer than the others, and she focused on Ricky's lips. She could tell he was shouting by the pulsing of the veins in his neck. Oddly, she didn't hear his words, but from the movement of his lips, she could tell he was screaming, "She's shot. She's shot."

She lifted her hand to her head and saw the blood run down over her fingers like bright paint.

CHAPTER 26

IVANA SHOULD HAVE been dead. There were some moments, as it all flashed back, when she wished she were. The bruises were beginning to heal. Her face looked like hers again, rather than the bloated side of a sick fish like the ones that used to hang in the market at home in summer. Ivana Pestova was not the girl she used to be. She glanced at the clock, pulling her mind from the things she wasn't supposed to think about.

It was almost six o'clock now. She was relieved that her first day in the new job was almost over. Just as he'd said, the woman took her in and gave her work. Ivana had changed the water and cleaned the basins and tools. She'd never had her nails done, so it was new to watch the women who came in and read magazines, turning pages delicately with wet fingernails.

The place she was living was much better. She slept in a small room by herself. There were others there. They shared a small kitchen where there was food. It wasn't fancy, but she could make tea and that was nice. She had her own key. She could come and go as she pleased. But, today was her first day out and only for her new job in the shop. Nothing else appealed to her. She hoped to save her money and go home, but the pay was small. It felt like it would take forever.

The woman in the shop was nice. She said there was another woman who would come by and that she was the owner. Or Ivana thought that was what she said. It was hard to communicate. The worst part was lying about her name and where she was from. He had told her not to give her real name until he came back and told her it was okay. He had told her that there was danger.

The men on the street by the salon, the few that came inside, they all scared her. She tried to hide herself, to keep her head down, but they always seemed to watch her. At the tavern where she used to work at home, she'd loved the men to notice her. She'd had Amira to protect her. Now, she had no one. Tears threatened to fall. She blinked hard and touched her eyelids with the backs of her hands.

By seven, she would be making her way back to the apartment. There, she would make something warm to eat from the cupboards and read her book. She'd found a tattered old copy of Little Women. It was in English, but she knew the story backward and forward, and so she was making her way through it slowly with the help of a Czech/English dictionary someone had left in the apartment. It helped to pass the time at night. She didn't go out. Her desires to see America, to experience it all, had disappeared.

There were a lot of things she didn't let herself think of—most of all, her mother and Michal. When she thought of them, she cried and couldn't stop. Her memories of their freezing apartment, her worn jeans and holed sneakers flooded over her. She wished she could go back. More than anything, that was what she wished.

She also avoided thinking about Anna. She worried that something terrible had happened to her friend. Worse than her own experience. That was the final thing she didn't let enter her mind—what had happened. It made her so sick and shaky that she couldn't sleep or eat.

She started when the front bell rang and another woman came in. Ivana rose and welcomed her the way Wanda told her to. "Welcome. How can we help you?" she asked awkwardly, tripping over the unfamiliar words and blushing.

The woman seemed confused. "Who are you?"

"I'm Iv—Katrina. Katrina Tatriva." Her cheeks burned.

Wanda emerged from the back. "Rosa. This is Katrina. She came in with a note this morning."

Ivana held perfectly still.

"What note?"

Wanda scattered papers on the desk and flipped through the appointment book before finally finding what she was looking for. She handed Rosa the page the man had given her. Ivana had memorized it.

Querida Rosa,

Not sure what Cameron has told you, but I need your help.
The girl is in some danger and needs a safe place to work.
I will help pay her if need be. I hope to be in touch soon.
Love to you and her and baby.

Tu Hermano, D

Some of it she hadn't understood. Wanda seemed a little confused, too. But, she let Ivana in. Now, it was up to Rosa.

"Brother?" Rosa said out loud, then gasped.

Ivana stepped back.

"A man brought you?"

Ivana was afraid she was about to be kicked out.

"About this tall?" Rosa said, reaching her hand above her own head.

Ivana nodded.

"Handsome?"

Ivana hesitated, swallowing slowly.

"Was he good-looking?"

She stared at her feet.

"Did he tell you his name?"

Ivana said nothing.

"Was his name Diego?"

"Yes," she whispered.

"*Oh, Dios.*"

Ivana feared that she'd said something wrong, but Rosa patted her arm. "And you speak English?"

She made a small pinch with her fingers. "I try. Only a little."

"I've got to call Cameron." Rosa pulled her cell phone out and punched something in. It was amazing how fast her fingers moved.

"Where are you staying?" Rosa asked with the phone to her ear.

Ivana wasn't sure who she was talking to—her or the person on the phone. "Katrina, where are you staying? Are you somewhere safe?"

"Yes. Yes, I am okay. I have need for the work."

"Okay. We'll take care of that. Have you worked in a salon before?"

"I've never been in a salon before," Ivana said.

"She didn't answer." Rosa typed something into the screen and put the phone in her pocket.

One of the other stylists took her purse from under the front desk and said good night. Most of the others had already left. Mondays were slow, Wanda explained.

"I texted her," Rosa said. "In the meantime, I've got a cut and color at eight so I'm here. Can you stay for a while?" Rosa asked.

"Yes," Ivana said. "Of course."

"I've got someone coming in at seven for a pedicure." Wanda pointed to Ivana. "That gives me time to give Katrina a little trim."

"Sure," Rosa agreed. "Does she want one?"

"She just said she'd never been in a salon," Wanda bantered back. "Do you want me to do your hair, Katrina?"

Ivana hesitated. Finally, she said, "I am Ivana."

"Ivana?" Rosa repeated.

"She's saying her name's Ivana, not Katrina," Wanda explained.

"I understand that. She's speaking English," Rosa snapped.

"Well, you seemed confused."

"I am. I thought you said her name was Katrina."

"I so sorry," Ivana explained. "I no mean to lie."

Rosa frowned. "It's okay, but tell us more about how—"

"Her name's Ivana," Wanda interrupted. "Are we doing hair? Would you like a little makeover?"

Ivana gripped her hands together. She knew "makeover" from her American magazines. "Oh, yes. Yes, please."

Rosa assessed her, head to toe. "Really? You're sure, uh—Ivana?"

Her chest seemed to fill with excitement. "Please. I love American style."

Rosa pulled her phone out of her pocket. "No word from Cameron yet. I'll order a pizza."

"Pepperoni, none of that all veggie shit," Wanda said, giving Ivana a wink.

Ivana understood only part of what Wanda said, but the way she talked, her smacking neon yellow gum, her golden blonde hair—she was so American.

"You like pizza?" Wanda asked.

"I think so."

Wanda and Rosa exchanged a glance. "You haven't had pizza?" Wanda exclaimed.

"Not in America."

"You've had it in Italy?" Wanda asked.

Ivana giggled. "No. In Šluknov—in Czech Republic."

"Czech pizza?"

Rosa scrunched her nose.

"Yuck."

"You eat meat?"

Ivana was in heaven. "I eat everything," she said.

The women laughed.

"Not with that tiny bod, you don't."

Ivana puzzled. "What?"

"Ah, forget it. Let's get your hair wet while Rosa gets us pizza." To Rosa, Wanda said, "Don't be cheap, Rosa. I want it from Goat Hill."

Rosa went back out the front door while Wanda led Ivana to a long chair with a sink at the head. She ran the hot water over Ivana's head and rubbed her scalp. She couldn't remember anything feeling so good. Rosa returned while Wanda was combing out Ivana's hair. She set the pizza down and pulled a bottle out of her bag.

It was a green wine bottle.

Rosa screwed off the top. "Wine?"

The only time Ivana had seen a screw-off wine bottle was when her uncle had come to the house. Her mother never drank wine, and the kind Amira served to the rare customer who asked for it had a cork.

"It's Boone's Strawberry Hill. You'll love it."

Rosa poured her a cup, and Ivana took a sip. It was delicious. Like dessert.

"See, I knew you'd like it."

"What is it?"

Rosa shrugged and poured herself a cup, too. "It's like a wine cooler."

"Wine cooler?" she repeated.

"Like wine and fruit, sort of," Wanda added, clipping Ivana's hair up with big metal barrettes.

Rosa opened the pizza box and Wanda groaned. "Not pineapples."

"It's pepperoni," Rosa countered.

"Pepperoni with pineapple."

"It's good."

Ivana felt her mouth water. What was pineapple?

Rosa handed her a piece and she took a bite. She tasted salty meat but also something juicy and sweet. She pointed to the yellow piece on the pizza. "What is it?"

"Pineapple," Rosa said. "You like it?"

Ivana nodded while she chewed. "Very good."

Rosa smiled at Wanda. "See."

Ivana took another drink of the wine cooler. This was heaven—American heaven. Rosa started the music, and she and Wanda sang out loud as they ate and drank. As Wanda worked on her hair, Rosa sat down and painted her fingernails. She moved so fast. They spoke quickly, and Ivana understood little of what they said but it was fun to watch them.

When they were done, Wanda spun the chair around and Ivana couldn't believe her own appearance.

"You don't like it," Wanda said.

Ivana shook her head, tears and a fit of giggles hitting her both at once. Her hair hung above her shoulders now; layers on the sides making it seem thick and healthy. She glowed. "I love it."

Wanda grinned. "Really?"

She spun back and leapt from the chair to throw her arms around Wanda. "Thank you. It is wonderful." She hugged Rosa, too. Tears rose in her eyes. She let them fall before wiping them off her face. "I am so silly."

Rosa was teary, too. "No, you're not. You're perfectly fabulous."

Wanda stood back. "And your hair does look great."

Ivana touched it again, still studying the mirror. "Yes. I think so also."

Soon, Wanda's client would arrive, so Ivana helped clean up the station and prepare the color and foils. They cleaned up the pizza and glasses. Ivana washed them by hand in the small back room, a little giddy from the wine and the night. When she came out, Rosa was holding her phone. "I never heard from Cameron," she said. "But, my eight o'clock cancelled, so I can drive you home."

"It's alright," Ivana told her. "I take bus." She knew the route. She packed up her things, but Rosa insisted on driving her.

Rosa played the music loud, the two talking only when Rosa needed directions. Ivana stared out at the night, her mind spinning. She was so happy.

At the apartment, she pulled out the single key Diego had given her and thanked Rosa again for everything. As she turned into the building, she waved goodbye to Rosa who was waiting at the curb until she got inside. Ivana ran her key along the mailboxes, making a long series of clicks almost like music, then paused at the stairway to do a little dance. It was almost like she belonged there.

CHAPTER 27

CAMERON SHIFTED ON the hospital bed. For hours, she'd been waiting for a doctor to clear her to go home. She was having trouble remembering the conversation with Diego. She needed time alone to try to pull it out of her subconscious. She had nine stitches in her palm and a nasty headache. Her little curtained cube hadn't been quiet for more than two minutes. Ballestrini, Lau, and Daley had all been in to check on her. Plus, two of the uniforms from the scene, followed by a detective. A crime scene tech had swabbed her hands in case she'd picked up any transfer from Diego. Had they touched?

"I thought it was a gunshot," Ricky said again. "You had blood on your shirt and shoulder. Your hand was bleeding and your head—" He exhaled a long breath. "It looked like your head was bleeding."

"You said that. Okay," Cameron snapped.

Ricky went quiet. His head dropped, hands clasped in his lap.

"I'm sorry. My head hurts, and I want to go home."

"Don't apologize," he said.

Cameron thought back to Diego's face. "He kept talking about a setup." She stared at the ceiling, thinking. "Why were there so many patrol cars at the house?"

"I don't know. I guess they were worried you were in danger."

Cameron sat up, sending a screeching pain through her temples. She grabbed her head.

Ricky jumped up, but she waved him off. Squeezing her eyes closed, she waited for it to pass.

"Nate," she said finally.

"What?"

"He said there was something about Nate on the news."

"Nate is with Señora Accosta," Ricky said. "We called her on the way over in the ambulance."

"I know," she answered. "But he said that Nate was missing. Kidnapped."

Ricky watched her with a worried expression. "That's impossible. We know he's fine."

Cameron tried to steady the room. Nate. "Diego had heard that Nate was missing. That's what he said. Diego came back to the house because he thought Nate was missing." Her pulse continued to throb inside her skull. "How could he have heard that?"

Ricky shook his head. "Are you sure that's what he said?"

She watched him as he shifted between his two feet. He pulled his phone from his pocket.

"What did you do?" She stood from the bed. Her knees buckled beneath her.

Ricky barely caught her. "Cameron, lie down."

She gripped the edge of the bed and he helped her back up onto it. As soon as she was safely seated, she shook off his touch. "You told Lavick about Nate."

Ricky's mouth went slack. "No, I didn't."

"Then who? You told someone. Who did you tell? I'm sick of waiting, Ricky. You owe me the truth."

Ricky's jaw went slack. He said nothing.

"Who did you tell?" she shouted. "Why did you tell?"

Ricky dropped into the chair.

"They set him up. They used Nate to set him up."

Just then, the thin blue curtain swung back and Lau walked in. "You okay?" he asked.

"No," she said to Lau and turned to Ricky. "Who was it?"

"No one that would have done this," he said softly.

"That isn't for you to decide. Tell me who knows."

Ricky hung his head, holding it in his hands. "Okay."

"Okay, what?" she demanded.

"I'll find out who used Nate. I'll find out today."

He wasn't going to tell her. "Get out."

Ricky didn't move. "Cameron…"

Lau crossed to the chair. "She said she wants you to go."

Ricky stood slowly and Lau led him away.

Why wouldn't he tell her? Who was he protecting that was so important? More important than her and Nate?

"You okay?" Lau asked her.

She fought off the tears. "Could you see if there is a doctor around? I need to get the hell out of here."

It was almost six o'clock when the doctor declared her fit to leave, but sent detailed instructions about being woken up every two hours to check for concussion. She gave these instructions to Lau. "My sister will do it," Cameron said.

Lau took her to Señora Accosta's house to get Nate and then walked with Cameron and Nate back to her house. A black and white was parked on the curb. Lau went over to talk to the patrol officers as Cameron headed into the house.

"Your sister home?" he called up to her.

"I'm sure."

He hesitated on the sidewalk in front of the house. "I'm okay," she assured him. "Thanks, Ryan. I appreciate you staying."

"Of course." He walked back down to his car at the end of the block.

Cameron watched Lau's taillights disappear around the corner, then made her way into the house. She laid Nate in his crib and listened to him fuss, hoping he would settle quickly.

Rosa wasn't home. It didn't look like she'd been there all evening. In the kitchen, a large, black case with evidence bags and tags and pens sat open on the kitchen table where it had been abandoned after the shooting. All the actual evidence that had been collected was gone, but in the rush to get to the new scene, they'd left stuff behind. Cameron knew that the case, and the rest of the police presence, would have to be dealt with in the morning.

For now, she had only one thing to do before she slept. Her gun in hand, she tucked the flashlight under her arm and slid open the back door. She closed it behind her, heeding the distinctive screech it made when it closed. She'd know if she heard that again while she was outside. Gripping the flashlight in her offhand, she walked down the three stairs to the side of the deck. Her head pounded with every step. She wished she'd accepted the last dose of Advil before she left the hospital. In the dark, she scanned for anything out of the ordinary. The light in the back switched on with her motion. When she was comfortable that she was alone, she got down on her hands and knees and shined the light under the deck.

"The DVD under the deck," Diego said. She was sure. She scanned slowly up, down, left, and right and then moved six inches clockwise and repeated the same. By the time she'd gotten halfway around, she was ready to give up. Up, down, left, right. Up, down, left… She stopped, spotting something plastic and blue. It was the bag the New York Times came in on wet days. She didn't get the Times, but Diego always had. Knowing she would recognize the bag, he must have grabbed it from one of her neighbors.

She set the light down and, checking behind her, got down on her belly to pull the bag out. She caught it between two fingers and yanked it closer. It was thin and hard. Not a newspaper.

She got her fingers around it and pulled it out, wiping the dirt across her pant leg.

She returned to the house through the back door, opened and closed it with a screech and set the alarm, before ducking into Nate's room. She moved the rocking chair in front of the small TV and DVD player where Nate watched Baby Mozart. She ejected his movie and loaded Diego's.

She was about to flip on the TV when she heard the beeping alarm. Someone was coming in the front door.

Moving quickly, she opened Nate's door. "Hello?"

"It's me," Rosa said. "There's a police car out in front."

"I saw it," Cameron said. "It's there in case he comes back."

Rosa ran her hands over her arms. "I'm glad we're setting the alarm."

"You were out late?"

Rosa rubbed her face. "Did you get my messages?"

"I lost my phone. I dropped it when I fell. Mrs. Yee brought it back this afternoon. She didn't speak a word to me. I know she speaks English."

Rosa frowned. "What do you mean—" She noticed the bandage on the side of Cameron's head. "What happened? Are you okay?" Rosa reached out to touch it and Cameron winced.

Rosa took her sister's hand and led her to the kitchen table, sitting her in a chair and flipping on all the lights. Cameron squinted under the glare of the kitchen lights as Rosa inspected her head.

"*Oh, Dios*, Cam. Did they come back? When did this happen?"

Cameron explained about seeing Diego, the story about Nate being kidnapped. Rosa gasped, turning toward Nate's room.

"He's fine. He was with Señora Accosta the whole time."

Rosa sank into a chair across from her.

"Ricky told someone in the department about Nate. Somehow someone got that information and they used it to lure Diego out. They used my baby as bait, Rosa."

Rosa let out a string of Spanish curses. "Why would Ricky do that?"

Cameron held her head. "I don't know."

"Are you all right, really? What did the doctor say?"

Cameron pointed to the counter. "You have to wake me up every two hours to check for a concussion."

Rosa read over the instructions. "Okay. Are you taking anything for the pain?"

"Just Advil."

The two were silent for a minute or so.

"I don't think he's guilty, Rosa."

"Oh," Rosa exclaimed, remembering something. "That's why I was calling you today. There was a new woman at work today. Wanda hired her, but she came in with a note from Diego to me."

"Diego's a pretty common name."

"No. It was a note from your Diego." She rose and disappeared into the front hall, returning with her purse. She pulled out a folded page and handed it over. Cameron read the words.

"She said Diego got her an apartment, and he offered to help pay her wages," Rosa said.

Cameron saw the last line of the note: *Love to you and her and baby.*

Cameron shuffled the pieces in her mind. "But, why? Why did he help her?"

Rosa shrugged. "I'm not exactly sure, but she looked like she'd been through something pretty rough." She rose from the table and glanced at the clock on the wall. "You need rest. I'll wake you up in two hours."

"How about three?"

"Two," Rosa said sternly. "So, you'd better get to bed."

Cameron hugged her sister and made her way back to Nate's room. She switched the TV back on, lowered the volume to two and pushed play on the DVD player. The video started in what looked like a warehouse. The camera was likely mounted somewhere near the ceiling and aimed down at a torn card table with three folding chairs. There was nothing on the table or wall, no windows in view. She increased the volume a few notches. There were voices, but she couldn't make out the words.

The camera view broadened, the motion of the image startling her. Two men stood on one side of the room. One she didn't recognize, the other was Ray Benjamin. Both of them wore bulletproof vests and raid pants and boots. Ray's attire struck her as odd. She hadn't thought of Ray doing much fieldwork.

Someone tossed a navy gym bag through the door and into the room, barking an order that she couldn't interpret, though she was pretty sure it was in English. She studied the bag. It was similar to the one Diego had, though she couldn't swear it was the same. Then, another bag was tossed in, and a man walked through the door, carrying a third. He was dressed in jeans and a sweatshirt, his head turned away from the camera.

His stride, the way he held his shoulders, Cameron knew him before she saw his face. He moved to the far side of the table, kicking the chair backward before heaving the bag onto the tabletop.

He unzipped it. As his hand came out with a fist of cash, she saw his face on film for the first time—Sergeant Michael Lavick. He held a couple of the stacks of bills up, smiling and shaking the money at the other men like some sort of lewd gesture. The other men were smiling, too, but it paled in comparison to Lavick's delight. She read the date stamp, written on the screen in awkward white block letters.

It was the week before she'd gone to the station—six days, actually—six days before she'd discovered that Diego Ramirez was alive. Who filmed this and why? Blackmail? Was it possible that Lavick didn't know he was being filmed?

Restless, she opened Nate's door and walked down the hallway to Rosa's room. She knocked, but there was no answer. Twisting the knob, she stepped into the room, hearing Rosa's heavy breathing. Cameron hesitated before sitting on the edge of her sister's bed. "Rosa?"

Rosa opened her eyes with a jolt. "Are you okay?"

"I have a question about the woman at the salon."

"What?"

"The woman that Diego sent in."

Rosa rubbed her eyes. "What are you talking about? What time is it?"

"It's midnight, Rosa. Listen to me."

She pushed Cameron away. "I have to wake you up in an hour and a half. Let's talk about it then."

"It can't wait."

Rosa sighed. "Fine. What?"

"The woman at the salon, what's her name? Where is she from?"

Rosa shoved at her sister again. "That's more than one question, Cameron. I'm tired."

Cameron felt desperate. "Just tell me where she's from."

"Fine," she groaned. "She's Czech."

"Czech?" Cameron repeated.

"That's what I said. Her name is Ivana, and she's from the Czech Republic." Rosa rolled on her side and pulled the covers over her head, effectively ending the conversation.

They said Diego killed an immigrant woman, wiped her clean, threw her in the dumpster and then he—or someone using his name—had taken another Czech girl and paid her rent and found her a job. It made no sense. He was either killing or he was helping. But, which was it?

CHAPTER 28

IT WAS SIX thirty on Saturday morning when Cameron texted Hailey Wyatt. *Call me.* She'd been up with Nate since four thirty. Between that and the every-two-hour wake-ups for her possible concussion, she was too tired to sleep. After five minutes, she texted again. On the fourth try, Hailey called back.

"This had better be really good."

"It is," Cameron said.

"Cruz, it's Saturday morning, and I'm not on call."

Cameron told Hailey what she'd learned about the woman who had been brought to Rosa's salon. "It's possible it's a coincidence, but—"

"I don't believe in those," Hailey said. "Worse than religion."

"It seemed too weird to be true," Cameron agreed. "Either it was him or someone using his name."

"I need to talk to this Ivana woman about the other dead girl. Where can I find her?"

"I'll get the address from Rosa. Where should I meet you?"

Hailey hesitated.

"I need to do this."

"Not a word to anyone, and if anything comes up, we never had this conversation."

"Deal."

"Meet me in front of the Hall at quarter to eight."

Cameron calculated how long it would take her to wake Rosa, feed Nate, find a picture of Diego, hide the DVD somewhere safe, and get to the Hall of Justice. "I'll be there."

"I'll be in a gold Taurus like every other guy at that place," she said, referring to the inspectors' cars.

"Except for the guy part."

"Maybe that's why I have so much trouble with this job."

"I'll find you," Cameron said and set off to wake Rosa.

Rosa agreed to watch Nate for a few hours before she went to work. Cameron promised to be back as soon as she was done with Hailey. Cameron waved at the cop car in front of the house and left without any explanation about where she was going.

Cameron stood in front of the Hall of Justice in a pair of black jeans, black boots, a black jacket, and a tan baseball hat. If it weren't San Francisco, she might stand out. As it was, she looked like almost every other woman on the street. Since it was Saturday, the business suits weren't out. In this district, though, a "business suit" meant a whole range of things—hookers and pimps at one end, the attorneys and inspectors at the other.

Her phone buzzed in her pocket. Ricky. "Cruz," she answered.

"You feeling okay?"

"No. I feel like shit."

"I'm sorry. I know you're upset with me."

"You don't know, Ricky. From where I'm standing, everyone is guilty and you put Nate in danger. How can I possibly trust you?"

"I understand how it looks, Cameron. I did tell someone. Someone I was involved with."

"Involved?" she repeated.

"I need a little more time and I'll explain everything. Evelyn and I are going to New York tomorrow morning to deal with her aunt's estate. I'll call as soon as I'm back."

She spotted Hailey as soon as she was within a hundred yards by the fact that her curly head of hair barely showed over the headrest.

"I have to go." Cameron ended the call before he could respond.

Hailey swerved to the curb and paused while Cameron got one leg in before driving off again.

"This is being treated as a low priority case," Hailey said. "They don't even want to pursue the prints on the girl."

"Why?"

Hailey glanced over, then back at the road, her foot to the floor. "I think because they've got enough to fry Ramirez already. Why spend the resources to prove whether he did or did not kill the Czech? We know he killed Benjamin. We have an eyewitness." Hailey motioned to Cameron.

"A postpartum, sleep-deprived one."

"Plus, I guess they found the gun used to kill Axsater."

"The one they matched to Benjamin."

Hailey's lips thinned. "Different gun."

"I thought the ballistics on Axsater were matched to Benjamin," Cameron said.

"That's what the lab told me," Hailey said. "But there was a screw up—some new guy explained it all wrong. It turned out they were two different weapons. They only have the one in possession. It's a .45, registered to Ramirez."

That was wrong. "No. He hated .45s. Too bulky for a backup, he said. He only had the one standard issue and a .38 backup. It was the only one he ever carried." It was the old .38 that he was superstitious about, but she didn't say that.

Hailey changed lanes. "The gun that killed Axsater was registered to Ramirez and it was definitely a .45."

"If you were going to kill a cop, would you register the gun you planned to use?" Cameron asked.

"Nope. And I wouldn't register the truck I was going to transport a bunch of illegals in either," Hailey said, then added, "Unless I was suicidal or a total fucking moron."

"Well, he's neither."

"I wouldn't figure."

For a few minutes, neither spoke. Hailey followed the dash's navigation system to the address in the Tenderloin where Rosa had dropped off Ivana the night before. Ivana wasn't due in the salon until ten, so they hoped to catch her at home.

Hailey double-parked, threw her police pass on the dash and the two women emerged from the car. The streets were quiet at this hour. It was too early on a Saturday morning for people to be milling about. Those who worked regularly got paid on Friday. It was a big night out, especially in these neighborhoods.

Cameron pulled open a cracked glass door that led to the apartment where Ivana lived. She studied some dried blood on the wall. It looked recent. Friday night was known as fight night—men came home drunk, women wanted to know where the money was. Men drank it away. She's pissed, he's pissed.

When Cameron had started with the police, general call took those. Friday was always the busiest. Now, the department had a division to deal with domestic abuse. Cameron couldn't imagine anything more depressing. The woman calls the cops, gets him hauled away on Friday, then wants him out by the end of the weekend so he can get back to work on Monday and do the whole thing over again.

Hailey examined the blood, too. "Looks fresh."

Cameron agreed. The color was reddish, not yet the dark brown it would eventually become with exposure to air. The two stopped at the list of apartments and scanned the names. Some were typed, others handwritten. They were all old and yellowed. Then Cameron spotted familiar handwriting. "This one."

"P. Warren?" Hailey asked.

"*All the King's Men*. It's his favorite book." She paused. "Or, it was."

"Let's try it." They walked up the stairs and knocked on apartment F. There was a lot of shuffling inside and finally, silence.

"We are looking for Ivana," Hailey said. "We're friends of Rosa's."

"She not here," came a small voice from inside.

"Bingo," Hailey whispered.

"Please, open the door."

No response.

"We need to find her. It's very important."

"She no come from work."

Cameron and Hailey exchanged glances. "She didn't come home last night?"

"No."

Cameron pulled a photo out of her jacket. It was one of her and Diego. Hailey watched as she folded herself out of it and showed the section with Diego. She lifted the photo to the peephole. "This man? Have you seen him?"

There were a series of whispers from inside. "No. No see him."

"You need to open the door," Hailey said again, laying her fist into it.

The voice came back loud and firm. "No."

Cameron kept the picture raised. They didn't have probable cause to go in, and forcing their way in wasn't her preference. "Who is your landlord?"

Whispers. "Down—number A," someone finally said.

Hailey tried a couple more tactics to draw them out without success. "Fine, we'll try the super."

They went back down the stairs and knocked on the door to Apartment A. After a few minutes, Hailey hit the buzzer twice and knocked again with her fist.

Finally, a petite Asian man opened the door, wearing only a wife-beater undershirt, striped boxer shorts and white athletic socks that came almost to his bony knees. He eyed Hailey up and down slowly, clearly enjoying the sights. Finally, he yelled like an insolent child. "What?"

Hailey looked him over just as slowly while Cameron remained back, holding the picture of Diego. The man blinked at them, then rubbed his eyes with his fists. He stood awkwardly, his toes pointed out, his back arched and his hips out. "What you want?" he said, swinging his finger at Hailey.

Cameron showed him the picture of Diego. "You know this man?"

The man grabbed the picture from her grasp and opened it up. He touched her face on the photo. "This you."

Hailey pulled her badge out and lifted it for him to see. "She asked if you've seen that man."

The man glanced down at the picture again. "I know him. So, what?" He shoved the image back at Cameron.

"How do you know him?"

He pointed his finger between himself and the photo, his back arched. "We do business."

"What kind of business?" Cameron asked.

"Not for police."

"Tell us how you know him, or we'll take you to the station and you can tell us there," Hailey said, the edge to her voice making her anger clear.

"He pay rent from me."

"Rent for an apartment?"

He nodded.

Cameron motioned up to the building. "Which one?"

"He not home. It for his friend." The man turned to Cameron and added, "His girlfriend." He offered a little wicked grin like he'd told a good joke.

"Which apartment?"

"F."

"What's the woman's name?"

"I don't know name. She have accent, brown hair, big boobs—" He pointed to Hailey. "Like you."

Hailey started forward. The man darted backward. He tripped on a chair that was precariously placed in the middle of the room and fell over it, landing on his backside.

Hailey reached in and slammed the door closed, she and Cameron on the outside, him on the inside. "Little prick."

They walked back to the car in silence. Cameron was struggling to sort out the details. "There were at least three other women in that apartment."

"He's not screwing those women."

Cameron didn't answer. She couldn't think straight. The cop in her was overshadowing the part of her that wanted to believe Diego wouldn't murder a woman and toss her in the dumpster. Rosa had said the girl was badly beaten. Even with the evidence, she couldn't get herself to believe he'd done that.

"I've got to get home," Hailey said on their way back to the Hall.

"Thanks for letting me tag along."

"If you can get me a name and description, I'll put something out on Ivana."

"I can do it," Cameron said.

"She'll turn up," Hailey said.

It didn't seem likely to Cameron.

"It's not enough, but I can't offer more now."

"I didn't say it wasn't enough," Cameron said. "I'm a big girl."

"You didn't have to say anything," Hailey said gently. "This whole thing stinks to hell."

Cameron thought about the DVD of Lavick but knew Hailey wasn't the right person for that. She wasn't sure who was. "You know anyone who can unlock a jump drive?"

"The Computer Intrusion Squad cop from Chicago is pretty cool," Hailey suggested. "You could try her."

"Think she's trustworthy?"

Hailey sighed. "As anyone else you've got."

When Hailey dropped her off, Cameron jogged back to her own car. She took the drive home at a much slower pace despite how anxious she was to see Nate. On the front mirror was a note from Rosa that she'd had to go to the salon and Nate was with her. Cameron noticed a round spot on the floor.

She crouched down and touched it, the viscous liquid unmistakable. Blood.

Cameron slammed the front door. "Show yourself!" she screamed in a whispered hiss, so as not to alert the police car out front. Stepping around the spot, she ran into the kitchen. It was empty, the evidence case on the table. She went from room to room and found nothing. Finally, she made her way back to the hallway and searched the floor for another drop of blood. She found it on the perimeter of the living room. And another beside the back door. She opened the door and scanned the deck, but there was no one there.

She started back inside when she thought about the DVD he had left. Down on her knees, she saw another blue bag.

He'd left something else. Excited, she crawled in and grabbed it. It felt empty, but her fingers touched something in the bottom. She pulled the bag into her lap and saw a smear of blood on the bag. She looked around, but he was gone. He'd been there and left. It meant he was alive, but for how long? She was supposed to want him punished, caught. She was so relieved he wasn't dead.

Despite what she'd seen with her own eyes, she believed him. Pushing aside her own battling emotions, she pulled open the bag and removed a folded white note. She recognized the paper from a small pad Rosa kept by the phone. Diego had been in the house. How long ago?

In the familiar scrawl, Diego had written:

> *I had to borrow the DVD back. Axsater wasn't me. Working on who. For now, guard this. We can frame it when this is over.*
>
> *P.S. D/W is old. What if someone ran it?*

She was stunned. It was like one of their old notes. He was shot and injured and making jokes about her bizarre hiding place? But, it also let her know that he had a plan. He was figuring things out. For the first time since all of this had started, she had hope.

She shook the contents of the bag into her palm and looked down at the warped piece of metal that had once been a bullet. A year ago, she would have laughed out loud. Diego Ramirez was fine. He'd been shot, but he was okay enough to sneak back in for the disk and leave her his bullet. Now, despite herself, a tiny smile rose from her chest. She was happy—not in the dumb, thrilled way that happiness sometimes was. Maybe it would never be that way again. That sort of giddy happiness required a naiveté that she had lost.

But, she was happy in a smaller, more instinctual way. Diego wasn't dead. She closed her fingers around the bullet as the happiness descended and was replaced by something else. It wasn't another emotion so much as the lack of one. It was acceptance that how she felt did not matter in this situation.

Happy, sad, angry, those were personal emotions. Ones she seemed to feel much more at the surface of her skin since Nate was born. Emotions couldn't guide what happened, but they did guide her response. It was that emotion, coiled in her gut, that led her to believe in Diego's innocence. She would follow that in an effort to right whatever wrongs had been done.

In the end, whatever she did might not be enough. She could still lose him. The realization that followed was how empty the fight for justice could be.

CHAPTER 29

LUIS LET HIS head loll back and tried to open his eyes. The light was blinding. "*Qué* hangover." He tried to sit up but couldn't. He pushed off the couch and onto the floor. He needed to go to the bathroom, but all he could manage was to press onto all fours and vomit. It splattered across his hands and arms. The stench of alcohol burned his eyes.

In the bathroom, he threw up twice more. Resting his elbows on the sink, he splashed his face and rinsed his mouth. He swiped toothpaste across his tongue and added water to make mouthwash. He sank down to the cool tile floor, holding his head in his hands. It had never hurt so much.

Moving slowly, he grabbed the aspirin bottle and shook three white pills into his palm. He took them with an old glass of water by the sink. The smell was slightly sour. He shuddered with nausea. For a few minutes, he didn't move. Last night was a blur. He got paid. He took a wad of cash and met with a couple of the guys at a strip club on Mission. He didn't usually do that, but Candi had other plans.

There was a girl. He rubbed his head, trying to remember her name. After splashing his face again, he yanked the hand towel off the bar, carried it into the living room, and dropped it on the pool of vomit to deal with later.

He half expected to find her in his room, but the bed was empty. The sheets were strewn on the floor, but that was nothing new. Twice a month, a lady cleaned and did his laundry. The rest of the time, it was a sty. It would have been nice if Candi tidied once in a while, but that probably would have cost him extra.

He tried to picture the new girl as he scanned the room. Where had they done it? He was sure they'd done it. He always did it with them. He glanced at the bedside clock. It was eight fifteen. An early riser. Candi never left before ten. Where the hell was Candi last night? When he asked, she said something bitchy about not having to answer to him. "Fucking bitch," he mumbled in English. His English was getting better, especially the curse words.

He couldn't make sense of anything now. The only option was to crawl back into bed. The pounding in his head softened as he pulled the sheet up over his head.

He woke to the noise of a jackhammer. At first, he was sure it was inside his head, but it was an actual jackhammer on the street behind his. The clock said ten thirty. He didn't hurt as much. Mostly, he was hungry. He dressed quickly and was halfway out the door when the phone rang.

"Oh, Luis, I'm so glad I caught you," Candi cooed.

He grinned. Calling to beg him back… well, maybe he was into a new girl now. He halted mid thought. What the hell was that girl's name?

"Luis—"

"What?" he snapped, trying to remember her damn name. How many drinks did he have? The first two with the guys then the round with her and one more. Four total. They talked price. She was cheaper than Candi. Not as pretty, maybe, but still pretty. A hell of a lot better than Laura. And big tits. Candi's weren't small, but these were the kind you could really sink into. He remembered admiring them while they were at the bar. She had bought that last round.

"Luis, are you listening?"

Candi sounded like his wife. "What do you want?"

"I need to come by."

"I'm going out for a while."

"I'll wait until you're back. Or, just leave it unlocked."

He thought about that. He wasn't really in the mood right now, but the guys always said a blow job was the best hangover cure. "Okay. I'll leave it unlocked. Be here in a half hour."

"See you then," she said, all sugar.

He hung up. His head felt a little better. Obviously, her date last night hadn't gone that well. He left the door unlocked, patted his coat pocket for his wallet and sauntered out the door. The city air was cold and wet. Used to the dry heat of Oaxaca, he normally dreaded the cold. Today, with his stomach tight and his throat dry, the cool weather felt good.

He walked the three blocks to his favorite pizza place and went inside. Mario was working and they exchanged hellos. "The regular?"

Luis thought of Candi.. "Sure." If Candi wanted pizza, she could get her own. While it cooked, Luis sat at the narrow bar, back to the wall. The smells were making his stomach toss around. He couldn't tell if it was because he was hungry or going to be sick again.

"Ready. Eleven dollars, thirty-seven cents," the woman said.

Luis sat up and pulled out his wallet, one hand on the pizza box. He wasn't even going to make it back to his place. He'd eat the first pieces right there. He opened the cheap leather wallet his boys had given him for his birthday and dug his fingers into the bill section. He halted. It was empty.

His stomach lurched as he held the wallet upside down, waiting for the rainfall of bills. He had more than a thousand dollars last night. He had planned to make a deposit in his safe box. He had been running late and the bank was closed. A thousand dollars. He can't have spent it all. He set the wallet down and patted his coat pockets. Nothing. He dug through them—inside, then outside.

The woman pulled the pizza box back, shaking her head.

"But, I have money. I don't—" He picked up the wallet again. Oh, Jesus. Where was the money? The wallet had nothing. His jacket had nothing. He patted his pants pockets but knew there was no money there either.

The woman behind the counter wore a nasty scowl. He considered grabbing the box and making a run for it. "I just forgot it." He felt the pizza box warm on his hands, its grease stains calling to him. "I'll bring it later. It's only eleven bucks."

She shook her head and took the pizza.

He didn't let go of the box. "I come all the time. I'm a good customer."

The woman shouted something he didn't understand. Mario shrugged without speaking.

Luis stood at the counter, breathless. He couldn't pry himself from the pizza, but he had to go find his money. The possibility that he'd lost it made his stomach cramp up. He tried to slow his breathing to keep from throwing up. Suddenly, he couldn't. He ran out the door and back up the street pausing to vomit behind a trash can. A cold sweat broke out on his back, and there was wetness on his upper lip and forehead.

That was all the money he had. He took the other money out of the safe deposit box to buy a new suit and shoes. Spent it all, and he didn't get paid again for a week. He stopped and heaved on the stair, but his stomach was empty. Oh, Jesus, how would he eat?

He reached his floor, close to tears and pushed through the door. Candi was in the living room, picking things up off the floor. "Oh, thank God you are here."

"I need the money you owe me, Luis."

"I can't find the money. I had it all last night and now—" He stopped talking and moved to the couch where his coat had been. He ripped the cushions off and dug into the couch frame before stumbling into the bedroom. Could he have put it somewhere?

Candi followed him. In her arms was a stack of clothes. Hers. "What do you mean you can't find the money?"

He ignored her and picked things off the floor, shaking them before tossing them in the corner.

It wasn't there. He knew it wasn't. He'd taken one thousand eighty-four dollars out last night and lost it. All of it. Oh, Jesus. He had to send money to Laura. His stomach clenched like a fist. He was going to throw up.

Candi started talking, but he pushed by her and ran for the bathroom.

His stomach heaved. There was nothing in him but stomach acid. He was sure he was going to die. He limped from the bathroom and crossed the room to Candi. He put his arms around her. "I lost all my money."

She pushed him off, holding his shoulders and shaking him. "What do you mean you lost all the money?"

He sniffled, his head swimming again. "I had it last night, in my wallet. We went out." He paused. "I met a girl." He thought about the girl. Oh, Jesus. His money was gone. She stole it. That bitch stole it. But, how was that possible?

Candi fastened a hand to each hip. "What girl?"

He sat down on the couch. The cushions were on the floor so he sat on the hard frame. He hurt too much to talk about it. "I don't know."

"What was her name?" Candi pressed.

He covered his head with his hands. "I don't remember." He cried.

Candi towered over him. "You don't remember her name? Where did you meet her?"

She was acting like his wife. This was her fault—she was the one who'd gone out with someone else. "A club on Mission. We had some drinks." He started to tell her that was all, but he didn't know. He scanned the room. Had the girl come back to his place?

"How many drinks, Luis?"

"Not that many," he said. "Three or four."

Candi was quiet. Luis nursed his headache by rubbing small circles on his temples. Eleven hundred dollars, gone.

He patted the couch. "Come sit down. Sit down and hold me, Candi. I hurt all over."

Candi paced the apartment. He didn't watch. He just heard her—clack clack clack in those damn shoes. His head throbbed. She was putting her stuff in a bag. "What are you doing?"

"I'm leaving."

He tried to rise from the couch but couldn't. "What? You can't leave."

She laughed. "Why not?"

Why not? "Because you my girl, right?"

"Wrong." She pulled the bag over one shoulder and turned for the door. Then, as though remembering something, she stalked into the bathroom.

"Wait, Candi. I can find the money or I'll get more. Just wait."

She came out of the bathroom with a bottle of shampoo that he was pretty sure was his, but he didn't say anything.

She tucked it into her bag and took a last look around the room.

"When are you coming back?" he asked.

"I'm not, Luis. This gig is over. No money, no Candi, and you already owe me two hundred from last week."

His head pounded again. "I said I'll find the money. I put it somewhere," he lied. "You wait. I'll find it and pay you."

Candi came over and her face softened.

He thought she was going to sit down. He reached up to her, but she didn't touch his hand. "I only had a few drinks."

"She drugged you, you idiot."

He blinked.

"Let me guess. She bought you a drink after you offered to buy her for the night. Maybe you went to say goodbye to your friends and when you came back, she had a drink for you. You drank it, got in a cab with her, and you don't remember anything else after that?"

He was sweating again. A little drip curved across his face. "I—I—" He couldn't form the words. "Why would she do that?" It was so mean.

Candi roared in laughter and the noise split his head. "Because she's smart, you fucking idiot."

"Please, don't go," he called as loud as he could. It came out a whisper.

Candi stopped at the door. "I'll be back for my two hundred bucks, Luis. You've got a week. If you don't have it, I'll send Marco." She left and slammed the door behind her.

He cried out at the sound. Candi had left; all his money was gone. He was starving. He pressed his face down on the bony frame of the couch and smelled vomit. He rolled over, his head pounding too hard to think. Pushing his face into the back of the couch, he cried a little.

CHAPTER 30

CAMERON WAS UP at the crack of dawn on Sunday in a decent mood. The investigation was done, the police presence finally gone from the house. A car would remain on the street while they processed the evidence and, ideally, made an arrest. Cameron remained doubtful.

Even better, she had a reply text from Sydney Blanchard. The note was quick: Mei Ling is great and can do, I'm sure. It was followed by a 312 number. Chicago. Cameron decided to text a little later so as not to wake Mei. She'd missed another call from Ricky, but he would have to wait. She needed some time to digest what he'd said. And what he hadn't. Cameron could only imagine the woman was Captain Ahrens. It made her sick that Evelyn didn't know. It was all too much right now.

It was a rare, cloudless day with a sky so blue it might have been painted on. Rosa was still sleeping when she packed Nate into the Baby Bjorn and took him on the eight-block walk to the small Latino bakery where she and Diego used to get churros on Sunday mornings. Rosa would love the treat. Even when Rosa swore off everything Latin, she never said no to fresh churros from Vida Dulce. They were the first to arrive and waited as a woman unlocked the door and unrolled the old canopy at seven thirty. Cameron removed Nate's hat, fluffed his hair and approached the pastry case.

There was an older woman who used to cover the weekend mornings. Sweet, she always recognized Cameron. The one who emerged was a surly looking young Latina.

The woman interrupted as Cameron started her order. "What you like?"

Fine, they would speak English. "A dozen churros, please."

The woman mumbled something Cameron couldn't make out before pulling a bag off the counter and snatching a tissue. She loaded churros into a bag.

Another woman called out from the back, asking where the clean aprons were. She emerged a moment later, tying one behind her back. She was older, but the same height as the first, and Cameron thought they might be mother and daughter. While they chatted in Spanish, Cameron took out her cash.

"Eight fifteen," the younger one said, setting the bag on the counter.

Cameron handed her a twenty.

As the younger woman made change, she glanced over at her mother and said, "The gringa bitch took all the fresh churros."

Calmly, Cameron took her change, put it back in her pocket, and leaned across the counter. Nearly a foot taller, Cameron peered down on the girl, one hand cradling Nate's head and the other holding her sack of churros. Cameron gave them a stiff smile and spoke in perfect Spanish. "That's because the gringa bitch got here first."

Cameron took the churros home and caught Rosa as she was heading into the shower to get ready for work. Cameron needed distraction but she also needed to clear her mind. She decided to go to church, something she hadn't done nearly enough after Diego's death.

While Nate slept in her lap, Cameron focused on the decorative ceiling of the Mission Delores Church. Padre Merafine read from the book of John. She felt calm now. The thoughts were all there but slower, more manageable. She had to remember that sometimes nothing sorted her out as well as sitting in God's house.

"Jesus went to the Mount of Olives," the priest announced. "Early in the morning he came down again to the temple...

"The scribes and the Pharisees brought a woman who had been caught in adultery; and making her stand before the people, they said to Jesus, 'Teacher, this woman was caught in the very act of committing adultery. In the law, Moses commanded us to stone such women. Now what do you say?' They said this to test Jesus, so that they might have some charge to bring against him.

"Jesus bent down and wrote with his finger on the ground. When the scribes and the Pharisees kept on questioning him, Jesus straightened up and said to them, 'Let anyone among you who is without sin be the first to throw a stone at her.'"

Who was truly without sin in the eyes of the church? This was her biggest hang-up about the religion of her youth. It was almost impossible to live in this age without being confronted with the obvious contradictions between traditional Catholicism and the modern world. Unwed motherhood was right there at the top of the list.

Cameron kept the truth about Nate to herself with the people at church. At first, she had worn a thin silver band on her left hand to services. There were those who would judge her, but she was confident that God didn't care whether she and Diego had been married. If truth be told, Cameron was pretty sure God had delivered Nate to her himself.

The truth was between her and God. She sat back in the pew and listened to the Spanish roll off the priest's tongue. Sometimes, just the language made her long for Diego. Rosa insisted on speaking in English. Aside from her brothers and parents, and a few random friends she saw less and less of, Cameron spoke English.

Though she and Diego had switched back and forth, he'd always spoken to her in Spanish when they were making love. The memory brought a warm flush over her.

"How easy it is for us to think that today's gospel doesn't apply to our modern world," Padre Merafine continued. "We don't throw stones. Our world is too civilized. But is it really?"

Cameron considered his words. Wasn't throwing stones her job? Assessing the evidence and deciding who deserved to be brought before a jury for stoning and who should be exonerated? At what point was it simply subjective judgment, no different from the woman in the story. Shooting Ray was a sin, but was his shooter necessarily a sinner? Didn't the circumstances matter?

Thankfully, it wasn't her job to condemn or acquit Ray or Diego. Even finding them was no longer her job.

She felt a tap on her shoulder. An older man leaned forward and handed her a note.

She took it.

"From the back," he told her in English.

"*Hablo español*," she replied, frustrated. "Who is it from?"

"The cowboy," the man told her in Spanish.

She saw no cowboy. "*¿Quién?*" she asked again, hoping he would point the cowboy out.

He just waved over one shoulder.

Cameron looked back again. She was sitting about ten rows from the rear of the church, which held six hundred people. She guessed there were at least thirty people behind her, and she tried to focus on each face. It was impossible to see them all. An old woman behind her waved her around, hissing at her to listen to the Lord.

At the same time, a woman beside her made tsking sounds and wagged a finger as though she was a child passing notes in school. Cameron gripped the paper, trying to focus back on the sermon. She wanted to read the note, but forced herself to wait until people had stopped watching her.

The priest was talking about the way modern society stones its people. Cameron listened to the woman tsking and wondered if she caught the irony.

Deciding God would forgive her even if the lady beside her didn't, Cameron opened the paper. She recognized Diego's handwriting and without hesitating, she lifted Nate into her arms, picked up her jacket and Nate's diaper bag and excused her way past the parishioners in her row until she was at the aisle. Head down, she moved quickly to the back of the church. Without waiting for a break in the sermon, she pushed open the door and walked outside.

Before reading the note, she took a few steps in each direction, peering down the surrounding blocks in search of him. One street over, she watched the J Church Street train rumble through the intersection. The area was residential—clusters of brightly painted row houses. A row of palm trees and grass lined the center of Dolores, making the street feel like something out of Beverly Hills. One block down from the church was a diner where the waitress behind the counter wore a yellow and brown uniform. The style of the uniform looked as old as the diner. But, no Diego.

She walked back to the church and sat on the pinkish cement steps. The concrete was cool through her slacks, so she pulled a blanket from the diaper bag and wrapped it over Nate, tucking it in under his arms, then pulled his hat down over his ears. Gripping the letter in white, cold hands, she opened it.

Querida, There's a meeting set for Wednesday. Details on that drive. We break it, we might catch them and end this thing. Mucho amor.

She stared at the words. He'd addressed her as "querida" and signed it "love." We break it. We might catch them. Diego was alive and out there, asking for help.

She stared at the note in her hand and considered her options. She did have choices, but there was only one that seemed viable. She would help him however she could. First, she needed Mei to break into that jump drive. Nate woke fussing so she tucked the note into her inside jacket pocket and texted Mei, then walked home, feeling Diego's presence the entire way.

She was on their block when Rosa called. "How did you know I'd be out of church?" Cameron asked.

"She was attacked," Rosa cried.

Cameron halted. "Who?"

"Ivana."

"What? Where are you?"

"She had my card on her and the hospital has been calling the salon since five o'clock this morning. I didn't get the messages until I got in. You need to come."

Cameron strode toward the house. "Rosa, slow down."

"Ivana, the girl from the salon—the Czech girl." She was breathless.

"I remember."

"She's in a coma, Cameron."

"Okay. I'm coming. Which hospital?"

"General."

Cameron made a mental list of things she needed to do before she could go. "I'll be there in forty-five minutes. Meet me in front." If she survived, Ivana would have answers. Now, she just had to survive.

CHAPTER 31

CAMERON CALLED SEÑORA Accosta and was at the hospital in fifteen minutes. She sent Hailey a text message and left a voicemail, hoping this might be a break for her, too. She found Rosa at the main desk, talking to the attendant.

"Rosa."

Her sister ran to her. "Oh, God. They believe she was attacked right after I dropped her off. She hasn't woken up yet. The only thing she had on her was a card for the salon. They called and left a message at the salon. When I got here, they warned me that I might not recognize her." Rosa pressed her hand to her mouth.

Cameron hugged her sister. "It'll be okay. I'll go with you. Where is she?"

"I don't know," Rosa whispered.

Cameron pulled tissue from her purse and handed it to her sister, who watched her strangely. It wasn't like Cameron to carry tissue. "For Nate's drool."

Cameron heard her name.

She saw Hailey Wyatt, wearing a navy business suit and heels.

"I came from a fundraising brunch at my mother-in-law's."

Cameron frowned.

"Don't ask."

"Are you a lawyer?" Rosa asked her.

"I'm a Homicide Inspector."

Rosa didn't make a comment, but Cameron was pretty sure a lot of people would have. Hailey, especially in a skirt, did not look like a cop, especially not one used to dealing with corpses.

"This is my sister, Rosa," Cameron said.

Hailey responded to that with one cocked eyebrow. "Let me find out what's happening." She went back to the desk and spoke in a low voice to the desk attendant. Cameron saw her pull her badge off the waist of her skirt and hand it to another skeptic. When the attendant seemed convinced that Hailey was who she said, she lifted a phone extension, dialed. After speaking to whoever had answered, passed the phone to Hailey. Hailey spoke with her back to Cameron and Rosa, then hung up.

She made her way over. Cameron could tell from her expression that Ivana was in no shape to give any account of what happened to her or who had paid her rent and why. "Okay—"

"How is Ivana?" Rosa interrupted. "Can we see her?"

Cameron tipped her head at Rosa and nodded, indicating that Hailey should tell Rosa about Ivana's condition.

"She's not awake right now," Hailey said, speaking with the flatness of someone who delivered exclusively bad news. "She hasn't been since they brought her in. Her condition is stable, so physically, she is out of the woods. It's just a matter of wh—when she wakes up."

Cameron heard the word Hailey hadn't said. Whether she wakes up.

"Can I see her?" Rosa asked.

"Sure," Hailey said. "I'd like to ask you a few questions. Can we do that first?"

Cameron glanced around. "Is there somewhere we can go?"

"I'll find a room where we can talk." Hailey was gone only a few minutes. Cameron tried to calm Rosa until Hailey returned, and they all moved to a small office and sat down.

"I'm going to take some notes, if that's okay."

Cameron studied Rosa, who nodded.

Hailey asked about Ivana, what she'd told Rosa about who she was, where she was from. Hailey asked her to confirm the information about Diego. Rosa paused.

"She's on our side," Cameron told her.

When Hailey was done, she looked back and forth between them. "You guys are really sisters?"

"Rosa was adopted," Cameron said, an old joke between them.

Rosa didn't crack a smile, and Cameron felt badly for joking. She touched her sister's hand. "We need to pick up Nate soon. Let's go see Ivana and Hailey can call if other questions come up."

Hailey skimmed over a page in her notebook as though another question was on the tip of her tongue, but she closed her book and stood. The three walked toward Intensive Care.

"She was pretty lucky," Hailey said as they made their way down the hall. "One of the other residents of the place came home and scared the guys off. Otherwise, I'm not sure she'd be here."

Rosa inhaled sharply. Cameron took her sister's hand as they stopped in front of a closed door.

"Was it one of the girls from her apartment?" Cameron asked.

Hailey shook her head.

These girls had suffered terribly, but she hated the idea that they didn't stick up for one another. She prayed one of them hadn't walked by Ivana without helping. Especially when the difference could mean life or death.

Hailey spoke to a uniformed security guard seated on a folding chair at the door. His name badge read R. Felton. Hailey showed her badge, and the three were admitted into the room with a tip of an invisible hat.

Rosa took a last backward look before entering. Cameron stayed close beside her. The room was larger and brighter than Cameron had expected.

There were no flowers on the bedside table, nothing personal. The woman Rosa had described wasn't a woman at all; she was like the girl from the dumpster—fourteen or fifteen at the oldest. She wore a dull white hospital gown with a small, green floral print. Her face and head were wrapped in bandages.

Rosa stopped.

"We don't have to do this now," Cameron told her, but Rosa insisted.

Cameron surveyed the damage. Her left arm was in a cast hung from a sling, and her right was wrapped in a bandage and set at her side. Whoever had attacked her had focused on her upper body. The police would come back to ask questions, but she wished Ivana was up to answering some now.

At the bedside, Rosa clasped the woman's hand.

Cameron watched Rosa's face.

"Boy Killer," Rosa said, running a finger over the girl's nails.

"What?" Hailey asked.

Rosa wiped her tears. "Boy Killer—it's the name of the polish I painted on her fingers last night." She motioned to Ivana's hands. "That's what she's wearing."

"So you're sure it's the woman you work with—Ivana?" Hailey asked.

Rosa tucked a strand of Ivana's hair behind her ear and cried. When she spoke, it was with a low rasp. "Positive."

CHAPTER 32

MONDAY FELT INTERMINABLE. Waiting for news from the hospital on Ivana's condition, waiting to hear from Hailey on any evidence about the attacker, and waiting on a break in Mei Ling's crazy schedule to meet and try to crack Diego's drive. It was more waiting than Cameron could take.

Worse, Rosa was distraught over Ivana's attack. Though they had sworn to keep this all from their parents, Mama had caught on. Now, she was planning a visit. After Nate's birth, Mama had come out for almost three weeks, and Papa had joined them for a week. Though Mama was back out again in March, it was hard to blame her for wanting to come again. She had four grandkids in Texas, but Nate was the newest and the one she saw the least. Still, the timing of her visit was awful. There was too much going on that would worry her sick.

Still, when Mama decided, there was no putting her off. Cameron had exactly twelve days to sort all this out before her mother arrived. Mei had planned to come by after work on Monday, but there was an emergency involving a high profile downtown bank and Mei was called in.

Ivana was awake for several hours over the course of Tuesday. Cameron felt the momentum of things again. She texted Hailey the news and hoped something would break. It was after ten p.m. when Mei texted that she was finished with work and heading home.

Cameron called her as she was putting on her jacket. "I'm staying with my aunt in the Richmond District, but she will be asleep for hours now, and she'll freak if I bring someone home. Especially a woman. My mother is worried enough about the move out here."

Cameron laughed. "I understand. Is there a place near the house that would work?"

"Actually, there's a wine bar called Blush on Castro between 17th and 19th. I stop there most nights for a glass and some food. It's pretty quiet on weeknights and the men are more interested in each other than in me, which is nice. Frankie usually saves me a spot in the back corner."

Cameron told Mei she was on her way and asked if she should bring a computer.

"Bring the drive. It shouldn't take too long. Most non-techies aren't as clever as they think they are."

Cameron arrived at Blush Wine Bar to a pretty full house. The jump drive tight in her hand, she worked her way through the crowd and found Mei hunched over a computer at the last table in the corner beside the kitchen doors. Mei had her back to the crowd and wore ear buds. Other than the glass of red wine and cheese plate beside her, she might have been at the library.

When Cameron sat down, Mei pulled out the ear buds. "Hi."

"I can't believe you can think with all the noise."

"You get used to it. I'm not always working when I'm here." She laughed at herself. "Yes, I am. Anyway, I have my Black Crowes," she added, touching her ear buds. "You have the jump drive?"

Cameron handed it over, and Mei slid it into the side of her computer without looking. While Mei worked, Cameron watched the crowd. She politely declined the waiter's offer of wine, while Mei ordered another. Occasionally, Mei reached over for a piece of cheese or bread, or took a sip of wine. The rest of the time her fingers flew across the keyboard like a concert pianist.

It was only a few minutes before she said, "I've got three of them. There's some serious encryption on these last ones. It's called Blowfish and I'll need a few computers to break it." Mei pushed the computer back so Cameron could see the screen.

"What's on the three you can open?"

"Let's take a look." Mei double-clicked on one and a spreadsheet loaded. The first column was a list that had to be people's names, first initial and last name.

Mei lifted her wine glass and was about to take a sip. "Whoa. Look at those names."

Cameron saw it, too. The list started with L. Chervoniy, V. Lavrinenko,

K. Novacek, R. Mahno… The surnames went on like that: Chaloupka, Juhno, Grabar, Popescu, Goncharenko, Moraru, Janak, Pesek. "Eastern European."

"Definitely," Mei agreed.

"It has to be the names of the women being trafficked."

Mei said nothing to that. Instead, she pointed across the columns. "These must be dates."

"Right. The date they were trafficked. The next column is the amount they owed or maybe what they've earned."

"I'd wager it's their debt. I can't imagine these guys keep accounting like this on earnings."

"Maybe not." Cameron pointed to the last column. "What about this?"

"Some kind of code," Mei said. "Alpha numeric, not dates. Maybe states? A lot of these are C's. California? Maybe the numbers are partial zip codes."

"What about the other files?"

Mei closed out the spreadsheet and opened another. It filled the screen. Cameron scanned a list of dates and dollar amounts.

After a moment, Mei whistled.

"What?"

She clicked through a series of sheets in the file. "This looks like a gambling ledger." She leaned in. "See how each page has a code in the top left corner? That's the gambler's code. Each page represents a different gambler." She scrolled right and displayed the line of tabs. "There are easily eighty or ninety."

"But, what makes you think it's gambling? Could be anything."

Mei clicked back to the first page. "We had a case like this in Chicago. These are obviously dates, and dollars." She clicked to the red and black numbers, "Winnings and losses. This last column, though. See these words."

"Shanghai, High Chicago, Queen, Texas. What are those?"

"Those are types of poker," Mei said.

Cameron had no idea how poker fit into the trafficking. "Are there any other files?"

"One more." Mei opened a third spreadsheet.

It was a list of dates and locations.

"*Sea Here Darling*, *Pesce King*—what are those?"

"Boats," Cameron said, feeling her pulse pick up. "Boats bringing in the women, I bet."

"Most are in the past," Mei commented, pointing to the dates.

"But that one is tomorrow," Cameron said, pointing to the *Pesce King*.

"That's right." She typed in a side bar. "*Pesce* is fish in Italian."

"I doubt these guys are Italian," Cameron said, getting antsy. "Anything else we can open?"

Mei shook her head. "Not yet." She pulled the jump drive out and handed it back to Cameron.

"You don't need to keep it?"

"I copied the unlocked ones onto the jump drive for you and duplicated the encrypted ones onto my drive," Mei said. "I'll get to work on them as soon as I get into the lab."

"Thanks."

"No problem." Mei closed her laptop and picked up her wine glass.

"You stay till they close?"

"No. I should be going before my aunt calls my mother." She sighed. "I need to find an apartment. Know anyone?"

"Actually, I do. Call Nicole Kennedy. She has a real estate company under her name."

"Thanks," Mei said.

Cameron nodded to the computer. "How long does it take to break the encryption?"

Mei paused. "It depends. A few hours to a few days."

Cameron tried to hide her disappointment.

"I'll work as fast as I can."

Cameron thanked her and walked back through the buzzing crowd. Instead of answers, she had more questions. Like, how the hell did a poker ledger fit in to a trafficking ring?

CHAPTER 33

WEDNESDAY MORNING, CAMERON woke early. She'd spent a lot of the night trying to figure out how she'd get the team to South San Francisco at four o'clock. A lot of it depended on what was on the schedule for today. If they had a recon going on or were called into a hostage situation, that boat might slip through her fingers.

Cameron didn't meet Lavick's eye in the morning meeting and pretended instead to be taking notes while he spoke. Holding his clipboard, he started into the day's assignments. Recon on a potential armed robbery gang holed up in a warehouse in Hayes Valley. "Lau, you and Kessler are lead on that." Cameron wrote that down to have something to do. "Daley, Ahrens has requested your help for the day."

To that, Cameron looked up. Daley was the worst misogynist of the group, and it was hard to imagine Captain Ahrens selecting to work with him on anything. Daley acted surprised, so maybe it was some sort of grunt detail. He didn't appear disappointed either, and the news didn't seem surprising to anyone else.

"Paules and Zagrafis, you two are joining Homicide on an early morning shoot out in Dog Patch." Lavick glanced up at the remaining officers. "The rest of you are on open patrol." When they weren't on a specific assignment, the Special Ops officers spent a good portion of their time roaming San Francisco as extra support for the patrol cops. They did everything from picking up parolees at large, to arrests and outstanding warrants, to enforcing traffic violations. Unlike regular patrol cops, though, they weren't tied to a particular area of the city. The Special Ops officers could respond to any call, so they tended to stay close to high-crime areas. They were rarely lacking for action.

Cameron and Ballestrini responded to a high-speed chase, an armed robbery at the San Francisco Jewelry Mart, and a rather nasty domestic call before taking a late lunch close to the Bryant Street Station. Ballestrini was in good spirits, talking about taking the family to see *Rock of Ages* at the Orpheum over the weekend. He was singing "Juke Box Hero" for most of the morning. At least it was a break from *Les Misérables* and *Grease*. One of his kids was applying to college, and he went on and on about which schools she was looking at and how his wife was going to take a little tour of some state schools with both kids. "They're only eighteen months apart. Might as well kill two birds, you know?"

Cameron tried to imagine what her life would be like when Nate was old enough to visit colleges. It didn't seem possible. By two thirty, things had slowed down a little. Ballestrini stopped for coffee. Cameron pretended to have a phone call, psyching herself up to lie to his face.

When he got back in the car with a steaming cup, he was humming "I Love Rock 'n' Roll."

She lowered the phone. "We've got a lead on a boat coming in."

Ballestrini frowned. "A lead from who?"

"Didn't give her name. A woman with a heavy accent—could have been Eastern European."

"She called your phone?"

Cameron nodded without answering. It was easier to lie if she didn't have to do it out loud.

"How'd she get your number?"

That was a great question. "I don't know, but she sounded legit."

Ballestrini pulled out his own phone and stared at it like he should have gotten the same call. "How would she have gotten that information?"

"Maybe she overheard someone talking."

He hesitated.

She tried to push him over the edge. "She gave me the name of the vessel—*Pesce King*. P-E-S-C-E."

He looked at her. "She spelled it out for you?"

Cameron stopped herself. "I'm guessing on the spelling."

"What is it? French?"

178

"Italian," she said. "For fish, I think." With a name like Ballestrini, it seemed like he might have known. But Ballestrini was about as Italian as Chef Boyardee.

He gestured to the clock on the dash. "We should check in."

That was the last thing she wanted. Surely, Lavick would call someone and reroute it. Or what if it wasn't coming in the first place? Her brothers always took every opportunity to show off. She hoped Ballestrini might do the same.

She took a breath and decided to play his ego. "We probably should. I hate to have Lavick round up the whole team if it's nothing. But, we can't handle this on our own. Not when it could turn into something dangerous like the incident with the truck. The sergeant would want to know what we were doing."

Ballestrini thought about that for a second.

Cameron leaned forward to pick up the radio.

Ballestrini caught her hand and pushed it back. "Maybe we ought to check out the location and all, make sure it's valid before we call in."

Cameron replaced the radio on the dash. "You're probably right," she said again.

"You want to take a pit stop?" he asked. "Might be our last chance for a while."

Cameron hated how he was always asking her if she had to use the bathroom, but since Nate's birth, it was like she always had to go. Cameron got out of the car and hurried toward the coffee shop's bathroom.

In five minutes, they were on the road. Ballestrini was quiet. Maybe calculating the boost his career would get from single-handedly catching a boat full of smugglers. Cameron's thoughts were on Diego. From the freeway exit, Cameron directed him toward the water.

"She gave you a street address?"

"She mentioned the UPS trucks. This has to be it," she lied.

Ballestrini peered around. "We're about a half hour early, but we'll need a spot to hide the black and white while we take a closer look."

They drove to the backside of the UPS building where there was a freight loading area and employee parking.

"This seems like a good spot," Ballestrini said.

From there, they could walk up a small grassy incline and see the water through a few planted trees. It was a great spot to watch from.

Cameron felt herself tense as Ballestrini parked. He popped the trunk, and they both got out.

Ballestrini put on his heavy vest. Cameron decided it wasn't a bad idea. Plus, the day was cold, and the wind off the water dropped the air temperature by ten to fifteen degrees. The vest would help keep her warm.

Ballestrini brought out a small black case that held binoculars and pulled the strap around his neck. He pointed to a similar-looking bag that held the camera. Cameron pulled it out of the trunk. They left the heavy weaponry in the car, and Cameron wondered if they'd need it. It would be the first time she'd been in full gear since her return.

The water was choppy and the white caps created a sea of little hats on the surface of the water. Ballestrini handed her the binoculars. "You want to try to find this *Pesce King*?"

She handed him the camera bag and brought the lenses of the binoculars close together, before pushing them to her nose.

Starting from the northern part of the bay, she scanned the water for boats. There weren't many. Like the other day in the Berkeley marina, it wasn't a good day for boating. A number of large tankers crossed the bay, but other boats were few and far between.

The first one she saw was a ferry crossing the bay north of them. She recognized the familiar blue and maroon striped logo on the side and the name *Peralta*. She and Rosa had ridden that same ferry from Jack London Square into San Francisco when Rosa had first moved to the Bay Area. Nothing else caught her attention, and yet, she couldn't shake the numbed certainty she felt in her gut. It was coming. This was happening. She sighed, trying to release the tension in her gut.

"It's early," Ballestrini said, mistaking her sigh for impatience. "Give it a minute."

Her muscles grew taut. She couldn't stay still. She handed over the binoculars and rolled her neck in slow circles. "Can I have the keys for a second?"

"You forget something?"

"I want to see if I brought my notes from the call," she said, an excuse to walk away if only for a moment.

He lowered the binoculars. "You have notes?"

Shit. "Keys?"

He patted both pockets before digging into his right one, pulling out the key ring, and tossing it to her.

She unlocked the trunk and checked inside. Everything was in its place.

"Call for backup," Ballestrini shouted. "There's a boat called the *Pesce King* moored to a buoy out there, couple hundred yards off. I can't see anyone on board."

Her fingers trembling slightly, she lifted the radio and made the call for backup. She hoped whatever was out there offered some evidence for the good guys because they needed some.

CHAPTER 34

CAPTAIN AHRENS AND Sergeant Lavick were in meetings at Bryant Street, so the next in charge, Ryan Lau, would pull together the troops. He contacted the Coast Guard for air and water backup and told Cameron to hold tight until they were given direction. Ballestrini kept watch while Cameron radioed with the team and set up a temporary headquarters. The wind had picked up and the skies were darkening. The boat remained anchored some two hundred yards offshore, which seemed odd.

It took over two hours before the team was assembled. Everyone was dressed in raid gear. Lavick arrived shortly behind them to give direction. He made a beeline for Cameron and asked sharp, pointed questions about her source. Cameron lied flatly, offering as little as possible to explain how she and Ballestrini had ended up there. The sergeant digested the story without much expression, but Cameron knew he'd swallowed every detail. She would need to repeat herself more than once over the next few hours or days. Oddly, she didn't feel tension from him. Maybe it was all a wild goose chase or perhaps she was wrong about Lavick.

The last piece to fall in place was the mode of transit that didn't look like a police boat. The Coast Guard came through with that. They were able to get approval to use a ferry from the Alameda/Oakland Ferry company. Within the hour, the team was shuttled north to a port out of the view of the boat to be loaded.

Captain Ahrens arrived as they were boarding the Coast Guard boat. She and Lavick stayed behind to man the situation along with four members of

ICE while the eight-member Special Ops team and a boat captain boarded the vessel.

"Remember," Lau started, pumping them up on the trip toward the boat. "Nuts to butts." His cheeks reddened. "Except you. Just the butt part for you."

"You love saying that, don't you?" she retorted, playing the game, although her mind was a million miles away. She thought about Nate. It was her first takedown since his birth. Those wide eyes, that tiny toothless smile. She'd never felt so vulnerable.

Because there was no way to do reconnaissance on the boat, the intelligence group had contacted the manufacturer to obtain the layout. That, in turn, was blown up, and a map of each SWAT member's course laid out. Each member would move with a partner to cover each other's backs. Cameron and her partner, Kessler, would take the downstairs aft compartment. She would buttonhook the door first while he covered, then he would cross while she covered. She watched Lau go over the plan again and again, until the monotony of repetition made it feel like she'd known it forever.

Lau and Paules would lead. No ram would be needed to get on board, but Lau would carry a weapon loaded with less-than-lethal. If he could, he'd drop the suspects with that. If not, they all had plenty of real ammo.

They checked and double-checked equipment. She had flash bangs on her right thigh, sting balls on her left. Both would be helpful in the lower cabin of a boat. She hoped she'd need neither. She crossed herself with a finger one last time, and thought of Nate and Rosa and Mama and Diego. She added an extra cross for Diego.

"Let's do it," Lau called out.

Nuts to butts, it was. The closer together they stayed, the safer they were. From there, they'd split up and search for their suspects based on the plan they'd agreed on beforehand.

At one nautical mile, the team lined up on the side hidden from view of the *Pesce King*. Cameron fell into succession between Ambley and Kessler. The tension was in every breath. For each of them. Though the cold wind whipped across them, sweat dripped down her back beneath the equipment and the extra layers of protection. She smelled the salt in the air, and it reminded her of blood. She'd never been much for the sea. The steady rocking of the boat did nothing to calm her nerves.

In her earpiece, she heard the call that they were within a minute of arrival. Every muscle in Cameron's body ratcheted tighter. She ignored the pain in her shoulder and the pull of the stitches under her glove and tucked the butt of the gun under her arm and held the muzzle cocked down slightly.

The final countdown started and before she knew it, the bodies were shuffling before her. The air filled with shouting. The first officer went below deck, the next following as cover. The next two went left, Cameron right, Kessler behind her. Voices shouted in the background, adding to the thumping of her heart and the stomping of feet to create an all percussion band.

She came around a corner and found Dino Zagrafis with John Paules. "All clear," Zagrafis said, a little pale. She wondered if he was remembering something from the war. But, before she could ask, he shook it off and kept moving.

She and Kessler cleared a final cabin and made their way back to the stairs with a close eye out for motion. Kessler leaned down the stairs and called out below. "Clear?"

Suddenly, there were harsh shouts and the pop of a single gunshot.

Kessler darted for the stairs. Cameron was right behind.

"It's a setup," someone else yelled. "They're all dead."

Cameron kept her gun drawn as a sick feeling rose in her gut. Below was dark with a steely smell that brought to mind a shark waiting to attack. Cameron moved slowly, following Kessler, covering, then moving again, covering, then moving. Finally, she saw Ambley from the back. His shoulders were hunched. His gun dropped to the floor.

Lau took him by the shoulders and leaned him against the wall, out of the line of fire. Cameron stepped inside the doorway, pressing herself against the wall as she surveyed the room.

At first, it looked like a pile of dirty clothes were strewn across the room. Quickly, the shapes took hold in her mind. There were bodies in the clothes—women. The dark stains were blood. The bodies were cast around the room as though slaughtered in some devastating fury. Knife wounds on necks and faces, a bullet on another until she had to turn away. She pictured Diego's dark eyes, his gaze holding hers in Mrs. Yee's store, and had to hold down the vomit.

The team was streaming into the room. Blood and some sort of mud surrounded their feet. The men were in shock. In their faces, she saw wives and daughters. Ballestrini's daughter would be going to college. She was this age. She scanned the room for him but was interrupted by Ahrens.

"Report your status ASAP," Ahrens called over someone's radio.

Cameron pressed the radio button on her shoulder. "Team is secure, Captain. There are no suspects. I repeat no suspects."

"The boat's empty?" her voice came back.

"No, ma'am." Her voice cracked as she spoke. She scanned the room again. "We've got twelve to fifteen bodies, Captain. All dead."

Ahrens cursed. "We heard gunfire," Lavick shouted.

Ambley raised his head. "I shot at her." He pointed to a woman lying closest to the door. "I thought they were suspects. I thought I saw a gun."

Beside the woman was a metal pipe, maybe the weapon she'd used to try to defend herself. Cameron watched the pool of blood growing beneath the bodies. "It's recent. They haven't been dead long."

How had this happened? Did someone know that she'd broken into the drive? She hadn't told anyone. Or maybe someone had spotted her and Ballestrini staking out the boat.

"Double check the premises for any suspects," Lavick directed. "Then, hold it down. We've got the Coast Guard bringing in a crime team."

"Yes, sir," Lau responded.

Pushing herself off the wall, Cameron headed back into the hallway to help secure the boat. As Lau gave orders, she tried to drown out the voice in her head that told her this was her fault.

She forced herself onward, knowing she had to own up to Ahrens. About Diego, about the DVD with Lavick. All of it.

CHAPTER 35

IVANA HAD NEVER hurt so much in her life. The visits from Rosa and Wanda had done a lot to lift her spirits. The rest of the time she slept between the visits from the nurses and the two policewomen. The smaller, curly-haired policewoman came with a picture of Diego that Ivana would have liked to keep, but instead, she told the officer that he was the man who had helped her. When they asked if he was her boyfriend, she blushed terribly and said no.

On another visit, Inspector Wyatt took her back through the strip club, her rape. An older woman with long gray braids sat at a computer and drew the men as Ivana described them in her broken English. It didn't seem possible, but when she was done, the drawing was almost as real as a photograph. At the end of that visit, Inspector Wyatt also brought her a piece of fabric. Ivana recognized it as Anna's. She fingered the small square of pink cotton. Anna was dead, Inspector Wyatt told her. Ivana clutched the fabric and cried.

They had also talked about her most recent assault. With that, she was almost no help. She had been singing when she walked in the door of the building. Her attacker was average height and build. He spoke to her, or she thought he did, but she couldn't remember anything he'd said. The doctors said that was normal, but Ivana really wanted to help the police. She was lucky to be alive. If not for the woman who had come into the building after her, she'd probably be dead. As much as Ivana tried, none of it came back.

Once, when Michal was first in school, some older boys had beaten him up. He'd only remembered one of their faces, saying the others had come from behind. He'd been unable to remember what happened after the first few punches. Ivana had always doubted the story, thinking he was too scared to identify all three boys. Now, it made sense to her. Alone in the hospital, the hardest thing was not to let her thoughts drift to Mama and Michal.

Rosa and Cameron both told her that she ought to call home to tell her mother that she was all right. The more she thought about it, the more she knew they were right. She didn't know if she'd go home or not, but it wasn't fair to make her mother worry. Plus, she desperately wanted to know that Michal was okay.

She was due to get out of the hospital in a few days. She would stay with Rosa for a bit and decide what to do. Despite all that had happened in her stay, Rosa's kindness had done a lot to help Ivana consider staying in America. Things weren't much better at home. Working for Rosa in the salon would certainly be better than any job she could get in Šluknov, especially at her age.

The door opened. "You awake?"

"Yes, Mr. Rusty," she answered, recognizing the voice of the guard the police had put outside her door.

He was a nice man named Rusty. "Rusty Felton," he'd said, tipping his head like he was wearing a hat. It made her laugh, which hurt. He'd only stayed a few minutes that first time, but he came back a few times a day before he went to lunch or for coffee. He offered to bring her something. Even though she had said she was fine, he came with a chocolate chip cookie on her third day. "I checked with the doctor," Rusty told her. "He said it was okay."

Mr. Rusty appeared from behind her privacy curtain. "I am going to get a little coffee. You want anything?"

"No. Thank you."

"Okay. Won't take me but fifteen minutes."

"When you come back, Mr. Rusty, maybe you can tell me a story?"

While she ate her cookie, Mr. Rusty had told her about a time that he was stuck in a canoe for fourteen hours because there was a grizzly bear and her cubs on the shore where he was going to take his boat.

"You bet," he said. "I'll think of a good one. Be right back."

Mr. Rusty left and the nurse came in to give her something to help her rest. She could hear them at the nurse's station, talking, chuckling or sometimes singing. The sounds had become familiar and she was close to sleep when the door opened.

She squinted at the curtain that surrounded her bed and waited for it to open, but it was quiet. She blinked hard, trying to stay awake.

"Hello," she said, listening for a response. "Mr. Rusty?"

No one answered.

She closed her eyes, ready for sleep. A shadow crossed the room. She sat up, but before she could speak, a heavy hand covered her mouth.

The face she saw startled her.

"Shh. Don't scream, please," the man said.

He was not one of the attackers from the bar. She began to feel more relaxed. Still, his presence made her uneasy, and she wished he would leave. Where had she seen him? She thought he was one of the men she'd seen on the street near the salon, maybe inside once or twice. He wore a police uniform now. She couldn't remember if he'd been in one before.

"You haven't told your friends or that other cop anything yet?"

She shook her head.

He slowly removed his hand.

"I no remember. I try, but I don't know," she said.

"That's good. You don't remember anything because if you do, I'll kill your friends before I come after you."

Ivana tried to sit up in bed, but he pressed her back down, his hands like vises on her arms. She opened her mouth, but he clamped a hand down on her. She studied his uniform. "You are police."

"That's right. There are lots of us. And if you don't do exactly what I say, we will hurt Rosa and her sister, too. Do you understand?"

She nodded quickly, her heart pounding. Why was he doing this? Why would the police hurt her? She felt herself starting to cry, wishing someone would come in and save her. But no one did. She would never be saved. She longed for her mother. She had been right. Ivana should never have dreamed of coming to America.

The man shook her. "Listen to me."

She fought back tears.

"If you care about your friends, you'll stay silent. I'll send instructions for you. As soon as you are released from the hospital, you follow those instructions and everyone will be fine."

"I will. I promise."

"But, if you talk about this to anyone, I'll come for your friends and you." His smile made her shudder.

Sobs choked her. She let them out in a shaky burst.

"Do you understand?"

Trembling, she nodded again.

"Good girl. I'll leave you instructions."

"Wh-where?"

"You'll get them when it's time. Tell anyone, and you'll all be dead."

He gripped her neck and she clawed at his hands. He was strong, much stronger than she. She begged for someone to come in, to see him, but no one did. "You won't forget?"

She shook her head.

"Good." He removed his hand from her neck.

Her eyes felt heavy and yet her heart was galloping, the drugs and the adrenaline fighting one another.

"Watch yourself." He disappeared behind the curtain. The door opened and closed again.

She waited, shaking, listening. A TV played in a room nearby. Ivana concentrated to try to hear it, listening intently for any sounds. Exhausted, she rolled on her side and cried. Eventually, the drugs took over, and she fell into a dead sleep.

CHAPTER 36

THE WEIGHT OF the dead women settled in to Cameron. She smelled them in her clothes and hair, saw their distraught faces, bloody and beaten when she blinked. She felt their horror as they watched each other die. It was obvious others felt the same. There were no jokes in the equipment room, none of the banter that usually accompanied this time of day. There were a few murmured exchanges about grabbing a drink, but most passed.

All of them needed someone to talk to about what had happened. None would actually discuss it. That's what this life was like—you absorbed it all, let it go in tiny ways here and there, hoping the emotion dissipated enough that you didn't explode. One of them would. One always did. Jamie Vail had, as well as Michael Lindberg of IA, who opened an investigation on any cop who looked sideways at him. Cracked. Some repaired, some didn't. Cameron could feel them in herself—the tiny fractures like a hot desert ground in the sun. That's what they were. Eventually, without enough irrigation, they would all crack.

Cameron spoke to no one. The usual camaraderie was noticeably absent. Even Kessler, who usually made it a point to say good night, avoided her. No one had cast blame, but she felt it anyway.

She wrestled her bag into its spot, shaking off Lau's attempt to help her. The weight of it dug into her shoulder and back as she pushed it up, but the pain was welcome—something to distract her from the grief, the isolation.

As she was gathering her things, Ballestrini came in to the locker room.

"Where the hell were you?" Ambley shouted at him.

Cameron was startled. She'd never seen Darren Ambley angry. The team medic, he often played the role of mediator and counselor for the group as well.

"What the hell are you talking about?" Ballestrini barked back.

"You weren't behind me. On the boat."

"Like hell I wasn't, prick."

"You were supposed to have my back," Ambley said.

"I did have your back," Ballestrini snapped. "You're pissed because you shot the only one who was still breathing."

Ambley charged toward him. Kessler stepped between them. "Take it easy, guys. Ballestrini got on the boat. We were all there."

Ambley pointed his finger in Ballestrini's face. "Well, if he got on, he disappeared after that. I got down to that room and he wasn't with me."

"I saw him behind you," Daley said. "Ballestrini's right. You're just pissed you blew your load on a half-dead chick," he added as he left the room.

"Fuck you, Daley," Ambley yelled after him.

Lau turned his back on them. Cameron acted busy.

Kessler pushed Ambley back toward his locker. "Everyone, cool off."

Ballestrini walked to his locker, mumbling under his breath.

Ambley moved toward Lau. "Check out his shoes," he whispered. "We're all covered in muck and blood from the boat and look at his."

Cameron glanced over at Ballestrini's shoes, then at her own. He'd definitely been on the boat with them, but his shoes were clean.

Lau, too, checked Ballestrini's shoes. He nodded to Ambley, and Cameron caught his eye. He clearly thought something was off. Ballestrini puffed his chest out like a peacock. "What? You guys believe this guy? It's a load of crap. I was there, same as the rest of you." He slammed his locker and left.

Cameron waited a minute, then headed out herself. As she made her way toward the bay, she caught sight of Ahrens coming out of the ladies' room.

She picked up the pace to a jog. "Captain Ahrens," she called out as the captain turned toward her office.

"Yes, Cruz?"

Cameron reached her and checked over her shoulder. No one was around. "Do you have a minute?"

"Of course—" Ahrens motioned to her office.

Ahrens watched her with an inquisitive gaze. She didn't act suspicious.

Was it possible that all this was happening in a vacuum around the captain? Cameron didn't know how much to share, but she had to say something.

When Ahrens walked into her office, someone stood up from a chair. Cameron saw Daley.

He held up a file. "I've got that report." When he saw Cameron, his expression seemed to harden.

Ahrens motioned to Cameron. "I am going to sit down with Cruz for a few minutes."

Daley didn't budge, his lips drawn and thin. "This won't take more than five minutes."

Ahrens watched him and blinked. Cameron stared. Was this his way of telling her off for being the one to call them to that boat? When Ahrens looked back at her, so did Daley. He raised his eyebrows in an expression that told her to back down.

"No problem," Cameron said, feeling more flustered than she hoped showed. "We can talk when you're done."

"You can wait around. It'll only be five minutes."

Daley nodded, smugly. "Maybe ten."

Ahrens glared at him, and he quickly sat down.

"I'll be in the bay." Cameron looked down at Daley's frumpy navy blazer. The first button hung by a thread. "You're going to lose a button," she said, the best comeback she could come up with. Pathetic.

As she made her way to the bay, she thought about the exchange. Daley was a pig and played hardball occasionally, especially if Cameron had outdone him in some way. But as long as you didn't cross him, he was a team player, certainly not nasty or vindictive the way some guys on the sharpshooter squad were. And yet, he was clearly angry with her. She wanted to dismiss him as an asshole, but he had a right to be angry for today.

Cameron disassembled her rifle and cleaned and oiled each component before reassembling it. The barrel slid smoothly into place and Cameron returned the gun to its case. Ahrens hadn't appeared so Cameron shined her shoes, too. When she was done, the smells of gun oil and shoe polish were pungent on her skin. She washed her hands twice to try to lose the smell and headed back into the main building with her equipment bag. Ahrens' office was dark, the door locked. She smacked the wall beside it. "Damn it." The locker room was empty as she put away her bag and headed for the parking lot.

It was after seven when Cameron revved up the Blazer and pulled onto the pitted Naval Station road. Her anger was directed at Daley. "Bastard," she said out loud, and tore up the road, driving too fast. Her phone slid onto the floor on the passenger side and landed with a thunk.

She needed a release. An hour at the gun range, which she wouldn't get for another week. Maybe a long hard run. Or one of those boot camp classes she used to take at the gym. Something to wring out all the anger. Maybe some music. She leaned across to grab her phone off the floor but the seat belt froze. She unlatched the belt. She checked the phone's screen, grateful it wasn't broken.

As she was pulling her seatbelt back across her chest, she was kicked forward. Metal crunched around her. She was stunned. What had she hit? There was nothing in front of her. In the rearview mirror, she saw a car, lights off. She pulled to the side when it rammed her again. The force of the blow threw her forward, her cheek smacking into the knuckles that gripped the wheel.

The car's headlights went on and Cameron sped up, reaching for her belt again. The car moved up on the passenger side and swung into her again. The belt stuck. She tried to pull it across her body, but there wasn't enough slack to fasten it. She let it go again, using both hands to swerve away from the car. With the headlights bright in her mirror, she couldn't make out anything about the car, other than it was a sedan. Her pulse a drumroll in her ear, she tried to calm herself enough to make a plan. She eased the belt out again but then jerked on it too fast. Again, it stopped.

Holding her breath, Cameron slowed down, forcing herself to watch as the vehicle got closer. When the car was ten feet away, she jammed the accelerator to the floor. Rocks and pebbles flew up behind her as her back tires swerved before gaining traction. She narrowly missed being slammed again. As she accelerated, she reached across and pulled the seatbelt out, warring with the desire to pull fast. She managed to get it latched.

Still gaining speed, she palmed around on the floor behind her seat for her purse with her gun and her phone. She couldn't feel them. She reached toward the other side, but the car caught up and slammed into her rear.

Her back window shattered. Her arm was wrenched backward as her body flew forward. The seatbelt snapped against her ribs. Her injured shoulder screamed, but the car didn't let up. Cameron floored it to keep distance between them. It was only a mile until they were out of the naval station. She had to make a quick decision about where to go.

The road in the naval station was almost always quiet. She wasn't going to get any help once she was outside its gates either. Out there, she had to deal with the projects if this guy ran her off the road. A Caucasian woman in these parts was not going to go unnoticed after dark.

Her best chance was either to turn around and get back inside the Bay, or to make it to the freeway. Inside the naval station, there wasn't a place to make a good loop without giving her pursuer a chance at her head-on.

Her heart pounding, Cameron started up the hill and shifted into second, listening to the engine rage as she picked up speed. She blew by the guard post, ready to honk for help, but it was empty. Where the hell was the guard? Pressing the accelerator to the floor, she spun out of the station onto North-ridge Road. The car bottomed out. A truck swerved to miss her, blaring his horn. The other car sped around the truck, too. He was on her tail again.

The streets grew busier. In front of her was a low-ride Camaro or maybe a Trans Am, cruising. Cameron didn't slow down. Pushing sixty, she darted into oncoming traffic, bearing down on another car to pass the sports car. She swung back into her lane as the other car passed. Behind her, the sedan was blocked momentarily, but not long enough.

The freeway overpass was three blocks ahead, shining like freedom. Between her and it was a red light. A sixteen-wheeler barreled through the intersection as Cameron considered running the light. She pumped her brakes with both feet, sending her car skidding left. The sedan was coming straight for her door, fast.

She stomped on the pedal. Screeching tires filled her head. Burnt rubber stuck in her nose. She flinched and rammed her foot down on the pedal. Nothing happened. She pumped it again and closed her eyes for impact. The Blazer responded to the accelerator, and the car jerked forward. She opened her eyes and gripped the wheel as she crossed the double yellow lines and stopped under the bright light of a Chevron station. She swung around in the seat, searching for the other car, but it had turned the other way. All she could make out were two red taillights burning in its path.

There was a knock on the door and she started in her seat. She saw a large man at the driver's side window. "You okay?"

He was black and young, in his late twenties or early thirties, and she did what she always did when her pulse was outworking her brain. She judged him by the statistics—a black man, young, in this neighborhood. She found herself fingering the door lock as he stepped back, his hands up. "Hey, lady. Chillax. I was only checking on you," he said, his voice resonating through the glass.

Cameron watched him shake his head, and she hung her own, knowing how she'd acted. She, of all people, was supposed to know better than to judge people by their skin. Goddamn it. She watched the man getting into his car and considered going after him. But, there was nothing to say. Instead, she dialed the police's nonemergency number to report the incident.

On hold, she revved the engine and steered the car onto the road toward home. She recited the events of the evening to one of her colleagues—not someone she knew, just someone taking down notes for another case. Another case to be opened. Twelve opened for every one closed—was that the statistic she heard?

Suddenly, she was exhausted. Depressed, scared, sad, but too tired to pinpoint which one stood out the most.

CHAPTER 37

IT WAS SATURDAY night, and Luis missed Candi. He'd called her a bunch of times, but she never called him back. He'd left a message that he had the money he owed her, hoping he might get to see her that way. But, she'd sent another woman to pick it up. That woman hadn't given him the time of day.

Aside from Candi, he really hadn't met anyone in America. His nights off had been spent with her and his days off in front of the television. At least, when he'd been getting free cable. He'd had a hundred channels and all sorts of great porn. To make matters worse, they'd shut his cable off. He didn't want to cough up the sixty bucks it would cost him to get the same channels again. He appreciated money more after spending days living on the beans he'd bought with six dollars, the change he found under the couch cushions and leftovers from whatever they fed the girls.

He found himself calling home more, which wasn't like him at all. And his wife was almost never home. How was she doing without him? Better, probably. Even his boys barely talked to him when he called. She'd probably poisoned them against him. He'd finally called one of his brothers-in-law to check up on everything. Paulo had insisted that Laura was fine and happy and that nothing had changed. Luis thought that sounded all wrong.

She hadn't been fine and happy when he was there. She'd been a nagging, whining bitch. So, things were different. He'd have to go home for a visit soon. He hadn't made a trip yet. While she'd bothered him about it all the time the first couple of weeks, she almost never asked now. Something was definitely not right with that. He was writing his pages as though they were letters to her. Letters he would never mail, could never show anyone.

The more he wrote, the more he realized that America wasn't so different from Mexico—colder, not so dry. But the same. People were mean and cruel, or stupid. Like him. He wrote, "Soy estupido." He signed it like he always did and folded it up to take to the bank. That was his only treat—going to his safety deposit box. The people at the bank had looked at him strangely, but they couldn't do anything. It was his box. He had paid for it. They told him the first day that he could come and go as often as he liked, so he did.

He studied the clock and thought about what he would do after the bank. He wasn't going to sit in another Saturday night by himself. That was for sure. He'd been paid and with no one to spend money on, he had a wad of it built up. Tonight, he was going to find himself a new Candi. He tried to be positive about it, but his latest realization—that he was stupid—made him wonder if it was a good idea.

He told himself he needed a little fun and forced himself to dress in his best shirt. The shirt, a plaid-button down from Old Navy, desperately needed ironing, so he smoothed it out with his damp palms, hoping to take some of the wrinkles out. He put on the cleanest pair of khakis he had and doused some aftershave he'd bought at the drugstore on his cheeks, flinching as it burned his skin. Using a little gel, he smoothed his hair back and took a look at his complexion. He sucked in his gut, which was bigger than when he'd arrived in America, and checked his profile. Not bad. Certainly not bad enough to get dumped by some floozy like Candi. Her loss, he told himself out loud, pulling the wad of bills from his pocket and flipping through it. Close to four hundred dollars. He knew better than to take it all and tucked half in with his letter for the bank and pocketed the rest.

He pulled the bottle of Maker's out from under the sink where he'd left it the night before. He picked up the cup from the side of the sink, sniffed it quickly and poured four fingers of whiskey into it. Downing it in two full gulps, he felt it burn its way down to his belly. He loved the taste of whiskey, especially since he could drink it without his wife's constant bothering. She hated the smell. Her brothers all drank tequila. As far as she was concerned, that was the only acceptable liquor. But it was so Mexican. Whiskey was more American. He didn't want to come across as some dumb Mexican when he drank in America.

He poured himself another glass and made a mental note to try to save enough money from the two hundred to get another bottle tomorrow. And food.

His head light, he thought about the bitch who had robbed him and wondered if he'd ever see her again. He wasn't sure he would recognize her. One thing was for sure. He was buying his own drinks tonight. He took a last look at himself in the mirror and headed out with his money, his writing, and two keys—one to his apartment and one to his deposit box.

He walked the three blocks to the bank and made his deposit a few minutes before it closed. The old biddy who worked Saturdays gave him a nasty sneer and made a comment about the smell of booze. What the hell. It was Saturday.

In an effort to show her that he wasn't some bum, he hailed a cab in front of the bank and told the driver to take him to the ORG Lounge, a place Marty talked about. If Marty could get some there, surely he could too. Luis watched the meter the whole ride over and by the time they reached the bar, it was almost twelve dollars. He had a bad pit in his stomach as he shelled out the twelve dollars plus a dollar tip. The bus would have taken longer, but it would have given him twelve more dollars toward drinks.

He was thinking about the spent money when he sat down at the dark bar and ordered a Dewar's on the rocks from a big bald guy behind the bar. He found an empty chair facing the stage and watched the women dance. One of them had breasts the size of watermelons. She watched him as she pressed herself against a pole on the edge of the stage, one melon on each side. What would it be like to be in bed with melons like that?

Candi had decent size breasts, certainly bigger than Laura, whose breasts always seemed like an extension of her belly. Even if she'd had any breasts, his wife wouldn't have let him enjoy them. She never let Luis suckle her breasts. She said they were for babies. So prissy. No wonder he was obsessed with boobs.

Just then, the melon woman crossed the stage to a man shelling out bills. They looked like twenties. Luis couldn't stop staring. The man was vaguely familiar. Maybe he'd been in the warehouse or something. The idea made him uncomfortable. He picked up his glass and made his way back to the bar. Over his shoulder, he noticed the man watching him. He hoped he wasn't in trouble. He finished his drink. Maybe coming to a place Marty frequented wasn't such a good idea after all.

He felt a little drunk as he set his glass down and walked unsteadily to the door. He hit the street, swaying a little on his feet. He leaned against the building and thought about getting home. He didn't have the slightest idea which way to go since he'd taken a cab and hadn't paid any attention.

He turned to his left, the direction the cab had come from and took a few steps. Damn, he was drunk. Twenty feet down the street, a homeless man pissed against the building. That was pathetic. He staggered a couple feet and stopped.

He thought about the woman with the melons. He wanted to go back inside. He thought about the man in the bar. He didn't want to bump into him again, but there were a lot of people. He started for the door when a woman walked out. "Hi," she said, pulling a cigarette out of her purse.

"Hi." He hesitated at the door.

"You need some company?"

She wasn't as skinny as Candi, but she had good boobs. She wore a sheer red top and a black skirt. She had straight, blond hair that poured over her shoulders, and bright red lipstick. He couldn't make out her face in the dark, but she was pretty enough.

"Sure," he finally said. The last thing he wanted was to be alone tonight.

"You want to buy me a drink?" she asked.

Not really, he thought, but this was part of the game. "Sure. What would you like?"

"Whatever you're having."

A woman who drank liquor, that was a nice change. She led him back inside to a stool at the far end of the bar. The man was still down by the stage. She sat on the stool beside him and crossed her legs, so that her knees rested against his thigh. He felt himself get aroused as he tried to get the bartender's attention.

He ordered two drinks.

She asked him about himself. Candi never asked him about him.

She touched his leg. "What do you do?"

Relaxing, he covered her hand with his. "Importing."

She leaned forward and touched his cheek. "Sorry. You had something on your face."

He felt buzzed and happy, almost deliriously happy. He was so thankful.

"So you work in importing, huh? That sounds cool. What do you import?"

"Labor." The word slipped from his tongue. The man had described their business that way. He shouldn't have said it, though.

But the woman didn't even blink. Her hand crept up his thigh. "You mean, you import people?"

He felt himself grow excited. "Yeah, mostly women." He told himself to shut up, but her hand was distracting him.

He finished his drink and they ordered another. They kept talking. He didn't normally like to talk, but she was so nice. It was like she actually cared what he did. They finished their drinks. He searched for the bartender, but he was nowhere in sight.

He wanted to get another drink, to keep the buzz going.

"You want to go get a bottle and have a private celebration?" the woman asked. "I know a liquor store around the corner."

Luis studied the woman and licked his lips. "Yeah, okay."

"You have some money?"

He thought about the wad in his pocket, thankful he'd only spent twenty of it. "Some."

"Okay." She got down off the stool.

"Uh, how much?" he asked.

"For the liquor?" she asked with a coy smile.

He smiled back, feeling warm and frisky. She was good. "For the night."

"A night with me?"

He let his gaze rest on her breasts. He could see their sharp points through her top. He couldn't wait to feel them on his tongue. Anxious, he hoped he could afford her.

"One hundred and twenty-five, and I'll throw in the liquor."

That was a lot, but it left him money for food. Maybe he'd get to keep what they didn't drink of the bottle. "Okay," he said, reaching into his pocket.

"Wait until we're outside." Before he could speak again, she was heading for the door.

He followed quickly, his step lighter than it had been in days. He watched her butt under the tight, black skirt, thinking how it was going to feel under his hands.

They walked out into the cold night air, and he glanced down at the homeless guy he'd seen before.

She walked several feet from the door and stopped. "I've got a car. This way." She put her hand out. "Pay up front."

He had been tricked before. He wasn't going to let it happen twice "I'll give you half now, but the rest after." He felt himself swell with pride. He was no dummy.

She shrugged. "Fine."

He pulled the wad from his pocket and stripped three twenties off the stack. "Sixty now, the rest later. And a tip, if you're good."

Looking satisfied, she tucked the money down inside her bra. "Believe me, I'm good." Putting her arm through his, she led him down the street.

He sucked in the cool air so different than Mexico's. A tune from the radio was playing in his head. He wanted to sing out loud. He was going to get some.

Halfway down the block, she paused before they reached the police cruiser. "Where's your car?"

She reached into her jacket and pulled out a gun. "Right there."

He glanced at the gun, his mouth drying up. "What?"

"I'm a police officer, and you're under arrest for solicitation."

Another cop emerged from a police car and walked toward him, swinging a pair of handcuffs.

Luis thought about Brad and Marty and the notes he'd been keeping. "Wait!" he blurted out.

The cop cuffed him.

"But, I have information!"

"Right," the one cop said, and pushed him into the back of the cruiser.

"No, it's true. There's a group that sells women. For sex," he rattled on, the buzz of the liquor hitting hard. "They bring them in by the boatloads."

The woman cop turned back to him. "You better not be shitting us."

"I'm not. I swear. They import them like drugs."

As the police cruiser pulled away from the curb, Luis pictured Marty's dead body, covered in flies, and wished he was the homeless guy pissing on the building.

CHAPTER 38

CAMERON LAY IN bed. It was impossible to sleep and too late to call Hailey Wyatt. News would probably get back to her soon enough. A story of someone gunning down a police officer in her car would spread quickly. Ricky no longer seemed trustworthy. That left only Hailey Wyatt.

Cameron's eyes closed, and she squeezed the lids shut, feeling the pressure mounted behind them release for an instant. She was tired and pushing herself too hard. She needed to rest. She focused on images of Nate, hoping he could keep her head clear. She pictured his smile, then saw the ocean behind him. Nate always led her to Diego, but she pushed him away, rolling onto her side. She was not going to think about him. Tonight, she needed rest. Her head felt heavy as she tucked her hands up under her chin and let herself drift off.

The waves were crashing against the rocks, the spray rising like white foam against the crisp bright sky.

She woke to the sound of something slapping. She sat up in bed, startled, and listened. She had to blink several times before the images of her room crystallized from blurry forms to recognizable landmarks.

Slap. Slap.

Her shoulder ached as she pulled herself out of bed and moved across the room. She listened before touching the door. Slap. Whish. Slap. The wind, she thought. Something outside. She pulled her gun down from the closet shelf and checked the magazine.

Poised to respond, she opened the door and stepped into the hallway, her back to the wall.

Her pulse thumped the heavy drumbeat of adrenaline. She opened Nate's door and peered into his crib. He was snoring lightly, his room quiet.

Back in the hall, she walked to the kitchen where the noise originated. At the end of the hall, she looked both ways and listened for the noise again. Swat.

She moved into the entryway, which had a coat closet on one side and a small window on the other. There, slapping against the small window was a small Japanese maple tree, swaying in the wind, smacking its branches against the pane.

Cameron was exhausted. She moved toward her bedroom when a hand clapped over her mouth. "Shh."

The pounding of her heart filled her ears. She tried to dig her heel into the foot behind her.

"It's me." The arms released her and Cameron turned around, the gun tight in her hand.

Diego raised his arms.

"I could have shot you."

"Sorry. I tried tapping on your window but you must've been sleeping hard."

"How did you get past the alarm?"

"I deactivated it. The code is still Rosa's anniversary with Ricardo."

It was true. They hadn't changed the code since they'd first moved in. Cameron released the magazine from her gun and checked the chamber for a round. Then, she set the gun down.

Diego closed the space between them. "I heard you got the location off the drive. Did you find them?"

She rubbed at the aches in her back. She couldn't do this.

He grabbed her arm. "What happened? No one's talking about it. What was on that boat?"

She struck her palms hard against his chest, knocking him back. "They were dead. They were all dead, Diego. Every single woman. Slashed and shot. Dead."

He looked sunken. "Oh, Jesus. Jesus Christ. Somehow, they knew you got it. What else was on the drive?"

"A ledger of gambling debts and a list of women who are probably being sold for sex right now. If they're not already dead."

"Gambling debts?" Diego whispered.

She pounced. "Who knew? Who are you working for? What bastards are behind this? Because I swear to you, Diego, I'm not going to rest until the whole lot of them is under water. Do you hear me? I'm going to hang you out—all of you."

"That's what I'm counting on. I need you, Cameron. I want them to pay for this as much as you do."

Those women were burned in her mind as she turned away from him. He took her arm and pulled her back. Every time his skin met hers, it was like an electric shock. "Was there anything else on the drive?" he pressed.

"Two other files, but they were heavily encrypted. We haven't gotten into them yet."

Diego crossed to the living room and perched on the arm of the couch. Arms crossed, he stared at the floor. The same way he always did when he was working through a problem. It was like nothing had changed. Nothing and everything.

"What's going on, Diego? What did you do?"

"I didn't kill those people, Cameron."

He sounded so sincere, so upset, so needy. She focused on the door, trying to block him from invading her senses. And yet, she could already feel it happening. His smell, his voice. God forbid he touch her again. "What about the other ones? What about the woman at the strip club? The one from the dumpster?"

"I didn't kill any girls."

"You were there. They found your prints, Diego."

"I took a girl out of that place. I brought her to safety. I even—"

"Why, Diego? How did you end up there? How did you find her?"

"I need you to trust me," he said.

She didn't meet his gaze. "How can I?"

"I've made mistakes, but I am trying to do the right thing."

She tried to conjure an image of him that was someone different from the Diego she knew—a dirty cop who gave in to the lure of money, who had to resort to murder to protect himself from being caught. Watching him, listening to his voice, it didn't seem possible. His voice was steady, but unsure. His eyes met hers, and he felt like the same Diego. Even the collar of his shirt was tucked under like always. She had to hold herself from reaching out to fix it. That's when things would become too real. She couldn't handle that. "The mistakes are so big, Diego. You can't make them go away."

"I can't undo what I've done, but I need to find a way to make things right."

She shook her head. "How can you make things right for the people who loved Ray Benjamin?"

"Ray Benjamin was a bastard, Cameron. He was the worst of them all. He was going to take that money and disappear. I had to stop him."

"So you could have it? So you could give it to your son as some sort of attempt to buy affection from us?"

He clasped his chest as though she'd physically hurt him. "Is that what you think?"

"Go," she pleaded, feeling weaker with every moment.

His face was close and she could hear the rasp of his breath, feel it against her cheek.

"Don't," she whispered.

But, he did. He pulled her close, and closed his mouth on hers. It was soft at first and sweet, like a fruit she'd never tasted before. And then, his tongue was there, pushing, begging for her to let go. She tried not to. She tried to push him away, but she couldn't. His fingers wound through her hair, his body pressed to hers. And the tears streamed down her face as she kissed him back. Immediately, she was drawn back into their world from a year ago.

From the distance, Nate cried.

He pulled back almost as fast as she did, his ear cocked down the hall. He licked his lips as they stood awkwardly. "Is that—"

She wiped her mouth as though she'd just eaten something that may have dribbled down her face. His kiss burned her mouth.

"Can I see him?" Diego's gaze on her with a longing she'd never seen, even for her.

She couldn't do this. She couldn't let him back in.

"Please," he begged. He held his stomach. She knew that feeling. She couldn't imagine being kept from her son, but she would do everything in her power to protect Nate.

"I swear I've done everything by the book, Cameron," he told her. "I've never lied. They've been setting me up. Not just me, though. Someone else, too. It's so deep, I don't understand it yet. Use everything I've given you. Help me get to the bottom."

She steeled herself. She wouldn't get sucked in. This was not an emotional decision. "I don't know, Diego."

"Please, Cameron. You're the only person in the world I can trust."

Like they were partners again. How could she walk away? "I will do what I can, Diego. But, right now, you have to go." She forced herself to step past him, to open the front door. Trembling, she motioned him out. "Please leave, Diego. Please."

He moved slowly, almost staggering toward the door. She could feel his exhaustion, both of theirs, in her bones. He turned back. "You have to watch your back, Cameron. You can't trust anyone. No one."

She was suddenly cold at the thought of who might be involved. "I won't."

She closed the door on him before he could say anything more. She set the alarm and went into Nate's room. He had fallen back asleep, so Cameron lay down on the daybed, trying to ignore the stream of tears that rushed down her face and the silent sobs that rattled her chest.

CHAPTER 39

CAMERON HAD NEVER seen the tension in Special Ops so high. None of them had seen something like on that boat. They'd done everything by the book. The fact that the women were dead, and the only live one had been shot and killed, hit them all hard. Especially Ambley. Lavick and Ahrens were in meetings at Bryant, so the team was left to the Internal Affairs vultures who were picking over the carcasses of that day.

As was protocol, everyone was interviewed individually by two IA officers. Cameron was interviewed last, because she'd had to pick up a rental car on the way to the naval grounds. Her Blazer was officially totaled. Once the first round was done, they were brought back in for a second round if necessary. Cameron had told the two men across from her exactly what she'd told Ballestrini. That she had received a phone call that there was a boat with hostages on the Bay. They immediately asked for her phone as she'd known they would, "It was broken last night during a car chase," she lied. "I'm not sure if you heard about that. I was leaving last night when—"

"We heard," said the talkative one.

They didn't have any questions on the car chase. A different set of officers was working that one. They would get her phone records. It wasn't hard to do, but the lie bought her a little time to talk to Ahrens first. Cameron had left Ahrens two voicemails, but she was gone from the department constantly now. The only communications from her had been a call instructing Kessler and Ballestrini to view the video and try to identify the car that had chased Cameron. Hailey and Jess had called to make sure she was okay. She had sent texts in response, assuring them she was okay. She wasn't ready to talk to anyone. There would be too many questions she couldn't answer.

Meanwhile, Internal Affairs was still at them the next day. Compiling the information from the Special Ops team, they had created diagrams and reenactments of the boat. They must have been up all night. It would have been her day off, but the captain wanted them all in—again.

Cameron felt like she was spinning in a hurricane of dust. She had twice tried to approach Ahrens and been interrupted by something Ahrens felt was more pressing. She e-mailed Mei and checked in with Hailey on Ivana. No one had anything. It was nearly six when Ahrens showed up. She gathered the team in the bay. It meant they all had to stand.

"I'll be brief," she said, telling the team to be on the lookout for Diego Ramirez. He was thought to be armed and dangerous. "He is also our chief suspect for the attack on Officer Cruz two nights ago."

Cameron felt the room shift to her.

"That's all," Ahrens said. "Ballestrini, I want to see that video clip you found."

Cameron approached Brian Kessler. "There's a video? Of what? Did you see it?"

Kessler stopped her. "Are you okay?"

"I'm fine."

"I mean, really. It's okay if you're not." She realized the men were staring at her. Was it because they knew Diego was Nate's father or because she'd been attacked? "The video, Kessler. What's on the video?"

When Kessler didn't answer, she walked out of the bay.

Anxious to talk to Ahrens and get home, Cameron threw her sweaty clothes in her gym bag and headed for Ahrens' office.

It was empty. She'd waited all day to talk to her and she'd left.

Cameron saw the light on in Lavick's office. Stepping closer, she saw Captain Ahrens inside. The captain looked up like she'd been caught at something. "I was trying to find a file."

Cameron glanced at the manila folder in Ahrens' hand and caught the end of Benjamin's name. She knew that file.

Ahrens looked around the sergeant's office like it was a room she'd never seen before.

"I'd like to speak with you, if you have a few minutes," said Cameron.

Ahrens straightened her shoulders. "Of course. Let's go next door." The two women walked to the captain's office. As soon as the door was closed, Ahrens turned, still standing. "What's going on?"

Ahrens' eyebrows rose.

Cameron sucked in a breath. "I believe he's somehow involved in the human trafficking."

The captain sank into her chair at the mention of his name, her chin pointing toward the ceiling, her eyes closed. "Damn him."

Right then, Cameron was confident she'd done the right thing talking to Ahrens. It had been too long since she'd felt that way.

"Where's the video now?" Ahrens asked.

"I don't have it."

"Who does?"

"Diego Ramirez."

Ahrens put her hands on the desk and leaned forward. "Tell me all of it, Cruz. Start from the night Benjamin was shot and go through everything—every detail."

Cameron explained how she'd come to see the *Pesce King*, the bankbook in her home, the break-in, Diego's appearance and his pleas for her help. She told the captain about Ivana, careful to leave out Hailey, and about the jump drive without mentioning Mei's computer genius. She planned to leave out the bullet he'd left her. It felt like such an intimate gift, but then she thought better of it and told Ahrens that, too. Cameron didn't say who Diego had been to her. She hoped they could leave that understood and unspoken. She offered every detail she could remember. When it was over, she felt incredible relief.

Ahrens seemed to have taken on her weight. Cameron felt glad to transfer some of it. It had taken almost an hour to go through all that had happened. When they were done, Ahrens thanked her. Cops didn't often thank each other, which made Cameron appreciate it all the more. It had been the hardest period of her life.

Ahrens was quiet at the end of their meeting. After several minutes of their silence, Cameron said good night.

Heading toward her car, she wanted to cuddle on the couch with Nate. Maybe she could get Rosa to fix her enchiladas. She could use some comfort food.

She unlocked her rental car and sat in the driver's seat. She texted Rosa to tell her she was on her way home. Next, she texted Ricky.

I told Ahrens all of it. I believe D is innocent. Hope we can prove it. C

Finally, she texted Hailey to tell her that she'd told Ahrens everything.

Left you and Mei out of it. Will keep it that way. See you at RC.

She had to believe that by the next Rookie Club dinner this mess would be over. As Cameron put her key in the ignition, the loudspeaker clicked on. The empty air filled with Ahrens' voice. They'd located another boat on the Bay. All officers were to report to the office for dispatch.

Another boat. Cameron's belly filled with dread. She didn't want to go back out. She wanted to go home. Her cell phone rang, and there was no getting away. "Cruz," she answered.

"It's Lau. Are you on your way home?"

"I heard the message. I'm coming back in."

She heard him tell someone she was still there as he signed off. Leaving her gym bag and keys, she slammed the door and headed for the bus that would transport them out again.

CHAPTER 40

THE RIDE TO the Bay was quiet and tense. After two days of the intensity of IA interviews interrupted by short, grueling drills that were no subtle form of punishment, it was hard to adjust to the stony silence of the bus.

Usually, the ride to a scene was filled with high energy—directions, talk, even jokes and laughing as they all worked off the rush of adrenaline. Today, they could have been a busload of strangers on their way to an execution. Maybe they were. It was partially the absences. Daley and Ballestrini were at Bryant on something for Ahrens, and Ambley was out for the shooting. To fill out the team, they'd borrowed a couple of Special Ops officers from the South San Francisco team and would run the op one guy short. The first was a guy named Minard, who was mouthy and a little too raunchy for Cameron's taste. The second was a guy named Henry Coppolillo, who was even bigger than Kessler. Aside from Special Ops, he was in charge of the canines for the South San Francisco department. From his demeanor, it wasn't hard to imagine that he could keep them in line.

The awkwardness in the group might also have been a result of Ahrens' presence. The captain didn't normally join them for calls. It was unclear whether Ahrens had joined today because Lavick was out, or if there were other reasons. No one asked.

The marina where they stopped was north of San Francisco beyond Tiburon, a wealthy town right on the Bay. The streets were filled with businessmen and women, getting into BMWs and Mercedes after a treacherous day of stocks or law. Cameron watched them, feeling more distant from the average person than ever. As the men around her pulled on protective suits and gear, she spotted a woman pushing a baby about Nate's age in a stroller. She hated that she wouldn't see him before he went to bed tonight.

After that came a fleeting fear that she might never see him again. She shook the thought from her mind as she strapped her vest on. Finally, she checked and rechecked her weapon, before following the others off the bus.

She only made it a few steps from the bus when she realized she'd forgotten her extra magazine. At the top of the bus stairs, she felt it in her vest pocket. When she rejoined the team, Ahrens whispered, "Please, God."

The water was calm with a slight breeze to relieve the heat trapped beneath their dark clothes and heavy equipment. The thick glass of the boat's windows magnified the setting sun, making her feel like meat on a grill.

As they approached the suspect's boat, they all listened for sounds of life. Cameron felt a sense of foreboding. She wondered if the others felt it too, but as they got closer, Ahrens gave few directions. Her voice seemed to break the ice. The familiar teasing started back up again. Slowly, the cold tension boiled into the adrenaline they all thrived on. They could do this. She could do it.

"You ready, Lucy Liu?" Paules joked.

"She's definitely Diaz," Kessler said. "Even have the same first name. Our Cameron's just a better shot."

"The other one's got a better ass, though," Minard said.

"You've got the best ass, though, Minard."

Minard wagged his butt for the group. "You know it."

"Good thing you like it, Paules," Lau teased. "Your nuts are going to be kissing it in about three minutes."

They all laughed, but to Cameron's ears, it felt hollow.

No people were visible on the boat. Everyone was wondering if this was going to be a repeat of the last one. As they closed in, muscles tightened around her. Guns raised, metal scraped metal as officers released safeties. Velcro slashed as final adjustments were made to vests and holsters.

As they approached, Ryan Lau set up the order, and they formed the lineup for entry. Coppolillo led. Cameron was second to last, directly before Lau. The change in the lineup meant something. Lau was a senior officer, so he normally went first, but perhaps Ahrens wanted an extra eye on Cameron or maybe it was a shuffle because of the change in team. Whatever it was, she pushed it from her mind. Stray thoughts were a distraction and distractions got people killed.

Suddenly, there was shouting from up ahead. The accented voice was male.

"They know we're coming," Lau said, his voice mixed with fear and relief.

Cameron shifted her gun higher. Hostile, agile, mobile.

Gunfire sounded and glass shattered somewhere over their heads. The line dropped down for protection, waiting it out. There would be no return fire until absolutely necessary. No one wanted to repeat what happened last time.

The accented voice called out again, "Move away."

Helicopters flapped in the distance.

More shots rang out, and she sensed the line grow tense. They were close.

"On three," Lau called.

The numbers flew by, and all at once, they were moving. Running, jumping onto the boat. Move left, move right.

Cameron followed a clear path to her position on the starboard side. There, she crouched until Lau was beside her.

His shoulder pressed to hers, he said. "I go on three."

She waited for his move. As soon as he went for the stairs, she shifted around the corner and covered him. She followed, keeping them covered from above, then sweeping left between the rails as Lau swept right.

She pounded down the remaining stairs, her boots clamoring against the steel. She backed straight to the wall, scanned left and right, nodding to Lau. The smell below was sour and pungent, like rotting food. The smells of her job were something she'd never gotten accustomed to.

In the corner, she saw motion, then a glint of light off a gun. "Freeze," she shouted, her finger ready on the trigger.

"Drop the weapon," Lau commanded.

The suspect's muzzle moved toward them. His finger reached the trigger. Cameron fired, the shot echoed by one from Lau's gun. The shooter fell. Cameron covered Lau while he checked the body. He gave her a quick nod and tucked the gun in the back of his pants. One down.

Her knees were unsteady as they moved through the narrow passageway, scanning left, right, up, down. She waited, while Lau buttonhooked into a small storage space.

"Clear," Lau shouted.

She moved slowly in a half circle, back safe to the wall, Lau on the other side of the space. "Clear," she said, holding her thumb up in front of her to designate her direction.

He motioned right.

She moved ahead, gun ahead, finger straight out, ready to take the trigger in the blink of an eye.

She paused at a closed door and waited until Lau was beside her, both of them on one side. They exchanged nods. Good to go.

He lifted a leg and kicked the door.

It tumbled open. Cameron entered, buttonhooking around the doorway and surveying the room. "Clear," she shouted.

Lau entered, crossing the doorway to the far side. Together, they moved, backs to the opposite walls and scanned the room.

They spotted motion in a far corner.

"Come out where we can see you, hands up," Lau commanded.

Four hands showed in the air as two women crawled out from under a table.

"Anyone else here?"

The women studied each other. Cameron ignored them as she and Lau searched the rest of the room. It was clear.

"Stay here," she said and closed the door behind them.

The next cabin was empty. The third and final cabin's door was closed. Cameron sensed it wasn't empty. She thought about the hostages and wondered how many there were. She assumed more than two. Most likely, they were in there with some of the suspects.

Kessler and Coppolillo arrived. "Upper level is clear," Kessler said. "One perp down. Paules and Minard are collecting the hostages."

"This is the last room."

"Expect a fight," Lau said.

She pulled a flash bang off one side and lifted it to Lau, who nodded. She staged the pin so it would be easy to pull when the door opened, and gripped the metal canister in her fist. Once it went off, the sound would effectively stun everyone in the room for five seconds, giving them a head start on making sure the hostages were safe.

Lau poised to open the door. Cameron got ready to pull the pin and throw it in. He wiggled the knob. "Unlocked." He twisted the knob and she cocked her arm. "On three."

One. Two. Three.

Lau kicked the door open. Cameron threw the canister inside.

They ducked behind the doors to wait for the burst of noise. The team covered their ears, but even then, the sound was deafening. It took several seconds before Lau and Cameron entered the room, guns drawn. Immediately, she saw eight or ten women on the floor. A suspect in the corner. "Freeze," she screamed, gun aimed. She covered him while Lau grabbed another suspect inside the door. He threw him out into the hall, where Coppolillo and Kessler took over.

Her suspect raised his hands and dropped his weapon. Lau crossed the room and took his gun before using a plastic cuff to secure his hands. She was about to drop her gun when there was a muffled cry from the far side of the room.

She spun around and spotted a third suspect partially hidden by what had looked like a wall, but was actually a divider in the room. Her gun high, Cameron stopped when she saw him.

He moved slowly into the main room with a young woman—maybe fifteen or sixteen—held in front of him. At her neck was a large, black-handled knife. The girl had a square jaw and dark eyes that darted back and forth between Cameron and Lau.

"Damn," Lau whispered.

No one moved. Cameron was both angry and terrified that they'd missed him. It was bad news to have a suspect behind you, especially an armed one. She held her aim on him, but there was no guarantee she could take him out without hurting the girl.

The man was medium height and paunchy. The girl under his arm trembled with fear. "Guns down," he screamed, pressing the knife into her neck as she clawed at his sleeve.

Cameron stopped moving. Now, they waited until someone made a mistake.

"I kill. I kill her."

"Put the knife down," Lau said.

"I kill!" he screamed back.

One woman tried to get onto her feet. Cameron waved her gun at her. "Stay down," she directed. The room filled with crying as the women cowered on the floor.

The man jerked the girl closer.

Cameron watched as the knife bit into her neck. A line of blood appeared.

The woman let out a cry. The other hostages screamed.

"It's going to be okay," Cameron said, adding a "Shh" for the others.

When the man glanced away, Cameron took another step closer.

The woman's eyes widened.

The man jerked her back again, pressing them both into the corner of the room. "Back. I kill." He shifted the point toward her neck.

Lau moved in closer to Cameron.

"I can take him," Cameron whispered, her chin tucked down to keep her voice low.

From the corner of her eye, she watched as Lau nervously licked his lips. "How?"

"Just get me some profile."

"And the woman?"

Cameron swallowed. As long as the woman didn't make any drastic moves, she'd be okay. She could hear other officers at the door. "I can do it," she whispered to Lau.

Lau shook his head to hold them off. The more of them there were, the worse their suspect was going to freak. "Don't, unless you're sure."

She squatted slowly and set her gun on the ground as though she were giving up.

The suspect watched her, then Lau. Lau held his gun and moved slowly back toward the first cuffed suspect.

Cameron put her hand close to her weapon and motioned that she was ready.

Lau pulled the cuffed suspect off the floor and pressed his gun into the suspect's back. "Tell your man to drop the knife," he commanded.

The cuffed man said something.

The suspect held the woman closer as he shouted something to the cuffed man. The exchange continued for ten or fifteen seconds.

Cameron focused on his head. When he had turned sideways, her breathing stilled. She just needed a little more space.

The woman leaned forward, sobbing. The suspect's head rolled back as he screamed something toward the ceiling.

Cameron lifted the gun, aimed, and fired. She watched the back of the man's head explode in a burst of red and pink tissue. He fell backward, dragging the woman with him. Hysteria filled the room, while Cameron felt the adrenaline drying up. She holstered her weapon. Someone patted her on the back. She watched as the woman was pulled away from the dead man's arms. A little cut on her neck, but she would survive.

She headed back to the boat's deck.

"Hell of a shot," Lau said to her, as she passed him, trying to get to fresh air.

"Thanks," she said.

"Hell of a week," Paules said.

"Hell of a week, for sure," Lau agreed.

CHAPTER 41

DIEGO HADN'T SLEPT since he'd left Cameron's house. There was no word anywhere on the boat of dead girls. He had almost no communication from the station and no word from Claudia in a week. It was all he could do to keep himself sane by pacing the corner as he waited for his man to meet him. This was his last resort. If this bastard didn't give him what he needed, he'd kill the son-of-a-bitch.

A man stepped out under the streetlight. "You're late," he snapped.

"You?" Diego was surprised at the man who emerged from the dark. They had dealt only in anonymous text messages until Diego broke him down and convinced him to meet.

He didn't look surprised to see Diego. But, as he walked closer, Diego could tell he'd lost him. He was unshaven and unwashed. He wasn't the contact anymore. They'd ousted him. "They set you up too."

The man fidgeted with the manila envelope in his hands. "I can't help you. They'll kill me." He was trembling. "Not just me, but the kids, too."

"What about Claudia?"

The man shook his head.

Diego felt his stomach roll. He clenched the man's arm and shook. "What about her?"

"I don't know. I don't know anything about her."

Goddamn it. "What's in the envelope?" he barked.

"Some things you might be able to use. Things they don't know about. Maybe they'll help."

"What?" he barked, anger boiling over. They'd gotten him, too. Their claws were everywhere.

"It's the list of all the accounts."

"What?" Diego asked, confused. "What accounts?"

"The ones for the deposits. Everyone who gets a piece has it deposited into a numbered account. That's always been my job—"

Diego took the package and tore it open. It was one piece of paper, the return receipt on a fax that had been sent. It was just a row of numbers, incomplete. "How do I tell whose accounts they are?"

"The bank knows. They're all there—me, Daley, Masse, Donnelly, you—everyone has one."

"Me?"

"They opened one for you."

"I never got paid by them. The only money I have is what came off Benjamin, and it's in safe keeping."

He shrugged.

Damn them. "Is there money in it?"

"Probably some, but not a lot."

"Enough to raise suspicion." He shook out a plain black tape from the envelope. "What's this?"

"The tape from Benjamin's car."

"What tape?"

"From the shooting."

A tape of him shooting Ray Benjamin. Jesus Christ. He tucked it into his jacket. "Is this the only copy?"

He nodded.

"Where was the camera?"

"By the rearview mirror. Rotates ninety degrees. I don't know what it caught, but the audio's usually pretty good on those."

He returned his attention to the paper. "You must have more than this. All this does is show how they set us up. What about Ray and Vincente? What about whoever is still in it? Where are their names and the amounts they were paid?"

"Whatever else I have is at the house," he said. "I've sent the kids away, and I'm never going back there."

"You have to go and get it."

"I can't."

Diego grabbed him by the collar. "You have to, damn it. You have to get the rest."

"They'll kill me."

"You think you're safe with me?"

He cried, blubbering. Diego felt his rage growing. He collapsed onto his knees. Diego raised a foot before stopping himself. "Damn you. Get up. You can't do this now. You're in too deep."

The man leaned over and continued sobbing.

Diego pulled out the gun, Benjamin's .45. He shoved it beside the man's ear and barked at him to stand. He did, slowly. "You're going to go to your house and you're going to get more evidence. I'm going to meet you on the north end of your block in two hours. No cops, just papers."

The man, blubbering, agreed. Diego helped him up, holding his gun at his side. In the meantime, he hoped Cameron had hacked into the rest of the files on the jump drive he'd lifted from Benjamin's house. He needed something that could blast them out of the water.

An hour later, Diego had been trying to form a plan when the black and white pulled up in front of the diner where he sat, its lights flashing. As he rose from the chair, another arrived. Then, a third. A fourth behind him. He was surrounded. More than surrounded. They'd brought out the whole department for him. Diego had walked right into the trap.

He raised his hands like a good boy. He didn't run. He didn't try to negotiate. That would come later. He had to convince them that he had something that made him worth more alive. At least for now. He had an idea of what he could use. They would be planning to get the evidence and squash him like a bug. He had other plans.

He walked out to the street and let them cuff him, shove his head down, and push him into the back of the squad car. There was always a buzz of giddiness around the arrest of a cop. He experienced a stab of panic when someone slapped the top of the car and it pulled onto the street. It was going to be okay. He wasn't going to fail. That wasn't an option.

CHAPTER 42

ROSA SAT DOWN beside Cameron and pushed a plate of hot enchiladas toward her. "You have to eat."

"I'm not hungry," Cameron told her sister. Food was not appealing after seeing those dead women. She was still reeling from how close she and Lau had come to missing that suspect. The risk of taking that shot, not knowing if she would miss and hit the girl. Mei was working on the last files from the jump drive, so she had nothing to tell Diego. But where was he? What was he working on, and was he all right?

"I made exactly what you asked for."

"I'll eat it a little later, I promise."

Rosa drilled her hands into her hips. "Are you at least going to tell me what happened on the boat?"

"I really don't want to talk about it."

Rosa got up from the table again. She picked Nate up from his playpen and carried him around the kitchen while she worked. Rosa's whole presence softened when she was with Nate. She didn't worry about her appearance or men. And talking to Nate was the only time Rosa spoke Spanish without being forced.

Now, she complained to Nate about his crazy mother and her job. She was right. Cameron's job was consuming her. She couldn't continue like this.

A month ago, she couldn't have imagined not going back to work. Now, she wished she could find a job where she'd have some peace of mind. But that would have to wait. She couldn't leave Special Ops until she knew what Benjamin and Lavick had done. She wasn't quitting until someone paid for those women and for the absence of her son's father. Then, maybe she would have peace. The fury drained everything from her.

She watched Rosa and Nate. Normally, the sight of the two of them together was one of Cameron's favorite things. Today, she couldn't muster any enthusiasm. She kept imagining all those women, all those mothers and daughters, dead. And worse than the image of them dead, was the possibility that Diego was being set up to take the fall. How thick was the trap? What if they couldn't free him?

Rosa brought out a container of ice cream and set it on the table. "Maybe this would help?"

Cameron knew that if she didn't eat something, Rosa would not stop pestering her. Plus, maybe she'd feel a little better after something sweet and some rest. "Ice cream and a nap."

Rosa clicked her tongue. "Only you can sleep after sugar."

"Ice cream always makes me tired."

"Okay." She bounced Nate on her hip. "You going to take a nap with your Mama?"

Nate made little babbling noises.

Rosa opened a cupboard and pulled out a bag of Oreos. Then, bringing down a bowl and spoon, she handed them to Cameron.

Cameron served herself a healthy scoop of mint chip ice cream and topped it with two Oreos. While Rosa and Nate danced around the kitchen, she forced it down, the ice cream cold in her tight throat.

When she was done, she put her arms out to take Nate. "Okay, buddy, let's nap."

"Wake up hungry," Rosa warned. "Because we're having enchiladas for dinner."

"We promise, Tía Rosa," Cameron said, taking Nate into the bedroom.

For years on the force, Cameron had napped. The days and nights of heavy physical activity and high-pressure situations had also provided her with enough built-up exhaustion to sleep any time of day. Since Nate's birth, she slept less, wanting to be with him as much as possible and using his nap time to do some necessary chores. Now, cuddling her son, she remembered the way she and Diego used to cuddle in his bed in the middle of the day, pull the shades down, and nap. Often, they'd wake at six or seven in the evening, just in time to shower and go for dinner at one of their favorite places.

The memory brought back the familiar ache. But now, it was combined with an entirely different emotion, fear. As she padded down the hall with Nate, the phone rang.

"I'll get it," Rosa answered.

She set Nate on his changing table and yawned as she pulled off his pants to change him. Rosa opened the door, holding the phone. "It's for you. It's about Diego."

Cameron left the room, but she could feel the weight of Rosa's stare on her back as she did. "Hello."

"Cameron, it's Hailey."

"Hey."

"Sorry if I've called at a bad time."

"Doesn't seem like any of 'em are good right now," she said.

"It'll get better," Hailey said, though the tone was anything but convincing. "What've you got?"

"Few things I thought you'd want. We got some prints off the wall of Ivana's building, where she was attacked. Matched them to a police officer."

Cameron sank down on the living room couch. "Shit."

"Yeah. None of the ones on the scene. It's been passed on to Assault and Internal Affairs. That's not mine, and they don't come back to the ORG Lounge. We did confirm that Ivana was there with the other girl, Anna. Her prints are all over the wall in one of the offices. We believe that's where she was first attacked and raped. Jamie's on that one. At least, the guys who raped her and probably killed the other one weren't cops. We've sent the composites all over the department, but nothing has come back yet."

Cameron thought maybe finding the real killers would clear Diego of at least the one killing and the rape. She shivered. The whole department was at work on cases that had stampeded their way down the center of Cameron's life.

"It gets worse."

Cameron leaned back into the cushions as though she might protect herself from the next hit. She waited to hear Diego's name.

"The knife found on the *Pesce King* came back from the lab. I'm not working that one—but Dale Hartung is. Know him?"

"No."

"Well, it's got prints on it. A whole set—perfect."

Cameron held her breath. "Diego?"

"Nope. Michael Lavick."

"He was with us that day. At the scene."

"At the scene, yes. But, what about before?" Hailey asked. "Someone said he was out while you guys were planning."

Cameron sank down. "That's right. Lau led it. Christ, what a mess."

"No kidding. It's raining fucking cops in here. Chain of custody is a nightmare. No one's allowed in. It's all being locked in a huge walk-in safe, and only one person's got the key until this stuff gets processed fully and reports finished."

"Jesus Christ. Who?"

"Cheryl Ann Palahniuk."

"The Chief's secretary?"

"Administrative assistant," Hailey corrected. "Everything goes through her and I hear she's taking the job very seriously."

Cameron thought about that.

"I'd watch it right now, Cruz. It's everywhere."

"Okay. Thanks."

Hailey was quiet a moment.

"Rosa said something about Diego."

Hailey exhaled. "They arrested him last night. He showed up at Lavick's house. The police were tipped off. No Lavick though." Hailey paused. "I'm sorry."

"Shit. What are they holding him on?"

"Murder one for Benjamin, but I suspect there will be more to follow," Hailey said, and Cameron knew she was right. They'd have a laundry list on Diego unless new evidence came up.

"I've got to run, Cameron. I'll keep you posted."

"Okay, Hailey. Thanks." Without saying goodbye, Cameron punched the off button on the phone. Diego had been arrested. He was behind bars. How could she help get him out of that?

CHAPTER 43

THE DAY HAD finally arrived when Ivana would leave the hospital. Dressed in the clothes Rosa had brought, Ivana was ready to leave the sour-smelling room. Rosa insisted Ivana stay with her and Cameron for a few days. She had finally accepted, but Ivana felt certain she would never make it there. Her instructions were to go straight to her old apartment. That's where the man was meeting her. If she didn't, Rosa would be hurt.

He was listening, the note said, so she kept quiet and waited until it was time to go. Whatever happened, she wasn't going back to that apartment.

She put her medicines in the plastic bag she'd found in the hospital closet and looked around the room one last time. She would stop at a pay phone and call Rosa to warn her. She could at least do that. After all, no matter where she went, it would take her some time to get there.

She opened the hospital room door and peered into the empty corridor. What if he was there, waiting for her?

Surely, she could lose someone in a hospital. She'd go out another exit. She had spent a little time exploring, and there were a lot of ways in and out.

The process of checking out of the hospital took forever. Finally, she was wheeled out of the hospital in a chair.

"Is someone meeting you?" the nurse asked, looking around for a car.

"A little later," she lied.

The nurse checked her watch.

"I wait on the bench," Ivana said.

The nurse frowned and took another look at her watch.

Ivana moved out of the chair and onto the bench. "I am fine."

With a quick glance over her shoulder, the nurse nodded. "Okay. Be careful now."

The nurse went back inside. Ivana waited for a few minutes on the bench before returning to the building to find another way out. If he was out there somewhere, watching, she wanted him to think she was inside.

She walked past the elevators, down a long, busy hallway, her heart pounding. She kept her head down and focused. No one stopped her. She didn't let herself consider dying. She'd almost died twice already. If she died today, so be it.

Instead, she thought of Michal and wished she could rub his back while he fell asleep one last time. She had a stabbing pain at the thought of him and her mama, but she pushed the thoughts away. She would see them, she told herself. Someday. Today, she had to be strong.

Trying not to attract attention, she stopped every fifty feet or so and pretended to tie her shoe or check for something in her bag as she studied her surroundings. No sign of him.

She made her way to the Emergency Department in the basement and went out the sliding doors where the ambulances parked. Then, she headed up a flight of stairs next to the building and walked toward a residential area away from the hospital's main exit.

Three blocks down, she found a bush to sit behind and for twenty minutes, she watched. No one had followed.

Next, she went to the end of the block and used a pay phone beside a bus stop. She dialed Rosa's number. When she answered, Ivana spoke quickly, explaining the policeman she'd seen and what he'd told her.

"I've seen him near the salon."

"The tall one, with the mustache?"

"No mustache," Ivana answered. "But, yes, he's tall."

"It doesn't matter about him," Rosa said firmly. "You do not go to that apartment."

"I am not going there, Rosa. But I also should not come to you. He said he will hurt you."

"I'll come get you. Tell me where you are."

"No," she said and lowered her voice. "I must not."

"You have to come. I'll call Cameron, and she'll have someone here by the time you arrive."

Ivana checked over her shoulder. "It's too dangerous."

"Do as I say." Rosa's tone reminded her of her mother's—firm and strong. Ivana longed to be in Rosa's arms, to be held like a little girl. She wanted desperately to go to Rosa, but she was terrified.

"Come straight here. Come to the back door," Rosa repeated. "If you see him, scream for help."

Ivana longed to say yes.

"Did you hear me?"

"Yes, but—"

"No buts. Just do it. I'll call Cameron now. Can you get here okay? Do you know how?"

Ivana worried her lip, trying to decide what to do.

"Ivana!"

"Yes," she said. "I have the directions you gave me. If you are sure."

"I am. Now, be safe and get here as quickly as you can."

"Thank you, Rosa. You are too good to me."

"Don't thank me. Just be careful." With that, Rosa hung up, and Ivana found another place to hide while she watched for anyone following her. When she was sure she was alone, she set off for Rosa's house.

It took her almost two hours to make her way. She was careful to stop often and take quieter streets. When she arrived at Rosa's, she hurried down the side of the house to the small deck in the back. There, she climbed over the short fence and onto the deck. The inside of the house was dark, and she hoped Rosa hadn't left. She cupped her hands on the cool glass and stared inside, then knocked. No one came. She bit into her lip, beginning to worry when she heard a baby's cry. It had to be Nate. She saw Rosa walk by with a bottle in her hand.

Excited, Ivana knocked again, harder.

Rosa waved when she saw Ivana.

Pulling the door open, Rosa scanned the backyard and ushered her inside, closing the door behind them. "I'm glad you're here. I called Cameron twice and left a message, but she hasn't called back yet. I want you to tell me everything about the man. As soon as she calls, she'll get someone to find him."

Ivana checked the lock. "He was dark, like you."

"Hispanic?"

"I don't understand," Ivana said.

"Did he have an accent?"

"No."

"And you're sure he was a policeman?"

Ivana's eyes went wide. "Yes. He wore the suit and a gun."

"But, you didn't see his name?"

Ivana shook her head. "Please believe me. I don't lie to you."

Nate hollered again.

Rosa touched her arm. "It's okay. We'll figure it out. Let me take care of him first. He's hungry."

Ivana followed Rosa toward the baby's room. The room was painted blue with thick off-white carpet under foot. A small rug the shape of an airplane decorated the floor beside a white crib. A bright mobile with little farm animals hung down over the baby.

On the other side of the room was a big bed, covered in thick pillows. Across from the foot of the bed, stuffed animals covered the top of a bookshelf stocked with books. It was the kind of room Ivana had dreamed of as a little girl. Instead, she'd had almost no toys. The few she had were bought at a secondhand store. Her bed was a mattress on the floor, and a threadbare sheet and holed blanket were her covers. Nate's room was heavenly.

Rosa put him on the changing table and unfastened his diaper, talking to him as she did.

Despite her fear, Ivana was taken with the baby. She remembered when Michal was that young. "Can I help?"

"Once I've changed him, you can feed him if you like."

Ivana felt a tiny thrill. She hadn't held a baby since Michal. Her mother had few friends and none with young children. Her mother didn't allow her to babysit the neighborhood kids because their parents couldn't pay.

Rosa put on a new diaper and snapped up Nate's outfit. "There you go."

A moment later, the doorbell rang.

Rosa and Ivana exchanged a glance. Rosa lifted Nate and placed the bottle to his lips. Creeping to the window, she shifted the shade slightly and peeked outside.

Ivana followed her gaze, but from her angle, she couldn't see who was at the door.

Rosa exhaled. "It's okay. They're from Cameron's work." Rosa handed the baby to Ivana. "You stay here. I'll be right back."

Ivana took Nate, holding him tight to her and settled into a rocking chair, rocking him slowly as he ate from the bottle.

From the other room, she could hear Rosa and two men. They were whispering. Ivana strained to make out what they were saying. Maybe they were talking about her. She thought again about the man. He would be missing her by now. How long before he figured out she was not coming?

"Why do you want to find her? Why does it matter?" Rosa asked. "She's been through enough."

The other voice grew louder. "We need to talk to her."

Ivana felt her skin crawl. She silently prayed Rosa wouldn't tell anyone she was there. She rocked the baby, needing to comfort herself as much as him. Please, don't hurt Rosa. Please.

"How should I know where she is?" Rosa said.

The voices rose and Ivana felt panicked. "Don't lie to me," a man shouted. There was a slap. Rosa cried out.

Ivana held Nate tighter to her chest. A wave of tears filled her eyes. She blinked hard. The baby made a small noise, and Ivana felt her pulse pound. She needed to hide. She saw the closet.

Opening the door as quietly as possible, she took the baby into the cramped space and pulled the door closed behind her until all she could see was a thin crack of light. She pushed the long dresses and coats to the side and backed to the wall, her knees under her, the baby's bottle pressed to his lips.

He made a grunting noise as he ate, and she did her best to muffle the sounds behind the clothes. Please, don't find us.

She could no longer hear Rosa. Her heart pounding, she swallowed the tightness in her throat. Forcing herself to sit as still as possible, she waited for something to happen.

The silence went on forever. The only noise was Nate eating.

Suddenly, the bedroom door banged open. Ivana jumped and Nate started, but she held him close, pressing the bottle to his lips and praying he didn't cry.

"I told you, she's not here," Rosa said and Ivana could tell she was crying.

She blinked hard, unable to fight back her own tears. Oh, God. Please, no. Not Rosa.

There was nothing for several seconds. She held herself perfectly still, praying that Nate didn't cry out, that it would all end. Maybe Cameron would come home. Please, something to save them.

Rosa didn't speak. Ivana strained to hear any noise from her. She leaned forward to listen, wishing she could see them. What was going on?

Rosa let out a strained whimper. "No," she pleaded.

There was the hard crunch of metal on bone. Rosa cried out. Nate whined. Ivana pressed him to her own pounding chest. She could feel his heart pounding against her, the rumbling of sobs in his little throat. She cupped him to her and bounced him, the bottle pressed to his lips.

When she finally opened her eyes, she saw Rosa's long hair against the white carpet.

Rosa wasn't moving. Ivana tried to hold still, to be invisible. The shadow shifted against her eyelids as the closet door opened. When she looked up, she was staring at the end of a gun.

Rosa lay motionless on the floor.

"Let's go," he said. Ivana held Nate tightly, wondering if she could possibly save either of them.

CHAPTER 44

EVERYTHING ABOUT THAT morning had been strange. Ahrens called them into the bay to announce their assignments, which she normally did in the team room. It was the first time Cameron had ever seen Ahrens so undone. At eight o'clock in the morning, her hair was in a ponytail that might have been done the night before. Strands fell loose around her face. The pantsuit she wore was one Cameron had seen earlier in the week. The blouse beneath it was wrinkled and stained with coffee.

The rest of the team didn't look much better. A few were missing altogether: Lavick, Daley, and Ballestrini were nowhere to be seen. Ahrens had reassigned all the teams and directed them to leave all personal electronics in the locker room. "I want us focused on work today," she had added, telling them that if there were emergencies, they could be reached on their radios through the station's dispatch. Cameron almost brought her phone anyway, but there were too many people in the locker room to do it discreetly.

Unlike normal patrol days, Ahrens also assigned them to districts and warned them to avoid any calls that seemed like they might require use of a weapon. They were police officers. What did she expect? Not that there was much in the way of violence in the Castro where Ahrens sent Cameron and Paules. Never partnered before, she and Paules made awkward small talk between calls.

The day consisted of a series of ridiculous calls. The first was a noise complaint that turned out to be three construction workers blaring Van Halen. A man called in a domestic dispute, which was actually a mother yelling at her ten-year-old to drink his prune juice. "He's completely stopped up. He has to drink it." The little boy was seated at the table next to a glass of what looked like a dark ale, crying.

"You could try blending it with some fruit," Paules suggested as they left.

The other calls were two suspected thefts, one from a coffee shop and one from a bohemian store that sold hash pipes in unique shapes and colors. The final call had come in as she and Paules were heading back, so they ended up being the last ones to return. Cameron had used the phone at the bohemian shop to call Rosa to find out if she could pick up anything for dinner, but Rosa wasn't answering the phone. And that, too, didn't sit well. Normally, they spoke at least a few times a day. Of course, Cameron also usually had her cell phone.

When they arrived at the station, Cameron made a beeline for her locker and found her phone. She had one missed call and a message from home. She dialed the home number. The phone rang four times and with each ring, her stomach clenched tighter. Rosa was always home by now. She tried Rosa's cell phone next. No answer there either. She punched the button to retrieve her voicemail when she sensed someone behind her.

She saw Ryan Lau and jumped slightly.

He put his hands up. "Sorry." Lau's mouth was set in a straight line. Something was wrong.

She lowered her phone. "What is it?"

He glanced over his shoulder. "I talked to Daley."

"What's going on?"

"This has to stay between us."

"Of course. I would never—"

"I know," he said, stopping her.

She gripped her phone in her hand. She wanted to talk to Rosa.

"I think he's done something."

Cameron studied Lau. "Something—"

Lau clenched his jaw. "Illegal maybe." His eyes cast downward. "Something bad."

Cameron thought about that night in Ahrens' office.

"You knew?"

"Just a sense, I guess," she said. "Where is he?"

"I don't know, but he sounded terrible. And he was babbling." Lau's frown deepened as he continued. "You know how he is normally. Cocky, full of shit. It didn't even sound like him."

"What did he say?"

Ryan looked up. "That he was trying to get out. That he had a lot of things to undo. He kept saying 'please, God' and 'God, help me.'"

Cameron heard those words, Ahrens' voice echoing in her ears, and suppressed the urge to shudder. Did it all relate to the boats, to the traffickers? "Did he say what he'd done?"

"No. He said it had gone too far. Some girl was in the hospital."

Holy shit! Ivana!

"And now something happened that can't be undone."

Shivers trailed across her shoulders and back. She thought again about not reaching Rosa, trying to convince herself that there were a thousand reasons why she hadn't been able to reach her.

"I don't know who to tell, and I can't get in to see Ahrens. She keeps putting me off."

She wanted to shake him, get him talk faster. Spit it out. She gripped her phone. "Call Hailey Wyatt. Tell her about Daley." Cameron recited Wyatt's cell number. "She can help. I'll call you from the road."

"I've got a new cell number, 415-555-9876. Want a pencil?" he said. She shook her head. She'd already committed it to memory.

She started for the door. Lau moved with her. "He kept talking about something happening by the water, at some warehouse."

The boats. "Where?"

"He didn't say."

"There was one more thing," Lau said.

She had to fight to stay still.

"He said your name."

The tightness in Cameron's stomach turned to lead. "My name?"

"He was mumbling, but I thought he said, 'I should have done something for Cruz.'"

Cameron's thoughts fired off like rounds from a machine gun. Was he talking about running her off the road? "Call Wyatt," she told him.

"I will. Call me as soon as you can."

Cameron tried to make sense of Daley's odd behavior. What did he mean, and how was he involved? And how the hell did it relate to her? Was this what Diego was talking about?

As she made her way to her car, she listened to the voicemail from Rosa.

"Cameron, you need to call us at home as soon as you can. Ivana said a police officer came to her in the hospital room and threatened her. She was so scared." Rosa's voice sounded scared too. Cameron felt a chill run deep inside her. "The policeman told her if she didn't follow his instructions, when she was released from the hospital, he would hurt us. He used our names—yours and mine." She paused and for a second, Cameron thought the message was over. "How would he know us?" Rosa asked.

Cameron was thinking the same thing. Her breath seemed to stop in her chest before releasing like a bullet. Adrenaline burned through her as she sprinted toward her car.

Rosa's message was still playing as she ran. "I told her to come here. Call me and tell me what I should do."

No, Cameron thought. Not there. Not with you and Nate. "Oh, God. Rosa." She listened to the recording tell her that the message had come in at two p.m. Oh, Jesus. Jesus, no! That was more than three hours ago.

Cameron twisted the key in the ignition and started the car with a roar. She shoved the car into reverse and squealed out of her parking place. Her gaze nailed to the road, she floored the gas and drove as fast as she could. She continued to dial her home number and her cell every few minutes, but no one answered either one. Finally, she dialed Ricky.

He was out of breath when he answered. "Hello?"

"It's Rosa, something's happened." She spurted out the story of Rosa's message until she'd told him everything relevant.

"Jesus, Cameron. A police officer? Is she sure?"

"I can't reach her, Ricky. I don't know where she is."

"Okay, calm down. I'm across town. I'll be there as soon as I can."

Her knuckles were white on the wheel. She gripped it as though somehow the effort might save Rosa.

She called Lau next and told him about Rosa's message.

"Do you want me to come?"

Daley's words pulsed in her brain like a neon sign. He should have done something for Cruz. She dropped the phone and scrambled to pick it up.

When she looked up at the road, she was inches from the row of cars parked on the side of the street. With a gasp, she swerved back into her lane.

"Cameron?" Lau was saying when she got the phone back to her ear.

She was shaking. "I don't know. I have to get home."

She was hanging up when Lau said, "If I don't hear from you in fifteen minutes, I'm calling for backup."

"Okay, thanks."

"Be careful, Cameron."

With that, she hung up the phone and tossed it on the seat beside her. She tried to think rationally. It would be okay. She had to keep it together. Ivana said a policeman had come to her hospital room. How had she known him? If she'd believed he was a cop, Cameron assumed he'd been in uniform. Daley could have been in uniform, or the sergeant, but what would they want with Ivana? Had she seen something at ORG Lounge that night? Had she seen them kill that other girl? Had Daley done something that terrible? Were they involved in smuggling the women? Murder?

Cameron arrived at her house, her mind filled with awful possibilities. Nate's face passed through her mind—his tiny fingers, his puckered lips. Rosa holding him in her arms, his tiny toes painted tangerine orange. Oh, God. Please not them.

She threw the car door open and ran inside. The front door was unlocked. "Rosa," she screamed as she opened it.

No one answered.

She ran through the kitchen and the living room, scanning for any indication of where they'd gone. Nothing was disturbed. She tried Nate's room next.

She pushed the door open and stopped as though she'd been hit with a baseball bat. The wind gone, her knees weak, she let out a piercing scream. There, lying on the floor, was Rosa.

"Oh, God. God, no." Cameron sobbed. She went to her sister, dropped to her knees and touched her face. She felt cool, clammy. Cameron touched her neck and felt a thready pulse.

"Damn you. Damn you all." She ran for the phone and punched 9-1-1. Choking and sobbing, she said, "I've got a woman down. Looks like head trauma. Send paramedics. Now. Now."

The dispatcher tried to keep her on the line, but she dropped the phone.

"Nathaniel!" she screamed, running through the house. There was no sign of him. His diaper bag sat beside the front door, his car seat beside it, but Nate was gone.

She returned to his room and dropped to her knees beside Rosa. "Oh, Rosa. Estás bien. No te preocupes," she said in Spanish. "You're going to be okay. I'm here now. I'm here, honey."

Tears falling down her cheeks, she ran her fingers through her sister's long hair.

The sirens began to wail, and she ran to the door to greet the paramedics. Ricky was coming up the front steps. "In here, hurry."

The paramedics ran in and Cameron led them to Nate's room. As Cameron stepped through the door, she caught sight of something she hadn't seen before.

"Oh, Jesus. It's him."

The paramedics moved around her to Rosa.

"Who?" Ricky asked. "Who did this?"

Cameron reached down and picked a button off the carpet near Rosa's foot. It was a standard jacket button, waves of brown and white and tan like cream poured in coffee. Strands of navy thread hung from it. It could have been anybody's button, but she remembered seeing one like it before. The button had been loose, almost off when they were in the captain's office.

"Brad Daley," she said.

CHAPTER 45

DIEGO WOULDN'T LAST more than twenty minutes in hold up. They weren't going to let him stay here where he might talk, but he hadn't gotten any visitors yet either. He'd relayed his message. The files off the jump drive would be enough to fry some of them. Or so he was telling them. He passed the word on.

He was amazed at who showed up. But it was there in his expression. He was in on it. Crooked. A man he'd spent a decade working with. Cameron, too. And she trusted him. Somehow, Diego had to find a way to tell her. Which meant he had to get out of there.

"What's with all the bullshit evidence, Ramirez?"

Diego held his expression level. "I'm telling the truth. I've got enough to go to federal court. It's out there. You can't erase it by erasing me."

The man across from him leaned back with crossed arms, so confident. "What did you do—send something to our friendly *Chronicle* staff?"

"What's that from—a movie?" Diego asked, his hands trembling as he shoved them in his pockets. Had they heard? All the evidence Cameron didn't already have was on its way to the only person he thought he could trust aside from Cameron—Renee Eberhard at the *Chronicle*. Had he been wrong?

Still staring, there was a brief nod and then, "What do you want?"

"Two things: first, I want to walk."

"On Benjamin's murder?"

"On all of it. I'll keep my insurance. You keep doing what you do."

"And second?"

"I want Claudia. Safe and sound."

The man frowned. "Can't do it. Too risky."

"It's not negotiable," he said, trying to sound like he was the one with the power. "If I don't make a phone call in twenty minutes, it's over for you guys."

The man didn't respond but walked away.

Diego felt himself melt against the cell bars. Was that it? He held himself strong. They probably wouldn't risk killing him behind bars. They'd likely move him first. That would be his only chance.

He made a racket, insisting on his right to a phone call, but his demands weren't answered. No one was giving him anything, and he wasn't sure who to call. Cameron? She was in deep enough and what could she do? Gather his evidence from Eberhard and take it—where?

Two men arrived to transport him less than an hour later. They were big and thick, not agile enough to be cops. They were more like bouncers. They were silent as they signed him out and walked him through the station. No cuffs. Not legitimate policemen. Just a couple of guys hired to do the dirty work. He held himself calm. He could do this.

"Where's the place?" the smaller of the two demanded as Diego was shoved at gunpoint into the back of their car behind the Hall of Justice.

"What place?" he asked dumbly.

"Where you've been hiding. We got to check it out."

Diego shook his head when the bigger one grabbed his left index finger and snapped it like a pretzel. Diego fell onto his knees, howling.

"You can make it easy or you can make it tough."

Diego allowed himself to be manhandled into the car. If he fought them, it would only make matters worse. He had to bide his time and make a plan. Leaning back, he gave them the address.

He kept his eyes closed, trying to map out a plan. Nothing was coming to him. He had no weapon, and he could tell from the familiar bulges at the waist and ankles that these guys were well armed. The safe house was on the second story. There was a fire escape, but it was a large room, and the chances he'd make it to the window were nil.

He heard the whisk of flame. He opened one eye, his heart pounding in his broken finger and watched the big, silent guy light a cigarette.

Diego was ushered into the cramped safe house and pushed into a far corner while the two guys went to work on it. Cardboard boxes lined the floor, and the big one was tossing them over, dumping out the junk inside them. The smaller one was destroying the kitchen. None of it was Diego's. He had nothing there except a few clothes he wasn't taking with him.

They needed something else from him other than the location of the safe house. Otherwise, he'd be dead already. At least, that's what he was banking on.

Diego noticed the gas main with its big red handle. "Where we going, guys?"

The big one spun around and fired his gun. The first sensation was like his leg was buried in a glacier. Then, it was on fire. "Jesus Christ." He touched the edge of his jeans where the bullet had torn a hole and taken a chunk of his thigh.

"Shut up and sit down," the other said.

Diego steeled his breath. "Can I at least have a fucking cigarette?"

The talker one deferred to the big one who shrugged, then tossed over his pack. It landed far enough away that he had to put weight on the bad leg. His eyes clouded with the pain.

He eased himself back onto his feet and lit the cigarette. He took a drag, focusing on the burning in his lungs instead of the fire in his leg. Moving slowly, he got up and eased his way to the wall where the gas valve was.

The smaller guy had moved to the closet while the bigger one was digging through boxes of crap. Diego took off his button-down shirt and made a tourniquet around his leg.

The big one had run out of boxes as Diego reached the gas main. Blocking it with his body, he palmed the red handle. The closest door was in the line of fire, so he was going for the window, a long fifteen feet away, especially with his leg injured, but it was his only shot.

The small guy slammed the closet door and cursed. The handle in his grip, Diego used his cigarette to light fire to a newspaper dated six months back.

He flicked the cigarette onto the ground. The big one turned around and saw the cigarette. Diego waved the paper, and they both watched him.

"What the hell do you think you're doing?"

He leaned down and dropped the paper into the closest cardboard box and waited as it caught fire. The two stepped toward it, looking pissed.

Diego twisted the handle. The gas came out in an angry hiss, as though reaching for the fire.

"No," the big one screamed as Diego ran for the window.

He saw a flash behind his eyelids and felt the torrent of heat follow him. His scalp punched through the glass, and he landed hard on the fire escape, knocking his head. He felt the searing pain and saw spots, but kept moving. As he crawled away from the window, glass chewed at his palms. He kept moving. Once he was clear of the blaze, he scrambled across the cold metal, using the handrails to support his bad leg.

The men were screaming.

The metal of the fire escape was wet from the fog, and he slipped and fell. He struggled to pull himself up to run. His leg burned, shaky beneath him. Without hesitation, Diego ran along the metal until he reached the corner of the building. He stopped at the last window.

He pushed on the jamb, and the window wrenched open. It stuck at eight inches, and he crawled in, catching his leg on the windowsill as he went. When he looked back, flames were pouring out of his open window. Fire engines wailed in the distance.

Diego pushed the window shut and locked it, then ran for the door. He hobbled through the empty warehouse space, which smelled like vomit and urine, and down the stairs, using the handrails to swing himself down three and four at a time.

When he was sure he was alone, he hit the street and hid behind a dumpster. He retied the shirt around his bleeding leg and half sprinted, half limped, until he could no longer hear the sound of the fire engines and he could not take another step without collapsing.

He found a quiet alleyway and sat down behind a mountain of empty liquor boxes. Resting for a moment, he gathered his thoughts. If they had come after him, he knew exactly who was next on the hit list. He had to get to Cameron.

CHAPTER 46

CAMERON PACED THE living room as Ricky spoke to the policemen in Nate's room. Though she couldn't hear his words, his voice was low and calm, and she thanked God that he was here. He'd called her parents and her brothers and had spoken to the police and the detective who had arrived shortly after. He'd sent men to Brad Daley's house and after Sergeant Lavick, but so far there was no sign of Daley, Lavick, Ivana, or Nate.

Cameron had left messages for Lau and Hailey, and Ricky had called Señora Accosta to sit with Cameron while the house was cordoned off and searched, prints taken, and evidence collected. She'd been home almost two hours. Two hours that Nate had been gone. Probably more. Nearly twelve hours since she'd last seen him. Twelve hours since the last time she'd spoken to her sister or held her son. And she prayed she would again.

Ricky entered the room and asked Señora Accosta to give them a minute. Señora Accosta stood up, withdrawing her hand from Cameron's. It wasn't clear if Señora Accosta was comforting her or vice versa, so Cameron was happy for the break.

"You hanging in there?" Ricky asked.

Cameron scowled at him. "I only called you because I knew you could talk to Mama. Calm her down. I don't have anything to say to you."

Ricky crossed and sat where Señora Accosta had been. "About ten years ago, Margaret Ahrens and I worked together on a joint Special Ops/Sharp-shooter project. Evelyn was going through menopause. It was hitting her hard. The final step in the realization that we would never have kids. She was pushing me away."

She didn't want to hear this now. "I don't care."

Ricky raised his hand to stop her. "We were involved, briefly. I broke it off, but I never told Evelyn. Not until yesterday."

"But, you still talk to Mar—Ahrens."

"We catch up over a drink once in a while."

"And you told her about Nate."

"I did," he admitted. "I thought the information would help her be sensitive to your loss."

Cameron processed the words. Maybe it was the truth, but right now, it didn't matter. "I need to get out of here, get some air, maybe go for a drive."

Ricky led her toward the door. "You won't go doing anything crazy, will you?"

"What would I do?" she asked, wishing he would give her an idea. She would do anything—crazy or not—if she thought there was a chance it would lead her to Nate. Right now, she could only wait until someone else had a lead.

"Just be careful. You'll have your phone?"

She nodded. "Call me if there's any word—"

"Of course, I will. As soon as I hear anything."

The sobs gathered like a volcano beginning to smoke, and she turned away before they broke free. She found her jacket under Ricky's on the chair by the door, put it on and zipped it to her chin as she left the house.

She made her way east on Cesar Chavez back toward work and cut south, heading for the marina where Diego had sent her. She didn't expect to see him there, but she had to go somewhere and it seemed as good a direction as any. Beside her on the passenger seat was a travel pack of baby wipes and two of Nate's diapers. Unable to stop herself, she let the tears fall down her cheeks.

Her phone rang. She pulled over, wiped her eyes, and took a quick breath before answering.

"Cameron Cruz?" It was a woman's voice.

"This is Cruz."

"It's Mei Ling."

"Hi, Mei."

"Listen, I broke the code to the last two files. That Blowfish encryption is good, so it took forever."

Cameron gripped the steering wheel. "What did you find?"

Mei was quiet.

"Mei?"

"Images. Women—" She stopped. "Girls, really. Nasty stuff. Strangulation, burning, water boarding, clamps, and every kind of torture you can imagine. Maybe twenty-five, thirty women."

"Christ." These were the men who had Ivana and Nate. "Is there anyone else in the images?"

"Not in most of them. But, two men show up in a few of the images. I'll send images as soon as we hang up."

Cameron felt sick. "Okay."

"There was one other file. A lease on a warehouse. The encryption on that file was as secure as the pictures, but I can't tell why. It's a standard lease for a company called Divka holdings."

"*Divka*."

"Means girl in Czech."

Ivana. "You speak Czech?"

Mei laughed. "I speak Google Translate. There's an address."

"Give it to me."

The address Mei gave her was off Illinois on Humbolt, a district of run-down warehouses south of PacBell Park.

"Send me the image of that guy, and call Hailey Wyatt and Jamie Vail. Make sure they get all of this, too."

"I'll do it now."

Cameron pulled back into traffic. "Mei?"

"Yeah?"

"I'm glad you're part of the team."

"Happy to help."

Cameron made an illegal U-turn and started north. She called Hailey Wyatt first, then Jamie Vail. Neither answered their phones. Her phone rang a few seconds later. "Cruz."

"It's Lau. What the hell's going on?"

Cameron updated him on Rosa and Nate. "Any word on Daley?"

"He's AWOL."

"I'm heading to a warehouse where I think they might have Nate. You want to be my backup?"

"Where's the lead from?"

"My source is legit," she said, aware that she wasn't answering his question.

He didn't push. They'd both been with the police long enough to respect when you couldn't reveal your sources. "Give me the address and I'll meet you there. Don't go in until I arrive."

With that, she disconnected and dialed Ricky's number, but got his voice-mail. She left a message, trying not to imagine what she would find when she arrived. The address was on the water, and she was familiar with the district of rundown warehouses south of PacBell Park. She prayed no one had touched her baby. She pulled her service weapon from the glove compartment and ejected the magazine. It was full. As she drove, she snapped the magazine back in place and loaded a round into the chamber so she was ready.

She cut back across Cesar Chavez and went north on Illinois. She passed Humboldt and slowed down, then pulled over a half block away. She peered down the street as though somehow she would know it by sight, as though she'd be able to tell that Nate was there from a set of tire tracks or a smell in the air. No, she'd have to go find him.

She decided to leave the car behind. It would keep it out of sight and also allow others to find her more easily. Lau would be there soon. She wouldn't wait. She couldn't. She had to go find Nate. Lau wouldn't agree with her decision, but she thought her chances were better alone. She could take them by surprise. Backup meant noise and warning. She didn't want Nate's kidnapper to have any warning.

She holstered her SIG and tucked her .22 in her ankle holster before pulling on her leather coat and stepping out of the car. In her baseball cap and jeans, she hoped she'd be mistaken for someone out for a walk along the water rather than a cop.

As she made her way toward the water, she spotted two warehouses at the end of a pitted, dirt road. In the lots next to them piles of rubble were stacked next to massive pits. Some sort of construction had been started and then abandoned. Cameron walked along the south side of the gravel hills, hoping to keep out of sight of the warehouses.

It was impossible to tell which of the warehouses—if either—was in use. Both were painted industrial gray and locked up. The windows had been painted black ages before and were now a worn dark gray. She wondered if someone could see out through them.

Once she was past the pits, she started through the construction site toward the closest warehouse. As she made her way closer, she spotted a parked car. It was an old burgundy-colored Ford Explorer like the one the sergeant drove. She wished she had a pair of binoculars. The car looked empty, but it was facing the water, and she could only see the passenger side clearly. She drew her weapon and made her way slowly through the dirt and gravel.

She was less than thirty yards away when she heard a voice. She dropped down, seeking cover behind a short stack of cement blocks. She counted to ten to catch her breath, then moved forward again. She could see a man's figure against the far warehouse. He appeared from behind the warehouse and stopped in front of a door on the southeast side. He reached for the knob and shook it. When it didn't open, he kicked it, ranting and raving. He was slurring and she couldn't make out his words.

At first, she thought it was just some drunk, but as he turned around, she recognized Sergeant Lavick. In his right hand, he gripped his service weapon, waving it in the air as he walked toward her.

She aimed her gun and waited until he was close enough to make a clean shot. The sergeant wasn't the shot she was, and if he was alone, she had clear advantage.

Maybe Nate was in the car. She had to hold herself from moving too quickly. She waited, poised to bring him down. He tried another knob and, when it didn't open, kicked again.

He stopped and the arm with the gun slacked to his side. Cameron made her move. She crouched close to the ground. She had no cover, but it would be harder for Lavick to hit her squatting than standing. "Drop the weapon, Lavick," she yelled.

The sergeant spun around, searching for the source of the voice.

"Drop it now," she said again.

He swung past her and stopped, then slowly turned back until he saw her. "Cameron Cruz."

"Where's my son?" she demanded.

"He's gone."

The gun trembled in her hand. She refused to believe they'd killed him. "Where is he?"

"I'm sorry this happened," he said. The gun hung slack at his side, but he made no effort to put it down.

Cameron took sweeping looks over her shoulder to be sure they were alone and kept her weapon carefully aimed at the sergeant. Her heart raced. She wanted to shout again, but knew better than to rush him. She didn't want this to end in gunfire. She wanted her son. Ricky or Lau would show up with backup, and Ivana and Nate would be safe. There had been enough bloodshed.

"I can't take it anymore, Cameron," he said.

"Tell me where they are, Sergeant. Where is Ivana? Where is Nate?"

"I thought they'd be here. I expected them, but it's empty. Those bastards." He scoffed.

"Who?" she called out.

"I trusted them," he said, walking with jerky, tired steps like a man who had crossed a desert. "I knew it was bad, but they swore I wouldn't have to be involved in the deaths."

She listened, gripping the gun.

"You play a couple hands. Get down a few grand. That's how they get you. Promising to forgive that debt. Add a little on top. Help pay for a few extras."

She wasn't following him. "What game?"

"The money was so hard to resist. Then, they get you. They threaten, and you can't quit. They used my kids, my girls."

She didn't want to listen. Only Nate mattered. "Where is Nate? I don't care about anything else. I just want my son."

He glanced around like he'd never been there before.

She thought he was drunk. Did he really not know? "Where's Brad Daley?"

"He's gone. It's good he's gone, because he was one of them. That bastard tried to take me, but I shot him. I shot him right in the head. Made a mess of the car." He swung the gun in the direction of his car and rubbed his head with his free hand. "The car. Bela's going to be so pissed."

The sergeant's car was too far away to see who might be inside. Where was Nate?

He moved toward her. "They said he'd hurt my family. They said it didn't matter where I was. If I were in jail, they'd hurt them. They'd make my girls suffer. Can you believe that? Mariela and Alexis."

She blinked back an onslaught of emotion, warning herself not to think of Rosa, not to get sucked in. That's what he wanted. She set a knee on the ground and shifted her position. She leaned her elbow on her knee, steady.

"I didn't believe they could do it. How could they hurt innocent girls?"

"You did that. The knife—it was your prints."

"I didn't," he said. "I would never kill anyone. That's the trick. They catch you up in it. They frame you—like they did me. Just like him."

"Who?"

"Diego."

Her breath escaped her lungs like a punch. "Diego," she whispered.

"They'll do the same to you. They'll use the thing they have on you." He faced the ground, his shoulders low and sloped. He seemed destitute and harmless, but she didn't drop her guard. She wasn't going to risk it. He took two more steps toward her.

"Don't come any closer," she warned.

He halted and looked around as though she might be speaking to someone else. He swayed on his feet.

He'd been drinking. Cameron felt herself begin to sweat. Where the hell was Nate?

"I didn't think they'd really hurt anyone," the sergeant continued. "They killed all those women—a whole boat of them. Women." He made a choking noise. "They weren't even women. They were girls, barely teenagers, and they killed them all." He let out a choked sob, and Cameron felt like she was being strangled. She needed Nate. "And they're everywhere. Be careful, Cameron. You can't escape them. They're everywhere."

"Who is 'they,' Lavick? You need to help me. You can save Nate. You don't want him to die." The words caught in her throat. "You don't want to be responsible for that, do you?"

Her arm ached from holding the gun, a tremor starting. Her knees were stiff from squatting, her leg cramping. She wanted to scream, to shake him and beat him until he told her. Instead, she did as any good cop would do. She waited.

He smiled, and she felt shivers down her back. "I've given them up. Now, it's only you."

She took aim. "Put the gun down."

He shook his head.

She put her finger on the trigger. "Put it down," she repeated.

"I wanted to warn you not to trust them."

"Where is my son?" she screamed, unable to keep the panic from her voice.

He waved the gun through the air.

She applied the slightest bit of pressure to the trigger. It moved ever so slowly.

His gun rested against his own temple, and it took a second to realize what he was doing. "No!" she screamed.

The gun exploded, and the sergeant fell sideways.

She sprinted for him.

His eyes were wide open when she got there, and his heart was pumping because the blood was flowing like a geyser.

"Where is Nate?" she said, shaking him.

He didn't answer.

Shaking, she pounded on his chest. "Where is he? Where's my son?"

His eyes rolled upwards until all she could see were the whites.

She ran for his car, kicking up dirt. She was sobbing, her heart pounding.

She pulled open the passenger door, and Daley fell out onto the ground.

She felt for a pulse, but there was none. The car was empty otherwise. Dead. He was dead, too. She leaned back over him, pressing her palms into his lifeless body.

It was then she noticed the button she had thought he'd lost on Nate's bedroom floor still hung by a thread to his navy blue jacket.

CHAPTER 47

LAVICK'S BURGUNDY EXPLORER was right below him. Diego had spotted Lavick's car driving by him at the safe house and followed him. Maybe it was Lavick's job to make sure Diego was done, or maybe he was there for something else. Either way, Lavick didn't seem to notice the tail, and Diego was suspicious about how easy it had been until he watched the sergeant blow off the side of his own head. He was short of breath. He would need to get to a hospital before too long if he was going to save his leg, or himself for that matter.

In the distance, he saw Cameron, pounding on the doors to the warehouse. Diego hurried to the far side of the roof where there was a ladder to the ground. He called out to her.

He dropped to the base of the ladder and came around the side of the building. By the time Cameron was in view, he was making an attempt to run.

When she heard him, she raised the gun instinctively.

"Are you okay?"

Cameron lowered her gun. "They have Nate. Where is he?"

The words knocked the breath from Diego's chest. "When?"

"Don't fuck with me, Diego."

"I'm not," he said. "I swear. I followed the sergeant. He's the only one I saw."

"Where's my son?"

He choked on his next breath. Not Nate. "Jesus, Cameron. I swear to God, I don't know. What happened?"

Cameron cried out, "Oh, Jesus. They're gone. They're gone."

Just then, there was the crunch of tires on gravel. A black sedan came toward them. Diego focused on the driver, praying it was someone who could help.

Cameron aimed her gun at the car and then lowered it dropped it as she recognized the driver. "Thank God," she called and ran toward the car. It was getting dark, and Diego couldn't make out his face behind the windshield.

The door cracked open. She heard a voice, Nate's name. Cameron cried out.

"Cameron," Diego screamed. "Don't."

Tim Ballestrini emerged from the car.

"He knows where Nate is," Cameron shouted and her gun hand dropped to her side.

"Cameron. No!"

He lifted the gun. He had no shot with Cameron there. He was fully exposed. Ballestrini was quick. He pulled the gun from Cameron's hand, aimed his own at Diego.

Diego dove sideways a moment too late. The explosion was followed by a searing pain across his left forearm. The next explosion came right on top of it. The bullet grazed his neck. Blood flowed under his collar. The ground rose to meet his face. Gravel and dirt scraped his cheek, and he felt it all build until all he could see or feel was fire.

CHAPTER 48

CAMERON CRIED OUT, starting for Diego. Ballestrini held her back. "He raised his gun. He was going to shoot."

"Let go of me."

Ballestrini didn't.

"We have to call an ambulance," she cried. As she pulled her phone out, she saw two faces on the screen. Photos from Mei. One was Ray Benjamin, and the second face belonged to the man beside her.

"That's not necessary," Ballestrini said, snatching her phone and pocketing it.

"You sick fuck." She thrust her palm toward his chin, but he was fast. He blocked her hand and struck her hard in the face. "Enough."

Cameron reeled as a second and third car came down the gravel road. She hoped it was Lau or Ricky, but the three men who emerged weren't police officers. Among them were the two men who had come to her house, posing as police officers. Tony Kelly and James Caltabiano.

"Where's my son?"

Ballestrini shoved her toward the warehouse. "Let's go see, shall we?" He walked ahead of her. "Check her out, Marty. Make sure she's clean."

The man she'd never seen before came toward her with a wide smirk like she was a party favor. "Let's take a feel for weapons." He palmed her breasts, taking his time. His breath was steamy and sour in her face. Cameron felt the rage grow. If there wasn't a chance Nate was in that building, she'd have kneed him in the nuts and taken the punishment. Instead, she took measured breaths. Saved it for when she would need it most.

Twenty yards ahead, Ballestrini used the toe of his boot to kick Diego's body onto his back. She watched it, lifeless, and started to shiver.

Marty worked his way down her back and over her butt, palming her front at the same time and pressing the seam of her jeans into her skin.

"Speed it up, Marty," one of the fake cops said.

Ballestrini pulled his foot back and kicked the dead body firmly in the stomach as though to test the deadness of it.

Cameron clenched her fists.

Finally, Marty stooped to feel Cameron's ankles. He groped the left one first, running his fingers from her crotch down to the top of her shoe. He grinned up at her as he started toward the second shoe. Cameron spit hard in his face.

"What the fuck?" He reared up and struck her, knocking her to the ground before wiping the spittle off his face. "Fucking cunt," he said as the others laughed. He started back toward her, but one of the fake cops waved him off. "Later, Marty."

Marty got up in her face. "I'm not done with you, bitch."

Cameron said nothing as she got to her feet. The guy behind her pushed her toward the warehouse. The hard shaft of a gun jabbed into her back. "Don't fuck with us. We can do this neat, or we can do it messy."

Cameron thought about Nate and gave a little nod.

As they got close, she thought she caught motion in her peripheral vision, but when she looked, there was nothing.

She was alone.

CHAPTER 49

AS BALLESTRINI REACHED into his pocket for the keys to the warehouse, Cameron thought about Diego. She could have saved him. Now, they were all going to die. She prayed she'd have a chance to tell him how sorry she was, if only in the afterlife. She tried to hold that faith, but it didn't feel like enough.

Ballestrini pulled open the door to the warehouse and pushed her inside.

Cameron scanned the room. In the far corner by another door, she saw Ivana. Her hands were bound behind her and a strip of silver duct tape covered her mouth. Beside her lay a motionless bundle of blankets.

Cameron cried out, trying to get free to go to Nate. She could almost smell him, and a rush of pain ran through her.

"Sorry," Ballestrini said. "You'll have to say goodbye from here." Kelly and Caltabiano took hold of her arms, holding her back.

"No!" Cameron screamed.

"Marty, handle the girl." Marty went toward Cameron. "The girl, Marty," Ballestrini snapped, pointing toward Ivana.

Marty crossed the warehouse, and Cameron tried to imagine how she'd get to her gun. There was no way she could take them all down, but she'd have to try. She took a deep breath and swooned, letting her body go limp. The two men stumbled forward as Cameron hit the floor.

"What the hell?" one of them said.

Cameron rolled into a fetal position and moaned, trying to pretend she was having some female melt down. Her fingertips found her weapon, and she drew it, aimed at the bigger of the two and pumped one into him.

Before she could shoot, Caltabiano fell. She spun toward Ballestrini who stood, stunned.

She shot out Ballestrini's left knee. He dropped howling, and she rose quickly. Before he could move, she kicked his gun across the warehouse floor. She took the guns off the other two and threw them as well.

Marty was halfway across the warehouse, running for Ivana and Nate. Cameron raised her gun and fired low on Marty's leg, careful that Ivana and Nate weren't in the line of fire.

He stumbled forward onto his knees, screaming, "You bitch. You fucking bitch." But, he didn't stay down. Within seconds, he had scrambled back to his feet and was running again. Ballestrini was wailing.

"Shit," Cameron yelled, taking off after Marty.

"I don't have a shot," a woman shouted from somewhere above her. "Mei?"

"No! I can't see him." Cameron recognized Mei Ling's voice. And Hailey Wyatt. They were here.

"We'll cover you, Cameron. Go get that son of a bitch."

"Cover me, Mei," Hailey shouted. "I'm going down."

Cameron took aim again, but stopped before pulling the trigger. If she missed Marty, Ivana was in her line of fire. She couldn't risk it.

Marty was getting too close to Nate and Ivana.

Ivana struggled against the tape on her hands. She rolled to one side, trying to fight the rope.

Cameron fired to the right of them, hoping to startle Marty into stopping, but he kept running. He was closing in. Cameron was too far behind.

Marty raised his gun and aimed it at the bundle on the floor.

"No!" she screamed.

Glass shattered and two shots rang out in quick succession. Marty was thrown backward. His gun fell from his fingers, and he landed, sprawled across the concrete.

The door opened slowly, but Cameron didn't stop to look. She sprinted toward Nate. She dropped to the cement floor and scooped him into her arms. He started to cry, and she clutched him to her chest, rocking back and forth.

The door fell open. Diego Ramirez stumbled through, dropping his gun, before collapsing to the floor.

Ivana sobbed. Mei Ling arrived and sat beside her, using box cutters to get her loose.

Phone to her ear, Hailey stood over Marty. She kicked the gun away from the body. "He's not dead yet."

From the distance came the symphony of sirens. She carried Nate to Diego, touching his haggard-looking face as she sank beside him. His eyes opened and she cried out in relief.

He spoke first, his voice raspy. "Is he okay? My son?" He tried to reach up to touch Nate, but the effort was too much.

She lowered the baby so Diego could see him. "He's fine. Help is coming. You hear the sirens?"

He nodded.

"Just don't die, okay? Not again."

To that, he almost smiled.

Two paramedics came in with Lau and Kessler, and Hailey directed them to Diego. Lau peered at Nate and whistled. "Jesus, he looks just like you, man."

Diego winced a chuckle as Lau gave Kessler a thump in the arm. "No wonder she wouldn't go out with you, man."

As Diego was being loaded onto the gurney, Cameron heard him say, "What the hell? If I wasn't shot in three places, I'd be taking you down now. Hitting on my girl."

She grinned and held Nate tighter.

Lau let out a hearty laugh and Kessler blushed. "You were dead, dude," he said softly.

"Okay. I'll give you that." The paramedics rolled Diego out.

Nate cooed happily in Cameron's arms as she crossed to Hailey. Ballestrini was lying at her feet, spewing venom at her and cussing about the pain. "What, Tim? No show tune to go with this one?"

"Fuck off, Cruz."

Cameron put her foot on his knee and applied pressure until he screamed out.

"Why don't you ride to the hospital with Diego?" Hailey suggested. "We'll be behind in a little while."

"Take your time," Cameron said.

"Oh, we will," Hailey promised.

Patrol officers and additional paramedics arrived. A woman officer wrapped a coat around Ivana's shoulders as the paramedics set up to examine her.

Mei crossed to Hailey and Cameron, stopping to run her finger under Nate's chin.

"Thanks you guys," Cameron said.

Hailey winked. "Of course. This is my favorite part."

EPILOGUE

Three days later

Cameron carried Nate down the hospital corridor. They had come from Rosa's room. Mama Cruz was still there, busying herself with pampering her baby during the day and coming home and cooking and taking care of Nate and Cameron and Ivana, who was staying with them.

Ricky had told Evelyn about the affair with Captain Ahrens while they were back east and Evelyn had agreed to go to counseling. While Evelyn was a little more reserved than usual when she visited, Cameron thought they would make it. It probably helped for Evelyn to have Mama around, whether or not she would share the story. Evelyn was certainly keeping busy, shuttling in groceries and supplies, and cooking with Mama. Ricky took turns staying with Rosa when Mama Cruz needed a few hours off.

Mama would be with them for another three weeks. After that, Ivana was going to take care of Nate for a while. The time would give her a chance to see how she liked America, and try to put what had happened behind her.

The idea was Cameron's. She thought they would all enjoy some extra people around for a while. Ivana had been through enough already—they all had. The only stipulation was that Ivana call her mother and tell her where she was. Cameron thought no mother should have to survive an hour not knowing where her child was.

The city's mayor had appointed a commission to investigate the ring of smugglers. With Ballestrini and Marty in jail, they were expecting them to roll over on each other. It was still hard to imagine Tim Ballestrini as the head of anything so awful. Everybody had a dark side.

Ballestrini had managed to ensnare other officers with an illegal poker game played above the ORG Lounge. The losses got big, the game illegal, and soon officers were searching for ways out. Ballestrini set them up to pay off their gambling debts by helping circumvent police attention from the trafficking business. Soon, though, keeping the police away wasn't enough. One by one, he dragged them in deeper, all the while establishing evidence to blackmail them into submission on the chance they decided to double-cross him. He'd started to threaten their families.

And Cameron had led him to that boat of women herself. While she and Ballestrini were supposedly on the lookout, waiting for the team to be assembled, Ballestrini had given the order that the women be killed as a message to the players.

Although the commission had already identified several leaders of the trafficking operation, it would take time to sort through the details of who killed the women on the boat, how the business had worked, and, of course, exactly who was involved. Ballestrini was careful to keep the police officers isolated from one another, so none knew that other officers were involved. That way, he reduced the risk that the group would turn against him. Ballestrini hadn't confessed to chasing her car that night, so she may never know who it was. It didn't matter. Certainly not in comparison to the other things.

Thankfully, a Mexican man by the name of Luis Rosario had kept a detailed account of his dealings with the traffickers in a safety deposit box. Between that and the sergeant's dossier on each of his runs, the commission had enough evidence to put away more than two thirds of the twenty-seven names they'd uncovered.

With Lavick and Daley dead, they would likely take more than their share of the blame. The results on the non-police participants were even better. Most had priors, and in addition to the arrest of Marty Redd, they'd rounded up a major player named Freddy Jackson and a busload of criminals who had been paid for services related to the trafficking.

The tipping point was that Ray Benjamin had a change of heart. While he hadn't come forward to confess his own role in the smuggling operation, Ray had decided to quit. He'd decided to keep that last bag of money and walk away. When Diego had fought him on it, Ray had been willing to shoot

Diego. Cameron sincerely hoped those were details Jess didn't have to know. It was a terrible thing to think badly of someone you loved after he was gone.

When the police started to investigate the smuggling, members of the team stepped forward to volunteer so that they could steer the investigation away from themselves. That was mostly Lavick's role early on. Then, Ahrens was strong-armed into looking the other way when her ex-addict son had racked up a seventy-thousand-dollar loss at Ballestrini's poker table.

Cameron hesitated in front of room 3203, Nate in her arms. He smiled up at her. Gathering her courage, she knocked on the door.

"I'm decent," a voice called back.

Cameron pushed the door open.

Diego held a remote in the air and was flipping channels. "Time for my bath?" he joked. Their eyes met. His jaw dropped slightly, and the remote fell from his grip. "Cameron," he mumbled.

Feeling awkward, she stepped into the room.

He picked up the remote and fumbled with it until the TV went off.

"Were you expecting someone else?"

He shook his head. "No. No one—" He waved her in. "I guess—" He pushed himself up in the bed. "I wasn't sure you'd come."

Nate cooed, and Diego noticed the bundle in her arms.

She watched his face and knew the emotion that ran through him. She was familiar with the swell that filled your chest when you saw your own child. She stepped closer.

He hesitated, watching Nate. "Is he okay? I mean—he wasn't hurt or anything?"

"He's fine." She stopped at the bed, holding her son to her chest. She should offer Diego a chance to hold him, but she couldn't get herself to let go. She watched Diego's face, those wide dark eyes. She could still picture their last night together. They'd talked about the future, made plans. And then, he'd been dead. Gone.

"Rosa?" he asked.

"She took a nasty blow to the head, but she's going to be okay."

"And Ivana?"

She watched him. "You saved her."

Diego squeezed his eyes closed. "Thank God."

"Why did you use your real name?"

He shrugged. "Everything was such a mess. A part of me hoped maybe you'd hear about it. Maybe after I was gone, it might convince you that maybe I wasn't so bad after all. Despite what they'd done to make it look that way."

"And Claudia's going to be all right?"

"I think so," he whispered.

There was a silence as they watched each other. His gaze made its way from her to Nate, and then Cameron, too, looked down at her beautiful son.

"The start was so uneventful," he began. "I was out with a group of guys one night. One of the few nights we weren't together. You had the stomach flu."

She remembered. It was actually morning sickness, but she hadn't known it at the time.

"Benjamin was there and I was asking about ways to get Claudia out of Mexico. He mentioned an ongoing case in ICE, cracking down on a human trafficking ring. My look—that's what he called it—made me a good candidate for an inside position. He hinted that maybe in return ICE could help get Claudia out.

"It was only supposed to be six weeks, so I jumped at it. My job was to meet with potential buyers, negotiate deals. Someone was capturing it all on film, collecting names. Then, there was the story that someone had made me, so they invented my death. Like a sucker, I bought it all.

"I never saw any surveillance pictures. I was in there seven months and sold some ninety women into slavery before I admitted to myself that something was wrong. There was no report on arrests. No takedowns, no feedback on the sting that should have been happening. But, I kept pushing."

Cameron shifted on her feet.

Diego winced. "They kept telling me that it wasn't like Special Ops, that things took time. Maybe playing the game for so long without asking more questions makes me an idiot. As I started to ask questions, they started to tighten the noose. At first, they used Claudia the same way they used the gambling debts on Daley and Lavick. When that didn't work, they started to paint a picture of me as the crooked cop. Some new Jaguar leased in my name, credit cards maxed out at the Bellagio's high roller suite in Vegas. I finally got my hands on that duffel of money to leverage a meeting. I didn't expect Ray Benjamin. And… well, you basically know the rest."

She stared at him, wishing it would all make sense but that would take a long time. "I'm sorry for what you went through."

"I'm sorry, too," he said, his voice softening.

They both studied Nate. Cameron held him a little tighter. "You never chose this. It was my choice." The words slipped from her tongue before she could stop herself.

Diego's body folded over itself. He shook his head and didn't speak.

Cameron watched him, then broke the silence. "You don't have to— We're okay."

Diego reached his hand out to stop her. "Yes. Yes, I do. This matters more than anything." He rubbed his hands over his face, and Cameron saw the hospital bracelet on his arm. It reminded her of Nate's birth. She and Nate each had a bracelet. There had been one for Dad, too. But, he hadn't been there. She tried to push the past behind them, unsure if she could.

She saw him watching her.

"I was trying to protect you."

The comment stung. "I don't need your protection, Diego," she said. "What I needed was your trust."

He gripped his hands. "I know. You were my partner."

"Your partner," she repeated flatly.

"Yes. No. I mean—a partner in everything. I should have let you in. I should have trusted you would be okay."

"You should have."

Diego blew out his breath. "I didn't want to risk it."

"It would've been my choice. I would have chosen to help—for Claudia, for you."

"I thought I could do it alone, save her and come back, make everything okay again."

"Well, you did save her. She's going to be okay."

"But, in the process, I lost what mattered most." His gaze swept over Nate, and he looked away, defeated.

With a deep breath, she held Nate out toward him. "You should hold him." Your son. She couldn't say it out loud.

Diego's mouth dropped and without speaking, he held his arms out. The tears fell.

Cameron set Nathaniel into his father's arms, and felt tears swell in her eyes, too.

Nate smiled at his father.

Diego stared at him. "He's gorgeous. He's so unbelievably gorgeous."

"He does look just like you," she said, seeing them together for the first time. It was still so easy to talk to him. As much as she hurt, she wanted him to know that he mattered. To Nate, at least.

Diego's eyes went wide. "Really? You think so?"

"I do."

Diego cradled Nate in his arms, running a finger over her son's cheek, then across his head. He was clearly in love.

"Does your arm hurt?" Cameron asked.

He was grinning. "Like hell."

She reached for Nate. "Let me take him, then. I don't want you to be in pain."

He made no move to give him back. Instead, he cradled his son gently. "No. Please, let me. I've never felt better." He shifted to give Cameron room to sit down on the bed.

She hesitated, then sat.

"This is what it feels like to be a family," he said, quietly, while watching Nate's face. "I don't ever remember us all being together before my dad brought me to the States."

She thought about Rosa and Mama and about Ballestrini and Lavick. Tears fell down her cheeks. So much had happened, and it was all so raw. It felt like an open wound. It hurt to think about it, to let it out into the air. At moments, even breathing hurt. "I don't know, Diego. I'm not sure I can."

He didn't look at her. "I understand."

She watched him—his tears, his gentle gaze on Nate. She hurt. Either way, she would hurt. How could she live without him? Again. And yet, how could she let go of all the pain? "Maybe." The word fell from her lips.

His eyes went wide. "Maybe?"

Her heart pounded. "Maybe."

He exhaled in a long breath of relief and smiled. "Maybe is a place to start."

"I think so," she agreed.

Nate cooed at them.

"You really think he looks like me?" Diego said.

"Absolutely."

"Damn, I'm cute," he said, grinning.

Cameron laughed, and so did he. She settled into the bed, and they watched Nate smiling at them. This was what family felt like, Cameron thought. Painful and imperfect, but all the pieces were there. Maybe it would be enough.

It was definitely a place to start.

AUTHOR'S NOTE

The first person I would like to thank is you—the reader. Thank you for reading this book and for following the Rookie Club stories. While we're at it, thank you for every book you've ever read. It is the greatest gift you can give an author like me. Without you, there would be no books, and what a terrible world that would be.

If you have enjoyed this book, please consider taking a moment to leave a review on Amazon or elsewhere. Reviews and recommendations are vital to authors. Every good review and every recommendation for one of my books helps me stay hunkered and warm in my basement, doing what I love best—writing dark, chilling stories.

To claim your free short story, to learn more about the Rookie Club or my writing, please visit me at www.daniellegirard.com.

Now, please turn the page for a preview of book four of the Rookie Club Series, Grave Danger.

PREVIEW: GRAVE DANGER

ROOKIE CLUB BOOK 4

CHAPTER 1

OYSTER POINT WAS not where one expected to find a police warehouse full of guns. Over the past couple of decades, the area had actually become a rather attractive corporate park. The adjacent marina housed expensive yachts, and a well-developed trail system ran along the water. Natural grasses swayed in the wind. It was all very quaint and peaceful, not at all the way the place had been twenty years earlier when it was basically the cheapest available office space in the area.

J.T. wasn't there to enjoy the view and didn't give a damn about natural grasses. The whole place could have gone up in flames. The only concern was that economic prosperity meant tight security, which translated into extra time to set things up. Eighteen years was a long time to wait for payoff. But maybe the waiting was done. J.T. smoothed the gloves one last time and followed the trail.

Even in the dim predawn light, the phone box was easy to find. Phone companies hired human monkeys, then gave them an impossible-to-screw-up set of instructions. In J.T.'s experience, the monkeys still managed to do things wrong, maybe half the time. Evidenced by the fact that the phone box wasn't even locked.

A pair of wire cutters and the lines would be down. Ten seconds tops, but first, Sam's cell phone jammer had to be working. At this moment, Sam was in the small apartment adjacent to the garage, predictably huddled over his desk. He was likely working on the night's third or fourth Big Gulp of Mountain Dew. The empties would be lined along the desk like fat children at the edge of the playground. Sam was waiting, something he did by playing Minecraft or breaking into small nonprofits and finding ways to occupy himself. Last week, he hacked into a San Jose animal shelter and changed the names of the residents. A six-year-old calico was now called Big Red Pussy, a Goldendoodle who had been named Betsy was now Curly Bitch, and a Rottweiler who had lost an eye in a street fight had been renamed One-Eyed Dick. Sam thought this was hilarious.

Thankfully, Sam was not a field guy. For one, he didn't even have a driver's license, but he was also about as stealthy as farming equipment. No, Sam was hardly even a behind-the-scenes guy. Sam was a train wreck, but Sam could also be managed. Mostly this was accomplished by keeping Sam away from other people, which wasn't difficult because Sam preferred the company of other online nerds, sitting in their own dungeons, drinking their own Big Gulps, and eating some similar diet to Sam's daily feasts of Cheetos and microwave burritos.

Now, to work. The backpack dropped gently on the ground. The cell phone jammer was in a small cardboard box, surrounded in bubble wrap. Sam tended to go overboard on packaging. The device was a silver box not much bigger than a box of Tic Tacs with a black antenna coming out of each end. In the center was a silver switch. In Sam's girlish print, the left side read 'off' and the right side 'on.'

Only gloves touched the box as the switch was flipped from 'off' to 'on.' The call to Sam's number failed, which meant the jammer was working. The clippers made a satisfying snip through the wires and, in under a minute, the first step was done.

At the front of the building, Hank waited in the black van. Hank was a monkey, too, but of a different sort. J.T. might have brought Karl instead, but Karl was smarter, and J.T. didn't want any extra questions. Plus, all interactions with Karl had been electronic. J.T. had never seen his face nor the other way around, and J.T. was hesitant to change that. The fewer people J.T. dealt with in person the better.

J.T. raised a hand, and Hank emerged excitedly from the van and slammed the door closed.

"Watch the noise."

"Sorry, boss," Hank said. He shouldered an oversized duffel that seemed mostly empty.

Monkey. "You have what you need?" J.T. asked.

Hank patted his bag and nodded.

"Okay. It's your turn."

Hank approached the warehouse's back door with its 4-digit entry lock. He, too, wore gloves as he pulled a crowbar from the duffel bag and worked the end of it into the narrow opening between the door and the jam, rocking it up and down until it was wedged in far enough to begin to muscle it. The trim came off first with a loud snap as the thin metal broke away from the front of the building. Hank's hands slipped, and he dropped the crowbar which made a loud clattering sound on the pavement. It rang out like a bullet shot. "Jesus Christ."

"Sorry," Hank muttered again. He removed a long pick-like tool and a rubber mallet from the bag and created a dent in the metal door just above the knob until the latch was fully exposed. With the crowbar, he wrenched it open. Hank was built like a tank. It took all of seven minutes before the door fell open.

They stepped into the warehouse together, and Hank let the door close behind them. Softly. A first. The space smelled of old paper and lemon cleaner. The smell meant someone still cleaned the place, so their footprints would be harder to track. That was good news. The lights were off across the warehouse and the temperature cool, not the kind of place where someone was working, especially not at this hour. Skylights lined the walls almost at the ceiling, which meant someone might notice if they turned on the lights.

J.T. pulled a flashlight out of the small side pocket of the backpack and flipped it on. "You got yours?"

Hank found his flashlight, and the two of them scanned their lights across the inside. The warehouse space was small and lined with shelves where boxes were piled high. Police case files. Overflow. This was not the interesting part. That was in the far corner.

"This way."

Hank followed, finally quiet, as they crossed the warehouse to the last aisle where a cage took up the far corner. J.T. stood back. Hank used his crowbar to open the locked gate in under a minute.

The cage was lined with metal cabinets, some green, some gray, all old-style and flimsy. The first took Hank approximately fifteen seconds to jimmy open. Hank whistled at the contents, the shelves lined with semiauto assault rifles, each tagged with a case number.

"Load those up. And the other cabinets, too," J.T. said. "We don't need all of them. You've got four minutes."

Hank pulled two empty black duffels out of the one that carried his tools and dropped them on the floor. He opened the first and started loading guns.

There was a more important task to be done while Hank stole the weapons. J.T. exited the cage and returned to the main area of the warehouse, using twenty precious seconds to scan the rows before deciding on the placement. The second row seemed the best, most out of the way. Against the wall, certainly, to allow Sam the best signal. J.T. chose a box from the second shelf, two down.

With the box carefully set on the warehouse floor, J.T. loaded the larger of two computers from the backpack into the box. The computer was an inexpensive one—an Acer—purchased at Walmart while dressed in a business suit and leather gloves and scarf for the chilly day. And a wig. With cash. Three months ago. Three others were purchased under similar circumstances in case Sam needed them. A disposable cell phone and an independent battery source were strapped to the computer with Hello Kitty duct tape. Sam's idea of a joke. Sam had bought the tape himself.

None of J.T.'s prints would be on anything. Sam had been warned. J.T. had gone so far as to bring him a box of extra-large sterile gloves to fit his big, chubby hands. But Sam was sloppy. Hackers, in general, were sloppy creatures, J.T. had learned. Careless criminals, they coveted bragging rights over anonymity. The process over the results. Easily manipulated, too, by the right person. Sam was no different.

The second device was a Raspberry Pi, a computer that was no larger than a deck of playing cards. That needed to be higher. J.T. tested the shelves. The metal shelving was inexpensive. Empty, they would be easy to topple, but the weight of the old case files held them steady. Even spacing made scaling them relatively easy.

J.T. set the small computer, with its own battery pack and cell phone, on the top shelf before climbing up and reaching to the ceiling. The acoustic ceiling tiles were loose; the first one opened up without any trouble. It was almost too easy. Lousy security for police storage.

The bundle weighed maybe 20 ounces, mostly from the weight of the battery. J.T. slid it up into the ceiling so it sat against the building's outside wall and rested on the metal crossbars between acoustic tiles. Checked it twice. The tile slid back down smoothly. It looked just like the others.

Everything was as it had been. J.T. climbed down, retrieved the backpack, and returned to the weapons cage where Hank was loading his last pack. As predicted, Hank had left nothing behind. The guns were superfluous, but Hank was a common thief and common thieves lacked awareness of when enough was enough. Without mention of his excessive exuberance, Hank loaded the remaining handguns into the duffel. Hank didn't ask about the four minutes of absence. Lack of curiosity and brute strength were Hank's best features.

Hank wiped his gloved hands on his pants. "That's all of it, boss."

The two made their way outside and pushed the door closed. Up close, there would be no missing the damage to the door. But, from a distance, it would be hard to see. J.T. flipped the cell phone jammer off before turning to the backpack to retrieve its packaging.

"J.T.?"

J.T. started and spun at the sound of Hank's voice. "Jesus Christ."

There was the sound of metal on metal. The jammer fell between the phone box and the exterior wall of the building. J.T. tried to retrieve it, but it was wedged down out of reach.

Hank backed up. "Sorry, J.T. I wanted to know if you wanted me to wait or go to the van."

J.T. said nothing. The jammer was off, but leaving it was a bad idea. This was supposed to look like a smash and grab. The jammer was too sophisticated for an average burglar. J.T. dropped the pack. "Give me the pick."

Hank rattled through the guns in search of the pick.

J.T. focused on staying calm. Eyes closed. Deep breath in, deep breath out. No breaking necks. Not yet.

"There it is." Hank started to pull the tool free, but it caught up on a gun. Suddenly, a shot fired.

They both ducked as a bullet struck the passenger's side window glass of a utility vehicle parked in back. Glass exploded.

Without hesitating, J.T. grabbed the backpack in one hand and one of the duffels in the other and started for the car. Hank was right behind with the other two duffels.

The jammer was gone. There was no getting it now.

"Shit, boss," Hank said, panting. "I had no idea the guns would be loaded."

"Don't speak."

"Did you think they would be loaded?" Hank went on, nearly whining.

"Do not speak," J.T. repeated, fighting for control. Hank was disposable, but, at that moment, it couldn't happen fast enough for J.T.

Thankfully, Hank went quiet, although he continued to make little sighs and huffs like a high school girl, the need to talk obviously making him crazy. Despite the broken glass, the streets were quiet as they opened the back of the van.

Hank was sheepish as he loaded the bags. J.T. slid in the side door and pointed to the driver's seat. "You drive. I'm going to sit back here and see what we got."

The take couldn't have been less interesting. That was not the reason J.T. chose the back. It was about not being up front with Hank. Especially if something went wrong. Something else.

"We heading home?" he asked.

"Yeah."

Hank pulled away from the curb with a jolt that knocked everything, J.T. included, toward the rear of the van. "Sorry, boss."

J.T. did not respond. It was over. A mile away, the text came in from Sam. "I can see the networks. Working to get in now."

J.T. knew Sam would ask for the jammer. As much as J.T. would have liked it, Sam would not be distracted by the importance of his task. He'd want his toy back, and he would not take the loss well. J.T. would have to pretend the jammer wasn't lost. Hopefully, Sam could be put off for a day or two while J.T. pretended to "find" it. Better to let him focus on one thing at a time.

The worst was over. Now it was a matter of some cleanup.

The light turned yellow and Hank accelerated hard. Again, everything slid to the back of the van. Then there was the loud honk of a siren turning on and the glow of flashing red and blue lights. A cop.

Fuck.

"Boss?" Hank called in a panic.

"Pull over, Hank. Stay calm." The cop car parked, and Hank twisted his hands over the steering wheel.

"Take your gloves off, Hank. And don't let on that I'm here. I'll tell you when to go."

The plates on the van were stolen. It wouldn't do to have them run. Things were about to get messy, but J.T. was good with improvisation. Hank, on the other hand, was not. The cop car door opened and a single officer started for the van. He had a blond goatee and a wide upper body, the kind of young officer who probably spent a lot of free time at the gym. His left hand hovered on the butt of his gun. A left-handed cop was at a disadvantage. J.T. was surprised he didn't come around the passenger's side. Instead, he approached the driver's side with his gun on the outside. Inside, the Sig Sauer P250, complete with silencer, was now aimed at his head through the van's tinted side window.

When the officer reached the back bumper, Hank started to roll his window down. J.T. released the Sig's safety.

The cop's stride reached the middle of the van. The trigger eased back. One. Glass exploded. Two. Bullets lodged themselves in the cop's head.

Hank screamed.

The officer fell to the pavement. There was a short twitch in his left foot, then nothing. Done and done cleanly.

"Let's go, Hank," J.T. whispered. The police car's camera would pick up everything. J.T. didn't want their voices recorded, but it would be hard to miss Hank's screaming.

"Drive now," J.T. hissed again, but Hank hadn't heard.

J.T. crawled up toward the driver's seat and, resisting the temptation to put a bullet in Hank's head, too, whispered, "Come on. We have to go."

Hank lurched forward, and J.T. held tightly as the van swerved into the street. At the corner, Hank turned right, driving in the opposite direction of home. He was hysterical. He made it around the corner and out of the view of the police car's camera at least.

"Okay, stop here," J.T. said. "I'll drive."

Hank stopped the car in the middle of the road. Obviously, he had never seen anyone shot before. And it was such a clean job, too. He ought to have been impressed.

The two switched places, and Hank sank down against the wall of the van and pulled his knees to his chest. He made moaning sounds for the remainder of the drive.

"It's okay, Hank."

There were no other incidents. The garage door slid open and soon the van was inside with the door closed behind them. Only with the engine off did Hank pull himself from his fetal position and move toward the door.

Hank had his hand on the van's door handle, the back of his head cleanly exposed when the two bullets entered the back of his skull. The bullets didn't break the glass, so the mess was contained in the van. At least that had gone right.

It would all stay there for a few hours. Right now, the only pressing matters were a shower and a beer. Even at 5:00 a.m., J.T. was ready for a drink.

CHAPTER 2

MEI LING SAT in the back corner of the Special Ops van and studied her computer screen in the strange glow of the van's red interior lights. Around her, officers donned heavy raid gear: thick, black suits and combat boots and helmets with goggles. Mei was working to make herself small in the crowded space. Not that she was large to begin with. The van was maybe twenty feet long and had seemed spacious when they were all seated, but with ten team members, the captain, and equipment everywhere, it felt significantly smaller now.

Mei was working to hack the login on the computer they'd seized from Will Weigman, who the police believed was the meth ring's money guy. If she could break into it before Special Ops got into the building, they could obtain additional search warrants and cast a wider net. Unfortunately, the Special Ops team was gearing up and the brute force password dongle she'd plugged into the computer's USB port was still working on cracking the password. Mei was also waiting for AT&T to respond to their subpoena for the guy's cell phone records. The lab had even gotten the DA's office to issue a subpoena to Apple to gain access to whatever they could see from his Apple ID. Anything to give them some added insight. But waiting was a lot of what they did.

Computer forensics was never a speedy process, but watching the program from the inside of the Special Ops bus made it seem slower. Even glaciers melted faster than computer forensics these days, what with climate change and all. All around Mei, the Special Ops team was moving. Quickly. Efficiently, in a way the computer team never could. Mei wished she'd opted to do this from the lab, although then she would have had to deal with Aaron Pollack and her new team and that was less than ideal, too.

Cameron Cruz sat down beside Mei and pulled on a thick black jumpsuit. "What do you think of Special Ops?"

"Uh—"

"A little different from the lab?"

Mei motioned to Cameron's suit. "No, no. I've got a suit just like that. I would've worn it, but it's at the cleaners."

"You'd look great in one of these," Cameron told her. "And men love this look." Diego Ramirez laughed and reached down to tie his wife's boot, but Cameron elbowed him away playfully.

Diego laughed. "It's true. We dig it," he said, giving Cameron a quick kiss.

Mei glanced at her computer screen.

"Get a room already!" one of the other guys ribbed the lovebirds. Mei couldn't remember his name.

"Seriously, you guys don't spend enough time together off the job?" another one joked.

Cameron and Diego were the only couple Mei knew who both lived together and worked on the same team at the department.

Diego waved them off. "Hey, we're making up for lost time." Looking back at his wife, though, he couldn't contain his smile and, when Cameron turned her back to pull on her Kevlar vest, she was grinning, too. It was like they were getting ready to go on a scuba diving trip rather than into the center of a known meth ring.

Despite the flirting, Cameron and Diego moved with purpose. No wasted time as they donned equipment—belts, helmets, gloves. Cameron might have been five-eight or nine, but she couldn't have weighed much more than a hundred and thirty pounds, and the equipment she had on had to weigh another thirty-five or forty. In law enforcement for more than ten years, Mei had never donned a bulletproof vest or a gun on the job. She did her mandatory firearms training, but she was way more at home with a mouse than a Glock.

Mei minimized the screen on the decryption program and pulled up the GPS coordinates. The tracking device they'd put on their mole still hadn't moved.

"Anything?" Special Ops Sergeant Lau asked Mei.

She shook her head and glanced at the timer that recorded how long the device had been still. "Hasn't moved in nearly fourteen hours."

The group sobered. The tracking device was his phone. It was possible the small tracking chip had been discovered and left behind. In Mei's experience, when a tracking device was discovered, it was usually dumped. She'd spent plenty of days tracking devices to dumpsters or off bridges and into lakes. It was also conceivable that their inside guy had left his phone. It was normal to see gaps in movement of between seven and ten hours. People slept, after all.

But, with the sensitivity of the tracker and her equipment, Mei could see the movement of the phone off the bedside table, even just a few inches, let alone if it moved across the room. People tended to bring their phones with them from one room to another. This one had not moved a millimeter in fourteen hours. That was not good. Nothing to do now but wait for the team to go in and check it out.

Ramirez led the team through the layout and plan, and Mei watched. Her phone vibrated. Her mother was calling again. She sent the call to voicemail and texted her mother for the third time that morning, *At a scene.* She'd take hell for that later.

Mei heard shouts. The team lined up, moved out. Sergeant Lau went with them and reached inside to close the doors. Mei was alone with her computer. Most days, she ran this kind of program while she was doing a half dozen other things. Computer programs always took twice as long when they were being watched. Mei heard the ding of the dongle. The password was Betsy1082. Quickly, Mei typed it in and, without a breath ran a recursive find command, looking for anything with a modified date in the last week.

Five seconds later, the images began to load. Mei moved through them quickly. The first two were black, most likely accidental. The next image was hard to see, taken from a distance. She double-clicked the thumbnail so the picture filled the screen. At first, the tint of the skin made it look like a costume mask tossed on a pillow. The skin was gray-green where the neck disappeared under the white sheet, the bulk of his torso under the covers. A dead man. Maybe Weigman, but she didn't know what he looked like.

Mei loaded the next image. Somewhere else. Two large green soda bottles sat on a countertop. They looked old, their labels long gone. Each was partially full. Rubber was wrapped around the tops and a single tube ran from one to the other. Beside them was a glass bottle maybe half their size. Its label was turned away from the camera.

Mei quickly scanned the next few images. They seemed to document the place in a full circle. Empty bed through the doorway. A single ratty brown couch in the living room. Kitchen with a '70s style refrigerator in yellow. In the center, a small card table with one chair and the counter lined with the soda bottles. She enlarged the photo. Beside the bottles was a small blue plastic bottle. Though blurry, she could read the words at the top of the glass bottle: ethyl alcohol, USP. Below that, in bright red letters, it read 200 Proof. Ethanol.

In the next image, she saw a label that read H3PO2. Her chemistry wasn't good enough for that one. Instead, she Googled it. It was a substitute for red phosphorus in the production of meth and highly explosive. A meth lab. Mei scanned back through the images to the one with the body. In the background was a window and a single shade.

Mei jumped up from the computer, catching her foot on the chair that was bolted to the floor. She stumbled across the van and pressed herself against the windows. Stared up at the building as she had been doing when they arrived. The team was walking into a meth lab.

"No. No. No." Mei turned and scanned the tabletop. The radio? Where the hell was it?

She sprinted for the radio on the dash. "Sergeant Lau, do not enter the building. I repeat, do not enter."

The radio was silent.

"Send backup. Sergeant Lau's team is entering a meth lab. Lau, don't go in there!" she called more desperately. She watched out the window, anticipating an explosion.

When there was no answer, Mei opened the bus door and ran down the stairs. "Cameron! Diego!" she screamed down the block. She wasn't exactly sure how they'd entered the building. "Get away from there! Clear the area."

Were they already inside? Even a cell phone call could trigger an explosion. Call 9-1-1. She ran back onto the bus for her cell phone, dialed 9-1-1.

"Dispatch. What is the address of your emergency?"

"This is Officer Mei Ling. I'm with the Special Ops team and we have a potential ethanol leak. It hasn't blown yet, but the team is up there. They don't know it's an active meth production. We need to get through to them and tell them to get away from that building before it blows. We need fire-fighters and a bomb squad and ambulances."

"Officer, slow down."

Mei glanced at the image on her computer. Two liter-sized soda bottles and ethyl alcohol. Maybe it wouldn't blow. But there had to be enough ethanol in that air to kill Weigman. "Send backup. This place is a meth lab."

There was a loud smack on the side of the bus and Mei jumped. Sergeant Lau's face appeared through the glass. He gave her a tentative smile, which was followed by the comforting thunder of heavy boots on the bus stairs.

"What's all the commotion?" Diego asked.

Mei watched them all flood back onto the bus. All ten of them, plus Lau. Only then did she finally take a full breath of air.

"What did you find?" Lau asked, coming up behind her shoulder.

Mei double-clicked on the image of the meth lab and turned the computer toward the group hovered around her.

"That could be anywhere," one of the guys said.

"Mei, what made you so sure that picture is of this place?" Lau asked.

In the distance, Mei heard the low whine of sirens. She navigated back to the image and zoomed into the window. She pointed to the broken blind that hung asymmetrically in the window. "See that?"

"The shade?" Cameron asked.

Mei nodded. "Look up at the building," she told them. "Farthest window on the right."

The officers moved across the van. It took them a minute to find it. "Holy shit," Diego said. "That place is a meth lab."

Mei sank into her chair. "That's what I've been telling you."

ABOUT THE AUTHOR

Danielle Girard is the bestselling author of *Chasing Darkness*, The Rookie Club series, and the Dr. Schwartzman Series—*Exhume, Excise, Expose,* and *Expire,* featuring San Francisco medical examiner Dr. Annabelle Schwartzman. Danielle's books have won the Barry Award and the RT Reviewers' Choice Award, and two of her titles have been optioned for movies.

A graduate of Cornell University, Danielle received her MFA at Queens University in Charlotte, North Carolina. She, her husband, and their two children split their time between San Francisco and the Northern Rockies. Visit her at www.daniellegirard.com.

CPSIA information can be obtained
at www.ICGtesting.com
Printed in the USA
BVHW030826140819
555861BV00007B/75/P